PRAISE FOR
REIGN OF MADNESS

"Scenes where Isabel finally shares with her daughter the sacrifices a queen must make, the realities of her own life at court,
and lessons in the art of self-protection are all the more affecting
for coming too late . . . At the end of this cautionary tale, we
understand better the reasons why Juana might have made the
choices she did—they so easily could have been our choices,
too." — *The Atlanta Journal-Constitution*

"Cullen's page-turning account depicts the intelligent, caring
woman behind the legend . . . [*Reign of Madness*] is a sweeping
study of political intrigue. But an equal focus on character
development and plot makes for a satisfying blend of romance,
family drama, and royal machinations . . . Juana is a sympathetic heroine, and lovers of historical fiction will love her
story." — *Library Journal*

"Lynn Cullen skillfully takes us on a journey through the life
and times of one of the most famous females in Spanish history, Juana de Castile . . . It is one of the greatest love stories
I have ever read . . . Captivating . . . If you get caught up emo-
tionally in what you read, this book will have you pacing
the floors. This is history presented as you have never read
before." — *BellaOnline*

"Cullen fleshes out Juana's fascinating story of love, betrayal,
and redemption and puts a very human face on one of history's
most famous rulers." — *Booklist*

continued . . .

"Endlessly readable, deeply fascinating, and often stunning."
— *Open Letters Monthly*

"To read *The Creation of Eve* is to experience that wholly delicious bookish pleasure of total immersion . . . I found this novel about the quest for fulfillment in art and love enormously satisfying and I'm grateful to Cullen for the pleasures of such a splendid read."
— Sara Gruen, #1 *New York Times* bestselling author of *Water for Elephants* and *Ape House*

"[A] finely textured fictional biography . . . Cullen does a magnificent job reinvigorating a still-life portrait of an all-but-forgotten maestra."
— *Booklist*

"A suspenseful, evocative tapestry of Renaissance life, art, and royal skullduggery . . . Cullen proves herself a master of chiaroscuro in the *The Creation of Eve*, celebrating one of the brighter lights of a shadowy era when religious dogma trumped education and sensuality became a lightning rod for persecution."
— *PopMatters*

"What a marvelous, rich and compelling novel! . . . Turn and find yourself in the sixteenth century. I was unable to put the novel down and lived in its world."
— Stephanie Cowell, author *Claude & Camille*

"Lynn Cullen weaves a glittering tapestry in *The Creation of Eve*, blending themes of art, gender and politics into a provocative novel that feels surprisingly timely."
— *BookPage*

continued . . .

REIGN *of* MADNESS

LYNN CULLEN

BERKLEY BOOKS

New York

THE BERKLEY PUBLISHING GROUP
Published by the Penguin Group
Penguin Group (USA) Inc.
375 Hudson Street, New York, New York 10014, USA

Penguin Group (Canada), 90 Eglinton Avenue East, Suite 700, Toronto, Ontario M4P 2Y3, Canada
(a division of Pearson Penguin Canada Inc.) • Penguin Books Ltd., 80 Strand, London WC2R 0RL,
England • Penguin Group Ireland, 25 St. Stephen's Green, Dublin 2, Ireland (a division of Penguin
Books Ltd.) • Penguin Group (Australia), 250 Camberwell Road, Camberwell, Victoria 3124, Australia
(a division of Pearson Australia Group Pty. Ltd.) • Penguin Books India Pvt. Ltd., 11 Community
Centre, Panchsheel Park, New Delhi—110 017, India • Penguin Group (NZ), 67 Apollo Drive,
Rosedale, Auckland 0632, New Zealand (a division of Pearson New Zealand Ltd.) • Penguin Books
(South Africa) (Pty.) Ltd., 24 Sturdee Avenue, Rosebank, Johannesburg 2196, South Africa

Penguin Books Ltd., Registered Offices: 80 Strand, London WC2R 0RL, England

This is a work of fiction. Names, characters, places, and incidents either are the product of the author's
imagination or are used fictitiously, and any resemblance to actual persons, living or dead, business
establishments, events, or locales is entirely coincidental. The publisher does not have any control over
and does not assume any responsibility for author or third-party websites or their content.

PUBLISHING HISTORY
G. P. Putnam's Sons hardcover edition / August 2011
Berkley trade paperback edition / May 2012

Berkley trade paperback ISBN: 978-0-425-24731-0

The Library of Congress has cataloged the G. P. Putnam's Sons hardcover edition as follows:

Cullen, Lynn.
Reign of madness / Lynn Cullen.
p.   cm.
ISBN 978-0-399-15709-7
1. Juana, la Loca, Queen of Castile, 1479–1555—Fiction.
2. Philip I, King of Castile, 1478–1506—Fiction.   3. Queens—Spain—Castile—Fiction.
4. Castile (Spain)—Kings and rulers—Fiction.
5. Spain—History—Ferdinand and Isabella, 1479–1516—Fiction.
6. Spain—History—Charles I, 1516–1556—Fiction.   I. Title.
PS3553.U2955R45   2011   2011006884
813'.54—dc22

PRINTED IN THE UNITED STATES OF AMERICA

10 9 8 7 6 5 4 3 2 1

For my daughters, Lauren, Megan, and Alison

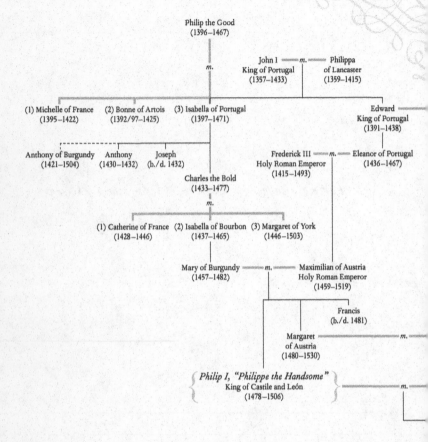

Philip the Good
(1396–1467)

m.

John 1
King of Portugal
(1357–1433)

m.

Philippa
of Lancaster
(1359–1415)

(1) Michelle of France
(1395–1422)

(2) Bonne of Artois
(1392/97–1425)

(3) Isabella of Portugal
(1397–1471)

Edward
King of Portugal
(1391–1438)

Anthony of Burgundy
(1421–1504)

Anthony
(1430–1432)

Joseph
(b./d. 1432)

Frederick III
Holy Roman Emperor
(1415–1493)

m.

Eleanor of Portugal
(1436–1467)

Charles the Bold
(1433–1477)

m.

(1) Catherine of France
(1428–1446)

(2) Isabella of Bourbon
(1437–1465)

(3) Margaret of York
(1446–1503)

Mary of Burgundy
(1457–1482)

m.

Maximilian of Austria
Holy Roman Emperor
(1459–1519)

Francis
(b./d. 1481)

Margaret
of Austria
(1480–1530)

m.

Philip I, "Philippe the Handsome"
King of Castile and León
(1478–1506)

m.

The Family of
PHILIPPE the HANDSOME

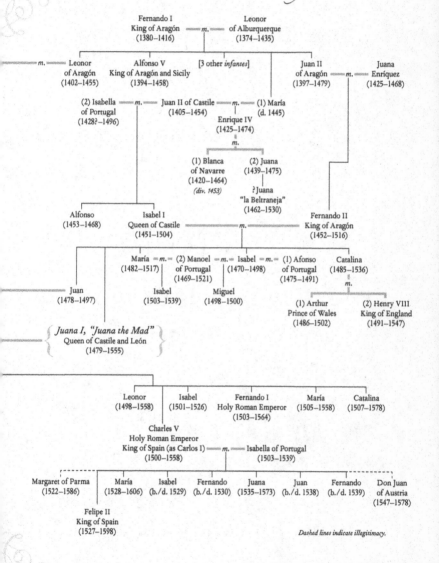

The Family of
JUANA of CASTILE

Fernando I
King of Aragón
(1380–1416)
m.
Leonor
of Alburquerque
(1374–1435)

Leonor
of Aragón
(1402–1455)
m.

Alfonso V
King of Aragón and Sicily
(1394–1458)

[3 other *infantes*]

Juan II
of Aragón
(1397–1479)
m.
Juana
Enríquez
(1425–1468)

(2) Isabella
of Portugal
(1428?–1496)
m.
Juan II of Castile
(1405–1454)
m.
(1) María
(d. 1445)

Enrique IV
(1425–1474)
m.

(1) Blanca
of Navarre
(1420–1464)
(div. 1453)

(2) Juana
(1439–1475)

?Juana
"la Beltraneja"
(1462–1530)

Alfonso
(1453–1468)

Isabel I
Queen of Castile
(1451–1504)
m.

Fernando II
King of Aragón
(1452–1516)

María
(1482–1517)
m.
(2) Manoel
of Portugal
(1469–1521)
m.
Isabel
(1470–1498)
m.
(1) Afonso
of Portugal
(1475–1491)

Catalina
(1485–1536)
m.

Juan
(1478–1497)

Isabel
(1503–1539)

Miguel
(1498–1500)

(1) Arthur
Prince of Wales
(1486–1502)

(2) Henry VIII
King of England
(1491–1547)

{ *Juana I, "Juana the Mad"*
Queen of Castile and León
(1479–1555) }

Leonor
(1498–1558)

Isabel
(1501–1526)

Fernando I
Holy Roman Emperor
(1503–1564)

María
(1505–1558)

Catalina
(1507–1578)

Charles V
Holy Roman Emperor
King of Spain (as Carlos I)
(1500–1558)
m.
Isabella of Portugal
(1503–1539)

Margaret of Parma
(1522–1586)

María
(1528–1606)

Isabel
(b./d. 1529)

Fernando
(b./d. 1530)

Juana
(1535–1573)

Juan
(b./d. 1538)

Fernando
(b./d. 1539)

Don Juan
of Austria
(1547–1578)

Felipe II
King of Spain
(1527–1598)

Dashed lines indicate illegitimacy.

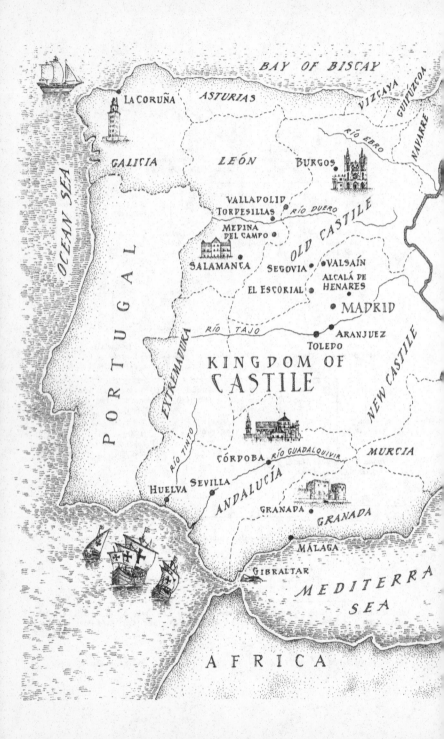

FRANCE

Pyrenees
CATALONIA
ROUSSILLON

KINGDOM OF
ARAGÓN

ZARAGOZA

ARAGÓN

VALENCIA

• Barcelona

VALENCIA

BURGUNDY
THE LANDS OF
PHILIPPE THE
HANDSOME

• BRUGES
FLANDERS

PICARDY
LUXEMBOURG

NEAN

• PARIS

FRANCE

DIJON

FORMER
BURGUNDIAN
POSSESSIONS

Prologue

Possibly Juana of Castile

2 May anno Domini 1543

A birdcage might be gilded, but it is still a cage. And so it is said of the palace at Tordesillas. For all its lovely balconies overlooking the churning waters of the Duero, its sun-warmed tile roofs, its royal pennants of scarlet and gold snapping merrily in the breeze, the townsfolk know the true purpose of the building. This is why farmers cross themselves as they pass before it with their wagonloads of wheat. Why the sisters of the convent of Santa Clara keep their eyes averted when in its vicinity. Why boys throw stones at its empty windows before they are rushed off by their scolding tutors. People are afraid of the place, as if the wrong that has been inflicted on its inhabitant might be catching.

Now its stone walls ring with the sound of trumpets, followed by the determined tap of fine kid shoes against tile. A page shouts, "His Majesty Don Felipe!" although everyone in the palace and in the windswept Castilian town over which it towers knows the identity of the slight young man leading the group of nobles dressed in velvet doublets and fur-trimmed robes. The young man—a youth, truly, new to the blond beard sprouting from his prominent chin—forges deeper into the palace. He strides past empty chambers that smell of the river, then through the arcade, which is shuttered though it is a mild day in early May, and past a chapel with a single votive flicker-ing wanly in the dark. He comes at last to a door and waits, twitching his jaw, a surprisingly heavy feature in his otherwise graceful face. A German guard, steel armor clinking, works the lock then throws open the bolt.

"His Majesty Don Felipe, Prince of Spain, Naples, Milan, Sicily, the Netherlands, and the Indies!" cries the page.

A woman whose bloom has long since faded looks up from the book she holds to the light of the only window of the chamber. She is dressed in the plain coarse gray of the Poor Clares. A wooden rosary hangs from her waist. Only the delicate Flemish linen of the coif beneath her thick veil—too fine for a simple Poor Clare—hints that she might not be a sister of that humble religious order.

The young man hesitates for a moment, working his considerable jaw, then strides before her and falls to his knees. "My Lady Grandmother, I wish to kiss your hands."

She hides her hands, one still clutching the small leather-bound book, in the folds of her rough skirt. "No."

The youth sits back on his heels as if snapped at by a dog he had judged friendly. The nobles behind him cease their jostling for position and exchange glances.

The lines etched around the woman's mouth speak of sorrow, aging her beyond her sixty-three years, but now, when she smiles with affection, it is possible to imagine how beautiful she once was. Indeed, in spite of her graying skin and brows, and having borne six children, all of them kings, queens, or emperors, in her mind she is still a young maiden. "Stand up, Felipe."

He hesitates.

She holds out her arms. "Come."

After they embrace, he says, "I have come to ask permission to marry."

Her smile fades. "My 'permission'?" She sighs. "Who?"

He pauses. Behind him, a cardinal coughs into his scarlet sleeve. "My cousin, Maria Manuela of Portugal."

"Catalina's child? My own daughter Catalina's child? Catalina *has not written me about it. No one has. But you would think at least Catalina . . ." She stops, then takes a breath. "When is the wedding?"*

"As soon as you allow it."

She exhales. "When, Felipe."

He lowers his eyes. "November."

"Thank you." Seeing his guilty look, she asks quietly, "Is she beautiful?"

His fool, a gangling fellow with eyes set impossibly close together and a head furred with melon-colored hair, jogs forward and knocks the prince with his elbow. "Is she beautiful? ¡Que bonita! *Who would not want to eat her peaches?"*

"Manuelito," Felipe says, "you've not seen her."

The fool slides forth a petulant bottom lip. "I have seen her picture."

Felipe glances at the walls, bare save for a painting of the Virgin Mary that is black with age. He reddens. He has not thought to bring a portrait.

The woman smiles gently. "You will find yourself more foolish than a fool if she does not seem beautiful to you once you have seen her."

Felipe's short laugh is one of sheepish gratitude. "Surely I will admire my cousin," he says lightly. "She has my same blood."

"Yes," says the woman. "She has my blood, too. Though that might not be the best recommendation."

Felipe reddens again. The woman sighs. She did not mean to embarrass him. This is what comes from being alone too much, she thinks to herself. I no longer know how to behave.

"She should count herself lucky to be of your line," Felipe says.

The boy has her delicate skin and its propensity to give away emotions, the woman thinks. He is a poor liar, just like her. Interesting, how lineage will tell, no matter how much you wish that it would not.

Looking at this boy, she can see her husband's heavy jaw and swollen lips, though on Philippe they were considered quite attractive, if you measured by the number of ladies who fell across his bed. There are women who, after gaining the affection of such a handsome man, must possess him completely or go mad. Philippe never seemed to worry about this.

He should have.

The Spains

Possibly Isabel of Castile

1.

15 April anno Domini 1493

I had gone to get Estrella. She was in my chamber on the second floor of the palace in Barcelona, chewing a slipper, no doubt. She was losing her puppy teeth, and I, the proud bearer of nearly fourteen entire years, believed with the confident certainty of a physician at Salamanca that her gums did pain her. I thought that my company would aid her. I would keep her in my sleeve, where she could burrow to her heart's delight. She would not piss if the ceremony did not take too terribly long. Surely a reception for a sailor, even one who claimed to have found a shortcut to the Indies, would not last longer than a Mass. She had made it through many a Mass when I thought that even I should burst.

My chance to escape came when Mother was deep in one of her discussions with her confessor, Fray Hernando de Talavera. The two of them were roasting themselves before the fireplace, which in the Saló del Tinell was large enough to house a peasant family and their beasts. My mother was the Queen of Castile, León, Aragón, Granada, Naples, Sicily, Toledo, Valencia, Galicia, Mallorca, Seville, Sardinia, Corsica, Murcia, Jaén, the Algarve, Algeciras, and, let us not forget, Gibraltar, with its apes, one of whom tried to bite me when I gave it an orange. But Heaven was not yet one of the places she ruled, and so she listened to Fray Hernando with a reverence she afforded few men. Certainly not Papa.

Fray Hernando was leaning over her, his head tilted to hear her over the din around them, an affectionate smile upon his handsome smooth-skinned face, when my brother, Juan, and his household clattered into the hall. Most of Juan's pimpled gallants had insisted on wearing their armor and, typical boys of fifteen years or so, were enjoying the pain they were inflicting on everyone's ears with their clanking. All they earned from Mother was a twinge of a frown, but my little sisters María and Catalina gazed at them worshipfully, as if they might be knights from one of the tales of chivalry that María so loved to read. My elder sister, Isabel, however, was not amused. Widowed and worldly at twenty-two, she was Queen in her own mind, even though, as a woman, she was behind Juan in the succession.

But while Juan acted like a clown, at least he was clever enough to realize that not even he was likely ever to be King, not with Mother's bear-grip on life. Good luck, Señor Death, trying to reel in Queen Isabel of Castile before she was ready. She had fought to win her crowns, battled the Moors to near extinction, and united the Spains, all the while wearing a man's breastplate as she urged her men on, her wavy strawberry-gold hair blowing in the wind. The woman was too ferocious to die. And though the motto she took with Papa was *"Tanto monta, monta tanto, Isabel como Fernando"*—Isabel and Fernando, they amount to the same— it was her fierce will and not Papa's quiet strength that was recognized as the force behind these wonders, as unjust as I thought that was. No, this was not a person who would lie down meekly to be collected by the Reaper. Perhaps this was why my sister Isabel took such pleasure in trying to dictate everyone's actions. In her heart, she knew it was as close as she would ever come to ruling.

Now my sister was exchanging disapproving glares with her ladies. Their own furrowed brows were tepid imitations of hers—indeed, some of their glances at the boys were passing flirtatious. *Bueno.* Let everyone chat, flirt, worship, or clank. I could slip from the chamber to get Estrella.

I had not gotten far—only to the chapel of Santa Agata, which Mother had newly redone, like everything else in the Spains—when I thought I heard a woman laugh. I stopped to listen.

Behind me, from the other side of the iron-strapped door I had so carefully closed to the *saló*, came the muted music of Mother's lutenists and the muffled din of the grandees, priests, and ladies waiting to receive Colón after his voyage. To the right of the *saló*, on the steps to the Plaça del Rei— those same steps on which a wretch had tried to take Papa's life only five months earlier—I could hear the pikemen stationed just outside the palace door, banging their poles and stamping their feet against the chill of the drizzly April morning. Drums pounded in the distance: Colón's procession. To judge from their sound, he had entered the walls of the city. In less time than it takes to sew on a button, I had to get Estrella in the far reaches of the palace, return, and melt back into the gathering, unnoticed.

But there—I heard it again. A soft titter, behind the heavy carved doors of the chapel, one of which was ajar.

I knew that laugh yet could not quite place it. And in Mother's chapel? Who would be in there now? All of us and our households were to be in the Saló del Tinell: Mother's orders. *She* believed Colón's claim that he had found a better way to the Indies—at least to the outlying islands—so the rest of us must be there to receive him, no matter if some, like Papa, whose line in all things I staunchly followed, were not convinced.

I heard the rustle of heavy cloth from inside the chapel.

I glanced around guiltily. Colón's drums were slowly nearing. My sister would note my absence at any minute and report it to Mother, bringing down both me and my former tutor, now governess, Beatriz Galindo, who was expected to keep control over me. But I had to see who was in there. Had one of Mother's ladies disobeyed her? Or, *Hostias en vinagre*, had one of my sister's? I would not want to be this person when Isabel found out. Even at my tender age I understood that a would-be monarch could be more tyrannical than a crowned one.

Carefully, as not to make the thick iron hinges creak, I put my shoulder to the door and leaned into the chapel.

Honey and orange peel. That's what I smelled, not the oily scent of the incense from Mass or Mother's musky perfume. Mother did love a good strong stink of civet. She dabbed a fortune of it on the nape of her neck each day. No, this was honey and orange, for certain. It was familiar to me, but how?

A woman murmured.

I followed the sound with my gaze to the portable prayer booth in which Mother was taken to Mass each day like a relic being carried to its shrine. The rustling came from inside the cloth-of-gold curtains. Whoever was inside was making the curtains sway.

I drew up short: There was a man in the booth. I could hear him breathe. Even a child knows whether it is a man or a woman by the sound of the person's breath.

I heard the smack of moist flesh. *¡Hostias! Hostias!* There were two people in there. I knew what they were doing.

My heart pounding, I took a step back and crunched on something hard. I lifted my heel. A ruby the size of a hazelnut.

I scooped it up and ran out to get Estrella.

When I returned to the *saló*, the drums of Colón's procession were rattling the timber floors of the chamber. He was entering the Plaça del Rei outside. Mother and Papa had taken to their thrones at the far end of the room; Papa was whispering in Mother's ear. She did not seem to see me slip between my little sisters, but Beatriz did. She rounded her eyes at me in outraged disbelief. Beatriz Galindo was only five years older than I, and already famed for her skill in Latin, having attended university in Salerno. She had been a brilliant tutor, but she was a terrible governess and for that I loved her. I feared that Mother would catch on to how lax a prison guard she was and relieve her of her duties. A chill from almost being caught raised the hair on my arms.

I was still breathing hard from my run, when, to the blare of trumpets and the pounding of kettledrums, Colón entered the hall.

Though he had met with my parents several times before his voyage, this was the first that I had seen the sailor. He was tall like Mother, and big-boned. He had her red-gold hair, too, but his chin-length locks, limp and darkened from the drizzling rain, were liberally shot with pale gray. He had a strong hooked nose and thick proud-set lips, and though he swept off his velvet cap in deference, he held up his chin when he dropped to his knees before Mother. Perhaps she recognized something of her own proud self in him, and favored him for it, for she raised one corner of her mouth in a smile. Papa, however, buckled his dark brow at Colón's arrogance. As with so many things, my parents' opinions differed markedly, and we children were left to take sides. My lot, as ever, was with Papa. I frowned at the puffed-up mariner.

Mother let him kiss her hand, then Papa's, then drew him up. "Cristóbal Colón, please show us what you have brought from the Indies. Come sit. Sit."

The grandees glanced at one another as Mother beckoned for a page to bring a chair. None of them had ever been offered a seat in my mother's presence. Nor, I realized at that moment, had I.

The crossed gilt legs of the chair groaned as Colón eased his large person onto the leather seat.

"Your Sacred Majesties Doña Isabel and Don Fernando, I thank you. With God's great blessings, I have brought you all nature of wondrous things." He clapped his hands. As the crowd murmured with approval, sailors dressed in red breeches and white shirts brought forth treasures: An open chest filled with nuggets of gold. Lengths of precious aromatic wood. Screeching green parrots in a silver cage. Exotic foods. One shriveled red fruit was so spicy that tears came to Mother's eyes when she tasted it, though she liked the toasted seeds called *maiz*. How she laughed when a pair of long-legged rodents were led in on leashes.

Colón grinned at her delight. "*Hutias*, they are called. Very good to eat. They taste much like rabbit."

Papa sat back as the hall stirred with increasing excitement. He was a listener, and a thinker, and, I thought then, the kindest person I knew. There was a reason he took the anvil as his personal emblem—you can strike it all day and it will remain silent and unbreakable. As much as Mother and others made of the perfection of their marriage, I did not think she appreciated him enough. *Tanto monta, monta tanto*—did it ever occur to her that he might be the stronger one?

"Did you bring back any other Eastern beasts?" Papa asked. "Marco Polo talked of monkeys, tigers, elephants. I don't recall any tales of edible rats."

"In truth," said Colón, "they are more like rabbits."

Papa studied him calmly. "Perhaps these rats were too unimportant for him to mention."

The smile faded from Colón's heavy lips. He gazed at Papa as if judging him anew. "Your Sacred Majesty, in the lands I claimed for you and Her Sacred Majesty the Queen, there were plenty of monkeys—a very loud type, as a matter of fact. I would not wish for their howling to disturb your peace."

Papa looked unmoved. "You are most thoughtful, Colón. Perhaps these, these—what did you call these rats?"

"*Hutias.*"

"—these *hutias* came from the City of Gold that Marco Polo referred to. Perhaps they are known to the Great Khan of Cathay."

"Perhaps," Colón said warily. "I have not had the privilege of meeting him yet, as I have already written in my letter to you. I did not linger in the Indies, for I wished to hurry home as quickly as possible to share the good news with Your Sacred Majesties. However, I was able to bring you these." He nodded at a sailor standing at the door.

The sailor disappeared for a moment. When he reappeared, everyone fell silent. Six wildmen, naked save for red breeches, edged into the chamber at the point of their captors' pikes. They each had a gold ring in their nose, fish bones bristling from their earlobes, and dull brown hair, as long as a girl's but stiff, atop which feathers were fixed. Colón's men held tightly to the chains that bound them as they crept forward, now lurching, now crying out, now staring wide-eyed at the crowd gaping back at them.

"Judas's soul!" My brother Juan peered at the men crouched shakily before him. "What are they?" Armor clinking, he reached out to one of them in wonder.

The creature flinched, then shouted at him in a foreign tongue.

The nobles, the ladies, Juan's boys, even the musicians, went rigid. Colón swelled up as if he would have liked to leap from his chair to murder the beast. This savage had shown disrespect to the heir of the crowns of the Spains. With held breath, everyone looked to Mother.

She gazed thoughtfully upon the wildman, who now cowered as though he knew he'd done wrong. "So." She tapped her finger against her lips. "These are my new subjects."

The hush in the chamber rose like a loaf of resting dough.

Slowly, she brought her hands together in applause. "Bravo, Cristóbal Colón, bravo."

Papa pulled his glance from something in the crowd, then clapped along with her. "Yes. Bravo."

His enthusiasm rekindled by relief, Colón animatedly described how he had found the strange men on what must be an outer island of China—perhaps near the famed isle of Cipangu. These were Chinamen or Cipangos or some such persons of the Far East. Men of the Indies, or "Indios," he called them.

"The land is populated with thousands more, just like these," Colón said.

"Are they cannibals?" asked my brother.

"In spite of their rough appearance," said Colón, "no. These men don't eat human flesh. Indeed, you have never seen a more gentle, childlike people. They are affectionate and without covetousness. They love their neighbors as themselves."

Yet they were chained as if dangerous. I did not understand. Only enemies of Mother or the Church were treated in such a way, like the Moors after Mother's defeat of Málaga. When I was seven, most of the population of that town—men, women, and children—had been put into chains for defying her. She had said that it was necessary, that they hated her, and the Church, and even me, and were threats to our security. When I asked her if even the children hated me, she sent me to Fray Hernando to be instructed, though it did me little good. Fray Hernando, with his warm brown eyes and smooth skin, had been so handsome and kind that I could not bear to look at him, let alone hear a word he uttered.

"Your Sacred Majesty," Colón said, "you should hear them speak. My Indios—"

"*Your* Indios?" Mother said.

Colón closed his mouth, then bowed. "Your Sacred Majesty, the deepest of pardons. My haste in marching to you from Seville must have weakened my brain. What I was trying to say was that *your* Indios have the sweetest speech in the world."

"Oh?" said Mother. "Have one speak."

Colón motioned for his man to rattle the chains of one of the Indios. He then said something to the creature in a foreign tongue.

The Indio shivered, be it from the cold of the stone hall, bone-chilling even in April, or from fear or illness, but he did not speak.

"Your Sacred Majesty, I apologize," said Colón. "As sweet a people as are your Indios, they must be taught how to behave. They are as unschooled and innocent as newborn babes."

Mother waved her hand. "Never mind. Tell us, how quickly can they be brought to the understanding of our faith?"

I studied the shivering man as Mother, Colón, and Fray Hernando discussed the conversion of the savages both at hand and across the Ocean Sea. Did no one else notice that the man was miserable?

Colón stopped speaking. Mother watched, puzzled, as he wiped his eyes on the sleeve of his blue velvet gown.

"Your Sacred Majesty," he said, composing himself, "forgive my tears of joy. I am overcome by how miraculous it is that we should be speaking of these things now, with these riches from my voyage before us, after so many years of opposition by so many of the principal persons of your household"—he paused, avoiding Papa's cool gaze—"all of whom were against me and treated this undertaking as a folly. I thought I would never see this day."

Mother leaned forward. "Look what you have done with three ships and your own implacable will. This is what makes the success of your voyage so precious to me. It proves the theory dearest to my heart: that if a person so wills it, he can achieve anything."

Papa pursed his lips.

Mother settled back. "I should like to greet your sons."

Colón bowed, unable to conceal his pleasure. "Your Sacred Majesty, we would be deeply honored."

He turned toward the boys in my brother's household, who until now had been holding their clanking to a minimum. Metal struck metal as they moved to allow one of Juan's pages to step forward.

The youth looked to be close to Juan's age of nearly fifteen; he held the hand of a little boy of perhaps four or five. Both were dressed in my brother's particolored livery of scarlet and green.

"Thank you, Your Majesty," Colón said, "for allowing my sons, Diego and Fernando, to serve your illustrious son the Prince."

Haltingly, Colón's sons advanced on Mother's throne. I had seen the older boy, Diego, before, with Juan's household, but did not know he was Colón's son. He was always on the edge of Juan's crowd, though he was handsome, in a somber way, with a narrow face, smooth black brows, and hair the shining brown of a bay stallion. I could not remember him jousting with the other boys, nor was he one to tease me when I passed, like the others. I had thought that his indifference to me was due to his being the ambitious son of a foreign duke, that he had found my rank in my family too low for his aspirations. I was appalled, therefore, to learn that I had been shunned by the son of a sailor. He must think me as ugly as a sheared ewe.

This Diego stopped before Mother and fell on his knees. Then, just as he leaned in to kiss her hand, his little brother dashed forward and pecked it. Laughter echoed from the low stone arches of the hall.

Mother pronounced, "This younger one has his father's bold will."

Diego Colón sank back on his heels, shock, love for his brother, and shame chasing across his face.

At that moment, one of the long-legged rats slipped its

leash. Estrella, tempted beyond limit of reason, leaped yipping from my sleeve and chased the creature under Mother's throne. I screamed as her guard thrust his halberd at my pup. The Indios thrashed against their chains and wailed in terror.

"Juana!" Mother's glare was more terrible than her cry.

I pulled Estrella from under the gold fringe of her throne.

"No harm done, Isabel," said Father. "It's just a rat."

I stood up, Estrella squirming in my arms. It was then that I noticed the row of hazelnut-sized rubies on the collar of Father's robe. One of them was missing.

2.

17 April anno Domini 1493

*I*n the family legend that Mother loved to recount and that my younger sisters clung to like mystics to the Cross, Papa, determined to win her hand in marriage, had tramped all the way from Zaragoza to Valladolid disguised as a muleteer. He'd had to come on the sly because Mother's brother King Enrique had forbidden the two cousins to marry. A marriage uniting the bloodlines would have weakened Enrique's own daughter's claim to the throne. But when my eighteen-year-old mother saw seventeen-year-old Papa in his rags, so handsome with his dark complexion, hooded eyes, and tranquil demeanor, she had to have him. They were married immediately. An hour after the ceremony, their attendants were on the balcony of their bedroom, holding out the stained sheets of their marital bed for all to see, proof of Mother's virginity at the consummation of their marriage. My sisters loved that part, even if they did not fully understand it.

As often as this story was retold within the family, it was not surprising that it should surface again that afternoon in the feasting hall of Cardinal Mendoza's palace. Colón had been in Barcelona three days and there had been a feast in his honor each afternoon—quite generous, Papa had remarked, for someone who had done nothing more for the Spains than return from a voyage with six terrified men and some rats.

"What color do you think Diego Colón's eyes are?" asked my sister María. Little finger out like the dainty lady that she fervently wished to be, even at age ten, she nibbled her meat from the point of her knife. "Greenish-gray or grayish-green?"

Lute music mingled with the hum of conversation as I spooned my own portion from the lamb stew. Over at our parents' table, Diego Colón sat next to his father, a look of undisguised happiness lighting his face while he alternated between bolting his food and gazing up at his father.

"Is there a difference?" I asked.

"Oh, yes," she said breathlessly.

On the other side of María, Catalina sat up from petting one of the dogs under the table. "What are you saying?" she said with her child's lisp. Seven years old and entering the gangling middle years of girlhood, she had recently lost both of her front teeth.

"You think everyone is handsome, María," I said, "even dusty muleteers carting stinking loads of sheepskins to the Medina del Campo fair."

"I notice one muleteer who *was* handsome," she said hotly, "and you will not let me forget it."

"Papa came to Mother dressed as a muleteer," lisped Catalina. "Even in his rags, Mother thought he was the most handsome man in the world, and married him on the spot." She smiled in gummy bliss.

I could not bear to hear the story again. "How do you like Colón's rats?" I said. "They're in that dish, you know. 'Very good to eat.'"

María pulled the spoon from her mouth and spat onto the floor. "They are not."

Catalina emptied her own mouthful with maximum drama.

I looked up with a grin only to find Mother staring at me from the high table, her face slack with disappointment. I turned away. I would not show emotion. Strike me all you want, I was an anvil like Papa. It was I who had stayed by him when that monster had stabbed him in the neck as we were leaving the palace. While my sisters had clung to one another in a wailing heap, and my brother had stormed the plaza with his sword drawn in a futile show of revenge, I had followed Papa to where his men, shouting and weeping, had lain him on the floor of the Saló del Tinell. He was bleeding onto his own cape, carefully folded under his head.

He had opened his eyes when I stepped near. "Isabel."

"No, Papa—it's Juana."

"Isabel, help me."

Mother was at a monastery outside the city, consulting with Fray Hernando. "It's Juana, Papa. It's me."

"Isabel," he whispered. But it was my arm he grasped when they lifted the bloody chain from his neck.

How dear Papa looked to me now, resting his chin on his hand as Mother, Fray Hernando, and Cardinal Mendoza questioned Colón. Listening, as always. The fur Papa wore covered most of the purple scar across his neck. He was not wearing the robe with the ruby missing from the collar—a relief to me, though I could not have told you why.

Laughter erupted from the table of Juan's household. Some of the boys were feeding the Indios great quantities of salted anchovies, then giving them unwatered wine to quench their resulting thirst. Juan had told me earlier that

Colón steadily plied them with wine to keep them tame. It was a miracle that they could still sit.

Suddenly the lute music broke off; trumpets blared. At the head table, Mother rose, her cloth-of-gold train rustling as it unfurled. Fray Hernando often took her to task for wearing such rich raiment, accusing her of wishing to draw the eyes of men to her person. How they argued about it, he with the heat of a jealous lover, she cold and angry, then contrite and tearful. You would think they were fighting about more than clothes.

Now Fray Hernando gazed up at her fondly; that old lizard Mendoza was smiling and nodding. She folded her hands over her belly and looked benevolently over the crowd.

"Cardinal Mendoza, if I may say a few words . . ."

The aged cardinal lowered his head, his chameleon's wrinkled jowls sagging. One of the tassels of his broad-brimmed hat dipped into his wine.

"Thank you, Your Holiness. Dear Cardinal Mendoza and my friends, I wish to announce the titles that I will be bestowing upon our good friend Cristóbal Colón"—she looked down at Papa—"unless you would like to take the honors, My Lord?"

Papa shook his head.

"Then I shall speak for both of us."

Mother bade Colón to stand. I watched Papa throw back a swallowful of wine as Colón rose to his feet, nearly knocking over the servant assigned to tasting his food for poison. Mother must have thought Colón valuable to have asked Cardinal Mendoza to provide him with a taster. I glanced around to see who else had tasters: Mother, Papa, Juan, my sister Isabel. There was one for our table of royal daughters.

We had our worth, too, as goods to be offered in exchange for political favor, though I tried very hard not to think of when our bill of sale would come due.

"In gratitude for the service you have rendered the crowns of Aragón and Castile, henceforth you will be known as Don Cristóbal, Admiral of the Ocean Sea."

The grandees and high ladies clapped politely at their tables, quizzical expressions on their faces. Admirals were not made. The title of Admiral was something you inherited. Yet Mother had just made one of this bag of wind.

"With this title," she said, "comes a stipend of ten thousand *maravedís*, annually, for your life and for the lives of your heirs."

There was a slight but discernible pause in the clapping. At the high table, the smiles of the grandees were frozen on their faces. When was the last time Mother had granted them a stipend? Indeed, for them it was always pleas for more money to finance her wars.

"With the help of God, Don Cristóbal shall find other islands, from which"—Mother turned to him—"you will receive one-tenth of any and all revenues gained from these lands. A goodly amount, especially once contact is made with the Great Khan and trade has begun. Furthermore, you have the right to propose officials and name your lieutenants in these lands. These rights, Don Cristóbal, along with the right to bear a coat of arms displaying the royal symbols of Aragón and Castile, are yours for life and for the lives of your children and their children."

She paused. The applause, when it came, was lukewarm.

"Don Cristóbal," Mother said, "the King and I would like you to sail again as soon as you are able. When persons representing other crowns hear what you have done, they will be tempted to try your route to the Indies themselves. We would like to outfit you with seventeen ships—"

A buzz of exclamation went up. Colón had been granted only three ships for his first voyage. Out of whose pockets would the money for these extra ships come?

"—and as many men as it takes to provide labor on your new settlements. In accordance with our wish for you to bring these new people to the Catholic Church, twelve priests will accompany the settlers. It is our desire to treat the said Indios very well"—she broke off to frown at the page who was lifting a cup to the lips of a swooning Indio—"and *lovingly*, and to abstain from doing them any injury. We wish for much conversation and intimacy to be established between us."

Save for servants removing dishes and for the aged Marquise of Chinchilla, doggedly gumming a bit of gristle at my table, Cardinal Mendoza's feasting hall had gone still. Even Colón himself, the great self-promoting windbag, was stifled for a moment.

"Your Sacred Majesty," he said at last, "I am overwhelmed. You will not regret your generosity. I shall do my very best for you, for the crowns of Aragón and Castile, the Indios, and for the families I bring with me to your new lands."

Mother's brow clouded. "Families? I did not say families. You shall implement colonies of laborers. No women shall be sent on this expedition. As I have been lectured by Fray Hernando on many occasions, no good comes from the intermingling of men and women."

"Us," María hissed in my ear. "We came of intermingling."

Just then I noticed the smell of honey and orange peel,

the same sweet scent I had caught in Mother's chapel. When I turned around to seek its source, I heard a jangle and a loud thud. I turned again. An Indio had slipped to the floor.

Later that night, Beatriz, poor prison-keeper that she was, hardly looked up from the volume of Aristotle she was reading when I slipped out to go to Mother's chambers. I thought my papa would be there, as he was most nights when he was not abroad. I wished to return his ruby to him. For reasons I could not explain, I was anxious to be rid of it, but Papa had been out hunting each time I had looked to give it to him. For the same inexplicable reasons, I was uncomfortable with giving it to one of his men or handing it to him in front of Mother. I would pass it to him in secret as he took his last glass of wine before retiring, while Mother said her prayers, as was their custom. Somehow I felt that he would appreciate this.

It was with warm anticipation of his approval that I came upon Mother's ladies, gathered outside her door. They straightened guiltily as if they had been listening at the keyhole, then bobbed in hurried curtseys. I smelled the sweet tang of orange peel and honey.

"What is that perfume?" I asked.

One of the ladies moved into my way. "If you are looking for your mother, she is in there having her confession heard by Fray Hernando."

The lady was new to the court since the year before, when we won Granada. She would have been pretty if she could ever trouble herself to put some expression in her face.

Beatriz had told me the woman's strange story. She said

that this lady, Aixa, was the daughter of the vanquished Moorish king, Boabdil. Mother had taken her into court as a gesture of goodwill when Granada had fallen. When I pointed out that the lady hardly looked Moorish, with her blond hair and light olive skin, Beatriz explained that this was because Aixa's grandmother was the daughter of a Castilian noble who had been taken in battle by Boabdil's father. The old king had made the Castilian girl one of his wives, and soon she became his favorite.

But, Beatriz said, there is good reason for a man to keep only one wife. The wives, each wanting her own son to be king, fought, pitting son against son, and sons against the father. War erupted throughout the Moorish kingdom. When everyone was fighting, Spanish soldiers swept in and stole Granada for God and Isabel of Castile, and that was how the daughter of the Moorish king became a servant— or a lady-in-waiting, as Mother preferred to call her.

I thought of Beatriz's tale now as Aixa blocked my way into my mother's chamber. She was a sullen thing. Why would Mother keep her as an attendant?

I stepped forward, sniffing like a hare. "Is it you who wears the scent of orange?"

Aixa raised her elbows. "You cannot go in there."

"Where is my father?"

Not waiting for an answer, I dodged around her and put my shoulder to the door.

Muffled crying came from the other side, followed by the rich calm tones of Fray Hernando's voice.

I pulled back.

Aixa's handsome face was as blank as a stone. "Perhaps you should come back later."

I stumbled toward the nursery, past pikemen standing guard in the halls, past a gray cat stalking its prey. I was hurrying along the stone arches of the arcade, the edges of Papa's ruby cutting into my knotted fist, when it occurred to me.

Since when did Mother make confessions at night?

3.

29 May anno Domini 1493

*I*t was the day after Colón had finally left Barcelona to put together his fleet, after weeks of milking Mother for praise and concessions. The morning was as sunny, new, and fresh as only a morning in May can be, even in quarters where dogs were kept and blacksmiths' fires burned and piles of manure attracted lazily buzzing flies. I had gone to the kennels upon hearing that Juan's favorite mastiff bitch had recently whelped. I wished to see the pups. Even though it was hardly proper for a king's daughter to wander about a service courtyard, Beatriz and I would not be there long enough for it to matter.

Hens were strutting among the doghouses as I gently separated a squeaking pup from its mother lying in the straw. Beatriz stood by absentmindedly, fingering the skirts of her plain gray robes—she dressed like a nun although she belonged to no order. She was reciting Horace in her head, I supposed. She would have been absentminded regardless of what I was doing, for the previous evening she had received another visit from her betrothed, and she always came away from such distant and distracted. My sister María, romantic that she was, felt sure this was because Beatriz was yearning to wed this gentleman, Francisco

Ramírez. He was one of Mother's young secretaries, very handsome and charming, always handy with a jest for us royal children and quick with his broad white smile. Mother had approved of the marriage in reward for Beatriz's tutoring services, or perhaps Beatriz, nineteen and beautiful, with a doe's liquid brown eyes, had been given to him in reward for his secretarial duties. I did not know which. Nor did I know why they did not go ahead and marry, though I was glad that they had not. I knew from experience that my next keeper would not likely be as tractable as Beatriz.

I was cradling the whimpering pup, Estrella prancing at my feet, when Beatriz stiffened, her gaze pinned upon a doghouse.

"What is it?"

"I don't . . . know."

I glanced at the blacksmith in a bay behind us, his pincers to the fire. In another bay of the arcade, a carpenter and his assistant planed a plank of wood. A hen tugged at something in the dirt near the hem of my gown. Nothing seemed amiss.

I put down the pup.

In that instant, a man burst from the doghouse and grabbed my arm. I screamed, then, seeing it was one of Colón's Indios, screamed again. He held on, crying out in his tongue.

The carpenters dropped their tools and ran, but before they could reach me, a page in Juan's livery sprang from the shadows of the arcade and attacked the Indio.

"Don't hurt him!" I cried, even as the page threw the Indio to the ground. The poor creature rolled in the dirt, cradling his arm.

"Are you well?" the page asked me.

With a start, I recognized Diego Colón. "Yes! He was not hurting me."

"And that is why you screamed?"

To the gathering crowd of workmen, Beatriz announced, "Her Highness Doña Juana de Castile!" as if I were favoring them with a Royal Visit.

The smith bowed, dripping sweat. "Do you need assistance, Your Highness?"

I smiled with all the dignity one could muster when one's slipper was sinking into a pile of dung while an Indio moaned at one's feet. "No. Thank you. Please do not let me keep you from your work."

The men backed away, glancing at one another, then returned to their tasks.

"Is he hurt?" I asked Diego Colón. Regaining my senses, I realized that it was the Indio named Juanito, after my brother, Juan. Mother caused him to be baptized, along with the five other Indios, in the cathedral four days after Colón's arrival in Barcelona. He was the only one to have survived more than a fortnight. Charmed by his name, Juan had taken him into his service as a page, but having learned of Juanito's ungovernable fear of horses, had promptly relieved him of his livery and relegated him to the far reaches of his outer circle. It would not do for a representative of his court to cry out in terror when seated upon even the gentlest mare. Not when a man's prowess was measured by how well he handled a horse.

"He should not have touched you," Diego said. "No one should touch a lady, let alone the daughter of the King and Queen."

"He did not know better," I said. "Imagine being among

a foreign people, unable to communicate your thoughts and desires."

"You assume that I have not been in that situation."

I could not think what he meant. Did he mock me?

"Why was he upset?" I asked. "What was he shouting at me?"

"Do you think I know his gabble?" When he saw my frown, he added coldly, "He is new to my care this day."

Never mind that this Colón was handsome in his narrow-faced way, and slimly muscular, and broad of shoulder for a youth my age; he was as arrogant as his father. I pushed back my headdress, which was slipping onto my brow. "Where is your little brother?"

He looked away. "Your brother the Prince has made him his mascot. They are out hunting."

"Why are you not with them?"

"The Prince gave me charge of Juanito," he said.

I laughed. "And your charge escaped and hid here in the kennels."

He stared coolly.

"Highness," said Beatriz. "Your mother must wonder where you are."

I turned to her. "My mother," I said, "is closeted with Fray Hernando, figuring out how to save more souls. Do you think that she notices where I am?"

Juanito, still crouched, held out his hand to Estrella, who had come creeping out from behind the mastiff and her pups. Estrella leaned forward and, gingerly, sniffed his fingertips. She waved her tail when he stroked her head.

"Dog," I said loudly.

Juanito looked up at me.

"Dog," I repeated. "She won't hurt you."

He scratched behind Estrella's ears with both hands. "Dug," he said woodenly.

"Good! *Dog*. Have you been teaching him Castilian?" I asked Diego Colón.

"That is not one of my duties."

"But wouldn't you want him to learn?"

He raised his chin.

It occurred to me then that it might not be an honor to be assigned to care for Juanito—not when it caused the assignee to be away from Juan's inner circle of attendants. Juan must not think much of Diego's company. And how much greater Diego must feel the sting of this, having his five-year-old brother preferred over him.

"I will not tell my brother that you lost your charge," I said.

He met my gaze. "And I will not tell your brother that I met you in the kennels."

I stared at him. Did he not recognize that I was showing him pity?

Juanito rose after Estrella, who, distracted by a fly, had leaped away. I was glad to see that he had not been injured on my behalf.

Diego stepped directly behind him.

"Must you guard him like you do?" I exclaimed.

"It's what your brother told me to do."

"If Juan told you to jump from the battlements of the city wall, would you?"

"I'm not in a position to question my prince."

"You should, when he leaves you behind while your little brother goes hunting."

He gazed at me long and hard, giving me ample opportunity to know that his eyes were more grayish-green than greenish-gray, should María ask again. "I am grateful for the honors your family has given me. I shall not forget what they did for us, even when I am—" He stopped.

"What?"

"Nothing."

"No. Please. What?"

Water gurgled from the stone spout of the fountain behind us. He pursed his lips. "Rich."

I raised my brows.

"Easy for you to laugh," he said.

"I did not laugh."

"Surely you are not so coddled as to not realize that others aspire to the comfort that you take for granted. Most of us must work hard and seize every good chance to make our way up in the world. Most of us are buffeted by disappointments and disillusions."

"You assume that I have not been in that situation."

He opened his mouth, then closed it. "Do you mock me with my words?"

"Not at all. Your words applied, and so I used them."

"I see. So a princess feels disappointments."

"At times—of course I do. If you scratch me, I do bleed."

A corner of his mouth turned up. "Then I shall be careful never to do so."

"I would appreciate that."

"Highness!" pleaded Beatriz. "I am certain we will be missed."

"Your lady calls you," he said.

I turned to leave, then turned back. "You should not make judgments about persons. Only the wearer knows where the shoe pinches."

"I did not think royal shoes could pinch."

"Ours might pinch most grievously of all."

"That is doubtful."

Beatriz took my arm. I resisted. "I wish you could walk in my shoes someday, don Diego. Then you would know what I speak of."

"Indeed," he said, "I should like to."

Beatriz drew me away by force. "I'm sorry, Your Highness, but I do not wish to lose my position."

I looked over my shoulder as we entered the arcade on the other side of the courtyard. Oblivious of the stares of the workmen, Diego and Juanito stood side by side, an unlikely pair. When he saw me looking, Diego gazed up at the arcade, as if something interesting had landed on the pillar above him.

I turned around, smiling to myself.

Oh, most definitely, his eyes were grayest green.

That afternoon, I was called to Mother's chamber. She and Papa sat side by side at a table, reading documents that Cardinal Mendoza was passing to Mother. A secretary waited to the right of the Cardinal with a stack of items to be read, while another secretary was poised to my parents' left with a shaker of sand, ready to sprinkle their wet ink.

I stood quietly. In the past weeks, I had not tried again to give Papa his ruby. Indeed, I had hidden it in a coffer in my room, and then forgotten about it as well as I could. There was something disturbing about it, something I did not wish to ponder.

Cardinal Mendoza's red skullcap flashed in the light pouring through the arched window as he tipped his head

toward Papa. "Remind your wife again how much her soldiers worship her. Should she desire, I believe she could
lead them to Jerusalem and back."

"I lost a child," Mother said flatly, "riding to war. A son."

Papa kissed her hand. "My darling princess. If someone
says black, must you always say white?"

"When we were preparing to lay siege to Loja, I felt the
first pangs of childbirth at the council table. The babies
came early—I lost María's twin. But I did lead those soldiers, oh, did I lead them. Just as I was told."

"Isabel," Papa said in a scolding tone.

She would not look at him. "I have done my part, Your
Holiness," she said to the Cardinal. "And I refuse now to be
cajoled into continuing the Crusade into Africa or across
the Mediterranean. Isn't it enough that we took Granada
and the Spains are now united?"

"We would win," said Papa.

"He's right, you know," said the Cardinal.

Mother held the old man's gaze. "Not only horses can be
ridden to the ground."

The Cardinal looked away, then, seeing me watching,
showed his tiny reptilian teeth.

Papa followed his gaze. "Juana." He smiled. "How is my
shirt coming along?"

Our old jest. I had been working on a shirt for Papa since
I was Catalina's age, but it had never passed Mother's
approval. Only her shirts were good enough for him. The
queen of more lands than any potentate in the world, and
she insisted on sewing for her husband.

"I should have it to you on Tuesday," I said—my usual
response.

"Then on Tuesday, I should look like a king."

My cue: "But Papa, you already are a king."

Cardinal Mendoza arranged his wrinkles in a smile as Papa and I grinned at each other.

Mother signed her document with a flourish, then slid it to Papa. "If you are quite done." I straightened my face when she looked at me. "Our portraitist has come from Toledo to paint your picture."

"My picture?"

Papa glanced at Mother.

"It shouldn't be too hard for him to catch your freshness and beauty."

She was calling me fresh and beautiful? Her usual manner was to home in on the areas in which I needed improvement, not to compliment me. An alarum sounded in my head.

"We need this picture to send to Maximilian, King of the Romans." She looked at Papa as if waiting for him to chime in.

Papa leaned forward, signed the document, then pushed it to the secretary to sand, silent as the anvil of his emblem.

Mother frowned at him before continuing. "He has a boy of marriageable age," she told me. "A healthy, intelligent-enough, athletic boy, a year older than you. Philippe is his name."

"Philippe inherited the title of Duke of Burgundy from his mother," said the Cardinal. "Mary of Burgundy was one of the richest women in the world. From his father's side he carries the title Archduke of Austria and brings the wealth and ambition of the Habsburgs. As his wife, you would live in splendor."

"I suppose he can mount his own horse," I said. I saw Papa hide his smile. I warmed with pride at amusing him. How many times had we heard Mother tell the story of how, as a girl, she had rejected the future King of France as a suitor on the grounds that he could not mount his steed unaided?

Mother's own look was long and displeased. "It is meet that we cement our alliance with Maximilian against Charles in France. Even your father agrees with that. I believe I can take care of the English question with Catalina."

"But Catalina's just seven." I glanced at Papa for support. Surely he would not agree to send either of us away. Not yet.

"She will go to England when she is of suitable age." She looked between Papa and me. "You know my mind, Fernando. Neither Juana nor Catalina—none of my girls— shall marry before sixteen. That is not unreasonable, not when the French and the English marry their children when mere babes."

"True, true," the Cardinal agreed. To me he said, "Poor Marguerite, Philippe's sister, was betrothed and shipped to France to marry Charles as a three-year-old, only to be rejected by him when she turned eleven. Then he would not send the poor girl home, thinking he might wed her off to his benefit. He has always been a scoundrel."

"You sent our Isabel to Portugal when she was ten," I said to Mother, "and she had to stay there for three years."

Mother looked pained. "That was an entirely different situation. I shall never forgive the Portuguese King for making her his hostage as a condition of our peace. Do you think I wished to send my—"

"Favorite daughter?" Had I gone mad? My tongue would be the end of me.

"I was going to say 'oldest,'" she said drily.

"You offered me in exchange for her!"

"That was just a ruse to get him to let her go."

Could she not see how this had terrified me?

"Will I have the right to refuse if I see fit, as you did when your brother tried to pick for you? You turned down the future King of France for not being able to ride a horse and the future King of England for being able to ride a horse too well." My heart pounded. I had never stood up to my mother before. *Hostias en vinagre,* who had?

"And I was right about both, wasn't I?" she said, unruffled. "The Duke of Berry was so weak that he lost his place for the throne, and when the Duke of Gloucester became Richard the Third, his zest for dominance drove his countrymen into rebellion."

"You are fortunate that your mother has your best interests at heart," said Cardinal Mendoza. "Her half brother the King cared not two pins for her. I need not remind you what a villain he was. You do remember what he did to his six-month-old daughter."

"Let it drop," Mother said.

The Cardinal turned his old turtle's beak to me. "When people suggested that the baby was not his true daughter, he had her nose broken to make her look more like him."

"This is why I am glad to be so removed from the succession!" I exclaimed. "I cannot bear what people will do to have the power of the crowns."

"You don't know the half of it." Mother flashed the Cardinal a look.

"I do know!" I said. "I don't want any part of it. I would rather be a—a miller's wife."

"Oh?" said Mother. "You don't think they have their own problems?"

Papa put his quill in his inkhorn. "Come here, Juana."

He made a ring with his thumb and his forefinger. "Can you fit your hand through here?"

It had been our game since I was little for me to slip my hand through the ring, he always feigning surprise at how I could make my slender hand do so, I always beaming as if I had performed a great feat.

When I leaned in to thread my fingers through his circle, I got the slightest whiff of orange peel and honey, as though it had transferred to his person when he had embraced someone. I looked up at him.

"Such a small hand," he said.

Something seized in my gut.

"Thank you."

"As long as it fits, you do not have to marry." He nodded in affirmation, perhaps thinking that was why I continued to stare.

"Really, Fernando," said Mother. "Why don't you tell her the truth?"

I glanced at Mother. Could she smell the perfume, too?

"I am," Papa said.

With a sigh, she dipped her pen into the ink, and signed the next document. She reached for another paper she had set aside. "Should we give Beatriz de Peraza the funds she requests to repay her?" She caught Papa's gaze. "She did supply Colón well when he stopped at Gomera on his voyage. She claims that as regent governor of Gomera, she is due the twenty-three thousand *maravedís* that she spent on him."

Papa looked surprised. "I did not know she was regent governor."

The Cardinal glanced at Mother.

Papa still held his fingers in a ring. "When did her husband die? He was so young. One would have expected him to live a long, vigorous life when you sent her to the outer isles of the Canaries to wed him. Could you have sent her farther away?"

"No," Mother said. "Though I would have if I could."

Papa drew away his hand, seeming to forget me. "Now that she is a widow, are you going to ask her back to serve you?"

"Should I?"

They stared at each other.

Papa did not wear perfume. And the scent on him was not Mother's.

"It's up to you," Papa said.

Mother's jaw tightened. "Then—never." Her pen scratching, she signed the paper.

Papa smiled when he saw me watching. "What is it, Juana?"

How could they speak of this lady from Gomera before me? Did they think that I could not hear, could not smell, could not think? No. No. The Anvil would never betray his wife of many years, no matter if she was difficult.

Yet he had given himself to other women. Though we did not speak of the circumstances at home, Papa had a son who was about the same age as my sister Isabel. There were no ill feelings—Papa had even made Alfonso of Aragón the Archbishop of Zaragoza. Mother allowed him to visit at court, and then Papa would take him hunting. Nobody was hurt. It was just something that had happened in the past. So it was implied.

Against my will, my mind's eye dragged me to the first reception for Colón in the Saló del Tinell. Even as I fought like a trapped creature against the vision, I saw Papa leaning in to talk to Mother. I saw the glittering row of rubies on his collar. As my sights centered on the space left by the missing ruby, I remembered what I had not let myself recall until that moment.

Papa had not been in the Saló del Tinell when I had left to get Estrella. He had returned only after I had heard the persons coupling in Mother's prayer booth.

My Anvil. Papa. Tell me you would not do this.

Oh, Papa.

4.

1 April anno Domini 1494

*I*t was a fresh spring morning; we were on the road from Valladolid to Medina del Campo. Drums were thumping in the distance like the heartbeat of God. From outside the hooded cart in which I joggled along with my younger sisters and Beatriz came the weary *clip-clop* of hooves, the hollow snorts of mules, and the groan of a thousand wagon wheels upon the dry Castilian plain. Far ahead, Mother and Papa rode on horses caparisoned in scarlet and gold, leading a caravan that raised the dust on the road for nearly a league.

Inside our cart, we saw none of this. We jostled in the gloom, Catalina singing in her child's clear voice while she brushed María's waist-length hair of strawberry-gold. Beatriz was asleep with an open book on her lap, a fly sidling its way up the breast of her nun's gray robes.

Sighing, I gazed toward the single source of light, a small barred window in the door. I was finding my entrapment within our rolling cage particularly hard to endure. The song Catalina sang was one then popular at court, a ballad about Mother and Papa's undying love for each another. It proclaimed how Papa's gallantry toward Mother made him the Last True Knight.

Hostias en vinagre.

I had not told my sisters about Papa's infidelities since learning of them the previous year. I could not bear for them to know that my hero had feet of clay. Nor could I stand to confront him with it. He was happily unaware of my knowledge, which in itself made me furious. I had to bear the burden of keeping his secret. I had to protect *him*, when he, as my father, should be protecting me. So I had made it my business to stay away from him, not only because I could not bear to face him, but also, yes, because I wished to punish him. As wrong and childish as it was, I wished to hurt him the way I had been hurt. Yet each time I punished him by turning away, I was punishing myself twofold. How I wished for the innocence of my sisters.

Catalina began the next verse.

"Must you sing that?" I cried out.

She paused with her brush. "What?" She appeared to be all teeth those days. Her new-grown front pair seemed too large for her mouth.

"Why not?" said María. "It's beautiful. I like the part where Papa saves Mother from the Moors."

Catalina lifted her reedy voice to resume. Just then, the caravan stopped. I banged on the leather walls.

"What's wrong?" María kept her head rigid so as not to ruin the fanciful hairstyle Catalina was creating for her.

A footman opened the door at the rear.

"Why did we stop?" I asked.

"Your Highness, to water the horses."

"Let me out."

Beatriz bolted upright. "Highness! Where are you going?"

"Don't worry. Take care of María and Catalina."

I pushed into the light of day. We had come to a lush valley lying within a fold of the arid plains. Small trees overhung a swift river flowing beside the road. The air had the woody green scent of leaves and wet earth. I closed my eyes and let the sunshine warm my face.

Catalina poked her head out the door. "Where are you going?"

"Nowhere." I hopped down, then, once out of sight, changed directions, hoping to throw Beatriz from my scent when she came looking, as I knew she would.

Holding up my skirts to free them from the long grass at the side of the road, I strode past horses being led, splashing, into the river. Stable boys swarmed up the banks, loaded with filled leather buckets for the mules still hitched to the wagons. Ladies emerged from behind the curtains of their litters, handed down by groomsmen. They dipped into half-hearted curtseys as I passed.

Near the front of the caravan, in the shade of a grove of oaks and surrounded by attendants, two lutenists, and a flute player, Mother rubbed her hands together as her proud lady Aixa poured water over them from a silver ewer. Papa leaned against a nearby tree with his sleeves rolled up and his hands still damp from washing, chatting with Cardinal Mendoza, who sat in a folding chair. The cardinal's litter rested on the grass behind him, its mules having been led to the river to drink. Whereas Mother and Papa usually rode horses, the Cardinal was carried in a litter like Mother's ladies. His old bones couldn't abide the back of a horse.

I wheeled around, hoping I hadn't been seen.

"Juana!"

I stopped.

"Juana," called Mother, "come here."

I did as asked. I curtseyed briefly to her; Papa kissed my cheek. I did not look at him.

Mother took the towel offered by Aixa without acknowledging her. "We never see you anymore. You're always chasing off with the Latinist. As a matter of fact, where is she? She should be with you now."

"Please, My Lady Mother. I would like to ride a horse."

Papa turned and told his man to call a stable boy.

"Fernando," Mother said, "do you think that's wise?" She handed her used towel to Aixa, who took a step backward, her eyes downcast.

"The child wants to ride a horse. Must you control even that?" He smiled at Cardinal Mendoza, who returned his mild amusement.

Mother lifted a finger at another lady standing by. "See if you can find me an infusion of chamomile." Her lady hurried off into the melee of persons freed momentarily from their conveyances.

"Does your belly ache, my princess?" Papa asked her.

Mother ignored his question. "I'm not denying Juana anything. Those girls ride in the wagon for their own protection. There are those who would kidnap them or harm them, like that villain did to you."

"It seems my wife will not let me out of her sight now," he said to the Cardinal. "The worst crime that little man did against me was to cause my imprisonment for the rest of my natural life."

"Don't joke about it, Fernando." She pushed her filmy veil from her cheek with the back of her hand. "You're right—I haven't gotten over it, and I won't."

"You weren't even there," said Papa.

Mother looked at him.

"Do not the Scriptures say to forgive and forget?" said the Cardinal.

Mother shifted her gaze from Papa. "It's not a matter of forgiving and forgetting. I have forgiven that little man. My sins take away the right to judge him harshly. But I do not take lightly things that endanger my family. Or my husband."

"You cannot fault a wife for protecting what is hers," said the Cardinal. He slid his gaze to Aixa and took a drink.

He lowered his cup. "So," he said to me, "you wish to ride like your mother? She's a legendary horsewoman, you know. She's been known to ride thirty miles at a gallop. Few horses are a match for her."

"Or men," Papa murmured.

The Cardinal laughed.

Did they not know how disgusting they were to me? "Never mind about the horse," I said. "I shall find Beatriz."

"Wait," said Papa. "Here comes our food. Eat with us."

A cook's boy, carrying a domed tray, followed by the cook himself, arrived at our circle. The cook, a short, florid man whose doublet was spotted with grease, lifted the cover and sliced a black *morcilla* sausage into pieces to sample a bite.

Papa motioned impatiently. "*Bueno, bueno,* nobody wishes to poison us today." The cook, still chewing, stepped aside. Papa helped himself as more cooks and their boys brought forth trays from farther back in the caravan, each dish tasted for poison. Soon a picnic of bread, cheese, dates, and honeyed pastries was at hand, though Mother still looked for her jar of chamomile infusion and I for a chance to flee.

"Have you heard from Fray Hernando lately?" the Cardinal asked Mother.

"Do you jest?" said Papa. "The good *padre* sent his first

letter before he was outside the city walls when he left us last year, and keeps them coming every week. It seems he cannot let go of his job as Isabel's confessor."

"Surely," said the Cardinal with a small smile, "Her Majesty has little to confess."

Mother watched as he bit into his cheese. "On the contrary. That is why I took your recommendation for my new confessor."

"Fray Francisco Jiménez de Cisneros—a more stringent self-martyr you've never met," said Papa. "The man lives in a hair shirt and sleeps on the floor."

"He teaches me about penance," said Mother.

Papa frowned. "He teaches you about misery."

The Cardinal took a drink. "Have you something to be miserable about, My Lady?"

She turned to Aixa. "Please—have something to eat. You look hungry."

"Your Majesty, I am fine, thank you."

"I cannot have you wasting away. Fernando, don't you have something for this lady to eat?"

Papa met Mother's gaze, then flicked his finger for his page to bring a tray.

No expression disturbed the cold beauty of Aixa's face. "I am not hungry, My Lady, but thank you for your concern."

"Fernando, give her one of those almond pastries."

Papa frowned. It was not for a king to serve a lady-in-waiting. Hesitantly, he took a wedge between finger and thumb.

"Feed it to her," Mother said.

Hatred flashed in Aixa's eyes.

"Do it, Fernando."

The lady opened her mouth. Papa put the piece on her tongue as solemnly as if it were a Host, then turned to Mother, his jaw clenched.

A stable boy approached with a mule bearing my saddle. I threw my honeyed pastry to the grass and ran toward him.

"Juana!" Mother called. "Where are you going?"

"Lift me up!" I told the boy. "Please!"

He boosted me onto the pillion. I placed my feet against the solid wooden bar of the footrest, snatched the reins, and chirruped my mount forward.

Aixa was one of Papa's lovers and Mother knew it. It could have been her in the prayer booth with him that day, her and her vile orange-and-honey perfume. Mother knew it. The Cardinal knew it. Papa knew they knew. How could they keep up their foul little game?

"Juana!"

I cracked the reins and soon reached a gallop. The pounding of the mule's hooves soothed my jangling nerves. I urged my steed along the river, sending the drinking horses farther into the water, splashing and whinnying. Behind the last of the horses was a clearing along the bank. I could cross to the other side and get away from this madness, at least for a moment. I braced my feet against the planchette and steered for the water.

No horses were along the river there, for a reason. As soon as we were in the water, the bottom dropped away. My mule, foundering, panicked.

I clung to the flailing animal. Shouts rose from the shore. When I turned to look, my pillion slid sideways, plunging me into the river.

Knives of water shot up my nose. My ears throbbed with the hollow swoosh of the mule's thrashing, and my own. I heard my burbled underwater cries. My leg was pinned against the belly of the mule, trapped between the planchette and the pillion. I writhed against my heavy tangle of skirts, clawing at the mule, the planchette, my leg. My lungs screamed for air.

A hard thud above my ear blackened my vision. My head roared with pain. I gazed up through the arm's length of river between me and life, my breath gone.

It was over.

Relaxed now, I watched as filmy rays of sunshine glided through my watery ceiling. A rainbow shimmered just beyond, soothing me with its hazy colors. Scenes from my life washed over me in calming waves: María and Catalina making faces to get me to laugh. María and I clutching each other with joy when Papa told us we had a baby sister. Baby Catalina holding my finger in her infant's grasp, her tiny nails as thin and pink as rose petals. Mother, tenderly pressing my head to her breast. I could hear the beating of her heart.

The soft colors of the rainbow whitened into brilliant light.

A hand clamped on to my ankle. Water whooshed in my ears as I felt my leg being freed of the saddle. A jab to my back punched me clear of the water.

I was so startled to be torn from the light that it took me a moment to breathe. Someone was tugging me toward the shore.

I blinked at the otter-wet head next to me.

"Swim!" ordered Diego Colón.

5.

2 April anno Domini 1494

"Quick! Juana!" María whispered. "Don Diego looks at you."

"Oh!" Catalina tapped her fingertips together in a frenzy of delight. "Look back at him!"

With effort, I left my foggy limbo and gazed across the hall, loud with the sound of spoons scraping bowls, goblets clinking against plates, dogs snuffling under-table, and bows sawing on the melodious strings of viol and vihuela. At Juan's table, Diego Colón met my gaze, then glanced away. He lifted a piece of bread to his mouth.

A vision of his water-slickened head flashed through my mind. I felt awed that he should try to save me, and grateful, yet strangely numb. I had long since been dried, clothed, and promptly sent to bed with a hot-water bottle, upon reaching our castle of La Mota at Medina del Campo the previous day. This evening, I was rested and newly clothed in festive crimson for a banquet given by the merchants of the town to honor Mother and Papa. Still, the sensation of having my life spill out before me played across my mind. Though I had not passed all the way over, I had not yet passed all the way back.

"He saved you," said María. "Everyone is talking about

it. He ran down the bank, jumped into the river with his boots on, and pulled you from that mule."

"We think he loves you," Catalina pronounced.

"Do you love him?" María demanded.

I gazed at their expectant faces.

"No."

I speared a mouthful of the dish set before me. The garlicky taste of partridge browned in butter brought me a step further into this world. In my lap, Estrella nosed forward in hope of getting a handout, then ducked back when María reached over me to take a pinch of salt from the cellar. My sister's scent pricked further through my state of numbness: I smelled the distinct sweet tang of orange peel and honey.

"Are you wearing perfume?" I asked.

"Do you like it?" María grinned. "Aixa gave it to me."

Catalina put out her wrist to me. "She gave me some, too. Smell."

"Don't take anything from her!"

Both girls pulled back in surprise. "Why?"

"Just . . . don't."

I searched the hall for Aixa. She was at the head table, removed from Mother only by my older sister. Papa, at Mother's right, was immersed in a good-natured discussion with Cardinal Mendoza. He smiled when he noticed me looking.

I looked away. How could he live with himself?

I finished my dinner, and then, when a dance commenced, begged off by professing my lingering weakness. Dances were rare at Mother's court since the attempt on Papa's life, and therefore were much cherished by the young. I remained at table, feeding crusty bits of bread to Estrella as my sisters clattered off in search of partners. Soon Aixa was performing the steps of a saltarello with her partner, the Marquis of Santander. Her languidly graceful movements infuriated me. Did Mother not realize that Aixa's conquest of Papa was her revenge against Mother for vanquishing her father the Moorish king? Why would Mother allow it?

I was smoldering with disgust when I noticed the Indio, Juanito, making his way across the hall toward me, Diego Colón a short distance behind him.

I gathered up Estrella in a panic. What would I say to them? Though I had seen Diego from afar in Juan's court, we had not spoken for almost a year, since our awkward encounter at the kennels. I had not even been able to thank him when he had hauled me from the river. He had fled upon heaving me onshore, leaving me to the ladies and gentlemen who rushed to my side.

Juanito dropped to his knees before me. "I am happy that Your Highness is live today."

I smiled with surprise. "Thank you. You speak well now, señor."

Juanito looked up. "Yes. I have good teacher."

I hazarded a glance at don Diego. "You taught him?"

"It came to my attention, once, that he might learn."

Our gazes met. His narrow face had grown more angular, his expression more grave, his gray-green gaze more searching. He was, I admitted to myself, unnervingly handsome.

Hostias, I was turning into María.

Juanito sprang to his feet. "He show me to ride, My Lady. Horses."

"Did he?" I said.

Diego gave a small shrug.

Juanito reached out to Estrella, who drummed me with

her tail. "I ride mules, ponies, anything," he said. "You should see."

"I'd like to," I said warmly. "Very much."

"Her Highness must be occupied now," said Diego. He touched Juanito's arm. "We should go."

"Don Diego," I said.

He paused.

"Thank you for saving me."

"I was glad to." He turned to leave.

I did not wish him to go. "I hear my mother has given you a length of golden cloth. I am sorry the reward was not greater."

He halted. The offended look on his face took me by surprise. "That is not why I did it," he said coldly.

"I did not mean—"

"I am sorry to have given you the impression that my care was for the reward."

"That was not my impression!" He had said once that he dreamed of being rich, but I did not think of that. "I was only thanking you."

"In fact, I tried to give back the cloth, but your brother said that your mother would be insulted. I only wished to help you—my reward was in seeing you safe."

"He give me the cloth," said Juanito. "I make good cloak of it."

"There you are!" Plump and pretty doña Magdalena, one of my sister Isabel's ladies, swept toward us. The tops of her breasts, pressed by her bodice, swelled nearly to her chin. I saw how Juan's boys kept her in the corner of their sights when they paraded before her in their armor. My little love for her grew littler when she exclaimed, "Are you not going to dance with me?"

Of course someone else had designs on Diego Colón. Even on the edge of Juan's crowd, his brooding handsomeness would not be overlooked.

Doña Magdalena latched on to Juanito's arm and stroked it as if it were a puppy. "Do you remember the steps that I taught you?"

"*Si, señorita.*" Sheepishly, Juanito let himself be led to the dance by my sister's lady. I found myself standing with Diego.

In strained silence, we watched Juanito anxiously hunch forward as he waited on the first beat, then bend his knees on the second beat, and with lips pressed together in concentration, rise on his toes on the third. He launched into a serviceable saltarello.

I could bear the silence no longer. "So Juanito dances."

"Yes."

"It was good of you to teach him. I suppose you've had no lack of partners at the feasts my brother gives. I daresay he has feasts nearly every night."

He glanced at me as if trying to decipher the meaning of my words. "She taught him."

"Doña Magdalena?"

He nodded.

"Oh, so you see much of Isabel's ladies?"

He drew in a breath, then let it out slowly. "I have heard from my father. He has sent back a fleet with Antonio de Torres. Don Antonio will report to your parents as soon as he has an audience."

My heart sank. He could not deny he was romancing one of my sister's ladies.

"Father writes to me that he has sent back thirty thousand ducats' worth of gold, just a little taste of what is coming. The rivers there are full of it."

"That is good," I murmured, crestfallen. Would he not ask me to dance?

He frowned at me before continuing. "What I wished to say was that he wrote that he still plans, at my request, to return to a certain land where he came across the tracks of lions and griffins, a wondrous place where there was all manner of fruit and flowers. But you should know why I asked him to go back." He seemed to steel himself. "I asked him to do so because he named the island Juana."

I looked away, trying to think why he was telling me this, only to have my gaze fall upon Papa. He was approaching Aixa as the pairs separated to circle around the floor. When he passed her, he touched his fingers to her hand. She gave him a lingering sidelong gaze before elegantly moving on. I scanned the dancers for Mother.

"I can see that is of little interest to you," he said.

The gist of his words sank in. "You asked your father to return because the island was named Juana?"

He would not speak.

Gingerly, I asked, "Was it a big island?"

He frowned. "Very."

"Because," I said, venturing a smile, "I would not want a tiny little island named Juana."

"Oh, no. He saved a tiny little island for your sister Isabel."

I laughed out loud.

A smile twitched on his lips, as if he was proud to have amused me.

"What about you?" I asked, gently now. "Is there an island named for you?"

"No." He grew serious again. "There is no need. I shall inherit governorship of them all someday, and the lands that he is yet to discover."

"That should make you happy."

"Happy? I don't know if that's the word. I feel a great weight of responsibility. I want to be a good ruler."

"If only Juan thought like that. His mind is completely given to hunts. But I suppose he doesn't need to think about the craft of kingship—he knows he will never come to the throne. Mother is much too stubborn to die."

He blinked as if I had just blasphemed God. "You should know," he said after a moment, "that I model myself after her."

"Holy blessed saints, don't!"

"You must not say that," he said firmly. "She is the most intelligent monarch in the world. She makes hard decisions, and doesn't flinch when making them, even if it causes her personal pain. I watch her very, very closely."

The hair prickled on my arms. "You do?"

"Yes. I am trying to learn." He looked at me. "Is something the matter?"

"Not at all." I drew a breath. "What would you do if you ruled?"

"Not if," he said, "when."

"When you rule, then."

He glanced as though to see whether I was mocking him. He seemed relieved to find that I was not. Had he no idea how handsome he was?

"What should I do?" he asked.

I could not help it. His face was so serious. "Name all your islands Juana."

A smile grew in his eyes. "All the new ones, yes, I could do that. I expect there will be many."

"Perfect."

He laughed. Watching the dancers, he asked, "Do you think that someday, after you have grown tired of seeing your name all over the map, I might name one after my mother?"

"One. Certainly. If she insists."

He smiled sadly. "I fear my mother was not one to insist upon anything."

I waited for him to explain.

"Not even for my father to stay. He left her to pursue his dream and never went back. I have not seen her since I was four." He shook his head. "I'm sorry. I don't know why I say this to you. I speak about it to no one."

"I know how that can be."

"What is it about you? I trust you." He touched his fingers to mine. "Thank you."

Heat charged through my fingertips as we gazed at our touching hands.

A page trotted up, startling us. He smirked at Diego before announcing, "Your Highness, Her Sacred Majesty wishes your company."

My heart pounded as I waited for the page to leave. "I shall be back," I told Diego, my voice strange in my ears. "Wait."

Mother was sitting on her throne, rubbing her chin in thought. She drew her eyes from the dancers before addressing me.

"Juana. I saw you standing idly with the Colón boy."

Warmth seared my cheeks.

"Your time would be better spent practicing your steps. I understand they are keen on their dancing in Bruges. It is meet that you can keep up with your husband."

"My husband?"

The keening of the vihuela and viol recommenced, this time accompanied by the rich tootling of a trio of sackbuts. "The portrait we sent was a great success. It seems young Philippe, Archduke of Austria, demands your hand post-haste."

"No!"

"We are still negotiating the terms of your dowry and an acceptable contract has yet to be drawn up, but I trust that his father—now Holy Roman Emperor, you should be glad to hear—will come to an agreement. His son desires you, and the Emperor desires an alliance. Preparations for a union of this exalted nature must begin at once. They could take months to complete."

"Does the Archduke know that I am but third in line to the crowns of the Spains?" I said quickly. "Further back than that, once Juan or Isabel has children. I am not such a bargain."

Mother laughed.

"But—I am not to go until I am older. Papa said."

Mother pursed her lips. "Your father says many things, as if saying them might make them true."

"I will not hear you speak against him!" I cried, surprising even myself. "He is an anvil."

She regarded me calmly. "Yes. He is."

Why did she not defend herself? Did she not think highly enough of me to take me into her confidence?

She exhaled an exasperated breath. "They would all be anvils and have us all be mush. I am so weary of the dance of deference that we must do. How often I have thought of this as I ride to yet another council to cajole my nobles into behaving, without my seeming to control them. I do believe that women might be the more powerful sex, with our agility of wits and our endurance. Yet we must not show our dominance to our men. We must act meek and docile. Why should this be?"

I shook my head. I wanted to return to Diego.

"I have come to see our relationship with men as being much the same as a horse's with its master. The horse could crush its rider at any moment, but has been led to believe it cannot do so. For fear of a little pain, it does as it is bidden. And so it continues forth, a noble, strong creature, kicked and spurred into docility by the little man upon it. Why does it accept this?" She stared at me as though I might have an answer.

Two of her ladies now returned. "May we get you some chamomile tea for your stomach, Your Majesty?" asked one.

Mother waved her off.

"Your Majesty took very little to eat at supper. I thought perhaps—"

"Doña Micaela, please. I am fine."

"Thank you for your advisement," I said, then curtseyed to Mother and left her to her strange musings so that I might find Diego.

But he was no longer standing near the dancers. I searched through the thicket of raised arms and swishing perfumed skirts, the whine of the vihuelas and the shuffle of slippers muffling the thumping of my heart. I ran out to the arcade, prompting a guard to raise his halberd against me.

He bowed when he saw who it was. "May I assist you, Your Highness?"

Save for the boys carrying dishes to the kitchen, only the rough warbling of frogs disturbed the lush quiet of the evening.

"No. No. Thank you."

The Habsburg Netherlands

Hans Memling, The Mystic Marriage of
Saint Catherine of Alexandria

6.

18 October anno Domini 1496

It was as cold and gray as Judas's tomb in the Flemish town of Lier. The sickeningly sweet scent of brewing malt filled my nose as my horse clopped over the wooden bridge and into the church square. The place seethed with nobles on brightly caparisoned horses, peasants with their legs wrapped in muddy buskins, and women in winged white linen headdresses. Church bells pealed and trumpets heralded my entrance along with my twelve Spanish ladies, all dressed in as many jewels as their families could afford, save Beatriz, who wore her humble nun's gray.

Ahead, in the shadow of the church tower with its thundering bells, a young lord awaited. His mantle of glistening sable, rich chain of gold, and jeweled hat marked him as the most noble of nobles. He held a hooded white gyrfalcon on his red-gloved fist even as he reined his horse sharply, forcing the animal into sidesteps and scattering the gentlemen around him in a move that would have earned a lesser man a cuffing. As it was, the nobles laughed. I could see his strong white teeth as he grinned in return.

My betrothed.

God, help me.

Philippe the Handsome, he was called—*Filips de Schone,*

in the tongue of the Flemish people, a loud lot with angular faces, wiry bodies, and hair the color of dust. And from what I saw now, they were well and truly right. His skin was golden, like the inner flesh of a plum; his eyes the clearest pale blue; his lips neat pillows of rose, set between slight winsome pouches at the sides of his mouth that gave him the air of a playful boy.

Already he had shunned me.

He had not been in Bruges when I arrived. I had been stunned to learn that he had tarried in German lands when he knew I was to arrive. Did he think me defective? No one left a bride of royal blood waiting. Tongues would be wagging all over Christendom. He had stretched his journey home over three leisurely weeks, and then, when he arrived here at last, had gone hunting for six days—six!—in preference of meeting me. How different it had been for Mother, with Papa, filled with excitement and longing, hurrying across the plains to her in his muleteer's rags.

Shuttered within a small brick palace with Beatriz and my ladies, I'd had plenty of time for my anger to freeze into fear. In my own land, when Pedro the Cruel had not found his wife, Blanche of Bourbon, to be pleasing, he had shut her up in a tower until he found the time to have assassins end her miserable life. Urraca of Castile so disgusted her husband, Alfonso the Feisty, that he tried to poison her, and when that did not work, he sent armies against her until she agreed to an annulment. History has proven that if a husband finds his wife undesirable, she can lose more than her simple pride.

Now my palfrey grew closer. I intensified my pleading with God.

Blessed Lord, show me how I am to be. Make him love me enough not to hurt me, I beg of you.

My betrothed settled his horse and bade his man hold the bridle. With the gyrfalcon still on his glove, he dismounted next to a linden tree that dropped its yellow leaves onto the church step. He was not so very tall, but he held himself loosely, as would one who had not a care in the world.

Trumpets blew in a fanfare. Over the deafening clang of the bells now directly overhead, my page shouted, "Juana, Infanta of Castile!"

My horse stopped, gentle traitor. The reins were being taken from me. The bells thundered in my ears as I was lifted down by the Admiral of Castile.

The Archduke came forward. I dropped my gaze and fell to my knees, grinding a prince's ransom of cloth-of-gold into the leaves on the wooden walkway.

"So this will be my wife." His voice was loud. On his fist, the falcon shifted with a jingle of tiny bells.

Over the ringing of the bells, I heard the jangling of bridles. An infant cried out somewhere behind me; a pair of ducks flew quacking onto the canal behind the church. I would not look up. A man did not want a woman who called attention to herself. I would be chaste and modest, as all the books on marriage urged. I would make him love me. I had to.

My betrothed coughed into his glove. "Well, the top of her head is certainly pretty."

The men next to him chuckled. I could feel the townsfolk edging closer behind me. A heart-shaped yellow leaf drifted onto the boards at my knees.

I heard him relinquish the bird to his falconer.

"Give me your hands."

My heart pounding in my throat, I held out my hands. Leather-clad hands clasped mine. Lips brushed against my knuckles.

"She trembles!" he announced.

I melted with humiliation as his men chuckled once more.

He kept his grip on my hands as I knelt before him. "I do like an obedient woman, but enough now. Madame, look up at me."

Would he find my nose too long? My lips too full? My eyes frighteningly green when the ideal called for gentle gray?

I raised my head and stared without seeing. I could feel his eyes inspecting my face, his gaze lingering upon each feature like a man searching for flaws on a horse he thinks to purchase.

"Stand, Madame."

Our hands still joined, I struggled to my feet.

"Are you well?" he asked.

I brought my eyes into focus. His expression was of puzzlement.

In his language, I said, *"Monseigneur, oui."*

"You speak French?"

"Monseigneur, oui." My prideful tongue—I could not help adding, in French, "And Latin and Spanish."

He shrugged. "Good, as long as you don't quack in Flemish like my subjects—though you are so lovely, I might not much care."

Lovely. He said I was lovely.

Over my head he called, "Is My Lady's chaplain here?"

I heard Fray Diego Ramírez de Villaescusa, the friar Mother had sent to be my confessor, raise his voice from behind me. "Yes, Your Grace."

"Would you be so good as to bless our union? I should like to take this fair lady as my wife." The sweetly petulant pouches at either side of his mouth added to the charm of his smile. "What say you to that, Madame?"

Was there to be no ceremony? No celebration? When my sister Isabel married Afonso of Portugal, there were five days of feasting, jousting, and presentations before she was delivered across the border to her husband. My betrothed had not even allowed for proper introductions to my attendants. Don Fadrique Enríquez de Cabrera, the Admiral of Castile, must be mortified. The highest-ranking member of Mother's court did not come all this way to be snubbed by an eighteen-year-old archduke.

I looked down the row of his gentlemen, dismounted and queued next to him, all smirking. A wife was not considered a wife, nor a husband a husband, until the marriage was consummated. We had spoken but a dozen words. Surely he did not mean—

The bells still tolling, Fray Diego made his way to my side.

"Say the words, my man," Philippe said. "Do your work."

Fray Diego began the rite. In shock, I made my mouth move when he came to the part of the vows where I was asked if I would take this man and obey him. Philippe then promised to take me, too, and we processed into the church for Mass. As Fray Diego's words echoed from the high stone vaults of the ceiling, I shivered from fear and confusion and the chill of the church, colder inside than outside at the steps. My new husband squeezed my hand during the Our Father, then took it again after we had received the Host. I stole a wondering look at him.

He smiled.

Dear Lord, did I truly please him?

After Mass, we walked hand in hand down the street from which I'd come, to the palace where I had stayed in wait for him. Behind us rode our ladies and gentlemen— mine looking confused and angry, his winking and laughing. Behind them danced the townsfolk, cheering and singing as if going to the wedding feast of the miller's daughter. Mother would be furious.

Philippe caught my glance. "Are you well, Madame?"

I had to do whatever it took to make him love me.

"Yes, Monseigneur, I think."

"You 'think'? Either you are or you aren't. It is as simple as that."

"Then I am well, Monseigneur."

His smile was sweet and genuine. "Good. You should always be what you must be. And at this moment, I'd say you are the loveliest bride in Christendom."

Once inside the palace, I was ushered by my ladies to my bedchamber, where I was stripped to a shift of gossamer linen, given a draft of warm wine, then tucked to my chin beneath the sheets.

Falcon on one hand, goblet in the other, Philippe arrived, accompanied by his men singing raucously, blowing horns and beating on drums. He passed his bird and his cup to his groomsmen. One of them, grinning, took his hat, his gold Chain of State, and his mantle and robe, then peeled off his heavy gloves. To loud cheers, Philippe's sleeves were removed, then his doublet, and then his shoes and hose. Dressed only in a shift, he bade his groomsmen leave.

He closed the chamber door behind him. The dim midday light streaming through the lumpy glass of the window caught the golden gleam of his hair where it curved below his chin. "My Lady Wife."

"Monseigneur," I whispered.

My gaze fled to the tapestry on the wall as he pulled at the strings of his shift. I was conscious of the weight of the fur counterpane upon me, and of the cool thickness of the linen sheets, discernible through my sheer gown. Even if I could have thought of something else to say, the pounding of my heart in my throat would have prevented it.

He went over to the fire snapping within the confines of its ornately carved niche and made to warm his hands before it, though his gloves had only just been removed. His groomsmen's merrymaking could be heard as they paraded through the palace.

In all her talk of the hanging of the sheets after the consummation of her marriage, Mother had never explained how she had performed the act. I had never gotten up the courage to ask her. Indeed, it was a subject I was loath to speak of with her. And whom else could I consult? Beatriz shied away from it as would a mare from a snake. She could not even be persuaded to marry. My younger sisters would find it a felicitous subject—oh, very much so—but their only knowledge came from troubadours' songs.

Yet I knew from watching horses couple that the man must introduce his member to a woman's purse, and from the sensation that I received in watching such in horses, I thought that receiving the member of a man I loved might be desirable. But this man was not my lover. Beyond my wedding vows, I had not yet spoken six sentences to him.

He came and stood over me. "I am afraid that they will not go away. The men," he said when I glanced at him. "They will not leave until they are satisfied."

Indeed, the gentlemen were now positioning themselves beneath our window, and were bawling out in lewd song.

This man had left me waiting for him for six days while he hunted. He had cared so little he'd not met me at the ship. Now that I had his eye, I could not lose his attention, not when displeasing him might mean he would send me back to Mother or lock me in a tower in the best of circumstances, or poison me in the worst. My hand shaking, I slowly pulled back the covers, uncovering my breasts, my belly, and then my thighs, sheathed in filmy batiste.

A smile played at his lips as he cast his gaze over my body. I wished to shrink away until nothing remained but my gown.

He swallowed. "Just be certain to shout loud enough."

"Shout?" I whispered.

"The Cry of the Maidenhead."

I shook my head, not understanding.

He frowned in displeased surprise when his gaze returned to my face. "You don't know of the Cry of the Maidenhead?"

Shivering as much from nerves as from the cold of the room, I shook my head again.

"In your land, you do not—I had thought that every-one . . ." He coughed into his hand. "Well. This is what it is: At the moment a bride loses her virginity to her husband, she is expected to cry out loudly enough for all to hear."

More groomsmen had found their way outside and below our balcony, where they shouted up sayings that would singe the ears of a whore. Philippe sighed. "I am sorry. They ex-pect your cry, and I do swear they will not leave us alone until they have heard it." I must have looked mortified, because he added, "At least there is a good bowl of hot cau-dle in it."

"Caudle?" I whispered.

"Once they've heard the cry, they'll bring in our bowl of

it, they'll toast, we'll drink, and then they will go away, I promise."

To what kind of rude land had my mother shipped me? Yes, in the Spains a bride was bedded with her husband after the wedding, but she was not expected to crow at her deflowering like a whore. Tears pricked at my eyes.

He sat down on the edge of the bed. "I am sorry. It appears you did not expect this."

A merrymaker outside blasted on his trumpet. My husband turned his head and shouted, "Would you shut up!"

I drew a breath. I could bear this. I could bear anything. "You must tell me when to shout, Monseigneur."

"When to shout?" He crossed his arms and puffed out his lips, accentuating their natural poutiness. "Should that not be obvious?"

I breathed a miserable sigh. A lump of salt swelled in my throat.

He studied my face. "I am sorry. It is not my purpose to dismay you, especially at the hands of my men."

"I shall be fine, Monseigneur."

"No. No!" He hit the bed with his fist, making me flinch. "I shall not let them tell me what I am to do with my wife. I am their lord, I can do whatever I want. They are not the ruler of me." He gestured at the tear under my eye, indicating that I should wipe it. "Do not worry. I think we might outfox them."

His men came, as promised, bearing a silver bowl of caudle, smoking torches, and fortifying bread. We received them in our bed, me up to my chin under the counterpane, he sitting up, uncovered to the waist. He grinned as they slapped his back and complimented his manhood while he drank from the steaming bowl. After he drank his share, he lifted my head so I might sip. The hot spicy wine still warmed my belly as they left.

The door shut. My husband sank under the covers to his chin. "Well done, *chérie*. That was a good and hearty shout, I must say. How did you know how to hoist such a yowl?"

"There are cats in the Spains, Monseigneur, as well as here."

He glanced at me as if considering me anew, then broke into a laugh.

The glow of pride I felt for amusing him dimmed quickly. For while we had tricked his men by having me cry out at his count of three, he had not tried to bed me. Did he find me so undesirable? Was his urgency to wed me just a show to impress his men?

"What troubles you?" he asked.

"I am not troubled, Monseigneur."

"Something does trouble you—you are as readable as a child's book of beasts. Come now, you must always speak your mind to me. I shall do the same for you."

I paused. "Do I not please you?"

He turned onto his side to look at me. "Please me?" He took my chin in his hand. I could smell his scent of musk and wine as he turned my face gently from side to side. Our gazes met in the flickering lamplight.

"I want to please you," I whispered.

Outside the wavy glass of the windows, rain commenced, first pounding in a curtain of gray, then softening into a silvery hum. He leaned down and touched his lips to mine.

Warmth spread through my body, the waves continuing as he pulled away.

"Then," he whispered back, "you shall get your wish."

Yes, it hurt, at first. And there was blood, but not much—the amount one would spill from a small cut. The next time he gave me more chance to understand. He showed himself to me, a dear jaunty fellow sheathed in dusky silk. I touched his turtle dove's eggs nestled beneath. And then he got on his elbows and explored me, talking to me gently as does a master to its frightened horse. Soon, very soon, the sweetness much outweighed the pain.

We did not emerge from my chamber until the following afternoon, and only then to eat and drink. He bade me try the beer of which the Flemish people are so fond, and when I spat it out, he laughed as though I were the cleverest girl in the world. Then we retired again to my chamber, which still smelled strongly of sex, and held back our laughter while a page hurriedly remade the fire, dropping the wood out of nervousness as we watched him from our bed.

We made love again. After that, he rose from me, washed his face in the basin, then threw himself on the fur spread of the bed. He propped his chin on his hand and touched his finger to my lips. "My sweet yowling Puss."

I kissed his finger, damp from his washing. "My Lord, I am reminded of a wedding custom in my country."

"Yes, Puss?"

"There is no shouting, mind you."

"No. Shouting is for silly Flemings—though you were quite good at it."

"After a king takes his new-wed queen to his bed, they display their sheets to their subjects as proof of their consummation, and of his queen's virginity."

"Lovely custom. How do they display them?"

"From their bedchamber balcony, Monseigneur. It is hung there for all to see."

He lifted the sheet below the fur on which we lay and peered at the sheet underneath. "If my people wished for proof of such, they should find much evidence here." He put down the cover and extended his hands to me. "Up! Put on your robe. We are giving my people a taste for things Spanish."

Our robes hanging loosely from our shoulders, we tore the sheets from the bed, then laughingly stumbled with them across the rush-covered floor. My husband threw open the shutters to the cold gray morn, and together we let down the proof of our happy union.

A stable boy leading a horse on the street below looked up.

"Behold!" called my husband. "The flag of Austria and Spain!"

The boy was still gaping when my husband drew me back into the room. He shut the window, and then tenderly gathered me into his arms, quieting my laughter with kisses.

7.

20 October anno Domini 1496

We had moved to the palace in Malines, a short ride from Lier. Shut within the hangings of the bed, I lay atop the sheets and with my toe kicked a tassel dangling from the bedpole. I was giving most serious attention to keeping the golden cord a-swing, for if I stopped moving my leg for the merest moment, the nauseating spinning would resume in my head.

How did these people drink so much wine? They drank vats of it at the suppers in the two days before our wedding ceremony of state, and then, at the feast after the nuptials, more wine flowed than does in all of Castile, León, and Aragón during the fiestas of Carnaval.

And these people ate, too, as if they had never glimpsed food in their lives. Entire forests lay upon groaning tables at the wedding feast: pheasants, partridges, stags, rabbits, herons, boar. There were peacocks roasted and sewn back in their feathers; chickens minced and molded into a large castle for Castile; jellied calves' feet formed into the shape of the Golden Fleece, symbol of Philippe's House of Habsburg. All these foods were served upon great three-masted ships sailing among our tables, with smaller vessels filled with spices and fruit—a salute to the fleet that had brought me from the

Spains. Course after course of this great bounty arrived, accompanied, to my ladies' horrification, by naked women painted to look like mermaids. There were horses tricked up as sea monsters and boys riding white whales made of wood. Then a capacious pie was wheeled in, from which burst a choir singing about the glory of the union of the Houses of Habsburg and Burgundy with that of Trastámara. Or had I imagined all this in my drunkenness?

I tried not to think of my overfull belly, while in the chamber beyond the drawn bed-hangings my husband poured water into a basin. I could smell the rosewater as he splashed it onto his face. Outside our door, men laughed and shouted— his ever-present men. The number of ladies bidden to Mother's chaste bedchamber when Father was abroad was paltry compared with the number of followers surrounding my husband. He was the handsome and vivacious lord of the land, and courtiers were attracted to him like moths to torchlight. Yet Philippe was anything but chaste. Far, far from it. My loins burned just to think of our coupling.

I heard the tinkling of little bells. Philippe's gyrfalcon must have been shifting on her perch. My husband had brought his much-loved bird into our rooms this evening, reassuring me that she could never free herself of her tethers and do harm.

The hangings were yanked open. My naked husband stood with the candlelight behind him.

"Well, Puss." He dropped onto the bed next to me, sending bits of down into the air. "What did you think of a real Burgundian wedding feast?"

"It was big."

He leaned over and kissed my cheek. "The Houses of

Burgundy and Habsburg like an excuse to show off. Was it better than in the Spains?"

I thought of when we celebrated my sister Isabel's marriage to the King of Portugal. There was feasting and jousting all the way to the Portuguese border, but there was also much attendance of Mass. And there was no wine for the ladies. No delicious, fruity wine. "Your sister won't have as magnificent a wedding feast as ours."

He blew away a bit of down floating before his face. "A pity. Marguerite's a splendid girl. As witty as a jester, and damn good-looking. Does your brother deserve her?"

"Juan has a good heart. He'll treat her kindly. She'll fare especially well if she likes to hunt."

"Likes to hunt! She has Burgundian blood in her—we would all rather commit murder than miss a good chase. My mother died hunting, you know."

"I am sorry, Monseigneur."

"Don't be. From what I hear, that's exactly how she would have liked to die. Come to think of it, me, too. At any rate, I didn't know her. I was not quite four when she died. Tell me—what did my sister have to say about me?"

"That I had better like hunting."

He laughed, then raised his voice. "Delilah!"

Through the open bed-hangings I could see his gyrfalcon, craning forward on her perch as if to listen to her master. She cocked her head to catch his voice, for she wore a leather hood and could not see.

He clucked at her. "Isn't she beautiful? And I'm not just saying that because she's one of the most expensive birds in the world."

"Would not a male of her type be more valuable?"

"Not at all. Female gyrfalcons are bigger and stronger than the males—quite the reverse of mankind."

I thought of Mother, dominating both council and home as Papa good-naturedly stood back. She loomed over him and everyone else like a single mighty oak over a grove of squatty olive trees. Perhaps I was wrong to have been disappointed in Papa. Perhaps it was Mother who was to blame. It was she, by her dominance, who had caused him to stray. I would do things differently. I would like the things my husband liked, do what he desired to do. We would be such kindred spirits that he would never be unfaithful.

"Does your bird always wear the hood?" I knew nothing of falcons. I would have to learn.

"Indoors, yes. Or would you prefer that she mark your ladies' little dogs as prey?"

I sighed, missing Estrella. My only comfort was in knowing she would hate it here—the cold, the wet, and now having to share a bedchamber with a falcon whose talons were as long as my fingers. She would have never come out of the bedclothes.

"What did my *grand-mère* have to say about me?"

I stopped pinging the tassel with my toe. A sense of discomfort penetrated my haze as I saw myself at the feast, with Madame la Duchesse perched immediately to my right. Margaret of York, Dowager Duchess of Burgundy, the third wife of Philippe's grandfather, held her receding chin aloft with the authority of a queen. Though the rest of her aging face was as bland as a skinned rabbit, a compelling, nay, intimidating, fire sparked from her eyes. Here was a woman used to going her own way. Indeed, my ladies have whispered that she once bore an English bastard. Surely that could not have been true. Charles the Bold, Philippe's grandfather, and in his time the richest man in the world, earned his name by demanding nothing but the best. He would not have accepted a soiled woman as his wife, even if she was sister to the English king.

At the feast, as the ships had sailed by with their splendid fare, the Dowager Duchess had taken little of the exotic foods offered to her, even though it was her glittering palace in which we were dining. She said even less, noting with disapproval every bite or sip I put into my mouth and every word that dribbled out. Trying to make conversation, I had asked if she might offer me advice on how to please my new husband.

She speared the single stuffed quail's egg marooned in the center of her golden plate. "My dear, my grandson always finds his pleasure. It is you who must find how to please yourself."

I had blinked at my own plate, overflowing with peacock, prawns, and roast boar dripping in truffle gravy. Was she testing my desire to be a good wife to Philippe? Evidently, they were close, she having raised him in the absence of his mother, who was Charles the Bold's daughter from his first marriage. "But, Madame, I want to make him happy."

"Make him happy! My dear child, he has no idea what unhappiness is."

"That is admirable, Madame."

She raised the quail's egg on the tip of her knife. "Is it? All his life, 'yes' is the only word he has ever heard. It has made for a man whose appetite grows larger from eating." She poked the white orb past her thin lips, then chewed, grimacing.

Now my husband stroked my arm. "Tell me what she said about me. She had to have said something. Grand-mère would not miss an opportunity to voice her opinion."

I resumed my play with the tassel. "She said you were happy."

"I am. Come now, surely she said more."

"Truly she said little else—save that the only word you know is 'yes.'"

The sweet pouches on either side of my husband's lips slackened, as they did whenever he was serious. Then he rolled onto his back and laughed. "I do believe that she might be right. Of course she is right—Grand-mère is always right. Well, I take that as a compliment. Being agreeable is an admirable quality in a man."

I had meant that he had heard only the word yes, not necessarily that he said it, but now was not the time to split hairs. "Indeed, Monseigneur. Being agreeable can never be bad."

He stretched his arms above himself. "You know what my people call me?"

"Yes, Monseigneur—Philippe the Handsome."

"Not that." He slid his lower lip forward in a pout.

"But Monseigneur, you should be proud."

He waved me off. "That is silly woman talk. My men call me 'Philippe Believer in Counsel.' I like it. I do try to say yes as much as possible—it's a good policy. Someday I will be called simply what my great-grandfather was called."

I kicked at the tassel. "What was that?"

"Philippe the Good."

"I shall call you that now: my good Philippe. Philippe the Good."

He grinned at me, his lids heavy with drink, then suddenly grabbed my leg. "And now, Madame, will you dare say yes?"

I rolled toward him, still caught in his grip.

"Yes, Monseigneur. Always yes."

"Mm." He kissed me hard. "You do learn fast."

8.

31 October anno Domini 1496

Our horses thundered through the dripping woods outside Malines. The wet undergrowth whistled beneath the bellies of the greyhounds bounding beside us. Men shouted, bridles jangled, and the bells on our falcons' legs jingled merrily. Starbursts of gray mud splattered against my yellow skirts as I wedged myself more firmly against the jolting seat of the pillion. I tightened my grip on the reins, though I had but one hand to do so; a hooded falcon dug into my thickly gloved left wrist.

Philippe's mother had died like this.

So my husband had reminded me before we took to our horses that morning, eleven days after our wedding feast. His falconer was setting a bird to my hand—a peregrine, with wings and back the shining gray of cold charcoal. Blinded by its hood, it turned its head from side to side, as if to see who I might be.

My husband stroked the bird's smoothly feathered wings. "My mother had a falcon just like this one, is that not so, monsieur?"

The falconer, a leather-faced man whose hooked nose and chin nearly met over his toothless mouth, responded in French strongly flavored with Flemish. "*Oui, Mijnheer.* The bird caught three ducks before your mother *la duchesse* fell, God rest her soul. It was a very fast bird."

He guided the creature onto my wrist. It took hold, the pressure of its talons painful even through my heavy glove. "She is well trained, Mevrouw," he said to me. "She will not give you trouble unless she thinks you are weak."

I looked up in panic. I was terrified of her. She would know this?

Philippe ran his hand down the bird's dark wing. "Mother was not expected to hunt the day that she died. She was great with child, and she would not have gone riding, even though the King of France had organized the hunt, had it not been for the Archbishop of Cambrai. After Mass that morning, the fool had given her a Book of Hours that contained an illustration of her hunting with her hawk while Death, bony and grinning and swinging a mallet, hunted her. Silly friar, he should have known she would take that as a challenge. There was a reason her father was known as Charles the Bold—and Mother inherited all of his fire."

"My mother killed a bear," I said. "With a javelin. Outside Madrid. Last year."

"What? Well. That's the spirit." He gave his falconer's back a friendly thump, then mounted his horse. "Make sure her bird doesn't escape."

Now our group galloped through a muddy field stubbled with the remains of the harvest. With a whoop, my husband urged his steed faster, slime slinging from the horse's hooves. Our party met his challenge with cries of delight, quickening our pace and loosing our own storm of muck. Blinking away the flying debris, I moved to wrap my reins more tightly around my free hand and thus startled my bird, causing her to fly up in protest. Her jesses halted her flight, jerking her back to my wrist, and in turn rocking me in my seat. My heart jumped as I fought to regain my balance.

Aliénor de Poitiers, the Viscountess of Furnes, one of the Burgundian ladies assigned to me by my husband, slowed to shout at me. "Are you well?" Her hood blew back on her shoulders, exposing a tumble of blond curls and a smudge of mud on her cheek. She glanced toward the party racing ahead of us. None of my Spanish ladies had come with us. It being the Vigil of All Saints' Day, they preferred to stay home and pray—it made a fine excuse for Beatriz to tackle the latest translation at which she was toiling. In truth, I had seen little of her and the rest of my Spanish ladies since my wedding, as much company did I keep with my husband. Save for Beatriz, who was of commoner birth and less rigidly formal, they clung to their Spanish habits as I sampled the delights of the Burgundian court. I had to adapt to Burgundian ways—it was that or lose my husband's interest.

"Yes, I'm well!" I shouted. "Go on!"

The dogs began barking with excitement. Our group was nearing the river—the destination of our eager scramble. It was there that our birds were to find good prey.

"Are you sure?" the Viscountess asked.

"Go! I'll catch you."

She took no further urging. Off she galloped, her blond curls whipping in the wind.

My unhappy falcon pranced upon my glove, jingling the bells on its legs, the short white-and-gray-striped feathers of its muscular thighs ruffling as they caught the breeze. I cautiously trotted forth. Alone, and at a manageable speed, I was able to marvel at the flat wet landscape, crossed by reedy streams and checkered with fields and forests, all

made dark and mysterious by the gloomy sky. Though the
Meseta, which stretches across so much of Castile, is dry
and stony, the skies are wide and high and the purest sapphire blue, their brilliance set off by white puffs of clouds.
I missed the bright broad skies, but not so much that my
husband's caresses could not cure me.

Hoofbeats thudded behind me. I looked over my shoulder
to see a gangling steed upon which rode an equally gangling
young man, his long limbs bouncing as he neared. Hatless,
beardless, and wearing tunic and buskins, he looked to be a
peasant's son, near my years in age.

My falcon hopped on my wrist, causing me to tip forward. I cried out and locked my feet against the planchette.

The long-limbed peasant's son rode up beside me. "Do
you have her?" he called over the sucking of our horses'
hooves in the mud.

I looked sharply to see if he might be mocking me, but his
eyes were bright with friendly curiosity. A grin lit his wide
and bony face as he gained my side. Bold, this fellow was,
approaching an *archiduchesse* this way. Perhaps he was a
huntsman's varlet, there to collect from the brush any birds
our falcons might take, though that hardly excused his im-
propriety.

Near the river's weedy edge several furlongs ahead, my
husband abruptly pulled up reins. Men scattered to avoid a
collision. He shouted to his falconers, who unhooded their
birds, untied the leather jesses, then cast the birds up from
their wrists. Bells tinkled from the legs of the falcons as
they soared into the sky.

The youth chirruped to his horse as if to join the rest
of the party. Feeling much the outsider, I found myself anxious not to lose his attention.

"My brother hawks," I called, trying to keep up.

He slowed and raised his brows, waiting for me to finish.

Beaters ran forward at the river, pounding their drums. Five ducks winged up from behind a stand of cattails, their alarm palpable as we approached the party.

"He hunts, too," I said, "with all manner of dogs."

The falcons circled high overhead, the melody of their bells faint here on earth. "Very well for your brother—"

Suddenly one of the falcons tucked in its wings and dropped like a dart toward the low-flying ducks. With an abrupt *ching* of bells, feathers burst from the back of a duck.

I gasped.

The falcon circled back and snatched the falling duck from the air. The fowl's feet dangled limply as the falcon flapped back toward its master.

The youth turned to me. "As I was saying, very well for your brother, but what about you?"

With a whistle from its handler, the falcon dropped the duck. The dead fowl plummeted to a thicket on the other side of the river.

The varlet's bold address disconcerted me. "Should you not retrieve the duck for your master?"

The carelessly beautiful Viscountess of Furnes brought her horse back to ours. "You have caught up." The smile on her sweetly bowed lips was not for me. "Dear Hendrik, so chivalrous you are, assisting the ladies. You do love your tales of King Arthur. Did he keep the dragons at bay, Your Grace?" she asked me.

She was flirting with this varlet at the expense of caring for me? No one would have ever treated my mother thus. "Yes," I said. "But who is going to get the duck?"

"Get the duck?" The girl blinked at me. The smudge on her face had dried, calling attention to the impossibly creamy skin of her dimpled cheeks. She broke into laughter. "Hendrik, I do believe the Archduchess thinks you are a varlet."

The stately madame de Hallewin, my husband's former governess and now, at his orders, my chief lady, dropped back to join us. "What's this?" Her features were as perfect, serene, and cold as those of a marble Madonna.

The Viscountess smiled merrily. "Madame la Duchesse has promoted our Hendrik to a huntsman's boy."

"I did not actually—" My falcon lifted her wings.

"You had better watch your bird," said madame de Hallewin.

"Whisper to your falcon like this"—the Viscountess put her lips to her own bird's hood—*"Hendrik is a bird boy."*

I wished to ride off, splattering great pats of mud upon their skirts draped so handsomely over the sides of their steeds, but instead I sat on my horse, feeling lonely and ridiculous.

"Look," said Hendrik, "a heron has been flushed."

Smiling, the ladies turned as a heron rose from its hiding place in the reeds and languidly flapped along the river, its pearl-gray wings gracefully skimming the water.

At the riverbank, my husband shouted something to his men, then unhooded Delilah and released her from his wrist. The great white bird shot after the heron, which, sensing its pursuer, sharply altered its course and lifted toward the clouds.

"It's going to dive!" exclaimed the Viscountess.

High above the nearest trees, the heron drew in its wings

and dropped toward the river in a spiral. Delilah mirrored its fall, each of her own spirals closing the gap between them until she slammed into the heron and broke its back. When the heron tumbled earthward, Delilah shot forth and snatched it in her talons. Faithful as a dog, she flew to Philippe and dropped the great limp bird at his horse's feet.

A cheer went up from the ladies and gentlemen. I found that I was lightheaded.

Philippe rode back to me, Delilah on his arm, her powerful yellow beak open to regain her breath.

"Puss! Where were you? What did you think of our catch?" He kissed his falcon on the snow-white peak of her head.

I struggled to smile. "Well done, Monseigneur. Well done, Delilah."

"Hendrik!" Aliénor sang out. "Are you not going to fetch the duck from the brush?"

Philippe looked between us, smiling good-naturedly. "What?"

The Viscountess brushed at her cheek, which retained a charming stripe of mud. "Her Grace the Archduchess thinks Hendrik is a huntsman's varlet."

Hendrik shrugged. "I didn't mind."

Philippe burst into laughter. "My Lady Wife, allow me to introduce Hendrik, Count of Nassau-Breda. At least, he will be when his uncle dies. Besides me, he's the ranking gentleman of our party. And quite a little shit, I might add. What took you so long to get here?"

"I was in Louvain." Hendrik moved to get down from his horse.

"Bothering your head with books."

Hendrik shrugged again, then bowed to me. "I wish to kiss your hand, Your Grace."

"You can do that later." Philippe hopped down from his horse, gave the reins to a gentleman, then opened his free arm to me. "Come, wife, and see the *curée*."

His falcon's eyes were large for her head and bright with intelligence. She craned toward the bird on my wrist, who, though heavy enough that my arm was growing weary from holding her, was only two-thirds Delilah's size.

"Hold her away from Delilah," said Philippe. "They'll get along as long as they're not too close. They know each other."

I held out my bird, then stepped within my husband's embrace. With his arm around me, and inhaling his familiar musky scent, I could be led to a hanging, for all I cared. In a rush of gladness, I rose and kissed his cheek, something my formal mother would have never done to my father in public.

"That's my Puss. Did I tell you the Spanish custom for hanging out the conjugal sheets?" he asked Hendrik. "You should have seen the lad on the street as we were putting them out. I wager he'd never seen a naked archduchess."

Hendrik glanced at me. I had not been naked when we flew the sheets—I had worn my robe at my husband's bidding. But I put my arm around my husband now, unashamed of anything he would say or do. If it enhanced his story to have me appear naked to my subject, I would hold my tongue. He was lord of this land and I was his lady, and I cared not a fig what other people thought, as long as he loved me.

Arm in arm, we approached the falconer, who was kneeling in the long wet grass next to the dead heron. The bird lay on its side, its long pale legs, tough as saplings, stretched out uselessly beneath its slender body. Tufts of plumage, a glowing gray above, the velvety white of fresh cream below, ruffled in the wind.

"Make sure Delilah gets the heart," Philippe said as a crowd gathered around us. "She does not work for no pay."

"Oui, Mijnheer."

The falconer rolled the limp bird onto its back and plunged a knife into its pale breast. He cut along the bone, then, as if opening a large oyster, pried it apart, reached in, and *slash, slash,* cut out the heart. He held up the smooth, fleshy orb.

"Here! Let me feed her." The Viscountess put out her gloveless hand.

With a nod from Philippe, the falconer slid the lump onto her palm.

She held the organ before Delilah's beak, as curved and sharp as a sultan's scimitar. I was not the only one who drew in a breath. The bird could snap off her fingers in a single bite.

Delilah snatched the heart, and with two shakes of her head tossed it down her gullet.

Philippe exhaled. "Pieter, give Delilah the legs, too. You," he told the Viscountess, "save your fingers." He smiled knowingly. "I am certain they can be put to better use."

Some in the hunting party chuckled.

The Viscountess gazed at him, then spread her palm, smeared with the blood of the heron's heart. "I am dirty."

"We cannot have that." Philippe put Delilah on the ground to let her hop to the severed legs now lying upon the grass. "Here." He offered the Viscountess his sleeve of white brocade, hanging from behind his heavy gauntlet.

"But I must not dirty you, My Lord."

"Come now, Aliénor, dirt is never so dirty on me."

She gave a silent laugh, then wiped her hand on my husband's sleeve. She took her time, leaving a bloody smear like that on our conjugal sheets.

I could not bear to stand by idly. "How chivalrous you are, my husband."

Both the Viscountess and Philippe turned as if surprised to find me there, though I was close enough to smell the mud on their clothes.

"To Philippe the Good!" I said staunchly.

Our party took up the cry. "To Philippe the Good!"

My husband beamed, then kissed me on the head, much as he had kissed Delilah, who was pulling the meat of the heron's leg into bloody strings. I drew in a breath. I had won the first battle for my husband's attention. I hoped that there would not be so very many more.

9.

14 November anno Domini 1496

hree choristers sang from the balcony above the feasting hall, their voices and the music of the flute and drum accompanying them unheard over the clinking of cutlery, the scrape of benches, and sudden roars of laughter. Dogs trotted under tables set with golden plates, gilded drinking horns, and fanciful ornaments worth a knight's ransom each. Wine spouted from the breast of a naked woman carved in wood in the most lifelike fashion, down to the swirls of hair on her mound. Tapestries depicting the legend of the Golden Fleece, with Jason's blond curls picked out in gold thread, rippled on the walls, moved by the drafts that seeped through the windows and walls.

I glanced at the table set perpendicular to ours, where Don Fadrique sawed at his meat with a frown. His tablemates— among them Philippe's sister, Marguerite, and Philippe's grandmother Margaret of York, the Dowager Duchess— dined unself-consciously, in Marguerite's case, laughing immodestly at the tales of the gentleman next to her. Meanwhile the Dowager Duchess held forth to a stunned and cowed Fray Diego on the superiority of springtime in England. In the Spains, usually only Mother dined at a table with men, and then only at feasts. Fray Hernando took her to task for even that. If he had his way, Mother would be as cloistered as a nun.

Here, though, nothing was thought of the mixing of the sexes. Truly, nothing was thought of throwing a feast. There had been one almost every night since our wedding ceremony of state, for every possible reason: for the union of our lands, for our health, for our children, for All Saints' Day, with a rest the next day to clear our heads and ride to Antwerp. The excuse for celebrating tonight was to say good-bye to Marguerite, who was to ride in a few days to Middelburg and then sail for Spain. Would she find irony in the fact that her new country, while eternally sunny, was direly somber, while her native country, perpetually rainy, was always gay?

Behind my husband, on a precious piece of silver sculpted into a tree branch, Delilah hunched with her hooded head between her shoulders, feathers fluffed. Antwerp in November was as cold and damp as a Cantabrian cave, and the castle, though blazing with fires on its many hearths, was as chill as the murky waters of the River Scheldt that flowed at its ancient feet. But what the castle lacked in physical warmth, it made up for in conviviality. How I wished for my little sisters to see the place. They would appreciate it, even if my tradition-bound Spanish ladies could not.

I was thinking of María and Catalina as we rested after the last course of candied fruits, when, next to me, Philippe lifted the decoration perched before me on the table. It was a perfect miniature in gold of the type of carrack that had brought me to my husband's lands. Tiny golden sailors the size of beetles clung to its gold-wire riggings; gold-leaf flags fluttered from its three masts; the rails of its fore and aft decks were wrought of delicate filigree. This wondrous little ship rested on the head and hands of a giant mermaid, whose golden naked body served as the vessel's stem.

"Do you know what this holds?" he asked. He gave the precious object a gentle shake.

My gaze went to my husband's lips. I could feel them upon my neck, upon my shoulder, trailing kisses down my back. *Hostias santas,* what was wrong with me? I wished to couple every moment. I lifted my eyes.

"Salt?" I said.

He laughed. "Only a Spaniard would guess that. Oh, don't be hurt, Puss. I meant no ill. But you have to admit, the Spanish prefer piety to fun. They have their sights fixed on Heaven, while we Burgundians are content to eat and drink and wallow around here on earth."

Even as I wished to protest, an incident from that afternoon came sharply to mind. My train of ladies and I had been about to enter the castle, concluding a foggy day's ride from Malines, when the Viscountess of Furnes stopped before the arched gate.

"Your Grace," she said, "it is the custom here for women who wish to bring babes to their wombs to honor a certain statue before entering."

I shifted upon my pillion. It was common to venerate relics and statues of saints in Spain. And I did wish for a child. Even more, I wished to acknowledge, especially to the Viscountess of Furnes, with her exuberant golden curls and overfamiliar ways, that Philippe and I indulged in sexual congress often. Very often.

"I would not be surprised if a child is already on its way," I said, "but I shall respect my people's customs. Where is it?"

"Above you."

I gazed up, my hood falling back. Through the drizzle I saw a small statue, perhaps the size of my forearm, which had been carved in relief over the archway, next to the door. But as I peered closer, I saw that the "blessing" this saint offered was its oversized turgid member, thrust from its body like a taunting tongue. The ladies laughed when I looked down in shock.

The Viscountess had straightened her pretty face. "You have just met Semini, the Norsemen's god of fertility. Robust, isn't he? Not that your womb would need his help."

Now Philippe waved the golden ship before me again. "Take another guess. What is in this pretty thing?"

I tried to get into the spirit of the place. "Aphrodisiacs?"

On my other side, Hendrik coughed into his hand.

"Puss, you scandalize me." Philippe lifted the top of the ship, exposing a sloshing hold full of wine. He swirled the red liquid under my nose. "Smell. Made from good Burgundy grapes."

"Mm."

He linked arms with me to drink.

"To good Burgundy grapes!" I exclaimed.

"To the sweet Spanish mussel." Philippe kissed me soundly on the cheek, winking at Hendrik, who shook his head as we drank.

Too fuzzy with wine to ponder what he alluded to, I reached for the other table ornament set before us, a tree no taller than my forearm, its golden limbs bristling with pointed leaves made of a hard gray substance not unlike the Dowager Duchess's eyes. A topaz as large as a walnut crowned the treetop. I had noticed this decoration at our table at other feasts. Perhaps it was a favorite of my husband's, though he had not yet used it—there were so many precious cups and filigree-encrusted horns and jeweled ornaments to choose from.

"Is there wine in this tree, too?"

"Now she's going to look for wine in everything," Philippe said to Hendrik. "Watch your sword, my man—she'll try to drink from it."

Hendrik raised his brows at me. One of his hazel eyes was noticeably larger than the other, adding to his cheerfully awkward appearance. "Whatever it takes to quench your thirst, Madame."

Laughing, I lifted the tree by its golden trunk, my long sleeves dragging onto the table. A guard rushed forward.

"No cause for alarm, Guillaume." My husband gently took the ornament from my hands, then nodded at the guard, who reluctantly receded into the shadows.

"What did I do?" I whispered.

"He takes his job seriously."

"Which is good for you, My Lord," said Hendrik.

"Which is good for me," Philippe agreed, "I suppose. Look." He unscrewed the topaz bauble at the top of the tree, which must have loosened a mechanism in the branches, for he was then able to pluck one of the spiny gray leaves from a golden bough.

He held it up. "If this turns red when I put it in our wine, you and I have just drunk poison."

He dipped the leaf into the red liquid in the ship.

Wine trickled down his hand as he righted the leaf. The petal remained gray.

"Evidently, we're in luck this time," he said with a laugh.

"What is that?" I asked in wine-fueled befuddlement.

"This"—he waved the dripping spear—"is a serpent's tongue that has turned to stone. A most handy device. It divines poison—very effectively. Truly, one need not dunk it in poison to get it to react. It will start to sweat if poison is near. That's why my dear good guards think they should keep some on my table."

"I have not seen serpents' tongues in Spain, Monseigneur. We just have tasters."

"Well, the tongues are very rare, though one of my huntsmen said they resemble the teeth of a shark he once saw washed up on shore. I don't know about that. But the guards do take the powers of these serpents' tongues most seriously and will not brook anyone's tampering with them. Apparently, not even my own wife's."

"I would never poison you!"

He grabbed my hand and kissed it. "I know. Who would?"

The warmth of his lips on my flesh sent a thrill through me. "They do right to protect you, Monseigneur. There are always those who wish to harm those above them. My papa, who would not hurt a flea, was attacked by a mad peasant and wounded most grievously."

"That is Spain. This is here. We are all too busy having fun for that sort of thing." He leaned closer to whisper. "Guillaume and his lot just do it for their pay. They have inherited their positions—they'd scream if we ended them. Besides," he said, louder, "Antwerp is a lucky place—has been, since a little fellow named Brabo killed the giant"—he turned toward Hendrik—"what was his name?"

"Druon Antigoon."

"—the giant . . . something-something Antigoon, who was wreaking havoc at the harbor by charging ridiculous tolls and lopping off the hands of those who couldn't pay. But the bully did not think so much of it when little Brabo came along and chopped off *his* great brute of a hand and threw it in the Scheldt. That is where the city takes its name, 'to throw the hand,' in the Flemish tongue."

An excess of wine may bring on an excess of sorrow as quickly as it does an outpouring of joy. Suddenly I was in the depth of despair. I did not understand this place, with its worship of food and drink and pleasure. I came from a land where refreshment was to be taken in moderation, and prayer with greatest zeal. How was I ever to fit in? I missed my sisters—dear María, dreaming of chivalrous men; eager Catalina, always trying to keep up. I missed Papa, with his quiet humor and his self-deprecating ways. I missed Mother, though the thought of how deeply she would disapprove of my current behavior gave me a jolt through my vinous haze.

"Puss, will you dance?" Philippe pushed back our bench and held out his hand.

I leaned on his arm as he led me to the assembling dancers, the weight of my skirts and hanging sleeves nearly unmanageable in my dizzy state. Philippe glanced at me, and then, with a mischievous grin, swung me into the jolly swell of sackbut, shawm, and drum.

10.

15 November anno Domini 1496

The somber chanting of the choir echoed from the cold stone vaults of the chapel ceiling. Oily curls of incense snaked through the dank air. Though I kept my gaze on the priest, whose pearl-sewn vestment clicked against the altar as he made the Sign of the Cross over the Host, I could feel the questioning looks of my twelve Burgundian ladies on me as I walked down the center aisle. Worse, as surely as if I had second sight, I could feel the studied resolve of my twelve Spanish attendants, including Beatriz, *not* to look at me, as if I were an object of such great horror they feared to cast their gazes upon me.

I had started out to Mass that morning with both factions after my dressing, a process made arduous by both the Burgundian and the Spanish ladies' insistence that they should have an equal hand in it. The result of this was that every lace to be tightened, every sleeve point to be tied, and every pin to be fixed in my headdress was an item for negotiation. Indeed, I had been made to stand naked in my drafty chamber, yearning for my warm bed and my husband, who had strolled unconcernedly from the room, until they could agree upon who should be allowed to change my chemise. (The Burgundians, it was decided, for the garment

was made of Flemish lace and was a gift from my husband.)
As we made our way through the ancient passageways of
the Antwerp castle, the footsteps of my retinue ringing from
the worn stone flags of the floor, I was already exhausted,
although, if I was to be honest, no small part of my weari-
ness was due to the festivities of the night before.

We were in the cloister that traversed the courtyard, with
the chapel bell ringing the call to Mass, when my flock encountered Philippe and his men, two of whom were pissing
in the courtyard.

Bows and curtseys were exchanged among ladies and
gentlemen; silence was kept in deference to our preparation
for worship. When I gained my husband's side, he ran his
finger down the back of my hand, sending a charge straight
to my nether parts. Our eyes met. Without offering expla-
nations to our attendants, we clasped hands and returned
in the direction from which I had come, bursting into laughter once we turned into the passage to my chamber and
away from the astonished stares of our attendants.

We did not make it all the way to my chamber. Devour-
ing me with kisses, Philippe pushed me against the door
of a storeroom, raked up my skirts, then took me on the
spot, even as a thin dog trotted by, unfazed by our animal
acts. When we were finished, panting from our exertion, we
righted each other's clothing, and then he led me, glowing
and swollen, back through the dark halls to the chapel.

Outside the door, he kissed my hand. *"Adieu, Madame."*

The chanting of the choir issued forth as he shoved into
the chapel. Head held high, he strode down the center aisle.
I saw his men at the front of the church turn to him grinning, and then the door swung back, leaving me alone in the
dreary hall.

In the Spains, to miss daily Mass or any part of it was a sin deemed barely forgivable. I could think of no day Mother missed hearing it sung at least once. If she was ill, her portable chapel was brought to her. If she was at war, a chapel was erected on the field before the first tent of her camp could be raised. If she was laboring in childbirth, her pangs were ignored until she could receive the Host. It is part of our family lore that Catalina just missed being caught by Fray Hernando at her birth. In the history of the Spains, women who gave up their lives to receive the sacrament of Communion when denied it by their pagan fathers or husbands were called saints. To willfully miss a part of Mass—there was a name for those women, too.

The longer I delayed outside the chapel, the blacker my reputation would be in the eyes of my Spanish ladies. I drew in a breath, then pulled the door open.

I took my place with my ladies in time to say the Our Father. Feeling keenly the Spanish ladies' disapproval, I knelt in preparation of receiving the Host. Fluid trickled down my leg. In the quiet marked only with an occasional cough or sniffle and the priest's murmured words, we were fed Christ's body. I prayed not for my soul, nor for the good of the Church, but that I would not drip onto the floor when I stood.

After we had been sent to go in peace, I spoke to my Spanish ladies about the weather, wondering if for once we might have some sunshine. They responded quickly, and kindly, though the current of disapproval that flowed under their polite words was as cold as the drafty air of the castle. Beatriz would not look at me. The Burgundian ladies watched our exchanges, glancing among themselves, and then, when they caught my eye, flashed me conspiratorial smiles. Uncomfortable with all of them, I sent word to Philippe, asking to meet me for a stroll along the river, but my message was returned by his page, who said his master had gone hunting with his men.

"Why is everyone acting so strange?" I asked Beatriz. The two of us were breaking fast in my antechamber, with cold meat and bread, a book of Livy spread open on the table. I had bidden the others to leave us so that I could receive a quiet hour of instruction in Latin. They seemed only too happy to comply. "Yes, I did exchange a few words with my husband during Mass, but—"

Beatriz's shapely brows disappeared under the white bandeau of her coif. "A few words?"

"A few embraces, then. I did nothing wrong. I was with my husband."

"Perhaps it was the timing of these embraces that offended."

"So it is true—I offended my ladies."

"Perhaps—"

"I cannot help it! He desires me. And I desire him. And oh, dear Beatriz, it feels so good."

She turned down her face.

"I am sorry. I am just being honest. If you would lower yourself to marry Francisco Ramírez, you would know of what I speak. He still waits for you, I know. María writes of it—the little dreamer cannot stand for you two to be apart. Why will you not wed him?"

"There are more important things besides marriage."

I laughed. "Truly? Like what?"

"Like teaching at Salamanca."

"You are jesting." I looked into her face. "You are not jesting. Why have you never told me this?"

"You have never asked."

"But you have already studied at Salerno—few women can make claim to that. You became so famous for your skill in Latin there that even Mother knew of you. She dragged you back here and made you teach every one of my family except Papa our Latin—how many feathers in your cap do you need?"

She gave me—for her—a defiant look. "I wish to be a professor."

"But women are not professors."

"Why not?"

"Because—" I stopped.

"You see? There is no real reason, other than tradition." Within the frame of her wimple, her delicate face was pinched with earnestness. "Believe me, Your Grace, I feel the pull of a man's body as much as anyone. Do you think that I am inured to Francisco's caress? Do you think I don't find him handsome? But once married, I will be expected to serve him only and to bear his children. I will have to give up my dream."

Margaret of York, my husband's step-grandmother, swept into the chamber, her two favorite ladies in attendance. The Dowager Duchess was a tall woman, taller than most men, and to judge from her face and neck—the only parts of her person not engulfed in yards and yards of costly stuffs—as lean as a hungry greyhound. She wore an ermine-trimmed surcot over a flowing gown of russet and gold brocade, and a black pointed hennin draped at the tip of its cone with a veil of sheerest lawn. This attire must have been the height of fashion in her youth, but now was so outmoded it would have been humorous on anyone but her. On her, it was an aggressive statement of personal taste. In keeping with the style of this tall headdress, a velvet loop descended from the base of its steeple onto her forehead, where age had etched fine lines into the soft skin. Her aging skin seemed to be the only tender part of her.

Around her arm she rewrapped her voluminous skirt, several lengths too long to allow walking—a fashion of generations past—then waved her hand at Beatriz. "You, girl who dresses like a nun. Be off."

Beatriz arose from her bench with a look of worry. It was not correct for the Dowager to send away my lady in my presence. That was my prerogative, not hers.

Once Beatriz was gone, the Dowager sniffed. "We have not talked for a while."

We had not talked ever, except at feasts, and then only she had done the talking, mostly about the superiority of things English.

"No."

"How are you finding our lands?"

"Most lovely, Madame."

"Truly?" She sniffed again. "A more dank prison on earth, I cannot imagine. Even England, with its tendency to rain, excels it, for at least in England there are rolling hills sweet with flowers in May. Here—mud and marshes, marshes and mud, with fields of plowed gray muck dug in between. But I did not come to talk about the scenery."

I lowered my head. "Madame, I shall never be late to Mass again."

"You were late to Mass? When? Today? I did not see. I did rest my eyes until my lady woke me to receive the Host. This is what comes with age—you cannot sleep at night or stay awake by day. Why were you late?"

I tried to find words.

"Come, come," she said. "Spit it out."

"My husband, he . . . desired . . ."

"He needed to sharpen his sword? Leave it to Philippe to want what he wants whenever the mood strikes him. Well, no harm in that. Your duty is to fill a cradle. I might have filled one myself had my husband stopped fighting his wars long enough to dip his lance with me. He seemed to think fighting would bring him more land than would producing children whom he could wed well. And look where it got him. Dead, in a frozen ditch, stripped of everything including his own two hands, in hale middle age. Where do you think that left me? No, it is your father-in-law and the rest of those overambitious Habsburgs who have it right: *'Bella gerant alli; tu, felix Austria, nube.'*"

"'Let others make war; you, happy Austria, marry.'"

The Dowager sniffed once more, a practice, I now realized, that she used in lieu of a smile. "Good. You know your Latin. You might be as learned as your ambassador said you were. I believe only half of what those little men say. They produce a portrait and call it the truth, as if we were so gullible as to think painters have no imagination. Why your portraitist felt he had to make your hair ginger-red, I do not know. It is a serviceable-enough brown." She tugged the rich cloth of her skirt off the floor and rewound it around her arm. "Well, how did your ladies take your late appearance at the liturgy?"

"They have said nothing to me about it."

"Did they smile and speak cheerfully to you afterward?"

"Yes. At least the Burgundian ladies did."

"That is what I was afraid of."

"But they were merry."

"They do not respect you enough to be concerned."

"Perhaps they do not know what transpired."

She snuffled bitterly. "Lovers think everyone else is blind."

"Then perhaps they were afraid of offending me."

She closed her eyes, then, shaking her head, opened them. "How old are you again?"

"Seventeen." Though at that moment I felt like a child of seven.

"How are we going to undo this damage to your ladies' respect for you?"

"Is there so very much?"

Her sniff verged on being a snort. "My dear, my dear."

Hugging her extra length of gown against her chest, she commenced to moving about my chamber, touching my possessions as if weighing their value at a market stall. "You may ask yourself, why does the Dowager come to me today? She is an old widow woman, with neither wealth nor health to recommend her. Why should she care about me, a little girl from Spain?"

Indeed, a little girl who grew littler by the moment.

"I remember when I came to meet my husband. I was older than you, twenty-two. I was the King of England's sister—well favored by an illustrious family, though, like you, at good remove for inheriting the crown. I was accustomed to the finest England had to offer, which was very fine indeed, but I was charmed by the efforts the Burgundians put forth to impress me. As I rode through the streets of the little Flemish towns, I marveled at the precious tapestries billowing from every building, the carefully painted tableaux, the rich costuming of the actors portraying great women from history—dramatic scenes were played out at every corner. Fountains flowed with wine in the market squares. Banquets

were held, the most magnificent of which was called the Feast
of the Golden Tree. Ask about it. They still talk about it in
Bruges. And it was all for me. All for me."

She picked up a jeweled cross given to me by Mother,
held it to the light meekly filtering through the thick glass
of the window, then put it down as if unimpressed.

"I was supping with my new husband in Ghent, watching
yet another spectacle of dancing unicorns and men bursting
out of hot pies in honor of my marriage, when one of the
ranking gentlemen at the feast leaned toward my husband,
a gold chain thick as a ship's rope thudding against his chest.
'Your Highness must wait to see what we have in store for
you in Brussels,' he said. 'It will make this banquet look like
an almsgiving.'

"And then, just as I was about to eat one more bite of
minced peacock pie overseasoned with cloves, I realized:
None of this was for me. Not the parades, not the tableaux,
not a single dancing unicorn. None of it. It was all for the
men, to show off to one another. Each was trying to prove
he was richest, and the marriage of the Duke to me, sister
of the English king—Margaret, if they bothered to learn my
name—was just an excuse to do so."

I turned away.

"Ah," she cried, "I see you know of what I speak! We
might as well be fattened beeves, sent by our kin to bring
political favor. We were never meant to rule, just gifts to seal
a treaty. Oh yes, I know how you feel. Though in your case,
you are lucky. My grandson is a merry sort, unlike my ferocious Charles. I think Charles hated me from the minute we
met and I had to bend down to receive his kiss, while he, all
set jaw and beetling black brows, had to raise up on his toes

to greet me. A man made to feel small all his life in comparison with his worshipped father does not take kindly to appearing short next to a woman."

"But I do love—"

She spoke over my words. "You, however, do genuinely charm my grandson. I can tell. You would be mad to not enjoy his caresses. And say what your ladies will, a husband's love is holy. Marriage is one of the seven sacraments, last time I heard. Your ladies are merely envious of your good match."

A page knocked on the door. He bowed to me, then bowed extra deeply, in true deference, when he saw Madame la Grande. He brought me a letter, then, with a petrified glance at the Dowager, bowed his way out of the room.

She refolded her gown over her arm. "Something from home?"

I frowned at the seal of the crowns of Castile and Aragón. Another letter from Mother. She had sent me six missives since I had left Spain. I had not responded after meeting Philippe, at first because all my hours were consumed by him, then because of the certain knowledge that my new life would displease her. I would have to account for myself soon, and I dreaded it.

"Do not let me stop you." She picked up the Book of Hours that Mother had sent with me from Spain and began to page through it.

I broke open the red wax seal and unfolded two thick sheets of paper. Tears pricked my eyes when I saw who it was from.

"Good news?" asked the Dowager.

"It is from my sisters, María and Catalina."

"How sweet. Is not the younger one promised to Henry Tudor's son Arthur?"

Seeing their dear handwriting was like feeling the warmth of the Spanish sun upon me. I wished to take the letter to a corner and savor it by myself. "Yes. They are to marry when she is a little older."

"Your little sister will be Queen of England someday. How do you like that, when all you can hope to be is Archduchess?"

"They are just titles," I murmured, perusing the letter.

"'Just'? A title is the least we deserve after being offered to our betrothed like wheels of cheese." She peered at the paper, then up at me, as if I should read it aloud.

"They do not say much." I wished she would go.

The Dowager turned a page of my Book of Hours. "They took the time to write. I should not mind hearing what they have to say."

I scanned the first few lines. María wrote first. Was I well? How did I find my new husband? Was he as handsome as was said? Was he attentive? Chivalrous? Amorous?

I sighed. My darling María, still yearning for a gallant knight.

The Dowager sniffed. "Well?"

I quickly moved down the letter. "My sister María speaks of . . . Colón."

"Colón?" said the Dowager.

"Admiral Colón, Madame."

"Oh, yes. The Genoan. Your Mother's golden goose, if only he shall lay. What did she say about him?"

I read silently from the letter, then paraphrased for the Dowager. "He has returned from his second voyage. Mother

and Papa received him in Burgos, in the Casa del Cordón."
I paused, picturing myself as a child, racing with María
under the carved stone ropes over the palace door, both of
us wishing to be the first to enter as we returned from Mass
at the cathedral. I had tripped on the threshold, only to be
scooped up by Papa, who carried me inside and gave me to
my nurse to bandage my bleeding knee.

The Dowager turned a page in the Book of Hours. "Read
it aloud."

Though my heart ached with homesickness, I had no choice
but to do as she commanded. "'He brought a coffer filled with
gold nuggets the size of chickpeas. He showed us several others the size of pigeon eggs, but when Papa asked, Colón said
he had not yet found towns roofed in gold. He talked instead
of God's Heavenly Hand delivering him from hungry cannibals and warring Indios on many occasions.

"'Colón says that the Indios are not the good souls he
believed them to be. They slaughtered the men he had left
behind on his first voyage, the ones who had stayed in the
fort he had made from the ruins of his ship *Santa María*,
when it had run aground. When the Admiral came back for
them a year and a half later, none was there to greet him.
His experience has made him a man of God. He now wears
the brown robes of the Franciscans. By my troth, he does
look like a friar, too.'"

"That should please a few people," the Dowager murmured. "The Spaniards and their piety. They think they
invented God."

I read on. "'He brought with him some cannibals who
had attacked him but whom he was able to subdue. I could
hardly bear to look upon them. They crouched like animals
and they hid behind great green-feathered masks through

which you could see their eyes darting. I feared the beasts would jump up and eat me!

"'Mother called for the page Juanito to speak to them in their language, to see if they intended to behave. At first they seemed to have some trouble understanding each other, then suddenly all of them shouted at him. When Mother asked Juanito if there was a problem, he said no. All they wanted was to know where they were, and when they were going back home.'"

"Seems reasonable," said the Dowager. "Who is this Juanito?"

"An Indio. The only one who remains from Colón's first voyage. My brother Juan has made him a page in his court."

"My Marguerite will be exposed to a cannibal?"

"He is not a cannibal."

"Oh?" The Dowager raised hairless brows and sniffed. "How do you know?"

I saw gentle Juanito, squatting next to the mastiff pups as he petted Estrella. I heard him at the reception in Medina del Campo, speaking Castilian, proud to have mastered the language. I saw him earnestly dancing the saltarello, as Diego Colón and I looked on.

"I know that he is good."

"Commendable, seeing goodness in a cannibal. Commendable, or mad."

But I was not listening. I was thinking of Diego. I had not seen him for more than two years. Soon after the evening in Medina del Campo, Mother had sent him to Salamanca, to study at the university.

The Dowager looked at me pointedly, then waved her hand. "Read on."

A knocking sounded at my chamber door.

"Come in," called the Dowager, though it was not her place to do so.

Eight of my Spanish ladies filed into my chamber with Beatriz. After curtseys to the Dowager and me, the highest-ranking of them, doña Blanca, petite and pretty as a rosebud, spoke up. "Señora la Duquesa Doña Juana," she said, her sweet voice somber. "Your ladies wish to beg your leave to return to Spain with the fleet that sails with our Prince's bride."

Beatriz spoke up quickly. "Not all of us. I shall stay, as well as doña Manuela, doña María, and doña Ángela."

I frowned in confusion as I faced the row of ladies, all dressed in rich cloth of Spanish black. The eight were the younger, unmarried women of my train. They were to stay for six months before returning home, unless Philippe found them husbands—it was expected that he do so.

"You do not wish to stay?" I asked them.

Their bowed heads were their response.

The Dowager held my Book of Hours to her chin, as still and alert as a fox.

I strove to smooth the alarm from my voice. "Is it homesickness? I am homesick, too. But I trust time will make it better, for all of us."

Beatriz drew in her lips and shook her head.

"I shall make sure Philippe finds you good husbands," I said, my panic rising. "I promise."

"Your Highness." Doña Blanca glanced at the others. "It is not husbands that we seek. Not Burgundian husbands."

"But they are rich!" I exclaimed. "And handsome. And gay."

The ladies gave doña Blanca significant gazes.

"Doña Juana," said doña Blanca in her silvery voice, "many of us cannot understand their ways. What we call gluttony and lasciviousness they call gaiety. They honor drinking well more than living well. We can hardly abide this court's perilous moral atmosphere."

"You judge too quickly! We have been celebrating my marriage and the marriage of your Prince Don Juan to Marguerite, as we all should. But I am sure that soon they will settle—"

The Dowager put down my Book of Hours with a thud. "Go! All of you! The Archduchess would be better served by those who value the great favor she has bestowed upon them. Go back to your chapels in the Spains and pray for husbands—see how quickly that brings them to you."

Doña Blanca's pretty mouth fell open. The ladies seemed to have stopped breathing.

"Go now," said the Dowager. "Shoo! We do not need you here. You. Doña Whoever. Show them out."

"Doña Juana," doña Blanca said woodenly, "I am truly sorry. If I may have your permission to leave . . ."

I put out my hand. One by one, they kissed it, then left.

I stared at my hand, still foolishly outstretched, as though the ladies would come back if I left it there long enough.

"You can do better than those sad-eyed madonnas," said the Dowager. "They think to try to outpray the Virgin Mary." She tapped the cover of my Book of Hours. "We shall have to order you a new one of these. The art here is so much finer than in the Spains."

11.

3 April anno Domini 1497

Heated water streamed over my head. I opened my mouth to let it pool on my tongue as steaming rivulets flowed down my sodden shift and into the tub in which I sat. I savored the warmth radiating into my scalp and skin and bones—and then Katrien's bucket was empty. Immediately, chill air breathed upon my wet hair and flesh, turning comfort into pain, even with flames crackling in the fireplace, the windows shuttered, the walls covered with tapestries, and the floors blanketed with woven straw mats. Although there were buds on the trees and other signs of spring outside, inside the Prinsenhof in Ghent, the black stone walls had absorbed two seasons of cold. A bucket of warm water was no match.

I sank lower into the cooling water, displacing the linens with which Katrien had so carefully lined the bottom of the copper tub. "Another bucket, Katrien, quickly."

"Yes, Mevrouw."

I paddled the water with my hands. Why had I not thought sooner of dismissing my Burgundian ladies and the remaining Spanish attendants for the day, and keeping only the stoic company of Katrien, the Flemish washerwoman? I was sad to have included Beatriz in the pack, but to show her favor overmuch would make it hard for her with the other ladies. Katrien was young, close to my age in years, yet she was as stout and strong as a pack horse, and though her hair might be white-blond under the curious winged linen bonnet that the local women wore, she was not especially beautiful with her round blue eyes and stub nose. But she was calm and efficient, and in her practical presence, I could relax in a way I never could when in the company of the Viscountess of Furnes, with her smug attention, or madame de Hallewin, with her quietly disapproving looks, or even Beatriz, who worried about me so much that it made me doubt myself. Katrien's blandness was a perfect antidote to the tension around me. And best of all, though I told myself this mattered little, she was too plain to attract Philippe.

She was waddling from the fireplace with a sloshing bucket when Philippe strode in with Delilah on his arm, followed by Hendrik and his old tutor, doctor François de Busleyden, now the Archbishop of Besançon.

"What ho! Good men, this is a sight meant only for a husband," Philippe said. Hendrik had already wheeled around and was disappearing out the door.

"We will wait for you in the antechamber," said the Archbishop, who then bowed and left as well.

"Go on, go on." Philippe waved at Katrien, stopped in her tracks with her bucket. "Do what you were doing. We do not want my wife to freeze."

She plodded forward. I winced as she poured the water over me, the pleasure of its warmth now gone with Philippe watching. I did not wish for him to see me this way, wet as a cat in the rain, my shift clinging to me and my hair hanging in sopping ropes.

He watched the water run down my breasts. "I do won-

der if you should bathe so much, Puss. It is a Moorish custom, isn't it, to splash around in baths every week?"

I glanced at Katrien. She stepped back with her empty
bucket, her eyes properly downcast.

Philippe put Delilah on the back of a chair, letting her
transfer first one clawed foot and then the other onto the top
rail of the headrest. "Didn't your mother's brother King Enrique favor Moorish ways? I hear he wore a turban and
carried a scimitar." He came over and stirred my water with
his finger. "And he took all those baths—no wonder your
mother relieved him of his crowns."

I leaned forward with a swoosh. "My mother did not 'relieve him of his crowns'! She was his rightful heir, and when
he died, she inherited them—though there were those who
unjustly tried to keep them from her."

He flicked some drops at me. "I wondered when I would
see that famous Spanish temper."

I covered myself with my arms. Though I might speak
out against my mother, it wounded me to hear others do so.
"When Enrique changed his mind and wanted his wife's
bastard child to be his heir, Mother was forced to fight for
the crown. La Beltraneja hadn't a drop of royal blood in her.
That's where she got her name—she was the child of a
courtier, Beltrán de la Cueva."

"I was just playing, Puss." He rubbed my arm. "You
shiver. All jesting aside, do you think bathing is good for
you, especially if you are with child?"

I looked at my knees, my teeth rattling with cold. We
had been wed for nearly half a year and still my womb had
not quickened. I was seventeen and healthy—or so I had
thought. When would he grow impatient with me?

"Katrien," I said, "I should like to be dried now."

She hurried over with a linen sheet, her wooden clogs thumping against the rush mats.

"I have news from Marguerite," Philippe said as I rose, dripping. I could smell Katrien's scent of hay and cheese as she wrapped me in the sheet.

Philippe pulled a letter from his doublet. Keeping the sheet around me, Katrien loosened the ties of my wet shift as Philippe scanned the contents of his sister's missive. "She said she arrived in Spain in March."

"Four months at sea." I moved my arms so that Katrien could tug off my chemise. "Did her ship run afoul?"

"So much so that she thought she would die. She even wrote an epitaph for herself, and stitched it to her waistband for when her remains were found." He lifted his letter and read.

"'Here lies Margaret, gentle damsel. Although she had two husbands, she died unwed.'

"Funny girl," he said. "Only she would find humor in being betrothed twice and never married—let alone in dying."

Katrien settled a hooded robe of marten upon me. I snuggled into the glossy fur. "How does she find my brother?"

"She said he was a gentleman, and lively, and intelligent, though of slighter stature than she expected."

"I suppose he is not as tall as she is. Poor Juan—as much as he loves to hunt and take his exercise, he has a small frame and a delicate constitution."

"Well, it seems that did not dim his ardor. He would have had them wed on the spot, just as you and I were, had your parents allowed it. Though they did get a dispensation to let them marry during Lent, your parents insisted on all the pomp and ceremony, with churchmen from the four corners of their kingdom to bless them."

"As is proper. They will be King and Queen of the Spains someday."

He took me in his arms. "I am glad we did not have to worry about that."

"Are you? Would you rather have wed me quickly than be King?"

He knocked back my hood as he nuzzled my neck. "I should want both," he murmured, "though at this moment, I could not give a damn if I were pauper or Pope."

I sent Katrien from the chamber with a look.

Philippe brushed his lips along my jaw. "What else did your sister say about my brother?" I whispered.

"He was quite impressed with the carriages she brought. Apparently, there are none in Spain."

"None," I said, unconscious of my words as he touched his tongue to my ear. "None in Spain."

He opened my robe. "Oh, I think something is going to be 'in Spain' soon, *n'est-ce pas*?"

Afterward, we lay on my bed, catching our breath. My gaze went to Delilah, sitting on the back of my dressing chair. Today she wore no hood. She turned to me as if aware that I was looking at her.

"Philippe?"

He ran his arm over his face. "Hm?"

"Delilah wears no hood today. How do you get her to be so still?"

"Much hard work, Puss."

"For you, or her? Her, I daresay. She seems exhausted. She moves her head though she remains asleep."

He lifted his head to look. "She's not sleeping." He put down his head.

"But her eyes are closed."

"In a fashion. They are sewn shut."

I raised myself. Peering from the bed, I could just make out the white thread binding her upper lids to her lower ones.

"You blinded her?"

"Don't sound so horrified. It's only temporary. We'll take the threads out later."

"But—it seems so cruel."

"It's for her own good. I had to starve her when I first got her—her spirit had to be broken for her to be of use to me. But now she gets the choicest bits from her catches, as you have seen on our hunts. I treat her like a queen."

I shivered.

"Soon she'll learn not to trust her own eyes, but to rely solely on me for direction. I won't even need to use the hood when we're outside. She won't fly away—you'll see."

"It doesn't hurt her?"

"No. Shhh. Go to sleep." He laid his arm over my breasts, then closed his eyes.

I thought he had drifted into slumber, so I started when he said, "Where were your other ladies this afternoon?"

I looked over at him. His eyes were still shut.

"I preferred privacy," I said. "In case you should come," I added.

"It is not proper for an archduchess to keep only the company of a Flemish peasant girl, Puss. Appearances, you know. What would the King of France say if he knew my wife's chief attendant was her washerwoman? Lord, if word got out, Grand-mère would be shrill. Anything that might lessen her in the eyes of the Tudor King Henry is anathema to her. She thinks he wears the crown that is her family's, you know. According to her, he stole it on the Bosworth battlefield. The Yorks haven't been on the throne for twelve years, and she still can't get over it."

"But—"

"Just keep your ladies about you. That is not asking for much, is it?" He opened one eye, then patted my breast companionably. "Now, go to sleep."

12.

20 October anno Domini 1497

We had been wed a year. On this sunlit fall morning, our party had dismounted in a stand of beech outside Bruges, and our horses—in the Dowager's case, the horses drawing her litter—were being led behind us. Yellow-dappled leaves hissed soothingly in the damp breeze. A nearby stream gurgled between reed-covered banks, mingling its muddy scent with the woody breath of the trees. Where the trees gave way in the distance to marshland, swaths of brown grass shimmered in the sun.

And yet, as we strolled along the weedy trail, my senses strained elsewhere. Specifically, they were latched upon the strip of skin between my husband's glove and the cuff of his sleeve, the sinuous, veined flesh revealed as he held up Delilah. I stared at this column of flesh while he told a story to Hendrik, who was trudging good-naturedly at his side. How did I keep walking and not groan aloud? Did others play lascivious pictures in their mind as they exclaimed about the color of the leaves—for the glimpse of Philippe's strong wrist put me in mind of something similarly blue-veined and upright, something for which I longed both day and night. Or was I simply going mad for love?

The Dowager, leaning on the arm of the lushly beautiful

Viscountess of Furnes as they strolled, spoke up behind me. "How is your sister?"

I started guiltily, as though my thoughts could be heard. If anyone could divine the thoughts of another, it would be the Dowager Duchess.

I hastily composed my face. The velvet hood of my headdress swished against my neck as I turned. "Which one, Madame?"

"The youngest one. Catalina."

"She is well, Madame. She and María send me letters. They are quite fond of Marguerite."

The Dowager swatted at her sheer veil, blown into her face from the tip of her hennin. "Who wouldn't be? Spain has never seen anything like that girl. Your brother was lucky to get her."

I swung forward. Lucky indeed. My sisters were full of news about how smitten Juan was with Philippe's sister. María, in particular, breathlessly reported that his doctors begged him to use moderation in bedding his wife, for in overindulging himself, he compromised his health. Juan would not listen, María said. He would spend every moment dallying with Marguerite, giving up hunting, jousting, and riding just to be with her—how that sounded like my impetuous brother. Mother was asked by the doctors to intervene, but she would not. What God had joined together, she said, she would not put asunder. How wondrous that Mother was not trying to control the situation, as indeed she tried to control me through her barrage of demanding letters, which I still had not answered since my wedding. It seems that what had started as my fear of being able to account for myself had turned into defiance, though I knew in my heart that it was merely a weak person's pitiful attempt at showing her strength. How easy it was, with the buffer of the sea between us, for me to insist that I would not be bullied.

"Will she be going to England soon?" the Dowager asked.

Still chuckling from the story he was telling, Philippe turned away from Hendrik. "Who, Grand-mère?"

"Juana's sister, Catalina. She's to marry the Tudor impostor's boy, Arthur."

"She is not yet twelve," I said. "Mother says she does not have to go until she is sixteen."

"Is there something wrong with her that she cannot be sent?" said the Dowager. "Our dear Marguerite was sent to France as a three-year-old. It was Charles's loss that he didn't keep her. Now he's chained to that brat Anne of Brittany, when he could have had our sweet girl. I bet he cries salty tears into his crown. Well. Regardless. Perhaps your mother will have a change of heart. Her daughter would be better spent elsewhere than on a Tudor."

"Grand-mère," Philippe said, "can we not just enjoy the leaves and for once not worry about the Tudors?"

"You should care!" the Dowager cried. "You were cheated from any chance at the crown for yourself when that dirty Welshman stole it!"

Aliénor patted the Dowager's hand on her arm and smiled in amusement at Philippe, as would an old friend at a long-standing familial argument. Would I always be the outsider?

"Was it ever within my reach, Grand-mère? Juana has a far better chance of getting her mother's crowns than I ever did to inherit the English crown through your side of the family. A good dozen folk would have to die before it got to me. Although I suppose there are ways to speed the process." Philippe gave the Viscountess a wink. "Grand-mère, did your brother King Richard ever say what happened to his two nephews? Did they ever show up after their visit to the Tower of London?"

The Viscountess widened her eyes in scandalized mirth. The Dowager's eyes bulged, too, but not with any sort of glee.

"If you think my dear brother would murder his own nephews just to keep his crown—"

"Philippe jests, Madame." Aliénor stroked the Dowager's hand. "You must not let him peeve you this way. He has needled you thus hundreds of times and still you take his bait."

The Dowager batted the air with a growl. Aliénor and Philippe exchanged smiles.

A familiar ache hollowed my gut. How easy my husband was with the Viscountess. But though I had been keenly watching the discourse between them over the past year, I had not yet caught them in any real improprieties. Yes, Philippe did choose to dance with her on many occasions. Yes, he did often race with her at hunts. Yes, when we went out for strolls, he often dropped back to walk with her, their falcons on their arms, to chat amiably. Once she sent him a gift of gloves. On that occasion, I had not been able to hold my tongue.

"What do you expect?" Philippe had said when I questioned him. I had found the gloves in his chambers, bound by a silvered-blue ribbon. "Was I not to accept them? She ruined my pair at hunt when she threw that bloodied duck at me—you saw her. She was only replacing them."

"I see the way you look at her."

"How is that? Like a man with eyes? My God, woman, am I not to look at people when they speak to me? Would you have my lids sewn shut like Delilah's?"

I frowned at the gyrfalcon, marbling the mantel of the fireplace with her excrement. "No."

"Whatever relationship you have dreamed up between us is completely in your head." He had taken my face between his hands. "Am I to shake it out of you?"

That time, as many others, he had defused my jealousy with a lingering kiss. And truly, I had never caught them in any real indiscretion, any more than I had discerned him cozying overmuch to the other ladies at court. He thought it harmless to pat a pretty girl on the rear, to nuzzle upon a girl's ears. I supposed it was Burgundian custom, though when I asked Katrien about this, she frowned.

"A duke can do what he wants," was all she would say.

At least he always came to my bed at night, unless he was on a trip with his men, and then I would insist that Aliénor and all the others he had patted or nuzzled stay with me. Their company would be proof of my chastity—as well as enforcing his.

The Dowager yanked on the velvet loop of her hennin to pull it lower on her forehead. "Too windy out here," she grumbled. "I don't know why you would want to come this way, Philippe. All I can think of when I walk these woods is the day your mother fell from her horse. It was right here," she told me. "Heiress to more lands than anyone, wife of a man who was determined to buy them crowns, and she threw it all away, chasing after a duck. She was so young and pretty. Sweet as a rose, too. It was a crying shame."

After that, the mood grew dull, though we did picnic by a pond fringed with willows. We returned to Bruges as convent bells struck None. Philippe then went with his gentlemen to play tennis, while I went into town to do good works, as was expected of the Archduke's wife. I chose Beatriz to accompany me, and armed with linens, bread, and a small bag of gold, we rode by closed litter to the Hospital of Saint John. There, joined by the prioress of the hospital foundation, the briskly efficient eldest daughter of a wealthy local family, we walked through the sick-wards built between the massive pillars of the halls. We stopped here and there to give cheer to those wasting away from disease or age, to pray, or for me to give my blessing, as if a not-quite-eighteen-year-old Archduchess had the power to relieve even the suffering of a gnat. The true work of the hospital was being done by the sisters who rushed along the rows of wooden beds with clysters and potions, or who sat at bedsides spooning gruel into slack mouths, or who directed dimming gazes to the many painted images of Heaven hung upon the walls, reminding those knocking at Death's portal of what glory waited on the other side.

The prioress paused to remind one of the sisters about the proper application of leeches, a procedure that seemed to fascinate Beatriz. She had studied medicine at Salerno, besides Latin, rhetoric, and philosophy, and soon she was engaging the prioress in a discussion on how to best balance the four humors of the body. I myself had to step away from the beds, dismayed at the suffering around me. I leaned against one of the stone pillars near the chapel to catch my breath. I was contemplating the vivid altarpiece, a triptych in glowing reds, whites, and greens, when the prioress spoke up.

"It is a splendid painting, yes? Saint Catherine receiving a wedding ring from the infant Christ. Master Hans did it."

"It is quite fine." I pushed away from the pillar, embarrassed to be caught resting in this beehive of mercy.

"Memling was Master Hans's family name, in case you

didn't know." She nodded to Beatriz as she bustled over to join us. Instinctively, she switched her address to my governess when it came to imparting knowledge. "I remember him walking the streets of Bruges when I was young," she told Beatriz. "His head was always down, as if he was hunting for dropped *stuivers*. When he looked up to cross the street, his face was pinched with startling intensity. He frightened me, but I was only a girl. Now I know it was not coins he sought but visions from God."

"The Saint Catherine is beautiful," Beatriz said.

"It is good that you think so." The prioress turned to me, drawing her long upper lip into a smile. "It is the Archduke Philippe's mother, the Duchess Mary. It's a true likeness."

I looked closer at the group of figures surrounding the Christ Child, who was sitting on the Virgin Mary's lap. The Saint Catherine, kneeling beside her martyr's wheel as she received Christ's ring, had perfect, sweet features, a soft brow, and contented lips. There was a serene intelligence on her face. This was modeled after the woman who cast aside care for her unborn child to hunt ducks?

"Do you like the Christ Child?" The prioress wore a trickster's grin.

"Yes," I said uncertainly.

"You should. It is none other than your husband, Philippe. He was born in Bruges, you know."

Even surrounded by a grim chorus of scraping gruel spoons, spattering fluids, and feet tapping urgently against the tile, I warmed. In the infant's bright eyes and long cheeks pouching by his rosebud mouth, I could see the man into whom the baby would grow. The child put the ring on his mother's finger with the amiable air so characteristic of Philippe.

"And do you recognize the model for Saint Barbara?"

Reluctantly, I shifted my gaze from the infant Philippe and peered at the woman seated to his left. Under her diadem set with precious stones, she scowled slightly at a book, as though perturbed that the tender interaction between the Christ Child and Saint Catherine had interrupted her reading.

"It is Madame la Grande, the Dowager Duchess," said the prioress. "She made Master Hans recast her likeness six times before she would donate a guilder to the foundation. It was her idea to show Saint Barbara concentrating on her reading. She would not be another vacantly smiling saint, is how she put it."

Not knowing what to say, I gave a breathy laugh and moved on to the next row of beds. I quickly came to understand that I had ventured into the area that housed those whose deaths were most imminent. Encouraged by the prioress, I prayed with a sobbing grown man and his broad-hipped elder sister over their aged mother, whose wasted face resembled more a wood carving than a living person. I had my hand gripped by a staring toothless man until the prioress painstakingly pried away each finger. After standing back to allow a man to be taken from a carrying chair and poured into his bed like a sack of wheat, I was relieved to join a young family sitting with their mother.

At first I did not know why they should be on this row. Was there not room enough elsewhere? The children—a toddling boy and thumb-sucking baby, bossed over by their imperious pigtailed sprite of a sister—gamboled at the woman's bedside, while her youthful husband, thin, balding, and as full of unsprung energy as a grasshopper, spoke with her cheerfully. I wondered why this mother had need for the hospital at all, happy as this family appeared.

The husband, after bowing repeatedly upon our introduction, asked me if I had met Colón.

"Colón?" I said, surprised.

He explained that he was a cartographer and most interested in the Admiral's findings. He took his wife's hand. "Paulien wishes to go to the islands that Colón has found in the Indies. She wishes to see the Indians."

"Your Highness." The woman's smile was weak but perhaps not so much so that a good rest might not remedy her. "Are the Indians so very fierce?"

"Moeder is not afraid of them," piped up the pigtailed miss. "Even though they eat people."

I bent down to talk to the little girl. "I have met one."

"A real Indian?"

I nodded. "Yes. And I can assure you, he did not wish to eat a soul. He was very kind. Do you know what he loves?"

The girl shook her head, pigtails swishing.

"Dogs."

"I like dogs."

"Me, too." I straightened to address the mother. "Perhaps you shall see some Indios for yourself, Madame. It is the Admiral's desire to bring back as many as he can." I did not add how, in doing so, he made Mother furious, according to my sisters' letters. The Indios were not his to enslave and transport, Mother said, being her subjects, yet Colón continued shipments. "Human gold," my sisters said he called them, much to Mother's displeasure.

"Yes, Mevrouw," said the little girl. "Moeder's going to go there. Aren't you, Moeder, as soon as you are well?"

"Marie-Paule." The mother put out her hand from under her blankets. As she reached for her daughter, an odor radiated forth, a stench that spoke of rotting flesh and decay. I stepped back, as much from shock as from the revolting smell.

The father took his wife's bony hand. "Yes, yes, Marie-Paule, of course Moeder is going."

The young mother's eyes sank into her head when she closed them.

I excused myself and quickly left the hospital, followed by Beatriz, who protested that our work was not done. But I would not have my tears upset this brave family. I drew the hood of my cape over my head and stepped out onto the bustling Mariastraat in the direction of the palace. I had only just passed the yard of the church of Our Lady when I saw a man's cloaked figure among the linden trees, heading toward the church door. Even in his voluminous hooded robe, I knew who it was, as must everyone in the city when he passed. Who did not recognize the rare white gyrfalcon riding upon his shoulder?

"I wish to—to go to pray," I told Beatriz. Before she could question me, I crossed the street. My husband had reached the side porch of the church and was opening the door.

A knot twisted in my gut as I hurried through the linden trees of the churchyard. Why was Philippe here? He said he was to play tennis. And why did he disguise himself? Was this how he had escaped detection during his assignations with the women I had seen him pet and fondle—meeting them in a church? A Spaniard would never sink to this wickedness.

"Stay," I croaked to Beatriz at the door. I could not bear for her to see how I was being shamed. "Or go back to the hospital. I want to pray alone."

I entered the church and made my way through the chill darkness. I could hear footsteps not far ahead. Why had I let him bring me so low? I had let myself need his touch so badly. But the things he did to me, the things I so desperately craved, he also did to others.

By the multicolored light filtering through the stained-glass windows of the nave, I could see the cloaked figure making his way to the front of the church. I held my hand over my mouth, as sickened as I had been when I realized that it was Papa who had been in Mother's prayer booth in the palace in Barcelona.

I was creeping down the side aisle when Philippe cried out: "Who dares follow me?"

I stopped. I glanced at the statue of the Blessed Virgin in the side chapel before which I'd halted, as if she might aid me.

Philippe craned forward, the bird mimicking his gesture. "Puss?"

"Do not call me Puss."

"Puss, what are you doing here?"

I edged forward, not ready to face what I was about to see. "I believe the question is, What are you doing here?"

"Fair enough, though I do not know why you should take such a tone with me. I have come to pay a visit."

He turned around. I saw now that he was standing before a black marble sarcophagus. From visits on holy days and other occasions when we came here instead of attending Mass in the chapel in the Prinsenhof, I knew whose remains this monument held: Mary of Burgundy. Philippe's mother.

He ran his hand over the smooth top. "The artisans have nearly finished carving the effigy to place upon this. It's of the finest quality—I've seen it in their workshop. It looks just like her."

Relief coursed through my body. "You've come to see your mother's tomb."

"You act surprised."

"No! No. Of course you came. Our ride this morning in the woods of Wijnendaele must have made you think of her." I almost laughed. How my mind had run away with me.

He stroked the marble, unaware, it seemed, of my struggle to contain my giddiness. After a moment he said, "It's amazing what you can remember from when you were not even four."

"You have a memory of her?"

"I don't know where we were—here in Bruges? Wherever it was, the canals had frozen over. I remember Mother insisting on going outside to skate with everyone else. Papa was shouting no, but the next thing I knew, she was chopping away on her blades and pulling me on a sled."

"You were on the ice?" I was gay with the delight of one whose execution has been stayed.

He brightened with my encouragement. "Oh, yes. I remember exactly how it felt—my fingers, face, and toes burned with the cold. I was laughing like an idiot. All around us, girls were cutting figure eights. Old couples were chugging along. Boys raced from one dock to the next. And Mother and I were like everyone else, freezing, laughing, and shouting *Hallo*. Then Mother pulled me to a place where an old woman had set up a stove at the edge of the canal. The crone gave me a waffle. I have never since tasted anything so good in my life."

Filled with contrite tenderness, I slipped my hand into his. Is this what passion did to your mind? Made you see things that were not there? No wonder the doctors of my brother Juan pleaded for him to cool his lust. It breaks down the mind as well as the body.

I smoothed the feathers on Delilah's back, keeping well out of the way of her beak. As often as I had to handle falcons, I still had not become comfortable with them. "What else do you remember about her?"

He thought a moment. "She wore a pointed headdress and veil like Grand-mère, and when she laughed, her veil would shake. She would draw it over my face, slowly, so that it tickled." He sighed.

"Your memories are so sweet. Tell me more."

"I don't remember much after that. I got passed around a lot after my mother died."

"Where was your father?"

"You know—I've told you before. Maxi was in Innsbruck. The burghers here in Bruges were holding me hostage until he agreed to give back the privileges Grandfather had taken from them. With my mother gone, they thought he should give up his rights to Flanders."

"But that didn't last long."

"No, thank goodness. I remember the sour looks on the faces of the burghers' wives into whose care I was given. When I was six, Father got me back and gave me to doctor de Busleyden. François was sort of the mother I didn't have—don't tell him that. I doubt if he sees himself as a mother figure."

Harsh doctor de Busleyden, with the jaw as sharp as a plowblade? Hardly not.

"Anyway, I told you why I am here. But why are you here, Puss?"

Candles flickered at the base of the Virgin's robes in the side chapel. Glowing spots of red and blue lit the floor from the stained-glass window. "You were quite frightening when you asked who dared follow you."

"Was I? Good! Perhaps I should take that as a motto: 'Who shall dare?' I need to frighten people more. Just because I am an agreeable sort doesn't mean I wish for people to doubt my authority."

"Monseigneur, people do not doubt the wisdom of Philippe the Good."

"Don't they?"

"Never."

He drew me to him.

We heard a *thunk* from the narthex of the church—the closing of the great wooden door—then loud footsteps. Doctor François de Busleyden, Archbishop of Besançon, strode down the center aisle, followed by Beatriz, blinking with concern.

He genuflected toward the tabernacle, in which the Host was stored, then bowed deeply to Philippe.

"Speak of the Devil," said Philippe. He peered around the Archbishop. "*Bonjour*, pretty little nun," he said to Beatriz. She half smiled, then frowned at the floor.

"She's not a nun," I said.

Philippe winked.

The Archbishop's sharp features remained unmoved as he took us in. He cleared his throat. "Your Highness, it is with terrible sorrow that I bring you this news."

"What, good doctor? What is so important that you

would have me know it by bursting before my mother's tomb in this way?"

The Archbishop jerked his head in a cursory bow. "The news is for Madame la Duchesse."

"Me?"

He trained his fierce gaze upon me. "Your brother, His Majesty Don Juan, Prince of Asturias, is dead."

13.

27 October anno Domini 1497

*T*he Dowager was drumming her fingers on the arm of her canopied chair of fine green velvet when I entered her study. I kissed her hand and the hand of my husband, whom I was surprised and relieved to find there, then quickly dropped upon the cross-legged stool to which the Dowager had waved me. I had hardly the time to realize that she should have risen to receive me and kissed my hand, as I was the ranking lady, when she spoke.

"We have been chatting."

Philippe glanced at me, then retreated behind the Dowager's desk, where he idly pushed around some of her papers.

A frown flashed across the Dowager's face as she watched Philippe touch her writing things. "How are you faring, dear?" she asked me. Her voice was rich with uncharacteristic concern.

I smoothed the black wool of my skirt. It had been a week since I'd received the news of my brother's death. We had promptly left Bruges, traveling at night as is proper when in deep mourning, and had gotten as far as Malines. We planned to continue to Brussels, where I would retire for six weeks. Yet in spite of all the formal expression of sorrow, I had yet to truly grasp Juan's passing. He was not still laughing with his pages at a supper? He was not crouched in a sea of wagging tails, patting his hounds? He was not leaning over his galloping horse, his blond hair flying? It could not be. A person so full of life could not simply . . . end. I adored Juan, worshipped him, everyone did. He deserved Mother's obvious preference, as sweet and merry as he was. And if I, separated from the sting of his death by seas and marriage, was yet unable to eat, how was Mother bearing it?

"You know, dear," the Dowager said, "crying won't bring him back."

"No, Madame."

"All the sobbing in the world couldn't raise my Charles from that frozen ditch." She looked pointedly at the portrait of her husband hanging on the purple-taffeta-clad wall. His was a coarse face, caught in a suspicious slight smile. The sullen eyes spoke of obstinacy and impatience. His thick lips were those of a brute. Well I knew how painters idealized their subjects. If this was the glossed-over version of the man, what kind of terror had he been in real life?

"Rogier van der Weyden did it," she said when she saw me looking. "You'd do well to collect his work. It will show up nicely on your ledgers. I have snapped up two copies of his *Descent from the Cross*—good moneymakers." She flicked her veil from her cheek. "As I was saying. I cried and cried. There went my chance at having children. There went my chance at enjoying a husband's love. My title as Duchess went straight to Philippe's mother, Mary. Charles had been *that close* to winning the lands that he needed to make him the first King of Burgundy, and now I had no more hope of being a queen. It was disappointing, to say the least. I didn't know if I was to be sent home or not, and to what? It was a sticky time in England. My brother Edward was on the throne, but my brother George, who should have known better, was putting it about that he himself should be wearing the crown. It was a surprise to no one that George had been drowned in a butt of malmsey—well, perhaps the malmsey part was a shock."

"Aren't you glad you stayed here," Philippe said flatly.

The Dowager scowled at Delilah, now stepping from Philippe's fist, first one claw and then the other, onto the back of the chair at the desk.

"You are the one who should be glad, boy!" she exclaimed, alarming me with her vehemence. "I don't know what your mother would have done without me. I made her marry your father. She fancied herself sporting in the marital sheets with the handsome French nobody who was wooing her, but I soon disabused her of that. Not when Maximilian was such a good catch. His father, Frederick, may have been Holy Roman Emperor, but all his wars had emptied his coffers. Maximilian was as poor as a church rat when we met him at Trier. But I knew ambition and potential when I saw it. Even though I had to pay his way here—who do you think paid for Maxi's clothes for the wedding?—I knew he was a good investment. Though I myself was just a widow struggling to hold on to her few properties."

I gazed at the paintings by Hugo van der Goes, Hans Memling, and Jan van Eyck wrung from across the duchy, at the ranks of illuminated books locked behind a wrought-iron grille, at the desk inlaid with precious ivory. Beyond the mullioned windows stretched acres of manicured gardens, orchards, and forests for hunting, all the way to the river.

"I'd venture to say you've done well for yourself, Grand-mère, for a poor defenseless widow."

The Dowager pretended not to hear Philippe. "I was thinking of you and Marguerite even before you were born. If your mother, with my duchy as her dowry, married the Emperor Frederick's son, surely old Frederick would make Maxi king. And I was right. Nine years later Maxi was King of the Romans—a nice title. Now he's Emperor. You will inherit his kingship and all his holdings one day. And you can thank me when you get them."

"The King of the Romans has no true subjects," said Philippe. "It's an empty title. Besides, I'd rather have my father alive."

The Dowager scratched at the velvet of her chair arm with her fingernail. "Generous sentiment for a son whose father prefers to putter around his castle in Tyrol than see his own boy. When was the last time he visited you?"

"He'll come when he has grandchildren," said Philippe.

I looked away. For all of its being plumbed, my womb still showed no signs of quickening. As much as he loved me now, at what point would Philippe consider me a poor bargain, as bad a value as a picture by an unknown painter in the Dowager's collection? What would become of me then?

"You should have seen this duchy when I first arrived. Richest land in the world. France, even England—no one could touch its wealth." The Dowager stroked her veil dreamily. "The feasts and tournaments we would have! People are still talking about my wedding celebration. There was plenty of treasure about, in addition to that ridiculous Golden Tree. Took fifty-two dwarves to carry it in—where in the world did they find so many? I swear Charles used to breed them—or perhaps his father did. Old Duke Philippe had his hands into everything. Now look at the duchy. Half your towns are out of your control, and all you care about is hunting."

"I'm not the fool you think I am, Grand-mère. Control means war. And you've seen what war earns a man—his head split in two and a permanent view of a ditch. You know what they say about your husband?"

"*Your* grandfather, I'll remind you, so watch it."

"That he never had one minute to enjoy any of the things he worked so fiendishly to own. He had sixty-five ambling palfreys that he had fed, curried, and exercised, yet he never took them out on a single jaunt. He had a whole menagerie of beasts in Brussels—he kept a lion in the castle courtyard—and never saw a one of them. Heaven forbid that he get down to his castle at Hesdin, with its trick fountains that sprayed the ladies from below, and mechanical contrivances that floured unsuspecting visitors from above. Such merriment was certainly not worth his valuable time. His father had a little workshop in which he played with making clogs, repairing glasses, soldering broken knives, that kind of thing. Your husband—*my* grandfather—laughed at him for tinkering with his toys, and destroyed the whole kit when he died."

"You are getting carried away here. What is your point?"

"My point is that it was all fight, fight, fight, and then he was dead. Did you ever even see the man?"

She tossed back her veil. "I saw him enough."

"Well, I myself would rather enjoy my life. I am proud that I gave back the town burghers their rights and privileges and that they, in turn, love me."

"You think they love you, because they call you 'Philippe, Believer in Counsel'? 'Believing in counsel' equals letting them do whatever they suggest. They can get you to do any-thing they want."

"That's not true! They love me because I will actually listen to them."

"Love. Love! What is this need for love? No Caesar has ever come to power because he was loved. Feared, maybe. Yes, fear has put more than a few people on the throne. You ought to talk to Juana's mother about it. Could you please get that bird off my chair?"

I was taken aback. Mother terrified me, because I feared her opinion of me. But she had won her subjects over with her care for them and her strength. She was so loved by the people that the title Queen was not good enough—they called her their King. Fear had not put Isabel of Castile on the throne . . . had it?

Philippe offered his wrist to Delilah, who stepped onto it with the grace of a princess. "You had better tell Juana what you were thinking. She is probably wondering what all this is about."

The Dowager sniffed, then grimaced at me. "I am sorry about your brother's death. I know how it feels—I lost one of my brothers and my father when I was but a girl of four-teen. You need to rest. And most likely to be bled. Copi-ously. My surgeons can do the trick. I've got the best one in all of Flanders. You'd do well to take his advice on diet and exercise. At any rate, I would like you to tarry here in your time of sorrow—past the prescribed period of mourning, I would recommend. You need to get well, to get strong . . . to get pregnant." She noted my downturned eyes before con-tinuing. "I shall give you my chambers, permanently, and will move to the little set of rooms by the river."

"Grand-mère!" Philipped exclaimed. "I did not know that you wished to give us your rooms. Please, we cannot take them."

She waved him off. "I insist. Heaven knows, this palace is too much for a poor widow like me. I would like to give it all, from mortar to mullions, to you both. It is my gift, just for the giving."

"Madame," I said, "that is too generous." These chambers were some of the most sumptuous in the world. Surely there would be a price to be paid to have them, and sooner or later the tally would come due.

"Do not worry about me. I shall be fine over there. My needs are humble." She folded her hands in her lap. "Enjoy."

"Madame, I"—I glanced at Philippe—"we don't know how to thank you."

"No thanks are necessary."

Philippe went to the window and looked out over the grounds. "I have always loved this palace."

"I am glad to see that I've cheered you."

I felt not cheered but trapped, the snare made all the tighter by my husband's glad acceptance of the bait. "You are most kind, Madame."

"Yes. Well. It is a sad time. But perhaps something good can come of your loss."

Good? When Juan died, the Spains had been robbed of their fairest flower, a tragedy beyond reckoning for my family.

"We can cry," said the Dowager, "or we can live. Which would you rather do?"

Philippe blew on the top of Delilah's head, ruffling her short white feathers. "Get on with it, Grand-mère. Please."

The Dowager gave him a stern look before continuing.

"Very well. To put it simply, Philippe must now declare himself Prince of Asturias. It is his right and duty to do so."

"Prince of Asturias?" I cried. "I beg your pardon, Madame, but only Mother and the Cortes of Castile can grant that title. It is the title for whoever is next in line for the throne."

"And who is that? Marguerite's child—if she has a son. If she is pregnant. A lot of ifs, when there is a vital young man right here."

"Women are allowed to reign in Castile. My sister Isabel is next in line if Marguerite should not have a child. And this isn't something that needs to be settled now. There is time to establish who will inherit the crowns. My parents are robust and healthy."

The Dowager raised her hairless brows, suggesting otherwise.

"Puss," said Philippe, "you don't have to give me the title."

The Dowager shook her head. "Why shouldn't she? What harm would come of it? As Juana says herself, this is not a burning issue. Just a show of respect toward her husband." She peered at me, her gray eyes bright as wet stones. "You do want Philippe to have the honor, don't you?"

"Yes, of course I do, but—"

"Do you hesitate because you want the title for yourself? As you said, women can rule in the Spains."

"I shall never rule."

"You won't with an attitude like that. Any ambitious relative with a claim will pass you right by. But just because you are not up to the challenge of ruling does not mean you should keep Philippe from it."

"I do not wish to keep Philippe—"

"Perhaps you would like it better if you both took the

title, like your parents. 'The Catholic Kings'—isn't that nice? 'The Princes of Asturias.' I like it."

"But—"

"I should think you would want to share all the rights and privileges that should come your way with Philippe."

"I do, but—"

"Then it is settled. You do have the power to make such a claim, don't you?"

To say no was to admit I was a powerless girl.

The Dowager spread her hands. "It is just a name."

I closed my eyes. I could see my wrathful mother, exclaiming to her ministers about my arrogant, spiteful, ignorant stupidity. *Persons did not name themselves Prince. It is bestowed on them by the Cortes. Where did she get this notion? Had she not been paying attention at court?*

I pictured Papa. He would not speak out against his foolhardy daughter. But it was not because he championed me. No, it was because he feared to speak up. Oh, Papa, an anvil never breaks, but it does not move, either. It may take blows and blows and blows, yet it will never accomplish anything.

"Truly," said Philippe, "you don't have to, Puss. I am happy enough as is."

The Dowager laughed. "Honestly, Philippe. Do you think of what you say? In the history of mankind, has there ever been a single soul who was happy enough 'as is'?"

I had the power to do this for Philippe. I had the power to do something besides watch and listen. I was not an anvil. I didn't know what I was, but it was not an anvil.

I opened my eyes. "Very well, Madame. I will do it."

14.

11 December anno Domini 1497

*M*ore water, Katrien."

Water splashed onto her wooden *klompen* as she lifted her bucket from the fireplace. Stray drops hissed in the great roaring conflagration she had built to keep me warm. *"Ja, Mevrouw.* Now coming."

I sank lower into the copper tub, feeling guilty about the work I had caused her. But I did love a bath, and it was one of the few activities that court custom had not turned into a ritualized ceremony, mainly because taking baths in the winter had not been considered by my husband's Burgundian ancestors. The need to make all my activities into a show had come to an excruciating head during my period of mourning for Juan. If I, by tradition, was required to sit at the foot of my bed for six weeks, my sixteen ladies-in-waiting (twelve Burgundians, three Spanish, and Beatriz, with a book in hand) insisted on sitting there with me. I was not allowed to read or make music or, if I had been a person inclined to do so, spin wool, but they could. And so I had been trapped in the beautiful rooms the Dowager had given me, listening to their banter, cringing at their songs, and going out of my mind with boredom while my husband was free to hunt, play tennis, or do whatever he pleased. I might as well have been buried alive.

When I was finally released from the prison of my mourning, freedom meant walking the frost-covered grounds with my ladies in tow, their servants following like drab ducklings. If there were any deer in the park, I never saw them. Not even the crows stuck around when a troop of gabbling ladies approached. Not that the ladies' gabbling was directed at me. In spite of all my efforts to get into the spirit of Philippe's court, I was still an outsider to the Burgundian ladies, and to my remaining Spanish ladies, save dear Beatriz, a disgrace.

So you can see why that afternoon, though it had been more than a week since the mourning period for my brother had passed, it suddenly became necessary for me to claim a private hour soaking before the fire. To achieve this, I'd had to tell my band that I was overcome with a headache and needed to be left alone. Madame de Hallewin insisted upon calling a physician, but I insisted even more strongly that doing so would only worsen my pain. The Viscountess of Furnes suggested, wryly, that she call a priest. I assured her that I should be fine, given a few hours in darkness. While the other ladies murmured their concern, Beatriz only watched me closely. I told them all that if I needed to retain anyone to attend to my needs, it would be Katrien, who then lifted her head in surprise from where she knelt at the fire. That way I should show preference to neither my Burgundian nor my Spanish ladies, I explained. Stalemated, they had left, after which time poor Katrien scoured the palace for a hip bath and hauled splashing buckets up two flights of stairs. Philippe need not know I was unattended. Surely he was busy at sport.

Now I hunkered lower in my tub. The fireplace in the former bedroom of the Dowager was as large as a shepherd's hut, and the chamber walls were hung with tapestries, but not even Hell could keep its heat in mid-December in Malines.

"Here comes."

The hot water burned soothingly through my wet shift as Katrien poured it over me. When her bucket was empty, she stood back.

"Is it me, Katrien, or do the Burgundian ladies disrespect me as much as I think?"

She cast down her gaze. A dog caught eating off the table would not have looked more trapped.

"You can tell me the truth, Katrien. I know that we have not truly spoken, but I should like to be friends. I promise, I shall be good to you."

She wiped her hands on her apron, her mouth pursed.

"I'm sorry. I did not mean to put you in an uncomfortable position." I plucked at my wet chemise and thought. "May I ask this, then—how do I get their respect?"

She swallowed, then frowned, before speaking at last. "They respect no one but themselves, Mevrouw. Not the Spanish, not the Flemish, no one."

"That is for certain. One must be born into the ruling families of old Burgundy, or forget it. What I wonder is, has anyone told them that Burgundy is gone? As rich and fabled as was the duchy, consult the maps—it has disappeared. It is part of the French King's lands now. Only the Netherlands remain. The duchy ceased when Philippe's mother died, the last of the Burgundian line. Call himself Duke of Burgundy all he wants, Philippe is a Habsburg, like his father."

"Do not tell him that," Katrien murmured, then glanced at me, scared.

I burst into laughter. "Oh, we definitely shall not. We must not burst the bubble of the new Philippe the Good."

"Mevrouw," she breathed, scandalized.

I sank lower into my tub. "This land is mad. It is the one place in Christendom where the Seven Deadly Sins are considered virtues. I wonder if Mother knew just what kind of place she was sending me to."

"Mevrouw?"

I let water trail from my fingertips. "Yes?"

"I found this when I was changing the sheets." She pulled a letter from her apron.

I sighed. It was from Mother. I had received it that morning, and as my ladies stared, had popped it under my mattress. I had not wished to open it. Likely Mother was responding to my claim to the titles of Princes of Asturias, for which I was duly ashamed. Not only was it improper, but monstrously cold. How heartless I must seem, grabbing at titles, when my dear brother had just died. If only she knew how much I grieved for him.

"Do you not wish to read it?"

Sighing, I held out my hand.

Katrien placed the folded paper in it. "Would you like my knife?"

I nodded.

She produced a small utensil from in her girdle. The Flemings, like common folk everywhere, were always prepared for a meal.

I slid the knife under the large red pat of Mother's seal, then shook open the letter—three sheets.

Dearest Juana,

By now you will have received word from our ambassador about the passing of our angel. I regret that I have not been able to write to you about it sooner, but in addition to keeping vigil for six weeks in my bed, I have been stricken with a strange illness, which has sapped my strength entirely. Indeed, I had been abed when your father and I received word that Juan was ill. It was the day after Isabel's second wedding. Being the mother of the bride is always exhausting, but that morning, I could not rise. I was wondering how in the world I could endure two more weddings——might we do away with some of the ceremony when María and Catalina are wed?——when a messenger came with a letter. I saw immediately from the way he would not look at me that something was wrong.

The news was worse than I could imagine. It was from our dear new daughter Marguerite, begging me to come posthaste to Salamanca. Juan had taken ill, and though doctors had bled him and purged him with herbs, his temperature continued to rise. She said that Juan had forbidden his men to send word of his illness to me, lest he alarm me when I was so weary. He must have seen what a toll the wedding festivities had taken on me when we had parted at Ávila, I for Alcántara at the Portuguese border, he and Marguerite for Salamanca, where they wished to set up housekeeping. I am mortified that he saw my exhaustion. Am I becoming such an old lady that people must tiptoe around me?

When I told Fernando of Juan's illness, he would not hear of my going. He said that Marguerite must be exaggerating. He would go see what was the matter; I should rest. And then he waited until I got back into bed before he would leave, which I did very quickly, for I did not want Juan to wait.

For a day I heard nothing. I thought I would go out of my head. Cardinal Cisneros prayed with me all night. And then express couriers came with the message: Juan is holding his own. Juan's fever has broken. Juan will surely recover.

Then, for two days, nothing more.

Finally, a messenger came. When the Cardinal insisted that he speak, he fell to his knees.

The messenger said that the King was dead.

I thought I must be hearing incorrectly. Fernando had not even been ill.

The messenger sobbed and had to be taken away. Cardinal Cisneros began to pray. I heard Fernando's name among his words.

I crawled on my knees to my prayer booth. I was in there, twelve hours later, when your father came.

It took me moments to find my voice. I told him I had heard that he was dead. He said, No, my dear, I am alive. Here I am. You have me.

I pulled away from him and asked, How is Juan? What about Juan?

He gathered me to himself, but I struggled against his arms to see his face.

When I met his eyes, he shook his head.

I hit him. Hard. On the chest. Then again. And again.

When I asked him why he had told me like that, he said that he thought that if I found out he was alive when I believed he was dead, it would weaken the blow about Juan.

I wanted to kill him.

We cried together like babies—your father, for Juan, and for his own loss, and I, for Juan, and for the folly of your father's thinking. For though your father understands many things, he does not know the relationship between a mother and her child. There was nothing

he, or anyone in this world, could ever, ever, do to soften the loss of
my angel.

"Mevrouw? More hot water?"
"Yes, please." I swiped at my tears with my wet hand and
read on.

Marguerite is pregnant. We look forward to the child's birth.
He might be the new Prince of Asturias, though he will never
be Juan.

All I have of Juan now is his dog, Bruto. You must remember
Bruto—the shaggy yellow cur that he insisted on keeping. He sleeps at
my feet now, with your little Estrella. They have become playmates—
though your Estrella is poor at sharing. She is fierce for such a little
thing. I suppose that is the way of the world—the smallest dog
barks the loudest.

Outside, the leaves have fallen from the pomegranate trees in the
courtyard. They were still green when I had taken to my bed. I feel
that I have awakened in a harsh new world, one in which I don't know
the language, the customs, or the climate. Is this how Colón's Indios
feel when they find themselves in the Spains?

I would like to ask how you fare, though I know you will not
answer. Why do you not write, Juana? It has been over a year. If you
wished to break my heart, you have succeeded. Do you punish me for
sending you from the Spains? Someday you will understand why I did,
and may not judge me so harshly. Until then, I will pray for your
forgiveness, and for the forgiveness of God for my sins, of which there
are many.

This 26th day of November, anno Domini 1497,

Your loving mother,
Isabel

I let the letter flutter to the floor and then sank in the tub. Had she not received news of my claim to the title of Princes? And she was caring for Estrella? Her kindness confused me. I knew only how to defend myself from her. But how did I begin to have a relationship with this woman? It was like trying to befriend a mountain.

Later, at dinner, my husband said, "You're looking pale, Puss." Servants were gathering our plates in preparation for an entertainment between courses. "You haven't said ten words."

The Dowager spoke up from my other side. "Perhaps she is pregnant." She raised her bald brows at Philippe. "If she is with child, she must guard her strength immediately. She must abstain from sweet milk and cheese, must not walk with a full stomach, or take any exercise at a fast pace. She must not walk at midday, or when it is cloudy."

"Is she pregnant, Grand-mère, or dying?"

She flicked back her veil with a scowl. "Do not mock me, boy. Both conditions will come in their own good time."

Madame de Hallewin leaned forward from the Dowager's other side to address me. "Your Grace, I have heard of a physician in Antwerp who can offer an elixir sure to stir a sluggish womb."

My lady-in-waiting, the aging and bewhiskered doña Eugenia, announced, "In the Spains, we turn to the mercy of Our Lord for our needs. When, after six years, Her Serene Majesty the Queen produced no more live children after the first, she undertook a pilgrimage to the tomb of San Juan de Ortega, outside Burgos. By the following year, she had conceived a son."

Philippe kissed my shoulder. "It should take you only

seventy years to walk to Burgos from here, if you avoid the midday and the clouds."

The Dowager gave him a warning shake of her finger.

I was saved from explaining the current state of my womb by a troop of dwarfs. To the blast of trumpets, they rolled out a great castle tower, the wheels of the cart that bore it creaking under the massive burden. No sooner had the dwarfs scampered away than men dressed as Saracens clattered in on horses, slashing their scimitars at us as they rode to the castle. Their steeds' hooves thudding against the rushes, they galloped around the castle and shook their turbaned heads.

The door of the castle fell open. Soldiers in armor dashed out and slew the terrible Saracens, save one. The soldier marched the unfortunate Saracen to our table and presented his sword to Philippe.

"Our enemies are yours to vanquish," the soldier cried. "Will you save us?"

Philippe, laughing, took the sword. "And here's where I say my motto, yes?"

"Yes, Your Grace," the soldier whispered.

Philippe waved the sword over his head. "Who shall dare?"

I watched, but my troubled mind was not engaged in it. I had succeeded in breaking my mother's heart, when all I truly wanted was her respect. The question was not whether I would forgive her, but whether she would ever forgive me. How could I repair the damage I had wrought, when I might not ever see her again?

The Dowager nudged me with her arm. "Get up. Your turn."

I rose, knowing my part in the drama for the evening. And while I had pronounced my motto at other entertainments and jousts, that night, though I was surrounded by hosts of smiling lords and ladies, the words rang true in a different way.

I laid my hand on my husband's. "I alone."

15.

13 March anno Domini 1498

*P*hilippe and I were in a chamber off the dining hall in Hendrik's palace in Brussels, readying for a Carnival entertainment in which we were to play a part. Hands on hips, Philippe turned his chin so that his man could fasten the brooch at his shoulder.

"Come now, Puss. How am I to be a good Julius Caesar when you are such a glum Cleopatra?"

The Dowager Duchess leaned on the arm of madame de Hallewin. "I was Cleopatra once. In a pageant for my birthday."

I wriggled under the darting hands of my Burgundian ladies, tucking my supplice into my belt, adjusting the circlet around my head, pinching the pleats of my skirt. The ladies hovered like bees at a honeypot, not out of concern for me, but to raise their own importance in the eyes of the court— and some of them, so it seemed to me, in the eyes of my husband. I had not caught Philippe wandering, but a nagging sense of insecurity had again crept into my belly. Not that I had firm evidence of his infidelity. No, all I had was a glimpse of his hand resting overlong on a lady's neck when he pointed to a duck on a hunt. Or the discovery of a long dark hair upon his collar. Or the sight of a lady turning away sharply when I entered the room in which she and my husband were together. When I had confronted him with these things, he had laughed and called me mad. Was I? I had begun to think it might be so. I felt tired and strange in the head.

"I am not glum." I put on a toothy smile.

"Puss, please. A snake looks jollier. Is it the letter you received from your mother today? I don't know why you even bother to read them, as much as they upset you. I hate to see them come." His brooch now clasped, he motioned for his man to bring him wine. "What did she say this time?"

The Dowager craned her neck forward, whisking her veil from her ear as if to improve her hearing.

I would not tell them about Mother's worry that she was becoming as hard as a diamond from holding in her grief. She begged for a letter, saying how much it would mean to her now. "She says nothing. She asks why I do not write to her."

"You haven't yet?" said Philippe.

The Dowager stiffened, like a fox picking up a scent.

The Viscountess of Furnes, resplendent in a gown of silvered blue, straightened the serpent on my circlet, grinding the band into my scalp. I winced under her heavy touch. "I recently wrote my first letter to her since our wedding. Our letters must have crossed."

"Your first?" Philippe wiped his mouth and guffawed. "Oho—that's my Puss! The most powerful woman in the world, and her little daughter won't take the time to write to her. That must get her goat."

"That's not why I haven't written," I said, though that was precisely why, at one time. It had been the only power her "little daughter" had over her. Now it shamed me to have taken the coward's route for so long. What a relief it had been to finally write her, though it had been difficult to think of what to say to vindicate myself. I had ended up telling her exactly what my reasons had been, childish as they were, and begged, sincerely, for her forgiveness. Now I both dreaded and longed for her response.

"I would not write to my father." Philippe handed his goblet to his man. "But he'd have me killed. Maybe your mother is not so powerful after all. How does she keep her holdings together without a few well-placed murders? It's the tried-and-true method in some lands." He shook his head. "Our English cousins. Who is more violent to their kin than they? Grand-mère's own brother snuffed their other brother. In a barrel of beer, no less."

"Malmsey," the Dowager said. "You make it sound so bad."

Philippe shook his head, grinning. "Grand-mère. To you, nothing is so terrible as long as Englishmen do it."

"How about the Florentines?" she demanded. "What about Giuliano de' Medici? He was murdered during Mass by his rivals, with the foreknowledge of the Pope."

"As for me," said Philippe, "I'm glad to have Habsburg blood. At least we have the sense to marry into our lands. 'Let others fight—you, happy Austria, marry.'"

"That's the Habsburgs," the Dowager said sourly. "So damn happy."

I picked at my Egyptian-style skirt. I wished Philippe would not harp so gleefully on the fact that his kin married with a keen eye toward financial gain. Our marriage may not have been made as a love match, but at least he could publicly acknowledge that we did love each other now.

"On the other hand," said Philippe, "Spaniards have ice

in their veins. How many relatives did Pedro the Cruel have to kill to keep his crown?"

"That was a long time ago."

"What was it, fifty years? One hundred? Two? Probably not so long ago that Grand-mère wasn't toddling around then."

The Dowager struck at his arm.

Philippe shied out of the way. "At least Juana's mother didn't kill her brother's daughter to take the throne. She just called the girl's mother a whore and the girl a bastard. A fairly brilliant piece of work, actually. Much less messy than a butt of malmsey."

The Dowager made as if to chase him. The Burgundian ladies tittered. I would have protested, the reaction he was going for—oh, how he enjoyed trying to provoke me, like a child teasing a cat—but that night I was feeling curiously weak and weepy. I had been feeling thus for days. I attributed it to the excesses of Carnival. How Philippe would laugh and call me truly Spanish if he knew how much I longed for the austerity of Lent. After more than a year in these lands, I still could not eat and drink as they did at this court.

"Nun," Philippe called to Beatriz, standing behind the Burgundian ladies. "Where is your costume? When are you going to give up that ugly habit?"

The Burgundians turned to watch with interest. But Beatriz was spared from having to answer, as Hendrik's master of ceremonies hurried into the room.

"Your Graces, it is time to enter the hall. I beg of you to follow me. All others, please, take your places at the banquet."

Philippe watched the Dowager and my ladies leave, his gaze remaining on Beatriz.

The master of ceremonies bowed and spread forth his hand. "Your Graces, this way, please."

"Does your mother mention my sister in her letter?" He offered his arm.

In late December, Marguerite had lost her baby, a poor misshapen thing too early for a name. Mother had attached a brief note to her ambassador's report, its very brevity revealing her pain.

"Not this time."

"She didn't say anything to you yet about our taking the title of Princes of Asturias? She must be on her deathbed, as quiet as she has been about it."

"You must greatly want to be a prince."

Philippe shifted under his breastplate. "Not really. Though what's so terribly wrong with it?"

"I fear the titles will not be ours, regardless. Mother reports that my sister Isabel is pregnant." I winced, hating to speak of such when my own womb was still empty.

"Ah, well, that's old news. François told me a fortnight ago."

I nodded. Of course. The Archbishop of Besançon knew everything. For a former tutor, he had risen high at court. Indeed, he was Philippe's closest counselor. He filled my husband's ears with state information important and trivial—delivered from a point of view that was always antagonistic to the Spanish. Should I be paying more attention to this?

"Does your mother say when the child is due?" Philippe asked.

"Perhaps the Archbishop could tell us."

"Puss, sarcasm does not become you."

I sighed. "August."

The master of ceremonies showed us to a barge, ready to be rolled into the banqueting hall by a team of servants dressed as mermen.

Philippe kissed my cheek as we took our places before the costumed oarsmen. "I still love you."

I glanced at him in alarm. Still?

Later, after we had been rolled into the hall to a roar of approval, and had acted our parts and finished our meal, I found myself, dizzy with drink, at the clavichord in Hendrik's chamber of state. I was playing a duet with Hendrik himself, to which one of Philippe's men sang suggestive lyrics, provoking drunken snorts and giggles from the ladies and gentlemen gathered around. No Spanish women were included, save Beatriz, who stood uncomfortably by the clavichord, hands clasped.

"Bravo!" yelled Philippe when we finished.

Our singer slumped to his knees, then onto his chin, before curling into a ball on the floor.

Philippe roared with laughter. Like a man with his tail afire, he made a charge for the tremendous bed Hendrik had constructed in the chamber.

"Everyone!" Philippe jumped on the mattress. "Join in!"

I watched from the clavichord as gentlemen, and ladies, too, scrambled onto the bed. Jewels thumping and brocades flapping, they began to bounce like so many spring lambs. Even the Archbishop of Besançon joined in, of a fashion, standing at the bedside and testing the mattress with his elbow.

"Glorious bed, Hendrik," said Philippe, jumping highest. He would have it no other way. "I must have one. How many does it hold?"

From next to me on the bench, Hendrik called out, "Fifty. Side by side." He gave me an apologetic grimace. "It was made to toss gentlemen on when they've had too much to drink. I never pictured the ladies joining in."

"Shortsighted of you," Philippe roared, somehow able to hear us above the jiggling hilarity surrounding him. The Viscountess of Furnes hopped before him, her pneumatic cheeks dimpled in a grin. She brought him into a contest with her jumps.

Hendrik saw me watching. "You'd better get up there."

"I think I should vomit," I said coldly.

Hendrik gave me a look, then idly plunked a key on the clavichord.

"Nun!" Philippe roared to Beatriz. "Join in!"

The Viscountess looked less than pleased, her expression resuming its gaiety only after Beatriz declined and she and Philippe had begun to jump again.

Suddenly Hendrik rose.

"My good guests! I should like you to see something special."

"Why?" cried Philippe, his leaps matched by the Viscountess. "Not now, man!"

"Trust me," said Hendrik. "You of all people will like it."

"Me?" He stopped jumping to kiss the Viscountess on the cheek. "Aliénor, you win." Laughing, he climbed down. "Where is this thing? It had better be good."

Hendrik grasped my husband's arm, then joined me to Philippe's elbow. He patted my hand.

"You will just have to see, won't you?" he told Philippe.

He took up a candelabrum, then started down the hall.

Snickering, stumbling, the noble party crawled off the bed and followed us down the stone passageway, until Hendrik turned into a small room and stopped. Before us, on a heavy table, was a massive wooden case nearly the size of a wagon bed. It was met with hoots of derision.

"What is this?" someone shouted. "An altarpiece? Did you take us to your chapel, Hendrik? We are hardly in shape for a Mass."

"That is the truth." Hendrik held up the candelabrum, illuminating the outside of the case. The outer panels, closed like the doors of a cupboard, were painted in dull shades of grisaille, depicting a shadowy world contained in a luminescent bubble. Silvery waves of water broke upon a land from which rose hills and trees and strange spiked life-forms. Threatening dark clouds receded from the glistening sky. In a quiet, otherworldly way, it was the most beautiful painting I had ever seen.

"What are you trying to do?" roared Philippe. "Put us to sleep?"

"Patience, Your Grace." Hendrick unlatched the case, laid open the outer panels, then raised the candelabrum. The crowd leaned in and gasped.

The center painting was a Dionysian scene of lust. In a riot of bright yellow, red, and blue, men and women copulated with each other, with giant fruits, with birds. Fantastical beasts and young people of many lineages cavorted in lakes and on lawns. Not a soul wore a stitch. All were serenely engaged in eating and other physical pleasure.

"What is it?" madame de Hallewin asked uneasily.

"You tell me," said Hendrik. "My uncle got it as a joke.

It's by a Netherlander called Hieronymus Bosch. I think he might be mad."

"It's the portrayal of the world if Eve hadn't sinned," Philippe suggested. "See what the bitch made us miss." He looked around, gratified, as the company laughed.

"I believe you are correct, Your Grace," said a gentleman. "That is exactly what it is. It's a very devout picture. Paradise. See all of God's children, tumbling in the hay, just as in the Bible."

"Where in the Bible?" doctor de Busleyden asked.

"I don't know. But it had better be in there." The gentleman burped into his fist. "Otherwise, Hendrik, I think you have yourself a hot piece of heresy."

Philippe slapped Hendrik on the back. "Don't worry. There are no inquisitors here. Unless my mother-in-law has smuggled one in. Or has she, François?"

The Archbishop shook his head. "Not yet."

I felt chuckles aimed my way, but did not give them the dignity of a response. Wine-fueled anger flared up inside me. What did they know of Mother? She who had sent Colón off to find a real Paradise on earth. She did not play with silly pictures, but sought new lands and great things, always pushing, always thinking. What must she think of my waiting so long to write her, balking at putting pen to paper like a child refusing to be tied into her bonnet by her nurse? I was sick with shame.

The party soon tired of the picture, and found their way back to Hendrik's special bed. I was not one of them. I was looking out the window at the moonlit forest spreading down Coudenberg hill, remembering the orange full moon smoldering in the blue-velvet skies of Toledo. If only I could go home again.

Philippe came over and kissed my neck, startling me out of my reverie.

"Puss. Come here." He grabbed my breasts.

I cried out in pain.

"What's wrong with you?"

I put my hands to my breasts, still radiating with pain. A green wave surged over my body.

"I think I'm going to be ill."

16.

15 November anno Domini 1498

So you are the one whose limbs pushed hard knobs out of my belly, as if a leggy fawn were curled inside me instead of a child. You are the one who tugged on my entrails when you shifted during that final month, though I thought you were clever—you could knock a plate resting on my belly. You were the one who amused me with your hiccups. From the days when you were but a flicker of butterfly wings, you were always on my mind, the inhabitant of all my dreams, though I could never imagine your face. And now I see you, my dear mysterious companion. You look at me with the same wonder with which I look at you.

The Viscountess of Furnes leaned over us, forcing her scent of lavender into our sacred space. "How sweet. A girl."

I raked the cloth-of-gold blanket higher upon my legs. So much gold thread had gone into its weaving that it was useless against the cold air seeping through windows and walls. Only its deep trim of ermine was warm. Philippe had it specially made for my recuperation . . . when he thought the child might be a boy.

Beatriz edged from behind the Viscountess. "She looks like you, Your Highness."

I gazed at the child sleeping in my arms. She had my

rounded forehead and Papa's dark hair and eyes, and traces of pouches at the corners of her lips, just like Philippe's. These things made me love her more, though I would have loved her even had she looked like a griffin.

"Has the Archduke been in to see her yet?" the Viscountess asked.

I touched my daughter's fingers. How could they be so perfect yet so small? Philippe had come in the hour before her birth. He had stood by, mouth open, while I gritted my teeth against the blue-black pain gripping my loins. I had no control—my womb was in a vise being cranked by a devil. And then, the pain had let go. Released, I gasped for air.

Philippe had come forward. "Are you well?"

I glanced at the midwife, who was pouring water into a cup. Katrien knelt by the fire, feeding it sticks. I had ordered my other ladies out, even Beatriz, whose terrified face frightened me, and my husband's gentlemen, too, not wanting any of them to see me, though it was their privilege to do so. My mother had asked for a handkerchief to cover her face to hide her terrible expressions, while allowing the nobles their right to keep vigil at her birthing bed. But I was not my mother. I had not her courage. Never had I felt such pain and such fear. How did I survive the relentless gripping? What if the baby stayed stuck in my womb until it died, and then I? Or if it came out and the bleeding of my torn womb could not be stanched? My sister Isabel had died in such a manner. Three months earlier, in August, a fact about which I had been informed in a tear-stained letter from María. Still, I could not imagine. Bossy, dear, imperious Isabel—gone? It could not be. I could not bear to think of her suffering. And now my own pains were worse, much worse, than I had ever imagined they could be.

All persons in this world have put their mother through this pain?

"You're doing fine, Puss." Philippe took my hand. "A little longer, and we will have a son."

A son. I could not promise him that. I could not promise him a live child, or even a live wife.

"My father is coming. From Innsbruck." Philippe kissed my knuckles. "He wishes to celebrate the birth of the heir to his lands and the Spains."

My brain was weak from exhaustion. I could not think how our child could possibly be the heir, even if he were a male child. My sister Isabel had died, but her infant had survived. A boy, Miguel. He would be King. I had heard this from the Spanish ambassador.

Why had Mother not written me these things herself? By now she must have received my letters, the first of which I had written nearly a year previously.

"Our son is not— We are not the true heirs. Baby Miguel is." At that moment, the vise clamped down in my womb. Its iron grip screwed tighter and tighter, taking control of my body. I dug my nails into Philippe's palm. He had caused this pain. It was his seed that had brought me to this state.

He wrenched my hand from his. "Ow. You hurt me." He examined his palm as he backed away. "What is wrong with you?"

A scream burned my lungs as he fled from the room.

Now I pressed my daughter's damp head to my lips, then met the gaze of the Viscountess of Furnes, looking upon me kindly. "I expect Philippe at any moment," I said.

She touched my child's fingers, the very soul of maternal sympathy, while dressed in a perfect silvered-blue gown, in the most current French style. The Viscountess had been absent a day here, a day there, during my confinement, days that coincided with Philippe's absence from court. Her throat had plagued her, she said when I asked where she had been; she had a weakness in her throat. In her throat or her lips, I asked, to which she blinked in pretty confusion.

In my final month of confinement, Philippe's visits dwindled further. Days would go by when I would wait for him, wait for him. I detained the Viscountess and she grew restless while in wait for him, as if she, too, worried about being eclipsed by another lady.

"Where have you been, Monseigneur?" I asked him when he appeared after a four-day absence. It was a bright afternoon in early November. The sunlight made rainbows on the edges of the windowpanes; a blackbird sang outside. I was buried alive, a swollen, living corpse, while the world was burgeoning above my grave.

Philippe shrugged, rustling the puffy tops of his sleeves. "Nowhere. Just hunting."

"What did you catch?"

"Ducks. A crane. The usual. Why?"

"Did Delilah catch the crane?"

He paused. "Yes. Yes, she did."

"Who accompanied you?"

"Hendrik, François—why do you ask these silly questions?" He bent down and kissed my forehead.

His familiar scent, the warmth of him near, loosened my tongue. "I am going mad, Philippe. I cannot bear these four walls."

"You'll be better once you've had our son." He sighed deeply. "François awaits with some papers. I must go."

I grabbed Philippe's hand. "What shall we name him?"

"Who?"

"Our son."

He shrugged. "Philippe."

"Yes. Or Juan. After my brother."

"We'll see. I must go."

I clung to his hand. "Your *grand-mère* wants to call him Charles, after her husband."

"Like hell." He pulled out of my grip. "I'll be back."

Five days passed before he returned.

I now gathered the baby out of the Viscountess's reach. She pulled back in oh-so-humorous offense. "New mother," she said.

Katrien came over, wiping her hands. "Mevrouw, may I bring you some watered wine?"

"I'll get it," said the Viscountess. "Flemish trash," she muttered under her breath. "Attending to the little mother is Beatriz's job," she said aloud. "Where is that strange bird?"

I tipped my head to get the Viscountess out of my sight, and drank in my baby's smell, sweet as blood. Surely the perfection of this child—her gray-blue eyes, her tuft of black hair, the tiny pouches by her lips—would be taken into account by those who would call me a failure.

17.

26 December anno Domini 1498

A cold wind flapped the yellow velvet hangings under which I sat and the lappets of my head-dress. Out on the boards of the lists, the flags snapped as if to be torn free and sent sailing into the crowd. I pulled my robe closer until the ermine collar brushed my lips. December, not the choicest month for a tournament. Not the choicest month for any activity in this cold, wet land, besides huddling before a roaring fire. But Philippe would have a tournament celebrating the birth, *now*—as he preferred all his activities, once he thought of them—and how could I complain when he told me that he had conceived of it to celebrate my churching. With the smell of ermine pelt in my nose, I clapped to the blast of six golden trumpets hung with my husband's standards. A herald rode before the stands.

"I bring this from the hand of a mysterious lady!" He unrolled a parchment tied in yellow ribbon and read aloud. "'To whoever receives this message: I am a fair and virtuous lady, held against my will by a giant. He wishes for my hand in marriage, but I have refused. Alas, he has taken my estates and locked me in a tower. I can be saved only by him who breaks one hundred and one lances in battle, or has one hundred and one lances broken against him, and then he must serve one hundred and one sword strokes, or have one hundred and one sword blows served against him. To him and him alone who endures this trial, the giant will release me from my tower. Until then, adieu.'"

Next to me, the Dowager tipped my way. "We had the very same play at my wedding, only bigger."

Philippe came thundering out on a white destrier thickly caparisoned in quilted yellow brocade. The yellow plume atop his helmet whipped in the wind as he spoke.

"I shall save this lady. Who shall go against me?" His lance pointing toward the sky, he reared up his horse. Its hooves flashed against its padded skirt.

A gentleman plumed in green urged his warhorse before the stands, then threw down his plated gauntlet. "I shall."

Philippe spread his free arm first to us in the stands, then to the crowd of city folk gathered on the other side of the lists. "It is done."

The sun came out. Its reflection glinted off Philippe's armor as he rode his horse to the far end of the lists, where his gentlemen lined up on their steeds, ready to take their place against him. How splendid he looked. He had not spared a *livre* on preparing for this tourney. Yet now, forty days after the birth of our child, he had not yet paid Leonor's nurses. He had not paid for any of my household expenses since I had arrived in his realm, a fact I had stumbled upon as I prepared for my churching. When I had asked doña Eugenia what she would be wearing to the Mass, she ducked her bewhiskered face until at last she confessed she would not wear something new. When I questioned Beatriz, she said that there was no money. I was horrified to learn that neither she nor any of my three remaining Spanish ladies, let alone Leonor's nurses, had been paid a *stuiver* for their expenses. None of them could pay for cloth, or shoes, or even tapers to carry into the service. Beatriz lifted her arm to show me her elbow. There was a hole in the coarse gray wool of the sleeve. The gown was the same one she had brought from the Spains.

I had turned to Katrien, washing the baby's cloths by the fire. "Have you been paid?"

She ceased her rubbing. Her flushed face became even more red. "No, Mevrouw."

He had not even paid the washerwoman? But he was to pay for my household expenses. This was part of the wedding agreement forged between Mother and Philippe's father.

"How do you eat?"

Katrien bowed her head. "My uncle is one of the Archduke's cooks. There are usually scraps."

It was my turn to grow red. No wonder so many of my ladies had departed so very quickly—they were given neither support in their faith nor husbands, and now, I was learning, not even an allowance for their daily needs. Why had I not been told this? How could Philippe be so negligent? Had it been his purpose all along, to drive away those sympathetic to me and the Spains? Why would he do so? An icy chill gripped my guts. Who was this man?

"He's coming!" said the Dowager.

Sand flew from the horses' hooves. My husband and his challenger bore down on each other with pointed lances, their steeds separated only by a low wooden wall. I clenched my teeth. I hated the lists, hated seeing men flying at each other with lances. In the Spains, they threw darts made of cane at each other in tourneys—Mother had outlawed the lists. She refused to lose a single man in the name of sport.

Papa had only smiled at her womanly weakness, but my brother Juan openly complained.

Lance crashed upon lance with a tremendous crack. When I opened my eyes, the splintered lance of Philippe's opponent was falling to the sand.

The herald shouted: "One lance for our Archduke!"

The Dowager batted at her sheer veil. "One hundred to go."

Another gentleman trotted out to challenge my husband. Again they rode hard; lances crashed; Philippe galloped away, his lance unbroken, the yellow scarf on its tip flitting in the wind.

All this yellow. My color was crimson. I looked down my row of ladies. Which one wore yellow? Not madame de Hallewin in her russet. Nor the Viscountess in her perfect silvered blue. Not one of my ladies, Burgundian or Spanish, wore yellow, nor could I remember any doing so, although since Leonor was born my brain did trick me. But Philippe's eye would not necessarily be restricted to my ladies. He could have taken as a lover any woman in the land.

The spark of suspicion grew like fire. I looked out across the tiltyard to the townsfolk of Brussels. In the sea of white winged headdresses, might one of these women be his lover? I saw a familiar face—Katrien. She stood with a balding man whose visage, even rounder than hers, bore similarities in the thick cheekbones and brows. Perhaps it was her uncle from the kitchen.

Behind her, a pretty girl stood on her tiptoes and shaded her eyes against the sun. A blond, like my husband. She looked to be fifteen or so, with full lips and large eyes. Already fresh-faced, her color was heightened by the wind.

Had Mother felt this madness? Had she cast her gaze

over a crowd, wondering which might be her husband's current lover? She had not replied to any of my letters. Yes, I deserved to be punished for not writing her sooner, but I needed her now. I was isolated and lonely and given to wild thoughts.

A loud splintering announced the third clash. I glanced up in time to see Philippe again ride free.

"You aren't watching," said the Dowager.

I looked at the lists. My husband was circling back from unseating another gentleman. The fresh-faced girl teetered on her toes, trying to get a look. Suddenly she stood down from her tiptoes, blushing. Philippe was peering her way.

Jealousy and fear flamed inside me. Where had he met her? Where were their assignations? He had rutted and roistered with no care to anyone, while I had languished, unloved, on my lonely bed.

Philippe shouldered his lance and rode to the end of the lists. I watched the girl, despising her innocent pink face. Hooves pounded below. There came a thud. A gasp went up. Philippe sprawled on the ground, his opponent trotting uneasily away.

Philippe took off his helmet, and the padded cap underneath, then shook out his hair. The girl came forward through the crowd.

I jumped to my feet. "Stop!"

The word echoed from the stands. Into the stillness rang the jingle of reins, a muffled cough. Rich, poor, townsman, peasant, all gazes were upon me. The girl drew back.

A page ran forth and pulled Philippe up. Sand crunching below his steel-shod feet, he approached my dais with his helmet under his arm. "Did you say something, Madame?"

"I beg of you, Monseigneur, stop this tourney."

"I have only just started." He turned and raised his arm to the crowd, who roared with approval. He turned to me. "And as you see, they desire it."

I could feel the blade of the Dowager's stare upon my back.

I groped for an explanation. "Monseigneur, I fear for your safety."

He laughed, then spread his arm to the crowd. "My wife fears for me. Womanly worries."

"Monseigneur, I fear for the safety of my child's father."

He glanced around. The slight pouches at his mouth puckered with tamped-down annoyance. "Is My Lady unhappy?"

I did not know how to answer. I sensed I was doing wrong. But how did I turn back?

"Yes. Please, Monseigneur. Stop."

"For My Lady, anything. And for our child, as well." He bowed to me, and then to the crowd, before mounting his horse. As he galloped toward the palace, the cheers made it hard for me to hear the Dowager's hissing in my ear.

"Stupid chit. Do you not realize what you have done? Your producing a girl child has unmanned him. Was it not enough shame when his father turned back to Innsbruck when he heard there was no boy? Philippe called this tourney to bolster his image in the eyes of his people—in his own eyes, too. Now look what you've done."

"He shames me!" I sought a reason that I could voice. "He wears another woman's yellow."

"Do you have a brain? If you'd listen to your French as you spoke it, even with your clumsy Spanish accent, you would realize how close '*jaune*' sounds to 'Jeanne.' The *jaune* pennants were to honor you, which even you would have understood, had you let him finish. You were the mysterious fair and virtuous lady he was going to free at the end of the tourney. He was going to present you with a nice fat emerald worth four hundred *livres*."

I smiled woodenly as the other gentlemen rode past, tipping their helmets. Dear Lord, I no longer knew: Who was my husband? A heartless man? Or a lonely boy?

18.

24 August anno Domini 1500

Cast ahead to August, more than a year and a half later. Insects sprang from the swaying grasses as our horses trotted through the marshes, their hooves sucking in the rotting muck. The sun beat down on my headdress, making me drowsy, filling my nose with the smell of hot hair, cloth, and skin, and the oily scent of horse.

"Is your falcon ready, Puss?" Philippe asked.

We were coming fast upon a pond. When we stopped, I was to take the hood from the sleek little falcon Philippe had given me. Unlike Delilah, she could not be trusted not to fly away the moment her jesses were loosened. She would go after what she deigned to be prey the moment she saw it, and hence I had to be sure that what she wanted to catch and what I wanted her to catch were the same. There was an art to handling a falcon; I suppose one might take pleasure being in partnership with one's bird. I, however, did not feel it, not when the object of our partnership was the death of an innocent.

I spat out a gnat that had flown into my mouth. I had more pressing matters to attend to than playing with birds. Was my new baby, Charles, still crying? He'd been inconsolable when I'd left him in the nursery. Six months old, and his life was a torture of swollen gums, gaseous bowels, and a red weeping bottom. I had ordered his nurse to take him outside to expose his raw buttocks to the sun, but she feigned to know no French or Spanish, only German, and I could not be sure what she would do. Philippe had insisted that she be his nurse—he owed her father a favor—so all I could do was hover nearby to make sure that she followed my wishes. It was I who had given him a root of licorice on which to rub his gums. The German girl would have let him cry.

Poor child. From his birth, he was not the strong, sunny child his sister had been, and at nearly two, Leonor was stronger and sunnier than ever. But Leonor had not his misshapen lower jaw, which pushed forward from beneath the upper one, hampering his ability to suckle. Even as fireworks were being shot from the bell tower of Saint Nicholas announcing the arrival of the Archduke's long-awaited boy child, I was in despair, watching my infant mewl at the base of his nurse's breast. As the citizens of Ghent celebrated on the streets, a succession of wet nurses was tried, to no avail. A nanny goat was introduced; my poor babe tongued at her leathery udder. But even if he had been able to latch on, how could I allow it? Charles might take on the beast's pugnacious character through her milk. At last a cow's horn was filed down and a hole put in its tip, through which the milk of a nurse of virtuous character was trickled. While out on the squares townsfolk were gulping the free wine that my husband delighted in drinking with them, my poor Charles was swallowing his first drop of milk. Only when his strained little gulps became regular was I able to fall into a sleep from which not even the loudest reveling in the crooked lanes of the Patershol could stir me.

Now a crane flapped out from the reeds. Philippe raised his arm. Our hunting party reined our horses, then undid the jesses around our falcons' legs. Delilah was off before I had removed the hood from my bird.

Philippe slapped Hendrik's back. "Look at her! I never get tired of this."

Indeed, he didn't. He could hunt with his falcon every day, even as miraculous things happened in the nursery. Leonor strung together sentences: "I not want chicken. I want sausage." Charles reached for the licorice root, put it to his own mouth, then, smiling, put it to mine. He sat without support, and chortled when Leonor clapped her hands to amuse him.

"Ah, she's got it!" Philippe cried. "She beat your tired old bird."

"That she did." Hendrik smiled at me.

"Not again," I said. I believe Hendrik had trained his bird to let Delilah always win.

Delilah brought in a crane and waited, lifting her feet in impatience, for the falconer to cut out the heart.

"Give her the legs, too," said Philippe. "She earned them."

He hooked me to himself and hugged me as we stood watching her eat. "You're quiet. Sad because your bird didn't win?"

I shook my head. Philippe relished the same interests and activities as when I had met him in Lier, while my life had changed so very much. No longer was I just Juana. I was mother to two children whose welfare depended on me. Their needs came before mine, and not only did I enjoy meeting them, but I took pride in learning what those needs might be, unaided by the wisdom and help of others, save Katrien, who had a natural talent with children, and Beatriz, who stood by my side though she was awkward with young ones. My mother had ceased writing to me directly; now she wrote only through the Spanish ambassador, which grieved me. I had so many questions for her. But she excelled me at punishment, as she excelled me in everything. Evidently she had not forgiven me for delaying my correspondence.

"Rudi," Philippe said, instructing the falconer, "give Delilah the back of the crane as well."

"There will be nothing left, Mijnheer."

"So be it. Let these other people's birds do something for once. Hendrik, your bird hasn't caught a bird since Easter. I would suspect that you mean for it not to make the catch, but I cannot see how. How does one stop a beast from acting upon its natural urges?"

I looked at my husband. How, indeed? But with my worries about the children, I had less time to ponder his activities. I had not been able to determine whether Philippe was monster or man-child or something in between. He came to my bed regularly. I found it best for my peace of mind not to ask him what he did with the rest of his day. Once, when he stayed out on a hunting trip a week later than he'd told me he would, I asked Katrien what she thought.

"Katrien, tell me the truth. I shall not be angry with you. Is my husband unfaithful?"

She sat back on her heels with her knife. She had been scraping the tiles where a candle had dripped during the night. "What do you call unfaithful, Mevrouw?"

I laughed uncomfortably. "The same thing that you would call unfaithful."

"In that case, no."

She turned away with the stolid finality so common to Flemings when they are finished with a subject, then leaned into her scraping. It had been an unsatisfactory answer, but it was all that I would get from her.

This night in August, after dinner, I was not thinking about Philippe's possible infidelities. Indeed, he had come to my chamber and had his pleasure upon me. I was thinking about Leonor. Did her knees turn in too much when she walked? I was trying to decide which physician to ask— doctor Meuris, who might be too harsh, binding her legs with laths, or doctor Gobien, fascinated with incantations and given to casting spells, who might be too mild—when a knock came at our door.

The page stationed outside opened it to the Dowager, holding a candelabrum. She had come in such haste she still wore the white bindings she tied under her chin at night. She looked like a body prepared for the grave.

"I bring you glad tidings."

"Good God," said Philippe. "What hour is it, Grand-mère?"

I shrank back under the sheets. What kind of tidings would so gladden the heart of the Dowager that she would let them disrupt her sleep? After she had partaken of her "special spices of the table" to aid with her digestion, and had her face rubbed with unguents and been trussed, nothing could rouse her once she had retired to bed. Especially not the good fortunes of others.

"What kind of glad tidings?" I asked.

"Glad for you, Juana, unless you are determined to get sentimental over someone you've never met."

Philippe signaled to his page to bring him a cup of water.

"Out with it, Grand-mère. I'm tired, and I am to hunt in the morning."

The Dowager raised the candelabrum to my face as if to relish my reaction.

"I have word from my man in Madrid. The child of your departed sister Isabel, the Crown Prince Miguel, is dead."

19.

7 November anno Domini 1501

*S*ome fifteen months had passed since the Dowager rousted us with her "glad tidings." Much can happen in fifteen months. A ship can sail to the Indies and back. Babes can be conceived and born. Courts can be uprooted and all the possessions and people who care for them packed piecemeal onto ox carts. Love can flicker and wane.

"So tell me," said Philippe, "what is she like?"

My gaze flew up from where it had been pinned to my horse's neck, bobbing in time with its clopping. I glanced at the oak forest through which we were passing, at the soldiers riding just ahead, the flags of the standard-bearers snapping. Philippe was watching me with an amused frown.

"I am sorry," I said. "What?"

"You were sleeping in the saddle."

"I wasn't." I was thinking about Charles, pushing the little cart I'd had made for him. Not yet twenty-one months old, and he was running behind his cart like a three-year-old. I could still hear him chuckling along with the squeak of the wooden wheels. What would he be like when I next saw him? Even if we raced through France, forged into the Spains, snapped up our titles as Mother's heirs, and then bustled back home, it would take a minimum of four months to make the journey. The day we had left her, my newest baby, Isabel, only three and a half months old, had just learned to roll from her back to her belly. She would not know me when I returned.

"Then what were you doing?"

"Thinking."

"About what?"

"My chickens."

A bored note crept into his voice. "You must stop worrying about them, Puss. Grand-mère has them full in hand."

It was the back of the Dowager's hand that worried me. She was liberal with the use of it, and she scolded me for protesting when she employed it against the children.

"They are to be kings and queens when they grow up," she had said, several days before we left. I had scooped up sobbing Leonor, the recipient of a slap. The child's transgression had been to touch her father's tree of serpents' tongues when she was allowed to visit us at dinner. "Do you want them to be spoiled?" the Dowager said. "I made the mistake of sparing the rod against Philippe."

Philippe had rubbed Leonor's cheek. "Don't cry, sweet." He leaned forward, grasped the tree, then pulled it back to her. "Be careful. The serpents' tongues are sharp."

With a provocative look at the Dowager, Leonor put her finger to a pointed leaf.

"That's not a toy, Philippe," the Dowager said. "What are you teaching her?"

"It's ridiculous that we keep these—they are relics from the past. This is a new day, Grand-mère. No one wishes to poison me. A man need not worry about his safety when he's not at war with half the world."

"Meanwhile," she had muttered, "your 'friends' are nib-
bling at your lands."

Did his friends nibble at his coffers as well? He had not
yet paid my servants or Spanish ladies. To cover their expenses, I'd had to pawn the jewels he'd given me. Yet on the
occasions when I had confronted him about their payment,
he'd gladly promised to do so, quickly stanching further
argument. My husband, it seems, truly was a master at saying yes. It was so much easier than taking real action.

A wind picked up, sending down leaves in a shower of russet. They crunched under the hooves of the horses. "I am
sorry, Monseigneur," I said. "I didn't hear what you asked me."

The curled ends of Philippe's hair brushed his shoulders
when he shrugged. His Flemish barber—riding ahead with
the baggage train that stretched for more than a league
through the French forest—was one of the one hundred fifty
indispensable servants who traveled with us, my humble
Katrien being one of the few assigned to me. "It was nothing. I had just asked what your mother was like."

He must have been nervous, to ask this question repeatedly. And rightly so. She was cold. Unforgiving. Hard. The
same woman who had conquered the Moors evidently did
not tolerate her little daughter's resistance. She had never
written back to me, though I had sent several letters begging her forgiveness. In truth, I was terrified to see her
again myself.

"Surely your man François has filled you in on my mother's character," I said. And not favorably, either. Only now,
after being at Philippe's court for five years, did I realize
how deeply the Archbishop of Besançon hated the Spanish
alliance—and me. How he must have fought against my

marriage to his protégé. It was Philippe's father, and the Dowager Duchess, who had promoted it, hoping for an advantage by being tied to the Spanish crowns. Who ever thought their gamble would pay off, and that I, so far back in the line of succession, would be my parents' heir? All I had to do was make this journey to the Spains, and the Cortes would confirm me as heir to the throne, and Philippe as my consort. And for a man who once claimed not to care about holding the title of Prince of Asturias, my husband most truly relished this outcome. Like a child sleepless with anticipation on the eve of his name day, he gleefully awaited his conferment, even though it was only for consort and not ruling king.

"I don't know why you and François cannot get along," said Philippe. "Anyhow, I make my own judgments."

Did he? Did he, now? Philippe let the Archbishop choose his policy, his ministers, his clothes. It had been Besançon's idea to betroth our little Charles to the daughter of the King of France while both were still in their cradles—a plan that unleashed scores of angry letters from Mother to her ambassador. And now, on our way to the Spains, we were going to meet the French King, against Mother's express wishes. All the world knew that Louis XII was her mortal enemy, with his penchant for dipping across the Pyrenees with war parties, and for entering into treaties with the English against Spain, even going so far as to claim Papa's lands in Naples. Now my own husband wished to parlay with him and I would get the blame. As if I had a soupçon of control over Philippe's thoughts and deeds.

"So tell me what your mother is like."

I drew in a breath. "She is tall."

"Tall like a giant? Or like one of the sturdy dames raised

on cheese and iron in Father's German realms? His own grandmother, Cymberga of Masovia, could crack walnuts between her fingers and pound nails into wood with her fist."

"My mother cracks more than walnuts. When her men were about to give up the siege of Baza, she thundered the thirty-three leagues from Jaén with us children in tow. As the Moors watched, astonished, from the ramparts of their fortress, she rode before her troops. 'Never give up!' she told them. 'Never give in!' Her men cheered for her, shouting, 'Long live our King Isabel! Long live Isabel our King.'"

"Had all that battle knocked the poor souls blind? Calling her a king. At least *I* know tits when I see them."

I could still hear the cheers of the men on the field before Baza. I had been ten, and upset. Did they not think how their shouts would make my papa feel?

"Well," said Philippe, "I am not afraid of her."

And he was a fool. Mother had won the crowns meant for her brother's daughter, had conquered the fearless Moors, had uprooted the Jews when they would not convert, and sent them from the land. What would she do with Philippe, Believer in Counsel?

We rode on to the beat of drums and our horses' hooves. The wind sent down bronze leaves like darts.

"So, Hendrik," Philippe said, "are you ready to see the pretty ladies of Paris? I hear the mussels are very sweet there."

"I am not looking forward to meeting the French King," Hendrik replied.

"Nor I," I said.

"Why? You can't be afraid of him, Puss. You are his equal, a king's daughter—unless you are ashamed to be the wife of an archduke."

"Of course I'm not."

"It does not bother you that you're the only one of your sisters to marry a duke, not a king?"

"I have no care for that. Who has been putting this notion in your head?"

He looked away.

"Philippe, the reason that I have no love for the French King is that, among other things, he jilted your own sister."

"Marguerite was a child. She wouldn't even remember now."

"There is where you are wrong, my friend," said Hendrik. "A woman always remembers a slight, even if she was just a girl at the time."

Philippe made a mock salute. "O Great Sage! You know so much about women."

"I don't," said Hendrik. "But I know horses. They are much the same."

Philippe laughed. "Women and horses are nothing the same. Are they, Puss?"

I blinked at him, wondering how a man who professed to love women so much could understand so little about them.

20.

22 November anno Domini 1502

*T*he rain drummed on the roof of the carriage. Although the leather curtains had been tightly fastened, a cold dampness blanketed the close dark space, sealing in a pungent miasma of madame de Hallewin's sharp breath, the acrid stink of the moldering old tome that Beatriz read, and the sour smell of my own anxiety.

"He should be here soon." Beatriz marked her place in the book with her finger and leaned forward as if to peer out the covered window.

She had expressed the same opinion since morning, when the carriage had first rolled to a stop outside the village of Blois. It did me no more good to hear these words now than it did when she first spoke them, the day I had left Paris in a fury. Philippe had acted amused that I should be angry about the two young French things he had dandled on his lap at our dinner in Paris, winking at our host as if my humiliation were part of the entertainment. I had expected him to follow when I stormed out, but I was soon disabused of that notion. I left Paris on my own and had waited in country lodgings surrounded by silent Burgundian ladies angry at being torn from the festivities, while a parade of familiar emotions tramped through my gut.

"Philippe will be here in his own good time," said madame de Hallewin. "Since he was a boy, he has always done things his own way."

"That does not necessarily make it the right way," said Beatriz.

"I don't question him," madame de Hallewin said lightly. "He is Archduke, is he not?'"

Their bickering did not help me. Philippe could do whatever he wanted, and there was nothing I could do about it, except perhaps hate him, just a little, in the bottom of my heart.

A faint blast of trumpets sounded in the distance. I sat up.

Beatriz untied a side of the curtain. At that moment, lightning illuminated the growing darkness, and through the veil of rain I could see the church towers on the hill above. Behind the church, I knew from staring at it throughout the day, sat the stony bulk of the palace, where the King of France awaited. We were four days late, thanks to my husband's reluctance to leave the pleasures of Paris.

"Close it," I said.

The trumpets sounded again. Now the ground vibrated with pounding hooves. Across the river, a church bell tolled five as Beatriz straightened my headdress. The carriage driver saluted aloud; the door groaned open on leather hinges. Philippe swung onto the seat before me.

My anger, shame, and fright distilled to a single rush of emotion: relief. Even in this new era of my disillusionment, Philippe still had the power to bring me to my knees.

"By Saint John, it stinks," he said. "How long have you been in here?"

It was a headdress of great value, with pearl-encrusted lappets, and rubies lining the edge of the short black velvet hood. The Queen of France had sent it for me to wear to the banquet that night.

I had not brought her a present of such value. Where would I have gotten the funds for it? Philippe controlled my monies and paid only those whom he wished to pay—my Burgundian ladies and servants who were loyal to him. The others I had to pay using my dwindling store of jewels. The ermine-trimmed gown that I wore was a gift from him. My own dressmaker, a kind man with thirteen children, had stopped coming on my orders—I could no longer pay him. No doubt Philippe had brought lavish gifts for the King and Queen, but would present them himself as examples of his own largesse and power. But I could not accept a gift like this without giving one of equal value in return—not if I and the Spains wished to appear to be the equal of Anne of Brittany and France.

"I wish to wear my own headdress."

Germaine of Foix, the young slip of a girl charged with presenting the gift, looked doubtfully at the glittering jewels on the French hood, then up at my head, as if trying to figure out how to get the piece upon it. She was a pretty thing, in a childish way, with the large eyes of a startled woodland creature and a wet red mouth that she seemed incapable of closing.

"My husband prefers to see me in my own attire," I explained. "My trunk over there—the headdress is in it."

She went over, opened the carved lid, then lifted out the

headdress, raising it high for its long veil to clear the edge of the trunk. "But it is so—" She stopped when she saw my look. Her mouth eased open guiltily, as though she had been caught with her hand in the sweetmeats jar. Although of noble birth, she was too young and naive to have learned to control her face. She would not last long at this court.

"Spanish? Yes, it is."

"Oh, I did not mean anything," she said hurriedly. "Spanish things are quite nice. I hear the Spains are a lovely place, so very sunny. You are not plagued by the dreary rains that go on here for days and days. It gets so very damp in all these layers of finery." She glanced at my clothing, then bit her lip. "Of course, you do not wear so many . . ." She crumpled her milky brow in thought, then brightened, seemingly proud to think of a diplomatic end to her rambling. "Perhaps you should save your headdress for when you will be dining with your husband."

"I'm not to see him tonight?"

"*Non, Madame.* The King has prepared a special entertainment for the Archduke." She wrinkled her pert nose. "Nothing that a lady would like."

Groomed and dressed, I wondered what this special entertainment would be that I would so definitely not like. I was still wondering as I was led down torchlit halls, my retinue behind me in a train of swishing skirts. How long would we have to tarry at this court? Each day away from my children was a torture.

We burst into the brilliance of a chamber lit with silver candelabra as tall as men. Their light danced against the scarlet satin of the walls. At the far end of the room, surrounded by ladies in dresses picked out with sparkling jew-

els, sat a small plump young woman about my age: Anne of
Brittany, the Queen of France.

Mademoiselle Germaine, holding my train, whispered,
"You must curtsey, Madame!"

The Queen was not a crowned queen but a queen consort. Her greatest title was Duchess of Brittany. My title as
Archduchess outranked hers. Furthermore, she was the
daughter not of kings, but of a duke and his wife. It was for
her to curtsey to me.

I continued walking.

"Madame," Germaine whispered. *"Non! Non!"*

I felt a tug on my shoulders as my train unfurled; Germaine had let go of it. If I were Anne of Brittany's lesser, I
should carry my train myself as I approached—a sign of my
deference. But I was not her lesser. Even if Philippe worshipped the French court, and treated me with mindless
disrespect, I was the daughter of Isabel of Castile and Fernando of Aragón. If I did not stand up for myself now, who
ever would? I continued with hesitant steps, my train dragging behind me.

A tall older woman with a sharp nose and the shiny black
eyes of an ermine stood by the side of the Queen Consort:
the sister of the King, Anne of Beaujeu. She positioned herself behind me as I came to a stop before the Queen. Her
Majesty's herald announced my name.

At that moment I felt a shove against my back. I fell. The
gems in my skirts dug into my knees like pebbles.

"No matter what they taught you in that barbaric land of
your birth," the King's sister said into my ear, "in France we
bow before our Queen."

I looked around at the woman. Her eyes shone with malice. "What are you going to do, girl, when there is no one here to save you?"

"I do not need saving."

"With that husband of yours? I should think so." She gave a throaty laugh. "I suppose he leads you on a merry dance."

I wished to slap her weasel's face. "You may tell the Queen Consort that the heir to the Spanish throne has arrived."

The girl queen looked at her handler, unsure of what to do.

"Kiss her hand!" the King's sister ordered me.

When I did not move quickly enough, she pushed my head onto the little queen's plump outstretched hand.

"How does French flesh taste?" the King's sister asked when I fought to rise. "Get a good taste."

She let me up. I wiped my mouth, tears of fury stinging my ears.

She smiled at my discomfort. "It is very sweet, yes? Ask your husband. He would know."

21.

23 January anno Domini 1502

*I*t was cold, and getting colder. Pellets of ice hissed against the carriage. I inched deeper under the lynx-fur robe with Beatriz as we busied ourselves translating Aesop. We were nearing the Spanish border. I had not spoken with Philippe in twenty-two days.

We had fought when we left Blois, from the moment King Louis, his narrow greasy face debonair with a long-toothed smile, had handed me into the carriage with a kiss and a wave, and Philippe had swung himself inside after. Philippe waited until the crunch of cobbles under our wheels became the thudding of wood against mud, then turned to me, his mouth twisted with cold contempt.

"Madame, just what kind of game were you playing at?"

The first time alone since we had arrived at the French court, and this was how he spoke to me.

"An odd question from someone who loves his games. Every time I asked where you were, it was, 'His Majesty plays at cards.' Or, 'His Majesty plays at tennis.' Or, 'His Majesty plays at chess.' Meanwhile I was being tortured by the French ladies when I wasn't attending Mass, Mass, and more Mass."

"You would think you would enjoy that, with your Spanish zest for wallowing in Mary's tears and the Sorrowful Mysteries. But not even in church could you handle yourself correctly. Don't think I didn't hear about it. You insulted Louis's wife. How was I to face him after that?"

"She gave me money to offer for alms, Philippe."

"And so did Louis to me."

I looked away, sickened by the anger in his face. Lords gave their vassals coins to offer for alms. It was a show of power and prestige, and to accept the coins, one acknowledged one's own servility. I was not going to take the money from that girl, no matter what Philippe said. Especially with the King's hateful sister watching eagerly for me to show my submission. Very well, perhaps I had made it worse by stalling in my pew after the little Queen Consort had stormed out in anger. I had hoped that by letting her go I could avoid a confrontation. I never thought she would stick with etiquette and wait for me in the narthex, though good manners dictated that she not leave the chapel without her guest. Her face was as red as a ripe boil when I finally left the church half an hour later. Her henchman, Anne of Beaujeu, had grabbed me by the arm.

"We offer you alms to give and you're too arrogant to take them. Are you too good to give to the poor?"

"I shall always give to the poor. It is the rich who trouble me."

"The whelp of the Spanish bitch Isabel is as rude as her dam." She had given me a shake before letting go.

Now Philippe said, "These are Charles's future in-laws, Madame, not varlets on the street. You cannot treat them however you choose with this mistaken sense of superiority that you have. What makes you think you are better than they are? Because your mother is King? You must think little of me, a mere archduke. Perhaps I'm not rich enough for your blood."

"I've told you before that I don't care about that."

"And then you came to dinner in that Spanish dress. I heard that the Queen had given you a rich veil but you refused to wear it. You show up looking like a nun instead. What is wrong with you?"

And this from the man who would not pay my dressmaker.

"You were with women," I said.

"Where did that come from? Anyhow, no, I wasn't."

"You were. Katrien told me when I forced it out of her. One of the King's laundresses talked."

"You will not bow down to a queen, yet you believe what a laundress would say?"

"Yes."

"Then you have a problem, not I."

I rubbed my gloved knuckle with my thumb.

He took my chin, then turned my face roughly. "I have not been with other women, understand?"

I met his gaze. "Just saying something does not make it true."

He tightened his fingers on my chin, squeezing into the bone. "I liked you better when you kept your mouth shut."

I would not acknowledge that he was hurting me. "I liked you better when you did not lie to me."

He increased his grip until his forearm shook. "Now that you've moved up in the world, do you need taking down a notch?"

Tears of pain seeped into my eyes. I wished to slap off his hand, though if I did, I feared, he would strike my face.

He let go.

My chin throbbed as if he were still pinching it.

He patted my head. "You were always a good girl. Stay that way."

A salty lump seared my throat as he settled against the side of the carriage. I choked on it, scarcely able to breathe until he fell asleep, exhausted, no doubt, from his festive week.

After that, he had ridden with Hendrik and the Archbishop of Besançon, taking a different route. Beatriz entered my conveyance to accompany me, and cried out when she saw the red mark on my chin.

I lowered my face as she sat next to me on the upholstered velvet seat. "What happened!" she exclaimed.

"I bumped against the carriage."

I could feel her staring. "Your mother is going to ask about this."

"It will be gone before I see her."

She said no more until the carriage rumbled forward. "I speak of this only because you need to prepare yourself for her questions. Your discord with the Archduke will look bad to the Cortes."

"I don't care."

"I thought you wanted Charles to be heir to the throne."

I did. It was my dream for Charles to be King of Spain one day, not just the husband of a French princess. If he was king, no one would dare make sport of his malformed jaw. They would revere and respect him for the man he was, not for what he looked like.

"If you cannot bill and coo like lovebirds," said Beatriz, "at least you could adopt a symbol of your marriage that gives the impression of a happy union."

"Like Mother's yoke and Papa's arrows. There is not a building in the Spains upon which they are not plastered."

"The Queen and King are wise. They know that people like to have something to believe in, no matter whether it is based upon the truth or not."

I glanced at her.

"Of course, their legend is one that is based upon the truth," she said quickly.

I had never told her about Papa's assignation in the chapel in Barcelona. It was not something I could talk about. But I had come to realize that anyone with eyes could see the trouble in my parents' marriage, although few got beyond the myth of their great love. It seemed that the legend carried more weight than did the truth.

"What shall the symbols of our marriage be?" I asked her. "A fountain to represent Philippe and his constant spurting forth? And perhaps a bucket for me, to collect his spilling seed?"

She sighed, then produced from her valise a volume of Aesop's fables. We spent the rest of the day, and the following ones, translating it from Latin. How soothing Aesop was. How neatly he observed human behavior, suggesting solutions in small, sweet tales, as if the worst that could happen to us was to be bitter about something we could not have, or to call alarm so often that others would not heed us in the case of real emergency.

We were working on the tale "The North Wind and the Sun," Beatriz with her portable writing instruments and desk, I with the book on my lap, the lynx robe tucked over us, when a great clattering sounded outside the carriage. Up rose the shouts of men, calling their horses to slow.

Beatriz undid the curtain, letting in a frigid sleet-laden wind. She stuck out her head.

Pellets of ice clung to her headdress when she pulled back inside. "There's water ahead—a river feeds into a bay."

The border of Mother's kingdom in the Basque lands lay on the Bidasoa River where it flowed into the Bay of Biscay. After weeks of inching along the muddy roads of France, could we have reached the first of the Spains?

The carriage rumbled on more slowly, until, with a thud, the wheels struck wood. We jostled as our conveyance clattered over the timbers of the pontoon bridge. Another thud, and the wheels thumped once more in mud. We were on the other side.

A cry went up to stop our train. Beatriz pulled back the curtain to take another look. "You will not believe this— there are mules out there. Scores of them, with muleteers. In this snowstorm!"

I smiled sadly, remembering how the thought of a muleteer would make my sister María swoon, as she pictured our handsome papa stealing to Mother. My dear María, such a believer in love and romance. A little over a year earlier, she had been made to marry our own sister Isabel's widowed husband, the stern King of Portugal, her elder by thirteen years. She was now due to be delivered of her first child, at which time she would successfully fulfill the reason for their union. Her much-dreamed-of love match had been a marriage of political necessity.

Trumpets sounded. The door opened. My heart jolted at the appearance of Philippe's elegant fur-robed figure, framed by the icy gray light. Behind him the grainy curtain of sleet was turning into soft pats of snow.

"It seems, Madame, that your parents try to control us

even in the middle of nowhere. They have sent mules onto which they insist we transfer our baggage and ourselves. They think our carriages cannot master the mountains ahead."

By the sound of it, luggage was already being transferred from cart to mule. Philippe scowled. "What kind of country are we to rule, where nobles ride mules like basest plowmen?"

Hendrik rode up, wrapped in a blanket to which the snow was rapidly sticking. He glanced at Philippe, then searched my face.

"Look at the beasts they give us," Philippe said. "In Maxi's northern lands, we ride sleighs through the mountains. Handsome, bell-trimmed sleighs, loaded with heavy furs, and pulled by teams of matching horses. What kind of person rides a donkey to meet his people?"

Hendrik shrugged. "Christ?"

Our train rode into the mountains. I was faint with hunger and cold when at last the mules descended to the town of Segura, where hundreds of Vizcayans, wrapped in furs and covered in snow, waited at the town walls.

Philippe dropped back for me to join him. "Hurry, Madame. Our subjects await us. I hope they've readied a hot bowl of caudle. Or do you have such a thing in this godforsaken place?"

I hardly heard him. At that moment the pain in my frozen toes and cheeks mattered little, and likewise the ache of bracing myself in my jolting seat for many hours, and even the sorrow of knowing that our love had grown cold. For over the hooded heads of the welcoming cortege hung a flag whose castles and lions were discernible despite the falling snow. The flag of the Catholic Kings.

I was home.

The Spains

Fernando of Aragón

22.

26 January anno Domini 1502

Flickering torchlight dabbled shadows on the walls of the castle as Philippe drank another glass of wine under the inquisitive eyes of our host, the Marquis of Denia.

"Not bad." Philippe smacked his lips. "In my lands, it is a touch more rich. But not bad for wine, not bad."

Denia, a young dandy with a great dark curl pasted onto his forehead, watched with stunned interest as Philippe drained his cup. No doubt the last person he had seen drink with such thirst was a plowman, tipping back a skin in the fields. It was our third day in the Vizcayan town of Segura, and Denia still regarded my husband with the unbelieving fascination one might have, should a satyr come to supper.

"I am glad that you find the wine acceptable," said Denia, "as you will now be residing in our lands."

Philippe lifted his brows at me over his cup. We had come to the Spains only for me to receive confirmation as rightful heir to the throne, with Philippe as my consort, legal foolishness to which I agreed so that my Charles could inherit the throne someday. For once, we were in complete accordance: Neither of us had any intention of staying any longer than for the Cortes to convene. We could not hasten

back to Flanders quickly enough—I to the children, and
Philippe to Delilah and the hunt.

Denia's eyes, as large and liquid as a bull's, registered
heightened interest as he noted our exchange of glances.

"I did like that joust with the darts." Philippe put down
his cup. "What did you call it?"

"*Jugar a las cañas.*" Denia switched back to French. "It is
Castilian for 'to joust with canes.'"

"Good name." Philippe stabbed a portion of meat from
the platter before him, nearly grazing the back of his hand
on one of the serpents' tongues of the poison tester brought
from Flanders and dutifully set before him by his cupbearer.
"*Cañas.* They might have just been canes, but those devils
were sharp."

"That is why we have shields."

"No jest. People are not shy about flinging their canes.
Still, I liked it. Let's do it again tomorrow."

Denia's glossy curl swung forward as he bowed his head.
"Permit me to substitute a running of the bulls instead."

I sighed. Our first stop in Spain, and already we were
obliged to stay for several days, days in which baby Isabel,
now six months old, might be cutting a tooth or Leonor
might be having a nightmare and needing comfort.

"Bulls?" said Philippe. "Excellent. I have always wanted
to see this Spanish sport."

"Ah yes, I hope that His Highness enjoys it. And I understand there is quite a surprise being planned for you in Miranda de Ebro."

The pouches at the sides of Philippe's mouth lifted. "What?"

Denia and his curl bowed again. "It would not be a surprise if I told you, but I assure you, you will like it."

"I will like it more if there is good Flemish beer."

To Philippe's left, Hendrik laughed.

Denia allowed himself a small smile.

Poor Hendrik, so coarse and thickly Germanic—he stood out in this elegant crowd. Not so the Archbishop of Besançon. He speared his meat with great delicacy while leaning toward Denia's wife, lending his ear with a cold, hard grace as she prattled on. I gazed around the crowded hall, loud with conversation and the clink of plate and spoon. Ladies and gentlemen sat at tables, the jewels on their bright silks winking in the torchlight. I could recall few dinners in the Spains attended by both ladies and gentlemen. Was the custom different in this area? Indeed, the nobles were dressed more elegantly than I remembered Spanish nobles to be. Two years before I had left the Spains, Mother, under the influence of her confessor, Cardinal Cisneros, had decreed that only grandees could wear colored silks and gold trims, and not even they could wear colored coats to match. But everyone in this assemblage was dressed as splendidly as a peacock. The laws in this land must have been different from those in the rest of the Spains.

"Would you like beer?" said Denia. "I shall make sure to find a brewer."

"Oh, I have a brewer," Philippe said, speaking through a mouthful of beef. "He is part of that pack of two hundred–some persons milling around your courtyard, among them my tailors, my glover, and my soapmaker. People I cannot live without. Oh, and Juana's washerwoman. My wife *would* have her, though I don't know why."

Perhaps because she was one of the few I could afford to pay after pawning the little necklace my sister Catalina had once sent? "How long will we be in Miranda de Ebro, señor?" I asked.

Philippe answered for Denia. "As long as our hosts would have us. Don't tell me you're in a hurry to see your mother, Juana." He swallowed, watching me. "Are you?"

Denia smiled politely. "Their Majesties are journeying from Granada, Your Highness. I understand you will meet them in Toledo."

"Yes." As much as I wished to hurry this visit, I was in no rush to meet my mother. Indeed, whenever I thought of it, a knot tightened in my stomach.

"Allow us to entertain you this evening. A little performance is about to begin." Denia picked up a golden bell next to his plate and, dipping his curl, held it to me. "Doña Juana?"

I shook it. At its golden jingle, wildmen bashed open the doors and stormed into the hall, shaking rattles made of bones and shouting gibberish. Eyes crazed behind green-feathered masks, they ran around the tables with loincloths flapping, making the ladies scream. One shook his rattle in my face, then jumped on the table.

Philippe sank back in helpless laughter as others leaped onto the table, spilling cups, knocking plates, scattering food. "Oho! What denizens of Hell are these? Watch out—he's going to get you, Puss!"

The door to the hall banged open again. In rolled a mock carrack on wheels, accompanied by dancing boys dressed as dolphins and pipers in blue. On the quarterdeck of the pretend ship, swaying to and fro as the wheels creaked across the rushes, a tall and portly player searched the horizon through his spyglass. When he saw the wildmen cavorting on the tables, he called out, "In the name of Their Sacred Majesties Doña Isabel and Don Fernando, I, Cristóbal Colón, the mighty Admiral of the Ocean Sea, claim you as my subjects."

The wildmen abandoned their tormenting of us. Brandishing their bones, they hopped down and swarmed the base of the ship. Three sailors rushed to the bow, then heaved a net over the frantic creatures.

"Look what God has given me!" proclaimed the actor playing Admiral Colón.

The crowd cheered, even the ladies. I looked around. Since when had ladies cheered at supper in the Spains? Since when were the entertainments so lavish? What had the Spains become in my absence?

The sailors hauled their writhing load aboard, and all disappeared into the bowels of the ship. Then Admiral Colón gave a speech about his special favor from God, puffing out his chest much like the real Colón of my childhood, to the sportive jeers of the crowd.

The wildmen reappeared on the quarterdeck, this time in chains, goaded by the boasting Colón. As they clinked their bonds and wailed their laments, another ship heaved into the hall. At its helm was another play-actor, scanning the horizon with his spyglass.

He snapped it closed when he saw Colón. "In the name of Her Majesty the Queen Doña Isabel and His Majesty the King Don Fernando, I, don Francisco de Bobadilla, claim *you* as *my* subject."

Francisco de Bobadilla? In the true world, he was Mother's good friend and a trusted public servant. I had known the kindly gentleman since I was a child.

The mock Bobadilla produced a weapon from his scabbard. He swung from a rope and landed with a thump on the deck of Colón's ship. Swords rang out as the players fell into a fight.

Philippe leaned toward Denia. "This is almost as much fun as the entertainments in my court," he said over the clanking, "though it lacks the naked girls."

Long lashes a-blink, Denia stared at Philippe as the play Bobadilla forced the weapon from Colón's hands. With Colón's sword still clattering on the floor, Bobadilla commenced wrapping the Admiral in chains.

Our host returned his sights to the players as Bobadilla displayed his conquest to the crowd. "Look what God has given *me*!"

The crowd shouted as if at a running of bulls. The players rolled away on their ship, Bobadilla with his sword drawn over Colón, the Admiral gaping at his chains.

Philippe stood up, clapping.

"Señor," I asked Denia, "what is the meaning of this play?"

He looked at me in surprise. "You do not know about the Admiral of the Ocean Sea?"

"My sisters told me he had returned to the Indies."

"Oh, he came back, Your Highness. In chains."

"He came home in chains? When?" Why had María not written to me about this?

"Let me see," he said, "it was November, a little over a year ago."

That was about the time María had been wed to the King of Portugal. The summer before her wedding, her letters had been full of breathless descriptions of the clothes being made for her, of the furniture she would take, and of her hopes that her husband would be dashing. Then, after her wedding, silence. It would be six months before I heard from her again, and by then it was no longer my dear, dreamy María who wrote. Whether it was her pregnancy or something else that caused her letters to become terse and short, she was no longer given to reports about the handsome sons of sailors.

"It was a matter of great amusement for the blustering fool to be brought so low." Denia looked at me closely. "But do not fear, Your Highness. The Queen had his chains removed immediately and restored the properties Bobadilla had stripped from him. In fact, she has granted him ships and money for another voyage, though he is to avoid Hispañola, where he made a great mess of the place. The colony was in an uproar when Bobadilla got there—Colón was hanging good Spanish men left and right for insubordination, and selling Indio slaves by the boatful though they weren't his to sell. It seems, Your Highness, that while Colón has a gift for the sea, he has not an inkling about how to deal with men."

Philippe glanced at me as I sat back, deflated. As much as I had scoffed at the windbag, seeing him brought low disturbed me. I cringed for Diego. He had been so proud of his father, seeming to tether his own worth to his father's star. The chains on the father must have weighed equally heavily on the son.

Trumpets sounded; bows were taken to violas da gamba; a shawm bleated as a player tried his reed. A tambour was beaten three times and the music commenced.

Denia and his curl bowed in full deference. "It is time to dance, Your Highness."

Philippe grabbed my hands and pulled me from our

bench. "I had Spain all wrong. Hendrik, grab a lady and get out here."

The Archbishop of Besançon watched me with expressionless eyes, then called to his scribe. The young fellow hurried over, wiping his mouth, then took out his writing case.

23.

19 February anno Domini 1502

*I*t was one of those winter days in Burgos when the sky was so blue and the sun so brave that you almost did not mind the season. Our horses plodded along the path by the river, their hooves thudding against the thick layer of rotting leaves over which yellow silt had been churned. The lilting song of blackbirds mingled with the hum of the rushing water.

"If I play one more game of tennis," said Philippe, "I swear I shall drop." He looped his reins around the horn of his saddle and with a groan stretched his arms over his head. His horse, Helene, his favorite ambler, brought with him from Flanders, needed no reins or guidance. She intuited where her master wished to go—a handy talent for a horse who had often to take her master home when he was senseless.

"You needn't play so much."

"And let Pedro show me up? No, thanks."

Since arriving in Burgos three days earlier, Philippe had discovered that Pedro Fernández de Velasco, the seventeen-year-old son of our host, Iñigo Fernández de Velasco, brother of the Constable of Castile, shared a passion for winning. They found tennis to be an agreeable field of contest and, each hoping to prove himself champion, slogged through matches day and night. Thus far they had won an equal number of games, and so their rematches went on. One of them had to concede to the other, something obviously not in their natures. Evidently Don Pedro had not received the missive that everyone else seemed to have received here in Spain, that my husband was to be spoiled and given his way. We could be in Burgos for weeks, proving who was the victor with the racquet, while at home, baby Isabel was learning to creep on her belly and Charles was speaking in sentences. My poor little boy with his overshot jaw, would his nurses understand him? Would he say, "I want milk," and be given a toy and left thirsty, without his mother's patient ear to hear him?

A green heron was startled from the bulrushes at the water's edge. It flapped over the pale bobbing tufts toward the town. The towers of the cathedral could be seen in the distance.

"By God," said Philippe, watching the bird, "I wish I had Delilah."

"Let's go home and get her."

He gave me a bemused look as he took up his reins.

"Might we return to Flanders soon?" I asked.

"I thought Castile was your home. Anyway, we should enjoy this place while we can."

And enjoy it he did. In Vitoria he delighted at the bull run held in the city streets. He cheered at the bulls' scrabbling on the cobblestones, and laughed at the children scrambling out into the road between bulls to fetch the sweets he had thrown there. He roared with happy trepidation when a bull approached and a child still hunted a morsel that others had missed. He did not understand why I left, upset, though the child had been unhurt.

In Miranda de Ebro, he clapped like an excited boy when a hundred horses thundered past the palace, the scarlet capes of their Moorish-dressed riders whipping in the wind. When a hundred armored horsemen rode up crying, "*¡Santiago y cierra, Espana!*" and engaged the turbaned riders in mock battle, he begged to join in. He was given chain mail and a warhorse and turned out onto the field, where his cries of "*¡Santiago!*" soon blended with the herd.

At least now in Burgos his energy was bent on a cloth ball, endangering neither men nor children, nor himself. Relaxed and cheerful from his exertions, he had agreed to accompany me to the Carthusian monastery of Miraflores on the outskirts of town—as long as we prayed little and left quickly.

Beyond the bulrushes, the Arlanzón flowed intently. Sticks, leaves, someone's glove—all were hostage to its mission to join other waters to reach the sea. The air smelled of wet plants and earth and the cold.

"Philippe, why don't we send for the children?"

"And risk their lives on the roads through France?"

"They can sail."

He gave me a look.

I did not truly think to endanger them in such a manner, either. I sighed. "I miss them."

He chirruped to his ambler. "What is so special about this monastery that you are dragging me to? Couldn't we just hear Mass at the cathedral? It's a big-enough place."

I trotted after him on my horse. "Miraflores is the burial place of my grandparents."

"It's a beautiful sunny day and you're taking me to see tombs? What did I agree to?"

"They are no ordinary tombs. Mother ordered them built when I was young. They are just now finished. The sculptor was Flemish."

"Of course. All good carving is Flemish, though I suppose the tombs won't be as nice as my mother's."

"Probably not."

He reached over the back of his saddle to me. "How about a roll in the rushes?"

"As appealing as that sounds, Monseigneur, no."

His pretty lips turned down, puckering the pouches by his mouth. "What happened to you? You would have jumped at the chance when we first married."

When we met I did not have three children. When we met I had not grown up while he had stayed a boy. When we met, I did not know that he thought a husband's infidelities were harmless, that a wife was foolish to let them bother her, when that is just what men did. But in spite of all this, should he stop our horses and take me in his arms, with some coaxing he could mold me to his purpose. A few kisses to the neck, the feel of his breath on my ear, his lips upon my flesh, and given time, my body would betray me. Perhaps that was merciful. How would this man who lived by the word "yes" respond to a heartfelt "no"?

The path led up a wooded hill cloaked in waist-high grass, which hissed as it bent under our horses' bellies. Above us, tuft-eared black squirrels leaped from tree to tree. I freed my skirts from the canes of a wild rose.

"It's not far now," I said.

Philippe frowned at the stone walls of the monastery

now visible through the woods. He snorted with exaspera-
tion. "Let's get this over with, then."

The Royal Chapel smelled of cold marble. A chill emanated
from the pale limestone floor, from the rough-hewn walls of
granite, from the white alabaster tomb before us that bristled with dozens of masterfully carved saints and animals.
How had the sculptor teased these beings out of stone? They
were lifelike down to their individual expressions, to the
very hairs upon their gleaming heads. Their magnificence
was matched in the carved wooden altarpiece looming overhead. The saints and angels—and Mother, kneeling in the
foreground—were drenched in brilliant gold.

"Juan the Second, King of Castile." Philippe leaned
against the intricately wrought gilded fence that surrounded my grandparents' tombs. His voice echoed from
the vaulted ceiling. "Was he a good king?"

"He was my mother's father."

"But was he good?"

I gazed at the robed figure reclining on the sarcophagus
of whitest alabaster. His crowned head rested on a stone pillow; a stone dog slept at his feet. Beneath him, a lion roared,
a wafer-thin alabaster curl of tongue lolling between its
teeth. "He had a favorite whom he let rule while he played at
his jousts and hunts and tourneys. Álvaro de Luna. He ran
Castile for my grandfather."

"That's unwise."

"Most unwise. Atrocities happened right under Grandfather's nose, but he could not see this. If people complained

to Grandfather, Luna had them killed. He poisoned Grandfather's first wife when she tried to sound the alarm, and still Grandfather did not see. He was too busy . . . hunting."

Philippe ran his hand along the fence rail, then inspected his finger to see if any gold had come off.

"Grandfather trusted him completely," I said. "Luna was like a father to him. Grandfather's own father had died when he was a toddling child, and Luna became his tutor." I glanced at my husband. Did he not see the resemblance to his relationship with the Archbishop of Besançon?

He looked up. "Go on."

"Luna was a hated name around our home, for making my grandfather look foolish, but even more so for what he did to her." I nodded to the marble figure lying next to my grandfather.

"Isabel of Portugal," he said. "The mad one."

"Who told you that?"

"Everyone." He shrugged. "Grand-mère. François. It's no secret that your grandmother was *zielsziek*."

"But she wasn't, unless it was madness to challenge a monster like Luna. When she tried to tell Grandfather that Luna had murdered the first queen with poison, and that Luna threatened to poison her, too, if she tried to expose him, Grandfather wouldn't listen. He couldn't imagine Luna as anyone but the kindly father figure who had bounced him on his knee."

"So did this Luna kill her?"

"You don't have to kill to do damage. He gave her just enough poison each day to sicken her. When Abuela was ill from the poison, he spread rumors that she'd gone mad, and she was too sick to refute him."

"But she got well?"

"Yes."

"Then why did she not simply tell people what he did?"

"She did. But it was too late. Her reputation for madness was sealed. It seems that an accusation is as powerful as the truth—once it is made, there is no denial that can completely erase it."

He looked at me a moment, then, grasping the finials, stared at the tomb. After a time he asked, "How did he administer this poison?"

"I don't know. But it was enough to temporarily damage her mind."

The bells of the monastery now began to clang, slowly marking the hour as if it were Time's last. I could feel the vibration under my skin.

Philippe pushed away from the fence. "Well, sad story, Puss," he said, raising his voice above the bells, "but Pedro will be waiting. I've got ninety pieces of gold riding on our match. Have you seen enough?"

I drew in a breath, shaken somehow. My poor grandmother. No matter what she had ever said or done, she would be known to history as mad. How awful it must have been for her to endure the false smiles on people's faces as they privately discounted every word that came from her mouth. Perhaps this had made her mad in itself. How does one keep one's sanity after decades of being disbelieved?

Philippe glanced at the lovely tomb carved into the wall behind us. Above the booming bells, he asked, "Who is that?"

"Alfonso. My mother's brother. The prince who was supposed to be King. He died when my mother was a maiden."

The bells stopped, though the sonorous reverberations continued in my ears.

"So there lies the true King of Castile," said Philippe.

"If he had lived, yes."

He cocked his head, appraising me as if I were a stranger to him. "Odd, how things work out. He was supposed to be King, but your mother ended up with the crowns. Your brother, and then your sister, and even her son, were to be your mother's heirs, but here you are, next in line."

"And you."

"Not really. In this land I am only to be your consort, not truly King." He took my hand and kissed it. "But you never know, do you?"

24.

7 May anno Domini 1502

We were on the road to Toledo. Behind us were mountains, distant and purple; ahead of us, an undulating carpet of grassland, dusty green against the endless blue sky. Here and there hillocks pushed up from the expanse, crowned with gnarled gray olive trees. Who tended these trees? Some fifty leagues to the north, on the plains near Zamora, farmers had dug homes into the sides of the hillocks. On progresses of my youth, I had seen them crawl out from their grass-roofed dwellings to plow the fields and mind their goats. But here there was no sign of life other than the bustards that waddled frantically through the grasses, panicked by the cavalcade that raised the ocher cloud wafting at our knees. The dust muffled the rattle of tossing bridles. It muted the tinkling of the thimble-sized bells hanging from the Canopy of State just before me, under which my husband's and my father's horses ambled side by side.

Plodding behind on my palfrey, I marveled at the sight of them. There was my papa, sitting upright, his scarlet cape spread over his horse's thick haunches, his black hair streaked with gray under a crown heavy with rubies and diamonds. There was my husband, father of my children, proud, young, and golden, in his purple satin doublet and robe. I had worshipped both, once. I wished I still could.

It had been two weeks since I had first seen Papa. After we had kissed and embraced, he had held me out from himself. I could hardly bear the apologetic look in his eyes; it was as if he knew that I no longer idolized him, and agreed with my assessment.

"Juana." His smile was heartbreakingly shy. "May I ask how that shirt you are making me might be coming along?"

Oh, Papa. So many things have changed. I am no longer a little girl. "Your shirt? I shall have it to you on Tuesday."

Hope flickered in his eyes. "Then on Tuesday, I shall look like a king."

My heart ached. For him, I would remain a child. "But Papa, you already are a king."

The sweetness of reconciliation had warmed me as we had embraced again. If only one could forget as easily as one forgave. But in spite of the guarded happiness our fragile new détente gave me, the knot in my belly clenched even as I watched him and Philippe riding ahead under the Canopy of State.

I would see Mother today.

The jewel on Philippe's cap swung out as he leaned toward Papa. "Monseigneur, how shall I address your wife when I meet her?"

"Isabel?" Papa grinned. "Isabel."

"I can hardly call her that."

"She's not one to stand on ceremony, my boy. Address her any way you like, as long as you don't wear that wig you wore in Medina."

They laughed like old friends. Indeed, they seemed to

have taken to each other immediately, in spite of Papa's
meeting Philippe under the most ignoble circumstances. We
had been two leagues out of Toledo when Philippe had succumbed to chicken pox. The father of three, Archduke of
Austria, Good Counselor, lover, and hunter, had been laid
low by a child's disease.

Father had ridden out from Toledo to meet us in our
makeshift lodging in Olias. Poor Philippe had to receive
him in his shift and shivering under a blanket, with clear
pustules bubbling upon his face.

Now Philippe said, "I wish you had been in Medina,
Monseigneur. The things you can do as the common man!
It was brilliant of Pedro to think of disguising me in the wig
and leather doublet of a soldier. I pinched all the titties I
wanted without having to flip some proud papa a *maravedí*
for the privilege. It's pay the piper if you have a title to
your name."

Papa gave him a sidelong look, then mostly regained his
amiable expression. "I dressed up once, to go meet my wife.
Her brother didn't favor the match and would have had me
murdered had he known I was in Castile. I was costumed
like a muleteer—did Juana tell you about it?"

"No, Monseigneur."

I had. He did not remember.

"Surprising," Papa said. "Well, it was quite a role to play.
I had to curry the mules and feed them. To tell you the
truth, I got to where I enjoyed it. Anyhow, my daughters
love that story."

Correction: Daughter. María. And to be honest, Catalina, too, now sixteen and in England, meeting, at last, the
boy to whom she had been two years wed by proxy. Would

she find young Arthur to her liking? Not that it would change her fate to become Princess of Wales, and someday, Queen of England.

A cough came from behind me.

I turned to see Beatriz, leaning forward on her pillion as she urged her horse ahead of madame de Hallewin's gray palfrey. She caught my eye and nodded toward Papa and Philippe, indicating that I should join them under the canopy. Rightfully, I was to be at the head of the procession, since I was Mother's true heir, not Philippe. Indeed, I was surprised to see Papa endorsing Philippe so openly. In this country, Philippe the Good was fast becoming known as Philippe the Drunken Reveler.

How happy he looked now, riding with Papa. He savored these ceremonies in a way I never could. But the more defer-ence the Spanish showed him, at least to his face, the more he seemed to hunger for the crowns. He was as his *grand-mère* had said: a man whose appetite grew more voracious from eating.

I heard quickened hoofbeats behind me. The Archbishop of Besançon trotted his horse up next to Beatriz, the lappets of his miter flapping. He guided his mount into her path, forcing her animal to step back so that madame de Hallewin's palfrey could come cantering around her. The Viscountess of Furnes, as creamy as ever in silvered blue, followed in madame's wake, a sweet smile upon her lips.

I turned around, the fist doubling in my gut.

"Does the Queen's health improve?" Philippe asked Papa.

Papa had come to Olias without Mother, who said she was ill. But it was rarely sickness that kept Mother in her bed. If her nobles disobeyed her, she would not punish them at the rack or by whipping but would stay under her covers, claiming her body suffered from the blows of their contempt. Only when they bent to her will would she get up, and then all of the Spains would seem sunnier. It did not bode well that she had not risen to meet me.

"The herald said she was sitting up," said Papa, "and able to take some broth this morning."

"I must admit, Monseigneur, that she frightens me just a bit."

Papa chuckled. "You must not worry. She has that effect on everyone. You should have seen the Moorish army when she charged up to the gates of Granada on a warhorse."

"I cannot see Juana doing that."

Papa smiled at me over his shoulder. "Oh, Juana's a good girl. I never have to worry about her."

Philippe twisted around in his saddle. "Are you doing well, Madame?"

"Yes, Monseigneur."

He nodded, then turned back quickly, as if afraid I might claim my rightful place in the procession.

Ahead, the towers of Toledo rose above the plains. Inside the city walls erected by the Visigoths, fortified by the Moors, and now flying the colors of Castile and Aragón, Mother awaited.

Dear saints in Heaven, save me.

Mother's hair was more white than I remembered, less red. In fact, I remembered no white at all. Pouches had been pulled out from under her chin, and gray bags from under her eyes, in the five and a half years that had passed. I could see them even at that distance across the hall. She wore

plain black and her favorite crown, the one of delicate filigree upon a wide plain band of silver. I had tried it on, once,
as a child, when she was meeting with her counselors. Its
thick rim had slipped down my head and dug into the tender flesh at the top of my ears. How did she sit under that
ring of pain for hours on end? I had prized it off and
promptly dropped it on my foot. I would not tell my nurse
why I was crying when she had come to get me, though my
toe had throbbed as if broken.

My husband now took my hand and we started forward
after Papa. I gazed in panic at the tapestries on the wall and
the ladies and gentlemen lined up before them, dipping as
we passed. Mother's dear friend Beatriz de Bobadilla stood
next to her, glancing nervously between my mother and me.
A young woman near my age stood on Mother's other side.
Only the highest grandee or my kin would have such a place
of honor. Did I know her?

Papa reached Mother and kissed her cheeks, and then
kissed the cheeks of the unknown girl. Was she the daughter of the Constable of Castile, the older gentleman on her
left, or of the Duke of Villena, at whose palace Mother was
receiving us? No matter whose daughter she was, shouldn't
she be on her knees, waiting to kiss the hand of her King?

Philippe squeezed my fingers. Though he held up his
chin and smiled nonchalantly, I could feel him tremble.

We came before Mother. We started to kneel.

I felt a touch on my shoulder.

"I had told your attendants that I would not have this.
Up, Juana, up. You, too, Don Philippe."

When I raised my eyes, Mother opened her arms.

She embraced me first. While we kissed, I heard the
scrape of my husband's shoes as he shifted nervously.

She let go of me, then held out her arms to him. "My son." When she was clasping him to herself, I caught the glance of the young woman I did not know. Dark-haired, olive-skinned, she kept flicking me looks as if she wished to stare but was afraid to do so.

Mother released Philippe, then folded her hands over her belly, which had grown more substantial. "What a lovely couple you make. My ambassador tells me your children are strong and beautiful. He says little Charles rides a pony like a man."

Did her ambassador also report my son's troubles with language? Or his small stature, from his difficulties with eating?

Philippe grinned, unaware of or unwilling to acknowledge his son's struggles. "I'll have him at the lists before you know it. I'm having a suit of armor made for him."

"There is time enough for that," said Mother.

"Juana." She turned to me and searched my face. After a moment, she said, "You remember doña Beatriz de Bobadilla?"

Mother's lady kissed my hand, then smiled coolly as if censuring me.

"And this is Juana of Aragón, the wife of Don Bernardino."

I put out my hand for the girl to kiss. So she was the young wife of the aging Constable of Castile. I blinked away the image of tender flesh being kneaded by hardened hands.

Her lips were pressed to my knuckles when Mother said, "She is your half sister."

This Juana raised herself, an uncomfortable smile twitching at her mouth.

I did not understand. I had no half sister.

"We welcome her to court," Mother said.

A half sister would make her Papa's daughter.

I looked to Papa, but his face was blank. The courtiers turned their gazes away as I sought an explanation in their expressions.

Concerned only with his own thoughts, and so immune to the tension throbbing in the air, Philippe spoke into the silence.

"Your Majesty—"

"Mother," Mother corrected.

"My Lady Mother, we visited the tombs of your parents."

Mother smiled with surprise. "You went to Miraflores? How is the work coming along?"

"Most magnificently, Madame. There was much gold everywhere, even upon the fence that surrounded them."

"Don't be fooled. A nugget the size of a pea can be hammered into a sheet as large as my veil. But it is beautiful, isn't it? It came from the Indies, you know. Admiral Colón's gold."

"Colón is bringing back more than slaves and pestilence?" Philippe grinned at the courtiers as if to bring them in on his joke.

"I should think so," said Mother, unsmiling, "or I would not be sending him back a fourth time." She gazed down her line of stone-faced gentlemen until she found one near the door. "Don Diego's father should be sailing from Cadiz any day now."

I followed her eyes to a young man dressed in her livery of scarlet and gold. Diego Colón bent into a slow bow. He was taller than I remembered, and thinner, but every bit as self-possessed, and, I found myself thinking, more handsome than ever in his quiet way. Had he returned to court from Salamanca?

Mother grasped my hand. "My dear son," she said to Philippe, "do you mind if I borrow your wife for a moment? We do need to chat."

I could hear servants talking in the courtyard as Mother led me down the arcade of the Duke of Villena's palace. There was a splash of water. I looked over my shoulder and saw Katrien, waiting in a queue of servants with her bucket, the wings of her Flemish headdress bright white in the morning sun. Outside, from the street, a mule brayed.

Mother pulled me under an arched doorway into a bedchamber—hers, I deemed, by the opulence of the portable prayer booth sitting near her altar, above which hung a painting by Rogier van der Weyden. I recognized the painting—the Dowager Duchess of Burgundy owned a copy of it. Did Mother think of it as a good investment, too?

"Sit."

I sank upon a cross-legged chair with a rustle of skirts. The bells of the cathedral began to ring. Terce was upon us. I breathed a sigh of relief. My interview would be short. Mother would not miss an opportunity to pray.

"I heard you did not ride into town under the Canopy of State," she said over the clanging.

She had just announced that I had a half sister, whom I had not known existed, and she had shunned me for years in punishment for not corresponding—and she was worried about how I had processed into town?

"Philippe wanted to."

"Fine. Philippe can ride under canopies all he wants. But you must ride under them with him, Juana. You are my heir—the Cortes must see you as such. They won't take you seriously if you're trotting along behind your consort like a servant."

"It didn't seem to matter. Philippe and Papa—"

"Your father! What was he thinking? It was he who took your place, not Philippe."

"Papa didn't take my place. He is King. He should take precedence."

"It wasn't Fernando's procession." She pushed at her crown. "He knew better."

Was that the problem—she was angry at Papa for producing this bastard? Why had she brought the girl to court? She could have hidden her away. I looked pointedly at the breviary lying on the altar, hoping she might keep the hour and start praying. This interview could end only in tears—my own.

"Why would Fernando take your position?" she muttered to herself. "I simply do not understand him."

If only we could just pray. Or could go back and join the others. There was safety in numbers. Mother did not like to make a scene.

"What do you hear of María?" I asked.

The bells stopped. Mother's voice welled into the absence of ringing. "She is in confinement. I expect to hear of the birth in the coming weeks."

I said what I thought she wanted to hear: "May she be delivered of her child safely, and may it be a man child."

She frowned at me. "Pretty words, coming from a woman child. Do you not find girls as valuable?"

So this was how she was to punish me, by bickering until she wore me down?

"How is Catalina?"

She drew in a breath, as though restraining herself. "She admires her new young husband, though he is very shy. I hear from her often, even if she is in England."

Now we were coming down to it. Very well. Let us get this over with. "I am sorry that I did not write, Mother."

"Sorry? Juana, what you did was unconscionable. You cut me to the bone with your neglect. Why? Why would you treat me this way?"

I was too ashamed to admit the truth. "I was busy with my husband."

"Busy!"

"You're the one who sent me to him. I was only trying to make the best of it."

"You didn't have one minute to put quill to paper?"

"I must work hard, Mother, to keep his eye."

She studied me for a moment. She started to say something, then thought better of it. The clash of galloping hooves striking cobblestones floated through the window; a courier shouted for a footman to take his horse.

"Do you love him?" she asked.

"Yes." I was too ashamed to admit otherwise. How would it make me look to not have made a success of a marriage to a man as seemingly affable as Philippe?

"I suppose you are so lost in love that my pleas to hear a word from you have meant nothing."

Her pleas? I had pleaded, too. I had begged for her forgiveness in my letters, once I started writing. What did it take for her to forgive me?

She blew out a breath. "Yet when the plea went out to claim your inheritance, you somehow found the time to come here."

"That is my husband's doing. I don't care about the crowns."

"Oh. So if you had had your way, you wouldn't have come at all."

I could hear the incredulousness in my laugh. How did she always manage to so effectively use my words against me?

"I am just trying to understand, Juana."

I sighed. "I do what my husband wills me to do. Isn't that what I am supposed to do?"

"Was it his will for you to not write me?"

She had punished me far longer than I had withheld my letters. I struck back, out of hurt. "Tell me about my new half sister. How nice to have one after all these years, and fully grown, too."

"Don't make a joke of it, Juana."

I was startled to see dismay on her face. Mother—who had frightened men who rode into battle with knives between their teeth, who had sent Colón and his crew into the yawning maw of the Ocean Sea, who had terrified me since birth with her calm exposition of my frailties—visibly cringed.

Questions regarding the age of the girl, her parentage, what this meant about Papa, played upon my lips. I had Mother against the wall, and yet, I did not want to pin her.

Someone knocked at the door. When she did not move, I went to open it.

Papa stood in the morning light.

"Juana, where is your mother?"

She stepped forward, her face composed except for a tightness around her lips.

"Isabel, I just received word. I am so sorry, my princess. Catalina's Arthur has died."

She stared at him. "Arthur? He is but fifteen."

"He is dead. God rest his soul."

"What is our dear Catalina to do? Who will it be next? Have I not paid enough?"

Papa gathered her into his arms, but she pulled away. Drawing a shuddering breath, she went to her altar and sank slowly to her knees. She was still praying when I slipped out, long after Terce had ended.

25.

8 May anno Domini 1502

Katrien stood in the doorway with a ewer of water.

"I am sorry, Mevrouw. I did not know you were here."

"Come in."

Outside, a blackbird whistled from a rooftop. A cart rumbled past, its wooden wheels thudding against the cobblestones. Estrella lifted her head. She was grizzled about her muzzle and eyes, and walked more slowly than when I had left her, but she had climbed onto my lap and hidden her head under my arm when brought to me on the night of my arrival in Toledo. Now she lowered her muzzle to her paws and closed her eyes, content in the sunshine beaming in through the arched window at which I stood.

"I have some water for you to wash with. Would you like some orange peel in it?"

"Orange peel, no. Why do you ask?"

"I notice the ladies of the court here scent themselves with it and honey."

A discomfiting memory of the smell and its association with my discovery of Papa's weakness flashed through my mind. Aixa was no longer at court. I supposed that Mother had sent her away, as she did all of Papa's lovers eventually.

I wondered to which remote place the mother of my "new" half sister had been banished.

"What else do you notice?"

She set the ewer on my table. Already taciturn enough on her native soil, she had become even more closemouthed since we had arrived in the Spains. She should have felt her ease here, as somber as were these lands of my birth. But then again, my homeland was not the solemn place I remembered. It had changed remarkably since I'd left. Even after we had donned our black *ropas de luto* to mourn Catalina's Arthur, the festivities continued. Papa had arranged for a tournament on this day, in which the gentlemen of the court would reenact the conquest of Granada. The Spaniards would be in brilliant armor, and the Moors would ride with short stirrups *a la jineta*, making them appear to stand astride their horses. Philippe had clapped when Papa announced it; Mother had made a slight pained smile.

"Are the other ladies still at the tournament?" I asked Katrien.

"Yes, Mevrouw."

I had claimed I had a headache, and needed a rest. Truth is, I needed to be by myself. I had much to think about.

"The wife of the Constable of Castile is there also?"

She frowned.

"Doña Juana of Aragón," I said. "Young? Pretty? Old husband?"

"She is there."

The night before, at the feast held to welcome Philippe and me, Mother had asked this new Juana to sit at the table with our family. Was this to honor the girl or to dig at Papa?

"Who's her mother?" Philippe had whispered into my ear, nodding at this Juana.

"I don't know."

He shrugged. "Bastards happen. My great-grandfather Philippe the Good had eighteen of them—that we know of."

I glanced at him. Let him not try to emulate his hero in this.

"I'll ask François to find out the girl's dam."

Now I asked Katrien, "What do the servants say about this other Doña Juana?"

Katrien shook her head, setting aquiver the wings of her white linen headdress.

Only Mother would inspire servants to keep their mouths closed about such juicy gossip. Out of respect for the woman who gave generously to the poor and spun wool just as they did, they would not speak of Papa's betrayal. They would pretend with her that she was not wounded.

"Do they say anything about my husband?"

Katrien kept her back to me. "What would they say?"

I laughed. "That he acts like a child."

She turned to face me. "Mijnheer is a gentleman!" she said vehemently.

I drew back in surprise. "So loyal! That is sweet, Katrien, but you are my friend, not his. You need not hold back in saying what you truly see."

She looked away.

"Katrien, you know that I trust you. Now you must trust me. Your words would never get past me. Nor shall I ever judge."

She wiped her hands on her apron. "If I may go, please, Mevrouw."

I nodded, hurt. I had thought that even if we weren't exactly confidantes—Katrien would never be one to confide in me, or perhaps in anyone—that we had some kind of understanding. How lonely I felt with Beatriz gone. She could not return from her visit with her family soon enough.

Later, Philippe strode into my chamber, awakening me from a nap. He wore the crested helmet of one of Mother's soldiers, though the rest of his attire was in the French style: a laced silk doublet laid open across his chest, a fine chemise underneath, and purple hose. He opened his visor with a screech of metal. "Do I look like a Spaniard, Puss?"

I sat up. "The very image."

He took off his helmet, then the padded cap underneath, and shook out his hair, which was several inches longer than the average Spaniard's. I had learned over the years that his barber curled the ends of it every morning, thus giving it the smooth curve that brushed the cords of his neck. Today the helmet had mussed the barber's work.

"I left it on to show you—the rest of the armor was inferior to mine at home. Where were you today? You should have come out. I think I slew about a hundred Moors."

"You didn't really hurt anybody, did you?"

"No," he said, then added, "I don't think so. Why didn't you come? It made me look bad to not have you there. I had to have your mother as my lady."

I smiled inwardly at the image of my bon vivant of a husband offering himself to my stern and forbidding mother. "I shall come to the next event."

"François found out about the girl."

I missed a breath. "The girl?"

"Your father's bastard. It seems that her mother is one Juana Nicolau."

My heart sank. "A lady of Mother's."

"François had to do a lot of digging. No one would talk. How much do you think your mother had to pay people to keep their mouths shut?"

"Nothing," I murmured.

He laughed. "And I'm a fool. François pointed out that my friend Pedro is your half sister's nephew by marriage. Bernardino Fernández de Velasco is Pedro's uncle. Small world."

What had it taken Mother to welcome this girl to court and grant her a high position? How it must have wounded her pride before her people to have this outward evidence of Papa's straying. Isabel the King could not hold her husband. What a chink it must have knocked in her glorious legend of marital fidelity and love.

Philippe chuckled to himself. "You should have seen this one ridiculous Moor at the tourney. I kept striking him with my blunted sword, and he kept jumping up to bow at me. Curious-looking creature, skin the color of quince jam. When his turban fell off, his hair stood out from his head like a parasol. It was stiff as a horse's cropped mane."

I looked up.

"Another fellow with him told him to stay down, but this fellow seemed determined to speak to me. He almost ruined the effect of the entertainment. Dead Moors are not supposed to rise and chatter."

There came a soft knock on the door.

"Enter," I called.

Katrien stepped in, bearing a vase of flowers. She froze when she saw Philippe.

"Come in, come in," Philippe said amicably. "Do what you were going to do."

She hesitated, then took the vase to my table.

Philippe crossed his arms and leaned against the table, making her alter her course. "What are those flowers?"

"Roses, Your Grace. The Queen sent them."

"Round Eyes," he said. "Is that what they call you at home, Ronde Ogen?"

"May I be excused, Your Grace?"

He saw me looking at him, then her. "Come here, Puss."

I did not come.

"Very well." He walked over and put his arms around me from behind. "I'll come to you." Where his sleeves were rolled up, I could see the ropes of veins in his forearms.

"I missed you," he murmured in my ear. "Did I tell you that?"

I nodded at Katrien, who hurried out.

"Woman." Philippe's breath warmed my ear. I could smell the spicy scent of his flesh. "Did you miss me?"

I broke free of him.

His brow twitched before he recovered his smile. "Is that how you're going to play it? You're going to be a skittish colt?"

"Not now, Philippe."

The playfulness melted from his face. "Then when, Juana? When?"

"Just . . . not now. Please."

"You make a lot of noise about my taking other women, yet you will not have me. Something is wrong with your mind."

"Please, Monseigneur. Give me a moment."

"A moment! You need a moment? Am I so unappealing that you must work up your desire for me?"

"No, it's just that—"

He grabbed my arm and pulled me against him. "I may be only your consort at this court, but by God, in my bed I am your master."

"Please, Philippe. Don't."

"You think you're too good for me now," he whispered harshly.

"That's not true!"

"Shut up." He shoved me against the bed. I was not ready for him even by the time he was finished.

He banged the door behind him when he left. I lay on the bed, seeping like an open wound.

26.

23 May anno Domini 1502

A shawm was playing from the balcony over the hall, the reedy drone infusing melancholy into air already thick with the smell of spices and roasted meat. As servers brought in another course, Philippe idly fingered the tree of serpents' tongues his cupbearer had dutifully set before him.

"I have meant to speak with you," I said quietly. "Perhaps you should retire your serpents' tongues from table at court."

He pinged one of the stony tongues. "Why?"

"It is offensive to my mother. No one wishes to harm you here. The tasters here are enough to protect you."

"They didn't protect that Luna person from poisoning your grandmother."

I looked at him in surprise. "You remembered."

"You must think that I am stupid."

"No. It's just that . . . I did not know you'd taken note."

He glanced at me, then cast his petulant gaze at the young men in their rich liveries, rushing about with their silver chargers of meat. "God, I am bored."

There were no naked frolicking mermaids or hilarious wildmen here. Mother had organized this feast to celebrate my confirmation as her heir by the Cortes. All we had was meat, meat, and more meat, cooked to where the juices no longer ran from it—the way Mother liked it.

A platter was set before him; the lid ceremoniously lifted. He looked less than impressed. "Another roast. Hallelujah."

"Shh," I whispered. "Mother thinks to honor you."

Philippe leaned forward to look at Mother, now engaged in a conversation with the Archbishop of Besançon. "She almost killed me today. If I had to look at one more ledger . . ."

"If you were King, you would be poring over those ledgers daily."

"Wrong. If I were King, my *men* would be poring over those ledgers daily. That is one of the benefits of being King."

Mother spun her own wool to make Papa's shirts, presided over her courts of law, and oversaw the plans for the churches, hospitals, and universities rising from the dirt all over her lands, when she could have been taking her ease. What benefits might she be reaping from her labors other than exhaustion? Yet she loved being Queen. She'd wanted the crowns badly, enough to battle for seven years against the nobles who backed her half sister's claim to them.

I felt someone's gaze upon me: Papa, on the other side of Mother. He smiled then lifted his brows at me.

I turned away. I felt estranged from him again since my abuse at Philippe's hands. What would he think of his sweet child, now reduced to a slit for a man to brutalize? Philippe had found our new sort of rough coupling to his liking, and was coming to my bed more often. As I sat at this table laden with food and silver, under my gem-studded skirts my loins were swollen and torn.

Philippe lowered the bite of meat at his mouth. "Puss, I can't believe it. The Moor who wouldn't stay dead is here."

"What?"

He gestured with the meat on knifepoint. "Over there. Good God, he's in your mother's livery. Is he her fool?" He gestured to his cupbearer. "See that man over there with the tan-colored tent of hair? Get him over here. I want to speak with him."

The cupbearer trotted off.

"Why?" I demanded. "What do you want from him?"

"Why do you care?"

The cupbearer spoke to the object of Philippe's amusement, who looked up, then peered across the hall and, seeing me, beamed.

Philippe chewed his bite of meat. "He acts as if he knows you."

"He does. His name is Juanito. Admiral Colón brought him from the Indies."

"A real wildman? Oh, excellent! Now the entertainment starts."

Juanito crossed the hall, his face lit with eagerness. He dropped to his knees before us. "My Lady Princess, Doña Juana."

I put out my hand. He kissed it hard.

I could not help smiling. "Philippe, this is don Juanito."

"'Don'? You address cannibals like gentlemen?"

Juanito let go of my hand and kissed my husband's with equal fervor. "I am your servant, My Lord."

Philippe pulled back his hand. "I remember you from the tournament the other week. Next time, you need to stay dead. Do you understand? You nearly ruined the effect."

Juanito frowned in apology. "I am sorry. Don Diego told me I should not have done that. But I wished to see the husband of Doña Juana."

"You do know him," Philippe said wonderingly to me.

Juanito bowed. "I serve the Queen as page now," he told me.

"The creatures you Spanish keep at court." Philippe peered at Juanito. "So, cannibal, tell me, what do people taste like?"

Juanito smiled apologetically.

"Are they chewy?"

"Philippe."

"Do you have a hankering for one now?" He stabbed his knife into the slab before him. "All this tiresome beef."

"Philippe, it's not funny."

"You side with a monkey, Madame?"

A trumpet blew, announcing the arrival of yet another course.

"He knows I am jesting," Philippe said. "Off you go, there's a good man."

I watched Juanito return to his table and his place next to Diego Colón.

"What?" Philippe said when I gave him a cool look. "I needed some entertainment. Your mother's feast is dull going."

For the rest of the meal, Philippe chatted with the Duke of Villena, to his right, who had been eyeing him with equal measures of disdain and fascination. After the last plate was removed, Mother surprised us by calling for dancing, though out of respect for the passing of Catalina's husband, it was to be a somber *basse danse*. She bade Philippe and me lead the other couples in the gliding steps.

After several measures, Philippe stopped, then turned me so that we became the end of the line.

"Will she release us from our misery soon?" he asked, bowing to me in the *révérence*.

"Shhh." On the dais to which they'd retired, Papa sat next to Mother, beating the rhythm of the music on the arms of his throne.

Philippe followed my gaze. "Won't she let your father dance?"

"He could dance. He chooses to stay with her."

He looked at my half sister, sitting with her husband. He smirked.

We moved forward as the next measure commenced. "In spite of what you think," I said, "on the whole, Papa treats her well."

"What are you implying? Don't I treat you well enough?"

I drew in a breath. Before I could speak, Philippe lunged to the right and grabbed the Viscountess of Furnes's wrist as she passed by. She gasped, then laughed. He let go of me and began processing with her. Her partner, the young Marquis of Santillana, gave a flustered bow, then stared after her as if he could not believe she had slipped from his hands. The dancers around me looked away in discomfort that I should be left standing.

A gentleman came into my side vision. I turned to find Diego Colón, his handsome face hard with seriousness. He held out his arm. "Your Highness. May I have the honor?"

I was nearly overcome with gratitude at this small gesture. I took his arm, aware of both my shyness and the warmth of his flesh through his sleeve. As we entered the line of dancers, I noticed his hand, balled into a fist.

I tried to remove all emotion from my voice. "I did not expect to see you here."

"Because my father was in chains?"

I remembered the play in which Francisco de Bobadilla imprisoned Colón. I felt my cheeks turn red. "No."

"I can see that you heard of it even in far-off Flanders. Of course. The world is eager to bring down a man who excels."

"I only meant that I thought you might be in Salamanca."

He glanced at me as if to see whether this was true.

I did not wish to spar with him. I was too weary from my dealings with Philippe. "I see that your father has sent gold from the Indies." We stepped in time to the music. "The altarpiece at the monastery in Burgos was resplendent with it."

"Gold is just the beginning," he said. "He has found the lands leading to a westward passage—he is going back to expand the route. Do you know how important that is?" He raised my hand at the beat.

"Yes." I sighed, then smiled. "There will be more islands to name Juana."

His eyes warmed. "Of course."

"Truly, I am glad that he has met with more success, and not just because of all the potential Juanas."

Diego inclined his head slightly. "Thank you. His success will benefit all of the Spains for generations to come. It will shape the way we trade, and provide unimagined riches to rebuild your parents' lands. But for me, at this moment, the chance of talking to the real Juana is just as rewarding."

I laughed. "Flattery. I could use a bit of it just now. Thank you."

"It is not flattery." His expression was serious.

I looked away. "You must wish to go with your father to the Indies."

"He insists that I stay here."

"It is a dangerous journey."

We took a step backward. "I don't care about that," he

said. "But I agree to remain here so that I may continue to learn from your mother. At present, the governorship of the Indies has been given to another person."

My embarrassment returned. "Surely you and your father will win back your rightful place as governor."

He set his jaw. "That is my plan."

"Perhaps your studies at Salamanca will aid you."

"You knew that I went there?"

I nodded.

"Did you hear, too, that I was expelled for fighting?"

I glanced at him in surprise. "No. I did not."

We faced each other at the end of the measure, then performed the *révérence*. "You must think less of me for acting the ruffian."

"No!"

"You should. I was too proud. I have since come to realize that if I were to fight each time I heard my father's name muddied, I would have no time to work on actually clearing it."

"I am sorry."

"Don't be. Your mother was kind enough to invite me back as a page. She wished to show her court that she still believed in my father, in spite of his failings. When I first appeared before her, and began to apologize for my black marks at Salamanca, she bade me speak no more of it. She said that to make good steel, the ore must first be put to the fire."

"That might be true, but it does not make the fire less hot when one is in it."

"No." He searched my eyes. "It does not."

"My Lady Wife."

We turned to find Philippe approaching with the Viscountess. The self-satisfied look on my husband's face became a puzzled scowl when he saw Diego.

Diego bowed.

Philippe did not return the courtesy. "Have we met?"

"Yes," said Diego. "Twice."

The Viscountess's interested gaze ranged over Diego.

"Philippe," I said, "this is the son of Admiral Colón, don Diego."

Philippe wavered slightly on his feet. "Thank you for reminding me, Puss. I would like to ask him how he is enjoying his inheritance of mosquitoes."

Diego smiled coolly.

"Counting up your cannibals, are you?" said Philippe. "You might be the first person to get rich by human flesh—no, I take that back. Procuresses already do that with their whores, don't they?"

"May I have back my husband, please?" I took Philippe by the arm from the Viscountess. "Pardon me, don Diego, mademoiselle Aliénor."

I led Philippe into the line of dancers.

"You're drunk."

"What else do you expect me to do at this godforsaken picnic?"

"To not shame yourself and me."

"My God, you are a prune. Hendrik!" he bellowed. He struggled to level his eyes at me. "Where'd your mother stash Hendrik?"

"Perhaps it is time to go to your bed."

"Only if you go with me."

Did he think his drunken smile was alluring?

He squinted at Diego, standing beyond the dancers,

watching us with concern. "What ho? Does the King of the Cannibals have a taste for my wife?" Blinking to clear his vision, he refocused on me. "Does my little wife have a taste for him, too?"

"Stop it, Philippe."

He lumbered to a halt. "Have I struck a nerve?"

I moved to turn away, but before I could do so, he thrust his hand into my bodice.

His beautiful face crumpled into a grimace as he dug his fingers into my breast. "You're mine. *N'est-ce pas?*"

He squeezed again, then let go.

I clutched at my broken laces.

"What are you looking at?" he asked the staring dancers. "Cannot a man admire his own wife?"

They turned away uncomfortably, as if they had witnessed a man beating his horse.

He led me from the floor. On their dais, Mother clenched Papa's hand. Papa, in turn, tightened his grip on his scepter, much as Juanito renewed his hold on Diego, wrenching to be freed.

I leaned against the windowsill, absorbing the moonlight as if it had the power to cleanse. Behind me, Katrien straightened the bedclothes, pretending that there was no stain upon them. My husband had had his pleasure, but instead of falling into a drunken sleep had stumbled off to seek more trouble.

"Mevrouw, your mother wishes for you to attend a court of justice with her tomorrow. You must get your rest."

"Philippe is the one who should preside with her. He's the one who wants to be King."

The moon shone on the stones of the street, dimly illuminating the warren of passageways between the buildings of the quarter. Across the way, the tower of the church of Santo Tomé stood square and silent against a plush black sky spangled with stars. A cat yowled.

"Mevrouw, unhealthy air rises during the night. Please come to your bed."

The clatter of metal on stone severed the quiet, followed by a burst of male laughter.

Katrien joined me at the window. An oath floated up from the darkness. It was in French.

Katrien inhaled sharply.

"You heard Philippe, too."

"It is some of his men, that is all."

"I have heard my ladies whispering. I know that he and his men roam the streets at night. They cannot keep their hose tied. There will be trouble. These Burgundian men don't understand how the Spaniards value their women's chastity."

"Surely the Prince is not among them tonight."

I glanced at her. "Tonight?"

She would not meet my eyes. "He is in bed, feeling the effects of his food and drink. You must go to bed, too. You will wish for this sleep in the morning."

The voices returned.

"Mevrouw."

"Shhh. That is Philippe. Listen."

Into the gauzy night air floated a man's teasing voice: *"Ronde ogen."*

I looked at Katrien. "Isn't that what he called you?"

"He's calling a cat. If that is him. Come, Mevrouw. You are so tired."

I let her pull me across the cool tiles. She tucked me in linen that had been pressed with flowers—I sniffed—roses. I breathed in their scent and listened, but not for my drunken husband, calling for cats and God knows what else. No, I listened, with all the ridiculous romantic fervor of my poor dear María, for what? For someone who would never come?

I drifted into the forgiving bosom of slumber and, for a few unconscious hours, was at peace.

27.

18 June anno Domini 1502

*I*t was a sight worth savoring during those months in Toledo: Philippe slumped glassy-eyed over the parchment that Mother's secretary placed before him, while Mother, her heavy green reading lenses perched on her nose, explained to him the significance of the document.

He massaged his temples as if to soothe a massive headache. His exasperated voice echoed from the coffered timber ceiling. "Truly, does it matter how many *reales* are allowed each day for bread for the pilgrims in the hospital at Santiago de Compostela?"

Mother looked over black rims as thick as a finger. "Yes."

He gazed over the document with a sigh. "Isn't there someone else who can do this? Must you oversee every hospital giving alms to every grubby pilgrim in the middle of nowhere?"

"Yes. And you must, too, as King."

"According to your Cortes, I am only to be consort."

"And do you as consort not wish to know what is afoot in your lands?"

His look of despair dissolved into a smile when he saw me watching from the other side of the hall. "Puss, come in here. You think this is all nonsense, don't you?"

I crossed the room and took the empty seat next to him at the table. "Sorry to be late, Mother. I was unwell."

She took off her eyeglasses and studied me.

I scanned the document. "Where are we?" I had vomited after Mass and felt desperate for sleep—familiar symptoms whose implication sent a charge of terror through me. I would not be allowed to return to Flanders if I was with child. The journey would be too risky.

"Perhaps you could take over for me," said Philippe.

"Do, Juana," Mother said airily. "If he is going to content himself with a minor role in governing our lands, you had better be prepared to take the reins by yourself."

"The King is not here," he said, as if that were a reason that he himself should not be subjected to this torture.

"The King," Mother said firmly, "is attending to other things."

Philippe sat back and folded his arms over his chest, letting it be known that if he must be there, it was under protest.

Several charters, three dozen petitions, and at least five rounds of cathedral bells marking the quarter-hour later, we were released, and then only after Mother had received a letter from Fray Hernando de Talavera. He had been sent to Granada before I had gone to wed Philippe. Evidently, his absence was still keenly felt, for she dismissed us, then closeted herself in an inner chamber, leaving us to do whatever we wished. I followed Philippe as he strode through the pillared arcade of the palace.

"Cabinet meetings every Tuesday, conferences with the royal auditor on Wednesdays, Thursdays and Saturdays holed up signing petitions and documents, and Fridays listening to ministers drone on about financial matters—by Saint John, the woman takes no break. And on top of that, she prays the hours whenever she can and, God forbid, does not miss a daily Mass. What a miserable life!"

He turned around to let me catch up. "Your father, now, he has the right idea. You don't find him sitting in the counting room, discussing how much should be allowed for alms for the poor in some dusty godforsaken town in León."

"Oh, you can find him in his counting room when he is in Zaragoza. He is quite particular about how matters go in Aragón, as those are the lands he inherited from his father."

"That's because he has power there. How do you expect me to take an interest in this place if I am second in power to you?"

"Neither of us truly has to worry about ruling. My mother has no plans of admitting her mortality soon."

"Well, when she does, you should leave it all for me to handle. I am experienced in ruling my own realms. You could be free to do whatever you desire—care for the children, sew shirts, spin wool."

"Whatever you wish, Monseigneur." It was easy to agree to something that was never going to come to pass. I, too, could have a happy relationship with the word "yes."

We neared the exit of the palace, where the guards awaited with raised halberds. "Where are you going?" I asked.

"Where are *we* going, you should ask." He led me into the hot white sunshine.

I followed him onto the Street of the Angel, the surprise of his attention lifting me out of my malaise. Townsfolk peered, stunned to see the Prince Consort and Princess of Asturias walking the narrow streets like commoners; they hastily bowed as we passed. Carters nodded as they rumbled by on their wagons. A stonemason chiseling a gargoyle on the eaves of Mother's almost finished monastery of San Juan de los

Reyes stopped long enough to squint down from his ladder and salute.

We passed onto the road to the San Martín Bridge, in the shadow of the yellow stone city walls on which soldiers paced, their crested helmets shining in the sun. With a nod from the gatekeeper in his tower, we began our way across the bridge, whose soaring arches, first built by the Romans, spanned the gorge through which the Tajo flowed. Philippe led me into an embrasure overlooking the water and, like a child, leaned against the stone wall to gaze down on the river rushing far below. I joined him, the taffeta of my skirt rustling against the wall.

Philippe stretched out his arms to the sapphire sky. "Splendid! The perfect antidote to slaving away with your mother. Thank God she got that letter from her lover—we'd be there still."

"What lover?"

"Fray Hernando."

I laughed. "Fray Hernando is hardly her lover." Shielding my eyes, I gazed at the hills rising from the far side of the bridge. Outcroppings of rocks, bearded with mustard-colored lichen, jutted from the slopes. Where there was crumbly saffron earth, gray scrub had sprung up, sometimes a gnarled tree. From childhood excursions to a hermitage in those hills with Mother, I knew that the brush, which looked so dead, was alive with birds and rabbits and darting lizards.

On the side of the bridge from which we had come, the gorge dropped almost straight down to the water from the city wall. The slopes were spiked with swords of aloe as tall as men. Swifts sprang from crevices in the face of the cliffs, to skim the water in twos and threes.

I followed Philippe's smile to the shore at the bottom of the gorge, where naked boys swam and dived in the water with a flash of their skinny flanks.

"You must have swum a lot as a boy," I said, "with all those rivers in Flanders."

"Actually, I didn't. Since the nobles and Father were fighting for my custody, I was under lock and key. I never so much as touched a puddle."

"But you got out often to hunt."

"With a gaggle of guards and nobles who posed as my friends. There was never anyone my age around. That is why I treasure Hendrik—he was the first person who was not gray in the beard to befriend me, though I didn't meet him until the year you came to my lands."

How lucky I had been to have my sisters and brother as companions. It was strange to think that all of them were gone now, to the realms of their foreign husbands or to Death, the effect of which was very much the same.

"I want my son to be able to enjoy these simple pleasures."

I glanced at him in surprise. He rarely mentioned Charles. I was glad that he should do so, though it caused me a pang of grief to be reminded of our sweet boy, so far away.

"I want to be a better father than Maxi was."

"He couldn't help being away from you. The burghers of Bruges held you hostage."

His glossy hair caught on his collar as he shook his head. "Even after he regained custody, he was always in his father's lands in Austria, and I was always in my mother's lands, with François."

"Let's go home, Philippe, to Charles and the girls. We can leave at once if you order it. Mother cannot stop us, if only you—"

"I remember my father getting me my first suit of armor. I was six, he had just regained control of me. He had bidden me to come before him in the armor, and asked me to save the helmet to be put on in his presence. I was already sick with fright from being screwed into a metal shell, so when his gentleman tied on my padded protective hat, then eased the helmet down over my head, I panicked. I couldn't see. I couldn't breathe. 'Put up your visor,' I heard him say, but my hands in my armored gloves couldn't find the opening. I could hear him roaring with laughter.

"The next thing I knew, my visor opened. François was looking in. 'I do believe it is King Arthur,' he said. 'Good sir, where might you keep your Holy Grail?'

"I cooled down enough to let him remove my offending lid. 'Lancelot,' I told him as soon as my head was free. 'I don't look like Arthur, I look like *Lancelot.*'"

Philippe's rueful smile charmingly puckered the pouches near his lips. In the handsome and confident man leaning against the stone wall of the bridge, I could see the lonely motherless boy.

"You didn't wish to be Arthur?" I asked softly.

He recoiled at the pity he must have seen in my eyes.

"That woman? He let Lancelot take his wife."

He pushed away from the wall, then stalked off, leaving me sitting.

I rose to make my way back to the palace. The guards looked down from the gatehouse; I would not meet their gaze. Once in the courtyard, I sank onto a bench in the shade of a fragrant orange tree to rest. I was thinking of my little Charles, wondering what kind of man he would become if he were to be separated too long from the love of his mother, when a shadow passed over the grass before me. I looked up to see a stork sailing to its nest on the rooftop of the neighboring church of Santo Tomé. No sooner had it landed on the jumbled sticks of its home than the white fuzzy head of a large chick appeared.

The father stepped forward awkwardly, then opened his great yellow beak. The chick reached in and gobbled until, satiated, it sank out of sight.

"You are interested in storks?"

I turned to find Diego Colón, standing in the arcade. He wore Mother's livery; a sword in its scabbard balanced on his hip. My heart, foolish traitor, beat faster.

"Yes," I said. "There are few birds more gangling and clumsy on their feet, or with homelier faces, yet I admire them. They make good parents. Both the mother and the father work at tending their young."

He came toward me, keeping his gaze on the nest. "It is said that they mate for life."

"If only humans could be as faithful as humble storks."

Our eyes met. "Some are," he said.

I drank in his nearness with the gratitude of a parched prisoner given water. "We would do well to study them."

Loud voices came from a distant part of the palace. We turned to see a physician striding through the arcade, his robes flapping, followed by two men in clanking armor. They were headed toward Philippe's quarters.

"Is there trouble?" said Diego. "Perhaps you should go to your husband."

"It is probably nothing. I suppose one of his men was cut while playing at swords, or perhaps someone fought over cards or was hurt in a wrestling competition. There is never a lack of sport among Philippe's men. You would know it if

Philippe himself were ill. He would call for every relic in Toledo with curative powers to be brought, and perhaps a magic charm or two. As bold as he hopes to act, he is most afraid of death."

Diego put his foot against the well. "What else is there to be afraid of, if not death?"

"I should be more charitable," I said hastily. "He never really had a firm foundation to grow upon. He lost his mother at an early age."

"As did I." He saw me wince. "I'm sorry. I did not wish to make you feel bad. I was just thinking that whatever faults I have, I would not want them blamed on her. It was not her fault that Father left her."

I waited for him to explain.

"Tell me about your children," he said. "Is your daughter like you?"

"My older daughter, Leonor?" I was easily led to safer ground. Just saying her name made me smile. "Not at all. She is a typical first child. She orders her nurses about—me, too, yet with such good sense that I happily obey. But she is most tenderhearted. She mothers her little brother like a hen. Though she was only a toddling child when he was born, she insisted on helping to swaddle him. And it was she who taught him to walk, coaxing him along with a ball."

He nodded for me to continue. I was not used to being able to utter a thought about the children without being interrupted with an exclamation about how clever Delilah was or when Pedro might ever be ready to play.

"It is Charles that I worry about. Perhaps you have not heard—his jaw . . ."

"Yes."

"It is a trial for him to eat, and hence he is of small stature and prone to fevers and illnesses. It made Leonor weep to see him lying listless in his crib."

"I am sorry."

"Oh, but he is so strong. I think he would have been dead long ago if he did not will his little body to live. In this way he is like my mother."

"Perhaps like his own mother, too."

I savored another of Diego's smiles.

"It must be difficult for you to be away from him," he said.

If only Charles's own father understood this. "Yes."

Diego reached inside his doublet, drew out a pouch, then shook something into his fist. He held it out.

"For you."

"Me?"

He opened his hand. On his palm was a pearl the shape and size of a pigeon's egg.

"It's beautiful. I have never seen a pearl this large." I looked up at him. "You must not give this to me."

"It is from the new lands of my father. He gave it to me to remember why he must be away from me, why we have made so many sacrifices."

"I cannot take this."

"Wear it as I have done, to remember."

"But how will you remember your father without it?"

His earnest expression softened. "I am not likely to forget him."

Footsteps pounded in the arcade behind us. A page dashed out into the sunlight. "Your Highness, the Prince wishes you to come to his chambers at once."

"Is there a problem?"

The page glanced at Diego.

"What is it?"

"Your Majesty, he ate some bad fish and fears he must vomit, and now he wishes you to hold his hair."

I lowered my face, ashamed that Diego should know my role as base servant to my boy husband. "I am coming," I said, then left without looking back.

28.

14 July anno Domini 1502

I will kill him!"

Mother paced as I stood before her in her chamber. I glanced at Papa, sitting at her desk, running the trimmed feather end of her quill across his palm. He lifted his brows at me as she continued in her lather.

"I cajole my nobles into naming him my heir after you. I beg everyone to entertain him to the point of personal bankruptcy. I say nothing when he misses daily Mass to go hunting. I even lift the sumptuary laws so that people could dress gaily to make him feel like he is at home in his own hedonistic court. So what does he do? Goes behind my back with a scheme that will destroy your sister."

Was Mother responsible for the changes in the behavior of her nobles that I had noticed since arriving in the Spains? Why would she go to this trouble for him?

"I do not know what you mean," I said.

"It is hard enough on poor Catalina, becoming a widow at such a tender age. But to replace her interests in the English court with his own selfish ones, after all we have done for him—I can hardly fathom his gall."

"What has he done?"

"Only to ask old Tudor to wed his young son Henry to

his sister Marguerite, instead of to Catalina, that is all. Old Tudor offered to wed Catalina himself and let his boy wed Marguerite, but that is hardly any bargain. Our Catalina with that withered old schemer—"

"Withered 'old' Tudor is five years younger than I," said Papa.

Mother blinked at him. "You know what I mean."

"Withered in his soul, perhaps," Papa said mildly.

"I find no humor in this. My poor child, to be sent home so ignobly."

"But Mother," I said, "won't she be glad to return here?"

"No. She wishes to stay. She is committed to making the best of our tie to England."

"She is sixteen!" I exclaimed.

"At sixteen, I was thinking about the interests of the Spains."

We are not, any of us, as heroic as you, Mother.

She shook her head. "Philippe is to be King of Spain someday—"

"King Consort, according to the Cortes," Papa said. "Not quite the same, Isabel."

"—King Consort of Spain someday and he still thinks like a duke."

I saw in my mind the image of the Dowager Duchess, stubbornly perched under her hennin in her purple-clad chambers, surrounded by paintings collected for their value in gold, not their beauty. With her lust to take back what was hers in England, I could see her leaping at the chance to put her granddaughter on the English throne.

"Are you sure that Philippe is the one who is bargaining with King Henry?"

Mother went to her desk and snatched up the paper lying

before Papa. "My ambassador acquired his letter. Your husband wrote it, from this very palace, though it is unbelievable, I know. You wouldn't think he'd have a chance to put pen to paper with all the frisking about that he does. Did you hear what went on last night?"

I glanced at Papa. He shook his head.

"You didn't hear?" Mother said. "Well, I shall tell you."

A trumpet blared. A page stepped into the room to announce Philippe's arrival.

"Come in, Don Philippe," said Mother. "Come in and tell us where you were last night."

He walked over to kiss Mother's hand, then Papa's, then my own. I gasped when he looked up at me. His right eye was purple and swollen shut.

"Monseigneur!"

He touched his eye. "I ran into a door."

"Is that what they call the husbands of townswomen these days?" said Mother. "'Doors'?"

Philippe looked to Papa, who lowered his gaze to the quill in his hands. Finding no support there, Philippe smiled at Mother.

Her mouth turned down with disgust. "Three men died last night in a skirmish near the San Martín Bridge. The night watchmen said the dying words of the men were in French."

Fright darted through Philippe's eyes. He blindly patted my arm. "Visitors to your city?" he asked Mother.

"Yes," she said grimly. "Visitors."

"A very sad tale, but for what reason did My Lady Mother summon me to her chambers? Though I am always honored to visit with you, I—"

"Why did you go to Henry Tudor and ask that he consider your sister's hand in marriage for his son?"

Philippe started to say something, then stopped. He crossed his arms over his chest. "The boy Henry is not married. Nor is my sister. I thought to make her happy. She cannot grieve for your son the rest of her life."

"Nor would I expect her to. You should have consulted me."

"I was not aware that you ruled the Netherlands."

Mother paused, then assessed him anew.

"Speaking of which, Your Majesties"—he bowed to Mother and Papa—"it is time that Juana and I return to my lands."

He turned to me with a smile. "Aren't you glad, Puss?" He pulled me toward him as if shielding himself from Mother. "My girl has been trying to go home since the moment we left. She does not like to leave her children."

"You wish to rule Spain, the Netherlands, and England," said Mother accusingly.

Philippe laughed. "I am not that ambitious. Ask my wife." He kissed the side of my headdress.

Now it finally suited him to go home, though I had been pleading for months to hurry our visit. The events of the previous evening must have been especially damning.

"You cannot leave the Spains now," said Mother. "If you are to rule here, you must get to know your people. As you might recall, it is one of the conditions of the Cortes. They insist that you learn to speak Castilian."

"They cannot be serious. Everyone I need to know here speaks French. In fact, yours is quite good, Your Majesty. I must commend you."

The pitch of Mother's voice rose. "You have yet to go to Aragón to be named heir of that land."

"I'll send a representative. François would go. We are needed at home now." He rubbed my arm. "Don't you want to see the children, Puss?"

"Juana wants to stay here," my mother replied. "She is to be Queen. We can send for your children, bring them here."

"Juana loves my lands, and her people there love her in return."

Mother threw the copy of his letter on the floor. "I have a notion to reconvene the Cortes and recall their confirmation of you as Juana's consort and of Juana as my heir. Clearly your interests are in governing your own lands. If you prefer to be a duke rather than a king, so be it."

Philippe glanced at the letter, then held up his chin. "You wish to keep your daughter from her birthright? Your grandchildren, too?"

"I have other daughters, unencumbered by traitorous husbands. Daughters who write to their mothers when separated from them."

I found myself drawn into their argument. "I wrote to you, Mother. I was wrong to take so long to do so. But it is wrong for you to never forgive me, especially when, in letter after letter, I begged for you to do so."

"What letters?"

"The ones I wrote to you from the Netherlands."

"I never got any letters."

Philippe looked between us. "Perhaps they were lost at sea."

"I entrusted them to a courier."

He shrugged. "Perhaps the couriers were lost at sea."

"I would have heard of it," said Mother. "I know if any of my ships or their crews are lost."

I stared at Philippe. Had he waylaid my letters? Why would he do such a thing?

"What?" His undamaged eye grew larger. "You're blaming me? I'm telling you, I don't know what happened to them."

Mother moved toward him threateningly. "I cannot believe a man would keep his wife from her mother. All the more reason for you to get on a ship and out of my sight."

"Please," I moaned. "Stop."

Mother closed her mouth.

Philippe frowned at me in annoyance. "What, Puss?"

Papa laid down the pen.

I drew in a breath. I was not yet ready to face the meaning of the words I was about to utter.

"We cannot leave the Spains. I am carrying a child."

29.

24 August anno Domini 1502

It was August in Toledo, when the air radiates with the heat of an iron pulled from the fire. Lizards, thin as a knife, darted tails a-slither over the hot stone walls of the houses and churches. Platter-eyed cicadas, big as one's thumb, wailed from the hills, their call building then throbbing then ebbing into the thick dusty air. Their cries accompanied my half sister Juana as she read from the Scriptures at dinner that afternoon, though we had not the good fortune for their screeching to blot her out. No, we were forced to listen to her labor her way through a passage in Ephesians as we ate, our spooning and sipping punctuating the verses that exhorted wives to submit to their husbands.

Oh, yes, I thought as I poked at a chickpea in my stew. I did submit to Philippe, even though most nights he preferred roaming the streets to sleeping with his newly pregnant wife. I let him take my body whenever he visited my bed, to preserve it from the damage it would sustain should I have resisted, yet I got no rest when he left me alone. As much as I wished not to care about his doings, I lay awake listening for the sound of male laughter out on the streets. When I heard it, or a murmuring in French, or a sharp female cry, my stomach would roil with anger and fear, until at last, sapped by the new life growing from his seed within me, I fell asleep.

My sister Juana turned a gilded page of her missal. "'So also ought men to love their wives as their own bodies. He that loveth his wife, loveth himself. For no man ever yet hated his own flesh; but nourisheth and cherisheth it, as also Christ the Church.'"

I laughed out loud.

Mother looked up, her spoon to her mouth. "Is there something humorous, Juana?"

I shook my head, then, in spite of myself, burst out again. How true—how greatly Philippe did love his own body. Had anyone ever indulged his appetites so generously?

Mother waited for an explanation. I saw Beatriz, returned to court after her visit home, press her lips together.

"I am sorry, My Lady Mother."

She watched me for a moment. "You seem agitated."

"I am well, Mother."

She frowned, unconvinced. "Eat. You need it for your child."

Spoons clicked against bowls as dining resumed. Mother's favorite harpist strummed softly, while outside, the rasping of the cicadas soared. The other Juana searched for the place where she had stopped her bumbling.

"Juana," Mother said.

Both my new sister and I looked up.

Mother's scowl designated me as her subject. "Your father says the Cortes in Aragón are prepared now to name you as heir."

I smiled as if that were happy news. Well, it was good that little Charles would have another crown to wear someday— the better to hold up his head against those who might scorn him.

The blast of the herald's trumpet alerted us to someone's approach.

A page opened the door and announced, "Don Philippe, Prince of Asturias."

I put down my spoon as my husband entered.

He kissed Mother's hand, then mine, then squared himself before Mother. Her ladies exchanged wry glances.

"I am sorry to interrupt your meal, Your Majesty."

She pursed her lips, then spoke. "Won't you sit with us?"

He cleared his throat. "I come from my own dinner, where I just learned that you have freed the Castilian men charged with killing three of my attendants."

"Sit, Don Philippe. Ladies, you don't mind?"

Philippe remained standing. "You freed murderers of innocent men."

"Don Philippe, if your men were innocent, would they not still be alive?" She went back to her eating.

"This is not acceptable!"

She lowered her spoon. "If you had cared to preside at the court of justice with me this morning, you could have had your say then."

"Pedro had arranged a hunt. I could not offend him."

Mother looked at him, then took up a piece of bread.

Anger and dismay twisted Philippe's beautiful face. All his life he had been coaxed and coddled into agreement. It was possible no one had ever challenged him directly. He certainly did not like it now.

"If you will not hang those murderers, I will—I will have

François reopen the case. I cannot have an uprising of Castilians against my men."

"And it is precisely because I do not wish for an uprising of Castilians against your men that I made the judgment that I did. Save the Archbishop's talent for arguing other cases. There should be plenty of them, the way your men are behaving."

"My men—"

"In the meantime," she said, overriding his speech, "I suggest that you instruct your men to repair to their own beds at night like the citizens of Toledo. It will be good for their health."

Philippe blinked at her. "What kind of country is this?"

"My daughter's. Someday. And yours, in a fashion, if you behave."

He looked to me. I glanced away.

"You haven't heard the last of this," he said to Mother. He strode from the room.

Mother's attendants slipped me expressions of pity. My Burgundian women watched with interest; Beatriz grimaced with her customary worry. I suppose I could have borne it had not my new sister stared at me with a look of bovine incomprehension. I excused myself, claiming that my early state of pregnancy necessitated that I take some air in the courtyard, in the cool shade of the orange trees. Beatriz got up to accompany me.

Our skirts dragging against the tiled floors, we made our way to the covered arcade. "Is there anything I can do for you?" Beatriz asked.

"You are too good. No, nothing."

"I have a new Latin text of Plutarch. Perhaps we could read it together."

I smiled. Only Beatriz would think that deciphering words of wisdom from an extinct civilization could bring one cheer. But perhaps it would comfort her. "Yes, please get it."

When she left, I leaned my cheek against the relative cool of a pillar, savoring the meager breeze limping across the courtyard.

"Are you well?"

I pushed upright. Diego Colón rose from a bench on the opposite side of the pillar.

"I didn't see you." I tried to hide my delight. "Here again? In this heat."

"May I claim that I'm watching the storks? Someone got me interested."

I glanced at the nest on the bell tower of Santo Tomé, then laughed. "You may claim anything you like."

"In truth, I have been making a study of them. I have come to see that this time in the chick's life is particularly hard on the parents."

I followed his gaze back up to the pile of sticks. A young stork clung to the edge of the nest, flapping its fluffy white wings. You could see the concern on the old-man faces of its parents as they watched it lurch forward, then flounder to regain its hold.

"The miracle is that the chick will learn to fly," he said. "What gives it the confidence to trust its wings and not drop to the earth?"

"Perhaps it knows no better. It does not know that if it doesn't move its wings, it will dash into the ground. If it knew the consequences, perhaps it would not be so brave."

"So it is a case of blissful ignorance."

I laughed. "Maybe so."

We watched the young stork flap again, this time with such enthusiasm that only one grasping claw kept it attached to the nest.

"He's almost got it," Diego said.

"It will leave soon," I said. "The whole family. The empty nests look so forlorn in the winter. I wonder where storks go."

"Africa, I think."

I looked back to Diego. "Truly?"

"I grew up in the monastery of Santa María de la Rábida near Palos. Every fall I would watch flocks of storks pass over, bound for the coast only a stone's throw away. From there, it is not far to Africa. Then every spring, I would watch the flocks fly over again. Some of the storks would stay. They would wheel in the sky, around and around, for days on end, until their mates came. Then they would have their happy reunion, throwing back their heads and clacking together their beaks."

"I have heard them. It sounds like rattling sticks."

"Stork love-talk," he said with a smile. "As a boy, I would stop whatever I was doing to watch them. I wished to show my father, but he was never there."

"Where was he?"

"Traveling." He saw my troubled look. "Oh, he came back now and then. Do not worry, the brothers were good enough to me. I was free to raise myself, which gave me the great luxury of letting me find on my own the person I should be. But there were times when I envied my little brother, who was brought up by his mother, Father's mistress in Córdoba, until he was taken to your brother's court. I envied him, and resented his mother—not very pretty emotions. I thought that they were getting Father's attention. It wasn't until later that I learned that none of us got it. He lavished it all on his most demanding mistress—the enterprise of the Indies." The father stork flew from the nest, its black-tipped white wings bright against the hard blue sky. "That is why I am a student of my beautiful bird friends here. They are free of ugly thoughts."

"Perhaps I can learn from them, too."

"You, Your Majesty? Are you not happy?"

I gave a dry laugh. "Have you ever met my husband?"

Shouts arose from Philippe's quarters in the palace. Shortly after, a page dashed through the arcade. He could be heard calling to a groomsman at the palace entrance. Hoofbeats announced the page's hasty departure.

I would not let them end this moment. "I now have no excuse for unhappiness. I am in possession of the luckiest of charms." I drew the great pearl from my bodice, where it hung from a ribbon around my neck.

A smile lit Diego's face. "You wear it?"

"Oh, yes. Except to sleep. It's much too lumpy," I said, which was only half of the truth. I did not wish for Philippe to see it when he ravaged me at night. It was not his jealousy I feared. Philippe would not dream that another man had given it to me. No one, he assumed, would dare. No, it was the size and perfection of the gem that made it vulnerable. My insatiable husband would have to have it for himself. But this one thing, regardless of its value—it could have been made of clay—this one thing was mine.

"You have woven a cradle for it."

I took it from around my neck and gave it to him to see. "Katrien made it, of black ribbon. I could not bear to put a hole in it, but since I wished to keep it close . . ." The sweetness of Diego's smile undid me. "Katrien is my washerwoman," I murmured.

"Yes, I know."

I gazed at him, wondering how he would know the name of such a low-ranking servant. Just then hooves thundered on the street outside. Before I could gather my thoughts, Philippe, clothed only in an open shift and breeches, stormed into the arcade with his men. They rushed past as if Diego and I were invisible.

"There is trouble," said Diego.

Guards clanked by in their armor. A trumpet blasted in alarm. A moment later, an anguished cry arose from Philippe's chamber.

Diego placed the pearl in my hand. "Go. He needs you. Godspeed," he said, but I was already running.

Nearly all the German guards who had come to the Spains with Philippe were already outside his chamber door when I arrived.

"What is it?" I demanded of them.

A guard knelt. "Madame, His Holiness François de Busleyden, the Archbishop of Besançon, is dead."

"The Archbishop? That cannot be. I just saw him this morning."

The guards exchanged glances but gave me no answer.

I tightened my fist around the pearl and made my way through them, my skirts crushing against their armor. Inside, Philippe stood at a window overlooking the church of Santo Tomé. He turned and, seeing it was me, opened his arms.

"Philippe, is it true?"

His body shook with silent sobs as he held me in his embrace.

"I am sorry," I said into his shoulder. "What happened?"

I could hear his pained swallows.

"Where is he?" I asked gently.

"In there. You can't go in."

Philippe cried out loud, then buried his face in my headdress. "God forgive me. He was more of a father to me than my own father."

"I hope he did not suffer," I said.

He pulled back, his face contorted. "Is it your purpose to make me feel worse? If it were not for me, he would be alive this moment."

"Philippe, hush. You did nothing but hold him in the highest esteem." I tried to gather him into my arms but he fought against me. "It was his wish to come to the Spains," I said. "He could have stayed in Brussels, but he wanted to come."

"Well," he snapped, "it wasn't his wish to be poisoned, was it?"

I put down my arms.

"Yes. That is what I said. He was poisoned. Poison meant for me."

"This is your grief talking."

"He was well enough this morning. Then he excused himself at dinner, saying he felt ill. I thought he left because he was angry at the news that your mother had pardoned those murderers. That's why I sought her out after I finished my own meal. Then I went down the street for a little entertainment—I never dreamed I would not see him alive again."

"But why would anyone—"

"Someone in my party made a Spanish lady's husband mad."

I searched his face.

"It wasn't me, if that's what you are thinking."

Realization iced my blood. His denial was his confession. "I suppose you'll say it was Hendrik."

"It wasn't Hendrik."

"Of course not. Though wouldn't it be convenient to blame him?"

"I promise you, it was not I who dallied with that woman last night. I did no wrong, yet I was blamed—the biggest dog always stands out in a pack."

"You would not be blamed for anything if you stayed in at night."

He ran his hand over his face. "I hate this godforsaken land. I want to go home."

"But we can't. Our unborn child—"

"I can," he said. "You can come later."

If he left, he could see to the children. People would be less apt to whisper about Charles if Philippe was at court. "Then go."

His look of relief narrowed into a squint. "Are you trying to be rid of me?"

"No. The children—"

"If I left before being confirmed by the Cortes of Aragón, only you would be acknowledged. Is that it? I should go, so that you will become sole heir for the throne of Aragón?"

"How little you know me if that is what you think."

He snatched my hand. "What is in here? You keep it closed."

"Nothing."

"Look at how you keep it clenched. It makes me wonder if you carry poison."

"Poison! Why would you even think that?"

"You yourself said that your grandmother was poisoned. And now poor François."

"Poison was Luna's madness. No one has used it since then."

"Open your hand!"

"Grief undoes you."

"Open it!"

He shook my wrist. The pearl dropped to the floor with a silken thud.

He picked it up. "Well, well. What is this?"

I swallowed. "It is what it looks like."

"Then you do not mind if I take it?"

"It's mine."

He stroked the pearl as if it were a little pet. "You will not part with a simple jewel, yet I am supposed to believe you care nothing for the crowns and all that comes with them."

"Take it, then."

"I can see why you are attached to it. It is a superior specimen. And what a clever little net you keep it in. Where did you get this?"

I shook my head.

"A secret, eh?" He closed his hand around the pearl. "Well, that can wait. But you aren't getting rid of me this easily. Since I was a boy, François prepared me for all honors that have come my way. It was his life's work. He lived and died in service to me. To leave the Spains without the guarantee of the throne of Aragón would be a mockery of all he did for me. So I shall go to Aragón"—he smiled at me, tears glittering in this eyes—"with you as my guard. No one will risk poisoning the precious Princess, and so in your presence I will be safe."

"You are mad. Grief has made you mad."

"If I am mad, it is your country that has made me so."

"And yet you wish to be its King."

He set his mouth.

"Philippe, let us go to Flanders and get our children. I shall not lose this baby—I am strong. Let us return there, and be to each other what we used to be."

"Stop talking." He rubbed at his forehead. "I am too sick to think. Leave me now."

"Philippe—"

"Get out!"

I could not reach him in this state. At the door, I turned to bid him good-bye. But he did not hear me. He was at the window, gazing at the lustrous egg resting in his hand.

30.

24 March anno Domini 1503

*T*he rain poured down in Alcalá de Henares, splashing in the puddles before our stand on the jousting ground, drumming on the velvet canopy, which sagged over our heads from the weight of the water. Drops fell from the center of the lake forming just above Mother, running onto her scarlet brocade headdress, then onto the shoulder of her robe, where they sank into the white thicket of ermine. It had been raining the entire week in which my milk had come in, and my breasts had been bound upon Mother's orders, though I had objected strenuously. Why not feed my beautiful black-haired little boy, whom Mother had named Fernando? My fertility did not matter. My husband, should he have liked to indulge in his cruel form of procreation, was in France. He had galloped off in December, after his men, in a drunken spree, had laid waste to a former mosque filled with priceless works of art in Zaragoza. Run off by the angry citizens like a band of brigands, he and his cronies had not stopped upon reaching the French border, but made directly for the French King. As soon as Mother had heard of Philippe's defection, she had documents for a treaty with the French King sent by express courier, to give the appearance that her son-in-law had left the Spains on a diplomatic mission. Only those who wished to be fooled by this explanation believed it.

Riders trotted before us in a spray of muddy water, then halted, the plumes of their helmets drooping in the downpour. Mother got to her feet.

"Stand," she whispered.

I was already nauseated from the odor of wet fur, damp smoky air, and manure, so an attempt at rising brought bile to my mouth. I eased back down onto the bench. I had never had this much trouble after giving birth. In truth, Fernando had come easily, pushing his way into the world after only four hours of labor, and I had felt wonderfully strong, instantly able to get up and walk to a garderobe, eschewing the use of the chamber pot offered by the midwife. But now, two weeks after my labor, I was suddenly foggy in the brain and weak, and my guts grumbled with sickness. I could not understand it. Yes, I expected after-pains. With the other children, the pangs in the days following their births were nearly as strong as the labor itself. But I had never felt this malaise.

Mother glanced down when I did not rise. "Are you ill, Juana?"

I tried to stand once more.

She frowned, then folded her hands upon her belly. "Doña Beatriz, take her back to the palace at once."

"No!" I would not provide Mother yet another reason for disappointment. *She* had not waited the forty days for churching, but had attended all of her children's Baptisms — once with a fever from childbed, another time during a minor earthquake, yet another while the Moors circled around her camp, riding high in their stirrups and shaking their spears. I would attend my son's celebration, too.

Beatriz slipped her hand under my elbow. I came to a shaky stand.

Mother turned to the mounted gentlemen assembling before us on horses in sodden housings. At her signal the pageantry began.

"Juana, if you are ill," she said when we were seated again, "you must return to your chambers. This damp will do nothing for your health."

"I am fine," I said, even as bile burned its way upward once more.

"Stubborn," Mother muttered.

Trumpets blared, and a herald announced the gentlemen who would first be running at the lists. They pranced forward, rain pinging from their armor. After a nod to Mother, they snapped their visors shut with a clink, trotted to the far ends of the lists, leveled their lances, and hunching forward, spurred their steeds. Mud flew from the horses' hooves, spattering the guards standing below us.

Mother turned to me. Although I straightened quickly, she said, "I am sorry that I reinstated jousts. I have a notion to end this."

"Would you have called off a celebration after you'd borne a child?"

Steely silence served as her answer.

I closed my eyes in an effort to muster my strength while several more pairs of combatants rode at each other.

"Your Highness," Beatriz whispered.

I opened them as another set of jousters rode their horses before us. Through his open visor I saw the somber face of Diego Colón.

I stared at him, willing him to meet my gaze, but his eyes were only for Mother. He took the scarf from his neck and held it out to her with a bow. Upon it was a crest whose top two quarters displayed the Lion of León and the Castle of Castile. I could not make out the lower two.

Mother raised her voice so that he might hear from the muddy grounds below. "Your new family crest?"

"Your Sacred Majesty, will you accept it as a token of my service to you?"

Mother beckoned for it to be brought to her. A guard took it on the point of his spear, and in that way raised it to her hands. She examined it.

"It bears the sea islands amongst the waves, as we discussed. But this last quarter was to display your father's symbol."

"A ship's anchor is his symbol, Your Majesty."

Behind me, I heard someone whisper, "Where are the mosquitoes?"

Mother did not seem to hear this slight upon the Colóns. She nodded. "Very nice." She handed it to me. I smiled, hoping to catch Diego's gaze.

Mother waved him on.

He closed his visor and galloped to the end of the lists. Bracing his lance against his breastplate, he looked to the master of ceremonies, who, with a drop of his flag, sent the horsemen charging. I held my breath as, in a shower of flying mud, Diego bore down upon his opponent. Lances crashed. Diego's weapon glanced off the other man's breastplate. The noble tumbled to the mud.

Cheers went up. Diego galloped to the fallen man and jumped from his horse with a clang of armor. He removed his gauntlet and stepped stiff-legged to where the man lay, then extended a hand to help him to his feet.

The man clasped Diego's hand, then yanked hard, toppling him into a puddle. Laughter went up from the crowd as Diego struggled in the mud.

At Mother's signal, pages ran forth and righted him and the other man. Both opened their visors and, dripping with mud, saluted to Mother. The crowd roared its approval as the noble grinned broadly in the rain.

They led away their horses. Not once had Diego met my eyes, though I willed him to see my look of sympathy.

A herald blew his trumpet. From the palace came Cardinal Cisneros, under a canopy flapping in the rain-laden wind. Next to him one of Mother's ladies carried a bundle of brocade.

The clouds cleared in my head in a moment of outrage. "He must go back! This weather is wretched."

"Shh," said Mother. "I asked for little Fernando to be brought out. The people need to see him. They need to know that we are like them, that we have children that we dote upon, husbands that we adore, families that need our care."

I stared at her incredulously.

"I am sorry, Juana, but this is how it is." After Cardinal Cisneros paraded my child the length of the stands and joined us on the dais, Mother asked him to give Fernando to me.

"She needs to take him back to the palace and rest," Mother said. "This is a difficult time for her."

Cardinal Cisneros smiled as I tightened Fernando's wrappings. "Pining for your husband? It is wonderful to be so deeply in love."

I glanced up. That is why he thought I was ill?

Mother spoke loudly enough for all to hear. "Oh, it is. What a blessing to have such a love for her husband. Go on, Juana. Go back and rest."

I felt the sympathetic gaze of the crowd upon me as I left

the stands, my child in my arms. Is that how I appeared
to them—a new mother suffering from the absence of her
husband?

Rain tapped on the canopy carried over my head as I
crossed the grounds, Beatriz hurrying behind me with a pair
of nurses. Once inside the arcade, I leaned against a column
to catch my breath. The walk—and the charade—had exhausted me.

"I am worried about you," Beatriz said.

"Oh? Do you think I am lovelorn, too?" I pressed Fernando to my lips.

"I can see why it is advantageous for others to think so.
For you, too, Your Highness. But the baby must be cold.
Give him to the nurses—"

"No!"

The nurses glanced at each other. I had not meant to shout
out. But they had the pleasure of feeding and caring for him.
If only I could hold my own son a little longer. Why must I
be so weary?

"Give him to me, then," said Beatriz, "and we will go to
your chambers to rest."

I closed my eyes, then, sighing, handed him to Beatriz. I
sank onto a bench against the inner wall of the arcade.
"Take him to his nursery. I will be there in a moment." I did
not tell her that I was too exhausted to move. Her fear for
my condition would only frighten me. If truth be known, I
feared for my life. Something felt terribly wrong. "Look, it
has stopped raining."

Beatriz gazed into the courtyard, where rainwater
dripped from the wrought-iron arch over the well. "Finally."
She was not easily thrown from her duty. "I shall return in
a moment."

"Make sure he is well tucked in."

"Yes, Your Highness." She smiled at the bundle in her arms. "Let us get warm, young man."

I closed my eyes and settled against the wall as she swept away with the nurses. I shifted under the bands pressing against my breasts and tried to relax my mind. Images from Fernando's birth cut through the fog, as vivid as the moment they had happened: the bearing down with my whole being; the giving way of flesh; the shocked, gusty wail; the baby's first murky gaze.

A metallic creaking, and then the groan of a crank being turned, jarred me awake. I opened my eyes and saw Diego Colón in the courtyard, lowering the bucket into the well.

He must have entered from the other side of the arcade and not seen me in the shadows. I stayed very still while he drew up the bucket, stripped off his muddy shirt, and began washing himself. He splashed water onto his face, then onto his muscular chest and under his arms, where it dripped from the downy black hair that grew there.

He was pouring water over the back of his neck when he saw me. He let go of the bucket. It jangled from its rope as he picked up his shirt from the edge of the well.

"It is muddy, you know," I said.

He pulled on his shirt.

"Your shirt—it's muddy."

He looked down, then wordlessly strapped his buckler around his waist. Was he not speaking to me for shame of his treatment at the lists?

"Don José was a scoundrel, pulling you into the mud like that."

He paused in his fastening as if about to speak, then changed his mind and continued dressing.

I stood up. "Why will you not talk to me?"

He bowed. "By your leave, Your Highness. *Adiós*."

"You punish me with your silence!"

"I am not trying to punish you, Your Highness."

"Yet you act as if you did not know me." A black fog clouded my vision. I tried to blink it away, even as a high-pitched buzzing whined in my ears.

Don Diego took a step forward. "Are you well?"

"Yes. Of course."

"Where is your lady?"

I dropped onto the bench.

He hurried to my side. "You are ill."

"I am fine." The ringing in my ears had become a pounding. "Just tell me why you will not talk to me."

"I was being foolish. Let me help you to your chambers."

I sank back against the wall. "You still have not told me why."

He drew in a breath. "I saw the pearl on your husband. But why shouldn't you have given it to him? A wife should give any gift given to her by another man to her husband. Stupid of me." He bent to help me. "I am taking you to Beatriz."

"No. Believe me, I did not give it to him. He took it from me."

"As he should. Everything that is yours is his."

"Yes, that is true, isn't it?" I said bitterly. "Even my children. I promise you, I did not wish for him to see the pearl. I knew he would take it if he did. I tried to keep it hidden. It was—special to me."

He studied my face. "Señora, I am concerned. You are so pale. I must call your lady."

"No! What is the news from your father?"

He sighed. "You simply won't be taken to your rest, will you?"

I shook my head.

"I know that you are trying to divert me, but I will tell you quickly—and then I am going to find your lady.

"As a matter of fact, I have not heard from Father in several months. His last letter was dated July of last year, after he had just survived a great maelstrom the Indios call a 'hurricane.' He had taken shelter in the mouth of the river in his town of Santo Domingo, heeding the Indios' warning about the coming tempest, but the governor, Francisco de Bobadilla, and five hundred men set sail for Spain against the Indios' advice. All of the governor's party were lost at sea."

The governor was much loved at Mother's court, so I had heard distressed talk of this. The fact that many—albeit without reason—blamed Colón for the governor's death surely contributed to don José's disrespectful behavior toward Diego at the joust. People now felt that the lands Colón had found were more trouble than they were worth.

I sighed. "It was a tragedy."

"It was. The worst of it is that Father feels compelled to seek even more new lands to cover the governor's losses. He speaks of finding the land from which the pearl that I gave you came. The Indios say there is a place in which the shores are awash with pearls the width of your thumbnail. And now no one has heard from Father for months." He drew in a breath. "My little brother Fernando is with him."

"I am so sorry."

"I should not bother you with this when you are ill. Why can I not control my speech around you? I buzz like one of the mosquitoes over which I am said to rule. Please forgive me."

"People are cruel and stupid. Don't listen to them."

"I don't. Not really. I know that someday I will govern Father's lands, just as you, someday, will govern the Spains."

I glanced away. If I were ever Queen, Diego's lands would truly be my lands and he would answer to me. As much as he wished to be equals, we would never be, even if his father's lands produced more than mosquitoes and misery.

A clattering of wood sounded against stone. We turned as Katrien entered the courtyard, carrying a wooden cask. She stopped with a final clack of her *klompen.* A fleeting look of surprise crossed her open face when she saw us, then a stronger emotion—fear?—before she put her head down, went to the well, and cranked the bucket.

"Listen to me, rambling on when I should be seeking your comfort," Diego said. He called to Katrien, "Señorita, please, the Princess needs a woman to accompany her to her rooms."

Katrien turned the crank slowly, her face still lowered.

"Now, if you please. Our Lady is not well."

Katrien glanced up. Again, a jolt of strong feeling altered her countenance for the briefest moment. But once she had brought up the bucket and come to my bench, she resumed her usual blank expression.

"I am fine, Katrien, really. I don't need help."

She braced herself against me to help me rise.

"You must like it here," Diego said to her.

Katrien, leaning into me, looked up.

"You are one of the few who did not return to the Netherlands with the Princess's Flemish train."

She avoided his inquiring gaze. Her arm around me, we started forward.

Diego bowed. "I hope you are better soon, Señora."

"I am better already."

The surge of happiness that I felt from our encounter fortified me as I started down the arcade with Katrien. It lasted even after Beatriz met us and took me from Katrien. The girl would not leave at first; then, biting her lip, she lowered her head and hurried off. But my mind was occupied with recollecting Diego's words. I thought no more of her.

31.

9 July anno Domini 1503

The litter jerked and swayed, the bells on its fringe jingling, as the mules picked their way over the tree roots that laced the rocky trail. The brisk mountain air smelled of cool stone, pine, and the moss that furred the ground: health-giving air, mind-clearing air. Surely it would cure me. Four months after giving birth to little Fernando, and still I was subject to the black clouds that floated through my head, blurring my thoughts and vision, robbing me of an appetite, weakening me. In response to an urgent post to the French court about my illness at the time of its inception, my husband insisted that I take a special Flemish preparation at dinner each day, administered by Katrien. He said that it had cured his *grand-mère* of a similar affliction. But I gained no strength from it. My bodice hung from the bones of my shoulders even after Beatriz laced it tight.

I looked down at Fernando, stirring in my arms. I kissed his forehead. It was not his fault that I was ill. I was not suffering from childbed fever, as some of Mother's doctors suggested. Nor was I pining away for his father—the ludicrous opinion of many, which Mother warned me not to dispute. It looked good for me to be missing him. The heir to the throne should project the image of strength within her marriage as in all other things. For the sake of my own pride, I did not fight her. But whatever it was that actually plagued me, what I needed in order to recover was to be with my children again. Just seeing them would give me strength. I breathed in another draft of air. This journey north to Segovia would bring me that much closer to the port of Laredo. From there, God and Mother willing, I could sail to be with my chickens.

"How are you?"

I looked over at Mother, who had ridden up on her mule. "We are well," I told her.

She pulled the collar of her robe closer, then braced herself more tightly on her pillion seat. Even in July, it was cool in the Sierra de Guadarrama when the wind swept around the boulders, bending the trees and sending pine-cones tumbling. "Why don't you give Fernando to his nurse, and rest?"

Next to me in the litter, Beatriz made a cradling motion with her arms. I shook my head. "I am fine."

Mother peered over my shoulder and smiled at my sleeping child. "You always used to travel well as an infant. You slept right through the pandemonium when the elephant given to us by the ambassador from Cyprus broke free from her handlers and trampled off into the fields when we were journeying to Madrid."

"We had an elephant?"

"Oh, you should have seen your father, leading the beast into Toledo, two weeks before you were born. He had on new silver armor, and a cloak thrown over his shoulder like a Roman general. My ladies said he looked like a Caesar. I called him the new Charlemagne. He liked that best."

"You were not in confinement for my birth?"

"Heavens, no. Only nine days before, I had made a solemn entry into Toledo myself, on the occasion of the Cortes' confirming your brother as my heir. The procession took hours, and then there was Mass, and then feasting—you know how it goes. I had no time to be locked away in a room."

I rearranged Fernando's wrappings. I had been cosseted and coddled before and after giving birth, yet still had not managed to recover. Would a time ever come when I would measure up to her?

"In fact," Mother said, "the day after you were born, I presided over the beheading of an enemy of the crowns—wicked old Alarcón, the alchemist. He had contrived to poison your father. They say they dropped Alarcón's head in a basket for garbage, but I did not stay to see that myself. I had granted an audience with the ambassador from England, who was waiting for me, and afterward I discussed the meeting with Fray Hernando, and then I was off to dress for yet another feast."

"I never knew that someone tried to poison Papa."

"Surely you don't think we keep food-tasters for show. As long as there are kings there will be people trying to poison them. It's the coward's way to power. My own brother was poisoned. I shall never forgive those people."

"Your brother? Alfonso? He was poisoned—by whom?"

She shook her head. "I should have been suspicious when they offered me the crown. At least I knew enough to refuse it then. If I had known they were behind Alfonso's death, I would have never agreed to take the throne."

"Whom do you speak of?"

Just then someone called, "Make way for the Lord of the Mosquitoes." I turned as Diego Colón urged his horse through a group of pages, who were now snickering. Most of them were younger than he. Many of the pages who had first come to court when he did had moved on, assuming their inheritances, taking their places among their peers who sat in the Cortes. I had encountered Diego several times in the past few months, coming from Mass or at dinner, and though we'd had no time alone, we found our gazes often meeting. I hoped that he had some message for Mother, thus giving me a chance to catch his eye. But once he broke free of the group of chuckling pages, he reined in his horse and continued alone, several horse-lengths behind us.

I could feel Mother gazing at me. Our mules' hooves rang against the rocks embedded in the mud. "Juana," she said, "now that your husband has been gone for many months, it is not the time to loosen your sleeping arrangements with your women. Have you made plans for your ladies to surround you in Segovia?"

"Yes, Mother."

Beatriz spoke up from my side. "I have made the necessary arrangements, Your Majesty."

"Good. She has needed to do something since those Burgundian women packed up and followed Philippe. When the King was gone, I made sure all could see that I had no opportunity to dally with another man."

I almost laughed. What man would have the temerity to approach the formidable Isabel of Castile? It would be like Estrella stalking a tiger.

"Chastity is the most important virtue in a wife," she said.

"More than love?" I said drily.

I heard Beatriz inhale.

"It is a form of love," Mother said.

We rode along, the bells jingling on my litter. "For all

men's talk of their needs," Mother said, "it is the female who seethes with desire."

"Mother!"

"I am trying to tell you something important." She switched the reins to her other hand. "We are rotten with desire," she said, "and in their hearts, men know and fear this. And so they restrict us, while giving in to their own passion, claiming they cannot control themselves. They think that if they simply say this enough it will make it true, and that we should believe this, too."

Fernando squirmed in my arms. My mother—a desirous woman. I cannot say the idea gave me ease.

"Because we are strong," she said, "we curb our impulses. Out of love."

"And what if we do not love?"

She gave me a long look. "Then we curb ourselves out of self-preservation."

She gathered her reins before I could speak. "Keep her warm, Beatriz. These mountains could take the breath away from Saint George's dragon." She tapped her horse, then rode on to speak with Cardinal Cisneros, bobbing down the mountain on a donkey, just ahead.

32.

I was strolling with Beatriz in the gardens at the foot of the Alcázar, in the grassy valley formed by the River Eresma. I had gone there to escape the early-afternoon heat, for while Segovia, nestled at the base of the pine-covered Guadarramas, was cooler than Toledo or Barcelona or Madrid, in late August it was warm enough to make one's shift stick to one's flesh.

Little Fernando lay in my arms, his dark hair damp with sweat. He grasped the withered willow leaf Beatriz twirled before him, examined the brown curl as delicately as a gold-smith appraising a jewel, then put it in his mouth.

Beatriz fished it out and dropped it to the grass. "Everything goes straight in."

I pressed my lips to his curls. He smelled of soured milk and sweet baby skin. "That is how he learns."

I sighed as Fernando grabbed the end of my headdress. I did not know what my little Isabel had been like at this age. Come November, it would be two years since I had last seen her.

"I have read a new text by John Chrysostom," Beatriz said, a little too heartily. "A bestiary, with excellent pictures, printed in Augsburg. I will lend it to you. I know you enjoy animals."

"I need to go back to Flanders, Beatriz."

"The picture of the unicorn is particularly fine, though I don't agree with his translation in the passage about the fox."

"I want you to help me convince Mother."

"You will travel once your mother thinks you are well enough."

"I am well enough now."

She loosened Fernando's pudgy grip on my veil. "You suffer from dizziness. You have not recovered your former strength."

I could not argue against this, but I had accepted and adjusted to my condition. I would not let it keep me from my children. "If we don't sail before the winter storms set in, the trip will be postponed until spring."

She kissed Fernando's fingers. "Are you really in such a hurry to be reunited with the Prince?"

It was true—with Philippe gone, I was at peace. I found it almost humorous that after Cardinal Cisneros's suggestion, and Mother's confirmation of it, many at court attributed my weakened state to my pining away for my husband. But as relieved as I felt to not be subject to Philippe's whims, I would gladly endure him if it meant being with my children. Soon they would not know me.

Fernando whimpered. I nuzzled his silken cheek. "Someone is sleepy."

"I shall take him to the nursery." Beatriz lifted him from my arms. "You rest. The footman will bring you a horse."

I did not fight her. With my strange ailment, I could not

walk up the steep hill to the palace entrance without help. But it was a fine day, if a warm one, and I was pleased to have a moment of solitude—as much solitude as could be afforded while Mother's men stood guard on the battlements overhead. I sat on a mossy stone bench under a tree, listening to the groan of the river. I thought about little Charles. Was he learning to speak clearly? When I returned, I would work with him, not punishing him as the Dowager Duchess surely did if he struggled, or giving him suits of armor instead of instruction as did his father.

A croaking and whistling penetrated my reverie. A flock of starlings wheeled against the sky in a now expanding, now contracting, fluttering black mass. I must have been very still, for as one they dropped down and alighted in the very tree under which I sat. I raised my face slowly, in order not to frighten them, even as another flock swooped in, and then another, until their shiny bodies blackened the branches.

The birds' frenzied screeching built as they called to one another. The din disoriented me, disconnecting me from my bearings. I felt something wild stir within me, a dormant creature that knew their call.

With a deafening rustle, the birds took flight. Someone approached.

"Are you well, Your Highness?" My heart jumped. It was Diego Colón.

"Oh! Yes. Very. Thank you."

He searched my face, concerned. His expression softened. "Perhaps you are making a study of starlings now."

I laughed. "Yes. I do seem always to be watching birds, don't I?"

He smiled. "Worthy subjects. I did not mean to disturb

your rest. I saw Beatriz with your child—she said you were here. May I accompany you to the palace?"

"Please."

When I got up slowly, he slipped one hand under my elbow and put the other on the small of my back to aid me. I could smell the leather of his buckler and the clean cotton of his shirt; I inhaled the rich scent of his skin. I imagined myself turning toward him and pressing against his body, then kissing him, long and hard.

Had I gone mad?

"You smile," he said.

I shook my head. "Where is Juanito?" I asked lightly. "I have not seen him of late."

"Did you not know? Your mother gave him a stake and excused him from court. He is learning the shoemaker's trade."

"He wants to make shoes? I remember when he could hardly walk in them."

"Isn't it true that we are most fascinated by that which seems the most unattainable?"

My senses trained on his hands supporting me, we strolled next to the riverbed as the breeze tumbled willow curls before us. High above, in the crisp blue sky, the flock of starlings swirled and eddied.

We stopped on a humped stone bridge and looked at the water below. Ahead, small brown ducks bobbed on the languid current.

"I have not heard from my father," he said.

I knew that he had not. No one had. The gossip around court was that the Admiral had been lost at sea.

"I do not know at what point I should step up and demand to be governor."

Did he even have claim to the governorship? Not only had the Admiral been relieved of that position several years earlier, but it was debated whether the Colón family deserved to retain any of the rights Mother had awarded him, as badly as he had mismanaged his settlements on the lands he had claimed.

Diego saw my frown. "I must think of these things. I am aware that I will be passed by if I remain silent."

"Have you spoken to anyone about this?"

"Who would that be?"

I realized then that even after all these years at court, Diego was still alone, with no friend or ally. What did it cost him to hold up his head, day after day, year after year, as his father tried and failed to find the Great Khan?

"How can I help you?"

He gave my back a gentle pat. "You are most kind. But I will help myself. I have a plan."

"To claim his lands?"

"Not only that, but to make them rich."

He saw my skeptical look. "I'm not speaking of gold. I'm speaking of the fruit of the earth."

I smiled.

"I am serious. I have thought about it quite a lot. Juanito has told me how his countrymen pluck fruit from the trees and produce from the soil all they need to eat, with a minimum of effort. What if production of these fertile lands was increased by using our Spanish method of farming, and then that bounty could be shipped overseas?"

"But—wouldn't the grain spoil?"

"What if it was not grain that was shipped, but cane."

"Cane?"

"Sugarcane. Distilled into hard cones. It does not spoil."

His gray-green eyes lit as he warmed to his subject. "The brothers at the monastery where I grew up tried their hand at it, having heard of it from Portuguese sailors returning from India. Father was intrigued enough by its possibilities to take sugarcane cuttings to his outpost, and his brother Diego mentioned in a letter to me that the cane has done well. Yet neither he nor Father sees the value of growing it on a large scale, as fixated as everyone is on finding gold."

"You have given this much thought."

He pushed a stone from the wall of the bridge. The ducks darted toward it, then, seeing it was nothing, darted away. "Yes. I must. I am aware of what people say about the outposts now, how unprofitable they are, how dangerous, with the wicked sort of fortune-seekers they attract. I am aware that faith in the Colón name is at a low. But with order and good sense, I will turn the outposts around. I will attract good men with families, not the swindlers, thieves, and murderers who sail to the colony now to escape their old crimes and wreak new ones on the Indios. I will bring order and prosperity—everyone will want a piece of my new world."

"I wish you well in it."

"I tell you this so you know that I do not just dream. I have given it countless hours of study. It is because I wish to be worthy of—" He took my hand, then looked into my eyes. "You."

"Me?"

"Is it wrong of me?"

My heart thumped. "It is noble to pay homage to those in the royal family."

"I am not trying to be noble, My Lady. I am not trying to pay homage. I want to raise myself in your eyes." He pressed his lips to my hand. "I do it for me."

"Then you do it for me," I said, "for I want what is best for you."

He drew nearer. "You are too good."

"I am not good at all," I murmured as he brought his lips, trembling, to mine. Their touch seared me to my core.

With the clatter of hooves on the cobblestones, Diego withdrew abruptly. A mounted footman leading a pillioned horse trotted through the Puerta de Santiago and down the road toward the bridge.

"Your horse comes," said Diego.

I blinked, as stunned and grieved as a babe removed from the breast.

The footman neared with my mare. Even as we faced forward at a respectable distance from each other, I could still feel Diego's lips upon mine.

I was helped onto the pillion. I braced my feet against the planchette, then jolted toward the gate in the city wall and, beyond that, the palace entrance. I did not say good-bye to him. I did not need to. My heart was with him still.

The clash of hooves echoed off the yellow stone mansions crowding the streets. Townsfolk cheered; the tiny bells tinkled gaily from the canopy shading Mother and me. I had not ears or eyes for any of it. Only hours before, Diego had kissed me. His words, his lips, his scent filled my head, making all other sensations weak and puny things.

Mother nodded at a group of nuns gathered behind the barred windows of the convent before which we now passed. "You seem distracted. Has your illness worsened?"

"No, Mother. I feel well."

She frowned, not convinced. "I am glad that I insisted you come. I've let you stay at home too much—it is right for you to be out and about if you can bear it. The people need to see more of you. They must get used to thinking of you as their Queen, for when the day comes that I am no longer here."

Reluctantly, I pulled my thoughts from Diego. "Mother, please. As long as there are the Spains, you will be here."

"I am mortal, Juana."

"You are hardly infirm." Indeed, she was as hale and hardy as a goat. She stalked, most days, up and down the hilly streets, visiting this church or that with bread, cloth, and alms. When she wasn't walking or praying or plowing through stacks of paper, she was riding with a party of men at hunt. More often than not she brought home game that she herself had speared, ordering, as she flung off her gloves upon returning to the palace, that the meat be distributed to the poor. I had no doubt she could wrestle the Archangel Michael, like Jacob in the Scriptures, and pin him protesting to the ground.

"I wasn't trying to worry you," said Mother. "I only wish for you to face your future."

Oh, I knew my future. I was to be saddled with a cruel boy for a husband while the man who was my true equal would hardly be allowed near me. If I lived long enough to see my children to adulthood, it would be while in a sad and disturbing marriage.

Our litter jolted past the cathedral and into the plaza before it. Mother stole appraising looks at me between nodding to her subjects, who were prostrating themselves in the dirt. I could feel her judging me.

I tipped my head toward the church of San Miguel, just

ahead. "Thirty years ago you were proclaimed Queen of Castile on those very steps—"

"Twenty-nine," said Mother. "In December."

"Twenty-eight years and eight months ago you were proclaimed Queen on that spot. How did it feel?"

"Horrible."

I looked at her in surprise.

"Your father was furious with me."

"Papa? Why?"

"As now, he had gone to Aragón to settle matters in his own kingdom. He thought that I should have waited to receive the crowns with him."

"Why didn't you?"

When we drew even with the church porch, a priest ducked through the low opening in the door and bowed to Mother. She returned the reverence before continuing. "That is a good question. With the luxury of hindsight, I can see how it hurt him, how it made him appear to be less of a man to have his wife grab the crowns without him. At the time, though, I saw no other course. Cardinal Mendoza sent word from the bedside of my brother the King the moment he died, and Mendoza's friends—my friends, I thought—persuaded me to seize the opportunity that instant to be made Queen. I was riding behind the Sword of State before poor Enrique had been wrapped in his winding cloth." She sighed. "How easily I was talked into it. How easily they used my vanity for their ends."

"But you saved Castile from a usurper. La Beltraneja had not a drop of your family's blood. Her mother was not faithful to your brother."

"That is the general line taken, isn't it?" Mother shook her head. "The things one believes when it benefits one."

I squinted at her, trying to understand as our litter swayed toward the city wall and the guard tower of the Puerta de San Martín.

Her gaze went to the crowd. "Is that not Colón's boy?"

I scanned the upturned faces.

"Over in front of the Casa de los Picos," said Mother.

I found Diego standing before the spiked façade of the house. He bowed when he saw me looking. Warmth poured through me like steaming caudle into a cup.

"I would stay away from him," she said.

I gave a false laugh. "I am never near him."

She judged me coolly. "Heed my words, Juana: Leave him be."

"But I do not have him to leave be. I rarely see him. You keep him running as your page. He worships you, you know."

"I am telling you this, Juana, for your own good. It only makes it worse when you cannot have them."

Our litter passed under the San Martín gate and entered the lower town, its narrow streets overhung with brick-and-timber houses. I wished to look back—how I longed for a glimpse of him—but fixed my sights instead on the Roman aqueduct just ahead. Its stone arches towered over the buildings of Segovia, out of place, out of scale. Though most believed it to be built by the Romans during the time of the Caesars, some thought it was the work of the Devil. The Devil's Bridge, they called it. The bridge to the gates of Hell.

"It is best if you immerse yourself in worthy projects," said Mother. "Pray a lot. Do good things."

"As much as I wish it, Mother, I cannot be as holy as you."

"Oh, I am far from holy."

"And that is why they call you the Catholic King?"

"I was given that absurd title because my 'friends' willed it so. It served their purposes."

I laughed. "Modesty is one of the forms of holiness."

Mother did not smile. "I am far from modest, and you know it. Yes, I have done some great things. But I have also done some bad ones."

She lapsed into silence as we drew near the aqueduct and rode along in the shadow of the arches. We lumbered up the steep hill, the arches of the aqueduct diminishing, until at last they fed into a squat stone pumphouse. Just beyond were the brick-and-stone walls of the monastery of San Antonio el Real, the destination of our uncomfortable jaunt. We had come to bring alms.

Once inside the brick walls, I trailed behind Mother and the prioress of the establishment, a tiny woman with the face of a shriveled peach, as they examined the treasures Mother had recently sent. The pieces were magnificent: a Flemish altarpiece, a Brussels tapestry, a painting from a master in Bruges, items of the quality usually reserved for the great cathedrals. Mother obviously preferred the place, though why she should do so above all the other monasteries near Segovia, I did not know. No miracles had happened here; no saints had ever visited. It housed no spectacular relic like the Holy Grail in the monastery of San Juan de la Peña in Papa's Aragón or the piece of the True Cross in Santo Toribio de Liébana in Asturias. Indeed, the place had originally been the hunting lodge of Mother's half brother, King Enrique, and only in the past few years had it become a house for the Poor Clares.

"The artisans from your husband's realms are quite clever," the prioress said to me as we walked the cool halls. "They are as adept in wood as they are with oils or thread.

We thank your mother for granting us so many treasures for our humble monastery." She took my arm. "Come to the refectory. We have just hung the lovely new painting that your mother has given us."

"No," Mother said sharply.

The prioress's veil brushed her shoulders as she turned in surprise.

"No," Mother repeated, more gently now. "We should not disturb the sisters' meal. They are eating now, yes?"

"Yes, I'm afraid that's true. I'm sorry that they won't be able to greet you properly. Meals are observed in strictest silence," she reminded me.

"I understand," I said.

"It's my fault," said Mother. "I was detained by the ambassador to England. I should have come sooner and not interrupted your mealtime."

"We are honored for Your Majesty to come anytime you please. But I would like Her Highness the Princess to see this since she is here. The sisters are especially glad for it. Now they have something wonderful to ponder when the sister chosen to read must stop to eat."

Mother argued no further, and soon we arrived at the refectory. The prioress opened the door to a room full of sisters in white and gray, their heads bobbing in the motion of eating, reminding me much of seagulls on the beach at Barcelona. The sisters stopped when they saw us, as did the children sitting among them, halted in the act of bringing their spoons to their mouths. The prioress made a motion with her hands for all to resume eating, which they did in silence. She beckoned me to the wall where the picture hung.

I inspected it briefly—a painting of mourners at the Crucifixion, with the usual doleful faces at which the Flemish artists excelled. As I came away, I saw a dark-haired girl of perhaps five years wave at Mother, who gave her a playful wink. She was a pretty little thing, with olive skin and hooded eyes.

The prioress drew us out of the refectory and shut the door behind us. "Again, I apologize that the sisters were not able to greet you properly."

"They did right," said Mother.

The swish of our skirts against tile echoed from the ceiling of the enclosed arcade. "I did not know that children were allowed to live with the sisters," I said. "Are they . . . siblings?"

She smiled soothingly. "Now and then a baby comes to us from the outside. We do not ask questions. It is a ministry that we are pleased to perform—it seems to have gained momentum in the years in which you were in the north."

"The mothers bring the children to you?"

"We don't see the mothers. We receive the infants as we receive other deliveries from the outside world—through the revolving window by the service entrance."

"Like a sack of flour?" I asked.

"Well, yes, but much more exciting. Whenever we swing the *torno* around and find a precious bundle upon it, we feel that the child is Heaven-sent. You'd be surprised how often that is, perhaps once or twice a year."

I had heard that unwanted children were often placed on church doorsteps. It was a common practice. But it surprised me that this richly endowed foundation took in orphans so readily. The parents of the girls who joined the order had to pay large dowries.

"Do the mothers ever come to see them?" I asked.

"The mothers? No. Once the child comes to us, it is dead to the world."

A silence descended. It hung over us, unbroken, until we came to the courtyard, where Mother exclaimed at the roses spilling over the trellises. "So many of them," she said.

"The ones you gave us five years ago. They have flourished."

The prioress led us into the sunshine and plucked a flower.

"So sweet," I said, smelling it.

"A second bloom," said the prioress. "Even as we give up on seeing another flower for the year, buds are forming quietly on the branches. We are always taken by surprise. Would you like a cutting?"

Soon the tour was over and we returned to our litter.

I sniffed the flower as Mother sank back upon her pillow with a groan.

"Do you know that little girl?" I asked.

She looked at me. "Which little girl?"

"The one who waved at you."

She opened her mouth to speak, then closed it with a grimace. "Get some rest tonight. You're looking a bit peaked."

33.

27 August anno Domini 1503

The cocks were still crowing when someone entered my chamber.

Beatriz bolted upright on her cot beside me. "Who goes there?"

I heard a rustle of cloth. "It is only I."

Beatriz rose and peered through the dim. "Doña María?"

"I am sorry to alarm you." Mother's lady stepped closer, clenching her hands. "I wished to bring word to the Princess that her mother is ill."

I rose now, too. "My mother?"

"I thought you should know. She has been vomiting since midnight."

"We will come directly. Thank you."

Beatriz called for my robe. When did Mother ever become ill? And for her lady to awaken me so that I should know—I could not remember when anyone had done this. Mother had been short with me at the monastery the day before, and had looked tired, but who wouldn't be after hunting in the morning and giving a three-hour audience in the afternoon? She had gone straight to chapel when we had returned, and spent much of the evening praying. I wished that Papa would come back from Aragón. He would put a check on her excesses when he was around, cutting short the hours she dwelt on business matters, demanding that she sup with him instead of spending hours on her knees at her prie-dieu.

Soon I was dressed. My ladies pinned Beatriz's veil to her bandeau, then left to quickly finish their own toilets since they had been called from their beds so abruptly. Katrien arrived, carrying the potion that my husband, in the guise of a caring spouse, had ordered I drink each morning. I downed it in one tortured gulp and handed back the white enameled goblet in which it was invariably served. "What is in this? It gets worse by the day."

Katrien lowered her face. What I could see of it beneath the white linen wings of her headdress seemed fuller of late. Her girth seemed to have expanded, too, though with her voluminous apron, it was impossible to tell.

She turned away to avoid my gaze. "It is only wine and some herbs that my uncle provides from the kitchen, Mevrouw. They have all been tasted for poison. He drinks a draft before he pours one for you."

"Poison? Why would you say that? I hadn't even thought of it."

She took another quarter-turn away from me, then stiffened when Beatriz stepped in front of her.

"This is not a game," Beatriz said sternly. "Be still when Your Majesty speaks to you."

"Yes, *juffrouw*," Katrien said coldly.

"Need I remind you that you are serving the future Queen?"

"You need not." She ducked away from Beatriz and stalked off, her *klompen* clashing against the tile.

I eased into the chair at my dressing table, relieved to

rest. Although I had become used to my weakness, it had not lessened over the months.

"Does it seem that she grows impudent?" said Beatriz, picking up my silver hairbrush. "She will not even face you when she addresses you." She commenced to brush my hair vigorously.

"She's never been the most cheerful girl. I don't know why she stayed with me when Philippe left. She could have gone chasing after him like my Burgundian ladies, though I must admit I would have missed her. We used to talk."

"I hardly think she could have borne traveling with the Viscountess of Furnes's train."

"True. I suppose that was one of the things that made her dear to me. She thought the Burgundian ladies were as ridiculous as I did."

"There is the matter of her uncle," said Beatriz. "I suppose she did not wish to leave him." She stopped brushing. "I just cannot help feeling that something is amiss with her, Your Highness."

I looked up at her. "The herbs the uncle gives her, you don't think . . . ?"

"She's the one who brought up poison."

"Don't even say the word. Why would she want to harm me? Why would anyone? It is mad to think it."

"Perhaps. But something is awry with her."

The bells of the cathedral began to clang, marking the hour before Mass. My ladies filed in, some of them with their corsets or headdresses askew from their haste to be ready.

"We go to visit the Queen," I said, "though I am sure she is well."

Mother lay upon the Bed of State, a small, still figure

under a vast sea of crimson cut velvet. As I drew closer, I saw that her eyes were sunken into darkened sockets, her mouth slack and open. Although her tightly tied coif gave her the innocent air of a babe, it was an old woman's face within its linen borders.

Her eyes opened. "Juana?"

A chill went through me. I had never seen her in such a weakened state.

"Good heavens," she said, "are you trying to terrify me with that expression?"

She struggled up onto her elbow, then made a dismissing wave at both my ladies and hers. "Thank you for your concern. You may go. You, too, Beatriz. Thank you," she croaked as they filed out. She jabbed her pillows as she fought her way upright.

"Mother, you look terrible."

"Who wouldn't? I have been up vomiting all night."

Was not vomiting an effect of poison? I had not thought of it until this moment.

"There's that face again. It doesn't make me feel better, you know."

"I'm sorry," I said quickly. "I'm sure that you are fine."

"Yes. I am sure that I am. Just give me a little rest. I don't know what all this fuss is about. Other people get ill."

"You never do."

"And I wouldn't have, if I hadn't ridden in the rain on Tuesday."

"When has rain ever stopped you? Did I not hear that once, in a downpour, while in the grip of childbirth, with a thousand Moors taking up arms against you, you speared a bear as you rode into battle?"

She gave her pillow an extra jab. "Don't be smart."

I smiled, relieved to hear her sound more like her old self. I saw a paper poking out from under her pillow. "What's that?"

"A letter." She looked at me guiltily, then held up her chin, cleaved in two by the strings of her cap. "From Fray Hernando."

"Can't you let matters of state go, if only for a minute?"

She smiled weakly.

"I am summoning Papa," I said. "He has been in his lands too long. Surely his generals can handle whatever problems are stirring on the Mediterranean."

"Bring him here because I spit up? No. I won't let you bother him. You know how happy he is in his own lands." She put her hand on her belly and winced.

"You are still sick."

"I am fine. Go to Mass."

"I'm calling doctor Soto."

"He has been called. I sent him away. Save him for the people who really need him."

"Why are you so stubborn about this? Why won't you let anyone help you?"

Her bluff expression slipped away. A young girl looked out from her eyes, determined to be brave, although frightened. "You will know why, when you are Queen."

"I'm not going to be Queen," I said with a heartiness I did not feel, "because you will not let me." I kissed her on top of the head. "Take a nap. I'll come back after Mass."

The young girl dissolved in Mother's face. She became the time-embattled leader of men once more. "Good. Pray for me."

"Very well," I said, "though that is like praying for a saint."

"Hardly."

I kept the smile on my face until I reached the hall and the door was closed firmly behind me. Beatriz was waiting.

"Speak," I said. "Why do you say nothing? Do you know something of her condition?"

"She is Isabel the Catholic King, as unbreakable as Toledo steel, is she not?"

"Yes. Yes, I'm sure she will be well." To say otherwise was unthinkable.

I saw the crowd gathering at the end of the hall. "I don't want to talk to anyone."

"Your Highness," called a lady. "Tell us how she is."

"Tell them she recovers," I whispered to Beatriz. "I'll meet you at the chapel."

I slipped into the adjacent hall, where I could avoid detection by leaving through the unused Throne Room at the end of the passage. The immense expanse of coffered ceiling swallowed the hushed pattering of my footsteps as I made my way across the dim room. People sickened all the time, I told myself, with much graver illnesses, and they regained their health. Mother had one bout of vomiting and everyone was in a panic. How dependent we all were on the health of Isabel the Catholic King.

I entered the darkened Throne Room, then stopped. Someone had partially unfolded a shutter and was gazing out the window.

Diego Colón stepped back from the window, then visibly gladdened at the sight of me.

I put my hand to my throat. "Don Diego." I was so relieved to see him that tears rushed into my eyes.

He bowed. "I heard that your mother the Queen was ill.
How is she?"

"She will recover."

"Of course."

I brushed at my eyes, hoping he had not seen. "You were
looking for something."

"Storks," he said gently, "I should say."

I came to the window. "I see none."

He laughed quietly. I could feel him waiting for me to
speak.

I shook my head. "Here I am, upset that my mother suf-
fers a simple ailment, when you have been worried for
months about your father and brother."

"You are right to care for her. She is an extraordinary
woman."

"I have struggled against her all of my life. I thought it
was she who kept me at bay, but it's me. I was the one who
never allowed myself to get close to her. I was afraid she
would reject me. And so I rejected her first."

"Go to her. It's not too late."

I turned toward him. "How are you so good?"

He looked down at me, his gray-green eyes intense. "If I
were truly good, I'd stay away from you. But I can't."

"I am glad."

He tucked a stray lock into my headdress, then laid his
hand, firm and warm, on my cheek. "I think of you night
and day. You have bewitched me."

I kissed his hand. "I am sorry."

He cradled my chin, then tipped my face to his. "Don't
be." Our lips brushed.

We drew back and beheld each other. Slowly, he bent toward my mouth. Our lips touched, then sought each other deeply.

"Juana!"

I pulled back from him.

Her robe roughly thrown around her, Mother leaned against the door, one hand gripping the frame for support.

"Mother!"

She pushed away from the door. "Go!" she told Diego.

"Your Majesty—"

"Shh!" she snapped.

"Your Majesty, I am grievously sorry for how this may appear, but I respect and esteem your daughter beyond all earthly things."

Mother waved him off. "I've not the strength for this."

"Your Majesty—"

"Go!"

He kissed my hand, regret and worry tumbling across his face. "Señora."

I watched him leave. My cheeks were so hot that I thought I would faint.

Mother tore at her cap strings. "I got out of bed to escape all their fussing. And now this. I can hardly breathe."

"Mother, we've done nothing."

"Do you think that I am blind? I'm sending you home to be with your children. I've kept you here too long." She closed her eyes and leaned against the wall, holding her stomach as if enduring a spasm.

When it was over, she straightened and sighed. "The boy has his struggles, Juana. Don't make it worse for him."

"What do you mean?"

"His father has been found. He's been marooned on the

island he calls Jamaica. One of his men paddled a canoe to Hispañola to find help."

"That's good news. He can come home. He has his little boy with him."

"Governor Ovando has denied him a ship."

"Then send him one!"

She pressed her hand to her stomach before continuing. "Ovando would let Colón rot in Jamaica, and there is no one in all the Indies to lift a finger to help him. That's how much the Admiral is hated."

"I'll send him a ship, if you won't."

"You'll send him one? That is a far cry from the child who took sides with her father in condemning the enterprise of the Indies."

"I did not know then."

She massaged her temples. "Oh, Juana, you still have so much to know."

"What? What things do you keep from me? Do you think that I am too dull or too weak to bear them?"

She shook her head, the untied strings of her bed cap swinging. "No. It is I who cannot bear this. It is I who cannot stand looking like less in your eyes. Do you think you are the only one who has loved someone she should not?"

"What are you saying?"

She sagged against the wall. "Not now. Take me back to bed."

I held her arm. We shuffled slowly through the hall, her sickroom scent of lavender, unwashed hair, and vomit wrenching my heart. Her ladies ran to us when we appeared at her chamber door, their exclamations continuing as they helped her up the steps and onto her sea of red velvet. I left them to tuck her in, then went to the adjacent chamber to collect my thoughts. I was looking out the window, my mind a stew of fear, joy, and confusion, when I saw a woman with a bundle in her arms. She was stealing across the tower yard below, the white wings of her Flemish headdress flapping in her haste. Suddenly she paused, drew the bundle to her nose, and then, holding it against her heart, bustled forward again.

Katrien?

The Habsburg Netherlands

Margaret of York

34.

16 May anno Domini 1504

id-May, and the marshes of Flanders burgeoned with life. Small birds flitted in the greening bulrushes; dragonflies darted at one another and at nothing; the very earth seemed to breathe and swell under our horses' hooves. A pair of ducks burst from the wild growth. I thought of Philippe and his gyrfalcon. Was Delilah again his constant companion, now that he had returned from France, six months before my own arrival? It had been two and a half years since I had last set foot on this sodden land. So many things had happened in that time: my oldest three children were no longer infants; I was now heir apparent to more crowns than I cared to think of; my love for Philippe had withered into a black desiccated thing, like a grape left overlong on the vine.

Beatriz swiped at a dab of muck that had flown up onto her cheek, smearing it onto her wimple. Still she wore the habit of a Poor Clare, although she was no more a nun than I was. "Too much mud in this land."

She had chosen to continue in my service, though Mother's secretary, Francisco Ramírez, pressed for her hand in marriage. Beatriz planned to translate a difficult passage of Aristotle over the next few months, then submit her work to the scholars at Salamanca, and so she thought being in my train preferable to a husband's caresses. I worried that she might be disappointed in the result, yet I was grateful for her company. I did not expect to be welcomed by many upon my return to my husband's court.

Soon we beheld the towers of Malines rising from the marshland. I wanted to sing aloud at the thought of seeing my children. My infant Isabel was now a toddling child; Charles, according to reports, a slight but willful four-year-old. Dear Leonor was five and a half and, from the nurses' reports, as bright and lively as a jay. A cloud passed over my heart each time I thought of my little Fernando—he had become sickened with measles the day my fleet sailed, and so had to remain with my mother, who promised to send him with her envoys as soon as he was stronger.

Not soon enough, I had passed within the tall white stone walls of the Dowager Duchess's palace. Nodding at the bowing ladies and gentlemen, I ran through the halls in my soiled riding dress. I threw open the doors to the nursery. There my three children, clad in identical black velvet gowns, sat in a row before the Viscountess of Furnes.

The shock of seeing my enemy with my darlings was overpowered by my joy. I fought back happy tears as I sank to my knees and opened my arms. "Chickens!"

None of them moved. Charles looked up at the Viscountess.

"We've been expecting you," she said.

I gazed from face to face. Behind each expression of fear or puzzlement or pure lack of interest was a kernel of the child I knew.

"Chickens, it's your mother."

"They know," said the Viscountess.

I had no more affection for the woman than when she had left the Spains with my husband's party, but to keep peace before my children, I would keep my tone friendly. "I am surprised to find you here."

"I am their governess."

I would not exclaim. "I thought the Dowager was in charge of their care."

"The Dowager is dead."

I sat back on my heels in shock. No one had told me. The old dame had truly allowed Death to claim her? He must have offered an acceptable price. Yet harsh as she had been, I preferred her to the Viscountess. The Dowager was the devil that I knew.

I glanced at the children. I mustn't speak of this now— talk of her passing might upset them. I reached out for my oldest child.

"Leonor, you have grown into a beautiful young lady."

The Viscountess's silk sleeves swished as she poked Leonor in the back. "Go."

Leonor took a tentative step forward.

"Go on, give her a kiss." The Viscountess shook her head at me. "I've told her that she must."

Leonor pecked my cheek, then shrank away from my arms. She ran back and took her place cross-legged on the floor.

"Charles," said the Viscountess, "go on, angel."

He inched forward. With a breaking heart I saw that his chin had grown larger. His upper jaw was completely subsumed by his lower. How difficult speaking and eating must be for him.

"Hello, Charles," I said softly. "I've missed you."

He grunted and lowered his head. I kissed the top of it before he hurried back to the Viscountess as fast as his spindly legs could take him.

"Isabel," said the Viscountess, "scoot, scoot."

Her baby belly thrust out, almost three-year-old Isabel stumped forward, kissed my cheek without a shred of feeling, then stumped back to her governess, where she burrowed her head in the Viscountess's silvered-blue brocade skirts.

"I wished to be here sooner," I said. "Children, I have missed you so."

Isabel piped, "You're dirty."

I gazed down at my skirts. "I am, aren't I? I've come from very far. Did your"—I frowned at the beautifully dressed Viscountess; she hardly seemed like a governess—"did the Viscountess tell you from where I have come?"

Charles lifted his chin to speak. "The Ffpainff," he said. "It iff a very big plafe. I am to rule it ffomeday."

My heart sang out. He could speak, and clearly enough. Other children lisped—he would not stand out so very much. "Yes. Yes, you are."

"Why do you call us chickens?" said Isabel. "We're not chickens."

I gazed at Leonor, hoping she would remember the old endearment and explain to her sister, but her frown remained fixed on the floor.

"I tell you what, I shall get clean, then I shall come back to hear all about each one of you."

They watched, silent, as I got up and left the chamber.

Tears stung my eyes when I stumbled into Beatriz, waiting for me in the hall. She looked at my face, then tucked my hand under her arm. "Everything will be all right. You'll see."

I was stepping from my bath into the sheet Beatriz held open for me, while Katrien stood by with a bucket to empty the tub, when a familiar voice sounded at my door. "Knock, knock."

Philippe stepped into the room, Delilah piercing the white satin shoulder of his doublet with her yellow claws.

"Your Highness," said Beatriz, "Her Highness is not—"

"—any less beautiful than ever, I see." He winked at her and then smiled at me. "*Bonjour*, Puss."

Beatriz flashed me an anxious look. "Please, Your Highness, if you can wait until My Lady is dressed."

"Nun, are you telling me that I have to wait for my own wife to be dressed?"

"Let him come in, Beatriz. He is right. I am still his property."

A clang sounded near the tub. Katrien snatched up her bucket even as water spread across the green tiles. She had remained as stoic as ever these past months, though she seemed to be making more of an effort to face me directly when she spoke. Perhaps it was to make up for refusing to tell me what she had been doing in the tower yard with that bundle on the morning of Mother's illness. I had not pressed her. I had too many other things on my mind.

"Let it be, Katrien," I said now. "You may go. You, too, Beatriz. Thank you."

I tucked my sheet more tightly around my chest as I waited for them to clear the room, Philippe watching them, his arms folded. When they were gone, I said, "I wasn't sure if I was to see you."

He put his shoulder to the mantel for the bird to step on it, then came over and kissed my hand. "Why wouldn't you? I'm your husband."

"You spent so long in France, I wasn't sure what you were to me."

"I have had nothing but the fondest regard for you during all of our separation. I did not think you would hold an illness against me."

I pulled back to see if he was speaking the truth. Time had agreed with Philippe the Good. He looked more at ease with the world than ever, like a man incapable of wounding his wife. "You don't look ill."

"Thank you. In fact, I am quite well now. But a weakness in my chest kept me abed there much of the summer and fall. Not that I wished to stay there. I am sick of those snobby French—this court is far more entertaining. I would have been back months earlier if I could have. As it was, I was only just able to see my poor *grand-mère* before she died."

"Why did no one tell me of her death?"

"You hadn't heard? I had written to you of it. I wrote to you several times since I returned. My letters must be following you across Europe."

"Letters seem to have a habit of getting lost between here and Spain."

He shrugged.

"Her death came as a shock to me. I did not think the Dowager was capable of dying."

"Why ever not? All the remedies and proscriptions in the world are no match for Time." He looked me up and down. "Speaking of remedies, have you been taking the one I recommended? I heard that you were quite ill, but I think you look well."

"I am better than I was."

"You seem it. I suppose my remedy worked."

"Maybe. I stopped taking it months ago."

He made a closemouthed smile. "When?"

"In late August." Although perhaps I was being silly, soon after Katrien had mentioned poison, I could no longer bear to take the potion. I had abandoned it even after Beatriz insisted on watching Katrien's uncle taste the concoction. According to Beatriz's report, he had poured himself a glass, and then my own special cup, and then sampled his own, to no ill effect. Though Beatriz witnessed this three days in a row, it did not improve my taste for the remedy. After I'd stopped it, my health had gradually returned. Perhaps my mind was so full of Diego that I worried no more for my body.

I turned away from Philippe. "I would like to get dressed now. I'm going to call Beatriz."

"No. Let me help you." He reached for the shift lying on my bed. "Is this what you need?"

He came over and stood behind me. "Lift your arms."

I raised them. Gently, he tugged on my sheet until the fold at my breasts came undone. The linen slid down my body.

He touched my nipple. "I missed you." I closed my eyes as he laid his rough cheek against my neck. "I heard that you missed me, too. My envoys brought tales that your longing for me made you so weak that you could hardly rise from your bed." He rested against me, his breath warm on my ear. "Is that true?"

It would be better for me if it were.

"Yes."

"Sweet, sweet Puss," he murmured.

I stared blindly at Delilah, preening the feathers of her shoulder, as his lips grazed down the sensitive skin of my neck.

I let him do what he had to. I was his wife.

35.

17 May anno Domini 1504

I sat outside under a spreading oak, sewing, as the children played chase with their father. Nearby, Beatriz bent over her book of Aristotle, her lips moving as she deciphered the words. We were being serenaded by canaries, melodious captives whose cages hung from wrought-iron arches upon which blooming roses climbed. Both the birds and the flowers were gifts my mother had sent to the Dowager Duchess when I was first married. These living things could adapt to new places; why could I not find happiness here if I truly tried? Perhaps Philippe had grown more caring since we'd parted. And it was not as if he were the only one to have transgressed.

Even now, as I pulled the thread through the cloth of Philippe's shirt, I could feel Diego's lips upon mine. I drew a shuddering breath. It was just a kiss, but with it I had given my heart. Even when I surrendered my entire body to my husband, I had no such love for him. Was not my loving another man more truly than I loved Philippe as great a betrayal as coupling with him?

For the sake of my soul and my sanity, I had to turn again to Philippe. I had to find something in him I could love again. But how, when I could not put Diego out of my mind?

I had struggled to do so from the moment we parted under Mother's ill gaze, during the weeks of my preparation to leave for the north and the time spent traveling from Segovia to the coast. Tormented by my longing, I had gone so far as to climb the ramparts of the castle of La Mota in Medina del Campo one evening in November, in a desperate attempt to clear my mind. I had been standing between two stone merlons of the battlements, listening to the eerie trill of a nightjar and the wind rattling the bare trees, when, to my utter shock, Mother climbed the stone stairs to join me.

I would have been no more startled than if the stars had begun to speak. She had insisted upon accompanying me to the coast, but usually spent her evenings alone, praying. "Mother, what are you doing here?"

She had thrown back her hood and gazed at the moon. It was nearly full, and bright, illuminating the clouds that scudded by in its white light. "You make the guards nervous standing out here like this," she said.

I looked down at the huddle of soldiers in the tower yard, stamping their feet against boredom, pikes to their shoulders. I could smell the oily smoke of the torches flaming from the walls. "I told them I am well."

"They were worried enough to summon me."

"I am sorry to trouble you. I suppose my explanation that I wished to listen to the woods did not sit well with them."

"Not when listening to the woods is all they ever do. It is probably a torture to them—they probably cannot imagine why you would choose to do it."

I sighed. "I love the forest."

She chuckled. "When I was a young child, I wished to be a woodcutter. All that time in the forest. It sounded wonderful."

"A woodcutter?" I laughed in spite of my bleak mood. "Mother, you were born to be Queen."

"Not really. Much of my childhood I had no notion of it. Papa was young and I had two healthy brothers ahead of me. I was as far from the crowns as—"

"Me."

"Yes." She regarded me. Clouds passed over the moon, obscuring her face. "I wonder now why I tried so hard to be Queen."

"Tried? You had no choice. You were next in line. La Beltraneja did not count."

Mother exhaled loudly. "You should really call her Juana of Castile, you know. She was no more illegitimate than you are."

"But—your brother was incapable of fathering a child."

"The louder the propaganda, the weaker the claim. How familiar you are, a generation later, with the lies that were spread then as truth."

"But you said so yourself."

"Did I? When have you ever heard me talk of my brother and his daughter?"

I thought, stunned. Had I heard her, or had it been just others?

"Listen to me. There were those who wanted me to have the crown. When Enrique died, they took me up on a mountain, so to speak, as the Devil took Christ, and offered me the world if I wanted it."

I was afraid to ask what she meant.

"Look, Juana, I'm no Christ. I said yes." She laughed ruefully. "I actually let myself believe what they told me, that I and not my niece Juana had the right to be Queen. I thought I was being generous by giving her the choice of taking the veil in a convent, or marrying your brother Juan when he grew up, though he was just newborn and she would have been a dried-up spinster by the time he was of age."

"I don't believe you. Why would you say this? Why would you take the crowns from their rightful owner?"

"Oh, Juana. You are not so naive as that."

The nightjar's trill waxed louder; it must have flown closer. There were plenty who would do whatever it took to seize the power of the throne. Luna had done it with my grandfather. Someone had poisoned Mother's brother Alfonso. To keep their line safe, the Dowager Duchess's brother Edward had killed his own brother George, and her other brother, Richard, had murdered his nephews. As long as there was a crown, people would kill to keep it. Or put their half brother's daughters in convents.

"Who were these others who helped you to the throne?" I asked, not wanting to know.

"Who would you think—those who then gained from it: Cardinal Mendoza and his followers. The Admiral of Castile." She drew in a breath. "The Archbishop of Granada."

"Fray Hernando? The most holy man in Spain? What cares he about earthly power?"

Mother grimaced. "He doesn't. He cares for me."

"What are you saying?"

We stared at each other. At last Mother bowed her head in the silvery moonlight. "I am not the hero you think I am."

A soldier called up: "Is all well, Your Majesty?"

Mother lifted her voice. "I am comforting the Princess. She is lost in love for her husband and needs my aid."

"Why do you say that?" I whispered. "You know that it is not true."

She shook her head slowly. "It would be better for you if you were."

A shriek from Leonor now jolted me from my thoughts. I looked up to see Philippe lunge at the children as they dodged around the climbing roses.

"Don't let him catch you, chickens!" I called, trying to sound cheerful. I thrust the needle into the cloth of Philippe's shirt. I had noticed it on the floor after he had taken me the previous afternoon, the shoulder torn by Delilah's talons. Mending it signaled my hope for reconciliation.

Philippe caught Isabel. He rubbed his face against her belly until she was breathless with laughter.

He put her down. Panting, she asked, "Why does she call us chickens?"

Philippe snatched her up again. "How about I call you 'gyrfalcon'?"

She pounded him with her balled fist. "I'm a girl!"

He grabbed her fist and kissed it. "I'm a boy."

She giggled. "You're funny."

"She thinks her father's funny," Philippe announced to me. He turned to her. "Will you think I'm funny when I'm King? Or am I funny only as a prince?"

Her soft brow buckled.

I pulled on the needle and thread. "She doesn't understand you, Philippe."

"Charles understands. We're going to be Kings someday, aren't we, Charles?"

"Yeff, Papa."

A tender look raced across Philippe's face, quickly replaced by a grin. He smacked his fist against his hand. "We're going to crush anyone who gets in our way, right, son?"

Charles pounded his own bony hand. "Cruff 'em."

Philippe laughed. "I wish your great-grandmother could see you. She rather liked crushing things."

I thought of my own mother. She was not as tough a creature as I had once believed. Perhaps I had been wrong to not question her about her failures. Perhaps she had only been waiting for me to do so. But it was I who was afraid to let her be less than a goddess.

Philippe motioned to a man standing nearby to bring him wine. "I'm having a feast tonight, welcoming you home." I watched him drain his goblet. "Nun, dress her up." Beatriz looked up as he came over and kissed my cheek. "My people need to start thinking of you as Queen."

"But I'm not their Queen."

"My father is making arrangements to change our titles here once I am King of your lands—oh, excuse me, Consort King. Anyway, here I will be full King, not some meek companion to Her Majesty. Finally, Burgundy will get its crown. Grand-mère would be so pleased."

"That may not be for a long, long while."

"You have not heard the reports of your mother's illness?"

I put down my sewing. "No."

He glanced away. "Oh, they are probably nothing. Her ambassador is given to exaggeration. The man would call a hiccup a death rattle. Do not give it a moment's thought, not on a pretty day like this."

I saw Isabel stumble and fall toward a trailing rose. She jerked her hand from the thorny cane and, with outrage gathering on her face, studied the thumb-prick welling with blood. Leonor scooped her up as she howled.

I took Isabel from her sister. When her sobs had subsided, I said to Philippe, "I would like to dismiss the Viscountess of Furnes as governess. Now that I have returned, I shall fill that role."

He signaled again to the servant for more wine. "You're a funny thing, more concerned about the title of governess than Queen." He took a drink. "But that is why you amuse me."

He gave the man his cup. "Look pretty tonight," he told me. And then, hunching like a monster, he chased after Charles, who ran, his little cries of delight distorted into growls by his deformity.

That night, music mixed with the clink of knives and spoons and the hum of conversation as we dined. In the torchlight, made brilliant by mirrors hung from every wall, the sharp petals of Philippe's tree of serpent tongues glistened as if wet. Drawn to the sheer malevolence of a pointed tip, I gingerly put my finger to it and slowly applied pressure.

"Watch out," said Hendrik, sitting next to me, "you'll cut yourself."

I drew back and smiled. "Dear Hendrik, thank you for your concern. But there are other things at this court more likely to wound me than serpents' tongues."

His broad face was etched with sympathy. "We are your friends, Your Highness."

"Some of you may be."

I glanced at the Viscountess of Furnes, leaning over her plate to flirt across the table with the Margrave of Baden-Baden. Like a fish being angled, the fresh-faced young man bent toward her as she spoke, then, as she sat back, bent farther forward as if tethered to her by an invisible line. She smiled privately, fingering a jewel suspended from a ribbon and hidden in her bodice. Whatever the gem was, it was large enough to make a lump under her neckline.

The past year and a half had only served to ripen the Viscountess, silkening her cheeks and intensifying her pale blue gaze. Her golden hair, upon which she wore her hood far back to reveal her sleek temples, gleamed in the torch-light. She shone like a goddess and she knew it.

Philippe turned away from the Margrave's wife, a plump young thing whose lips looked as though they had been inflated like a sheep's bladder. "What are you saying?"

"Nothing, Monseigneur," I replied.

"Where's my surprise, Hendrik?" Philippe took a swallow of wine. "Hendrik said he had a surprise for me tonight."

"I'm sorry, Your Highness," said Hendrik, "you misunderstood. The surprise is for the Princess."

"For me?" I asked.

"For her?" Philippe stuck out his lip in a pretend pout.

"The feast is in her honor, is it not?"

"Well, it had better not be a silly painting," Philippe grumbled. "I remember that ugly piece you tried to jolly us with in Brussels a few years back." He nudged Hendrik's arm. "If you are aroused by the sight of a man doing it with a strawberry, fine. I prefer women."

"I liked that painting," I told Hendrik. "I like to imagine what the artist might have meant by it."

Philippe knocked back his wine. "He was drunk."

"Have you decided what that might be, Madame?" Hendrik asked.

"I think he meant it to illustrate how the natural world would appear if Adam and Eve had not fallen in Eden."

"Correction." Philippe stabbed a piece of fish with his knife. "Eve is the one who fell. Adam was forced to follow her."

I could no longer ignore him. "So you think that women are the weaker sex?"

"Of course they are." He grinned. "We like them that way."

Hendrik cleared his throat. "I think it might be time for the surprise." He whispered something to his man, who went to the musicians' balcony.

Trumpets blared. Diners stopped their conversations and the great wooden doors swung open. Into the chamber danced Flemish men dressed in red loincloths and clamshells, great green-feathered masks upon their faces. Some carried parrots on their shoulders. Others paraded with monkeys on silver chains or, in the case of little greenish monkeys the size of squirrels, balanced atop their heads.

I laughed when a costumed gentleman led in a herd of long-legged ratlike creatures with crimson ribbons. *"Hutias!"* I exclaimed. "Admiral Colón brought them to court when I was a girl. My dog chased after them." I marveled how I could say the name Colón as if it meant nothing to me.

Hendrik grinned. "I wanted to remind you of your lands, where many worlds come to pay honor at your court."

I squeezed Hendrik's hand. "Thank you."

"If you were really going to do something for us, why didn't you get us some real natives? By all accounts, the she-Indios are quite the tigers—in a good way—once you pin them down."

I shifted away from Philippe. All his natural sweetness evaporated when he drank. "The Indios are people, Monseigneur, and as such are Mother's subjects. She specifically has granted them her love and protection."

"Your mother," he grumbled.

"There are times when I see her great wisdom." I looked at him in wonder. "How long it has taken me to say that."

Now the trumpets announced a call to dance. The players of Hendrik's surprise exhibition marched out of the hall with their beasts. Soon I was with the other dancers, holding Philippe's hand while performing the lively leaps of a saltarello, wishing the evening would end so that I could go to bed. I would be rising early—I had promised my children that I would take them for a walk along the river in the morning.

Philippe jerked me toward him. He gazed at me as I righted myself from my stumble. "Do you love me, Puss?"

"You're drunk."

He stopped dancing. "I asked you, do you love me?"

The other dancers exchanged uneasy glances.

"Yes, of course I do." I looked away, upset that others should see him like this.

A gleam caught my eye. I followed it to the Viscountess, where a great egg-shaped pearl had slipped from beneath her bodice and now rested on her breast.

As awkwardly as a man underwater, Philippe followed my line of vision. He squinted, then frowned, then looked at me. "It means nothing," he said.

I pulled out of his grasp.

"She is the children's governess!" he called after me as I strode across the floor. "I rewarded her. What's wrong with that?"

I kept walking.

There was a disturbance behind me, then a woman's gasp. I heard the plodding of Philippe's uneven steps as he strove to catch up with me.

He thumped my shoulder. "Here."

When I turned, he thrust the pearl before me on his palm. "You want it. You keep it. It doesn't matter to me."

I gazed into his face, beautiful even when distorted with drink. "Dear Philippe, that is precisely the problem." I turned to go.

"What does that mean?" he cried. "What do you mean?"

As I strode by, my skirts brushed against the tables emptied of all but those nobles who were too infirm or aged to dance. Lesser court officials stood against the walls, gaping.

"Stop!" Philippe ordered. "You cannot leave until I've dismissed you!"

A dog gnawing on a bone jumped out of my way.

"She's not stopping!" Philippe sputtered in amazed fury. "Do you not hear me? I command you to stop!"

I pushed through the doors, leaving the roar of shocked silence behind me. Alone in the torchlit passageway, I did not cry, but felt the hollow black ache of despair.

36.

18 May anno Domini 1504

The following day, the children's little spaniel raced ahead along the riverbank, ears flying, belly fur raking refuse, mouth pulled back in a wide doggy grin. "Catch her!" I called after Leonor and Charles, who ran after her, shrieking. Behind them Isabel churned through grass up to her knees. She stumbled, fell, then popped up, crying for them to wait.

"I've been reading," said Beatriz, strolling next to me. It was a fine morning. The air smelled of the muddy river, where ducklings scudded after their mothers, and of the wild roses blooming along the towpath, to which fat-legged bees paid visits like greedy proprietors checking on their holdings.

I laughed. "When are you not reading, Beatriz?"

Her graceful features were arranged in a frown within the white oval of her wimple. "I'm a little . . . concerned . . . about something."

"Yes?" I said absentmindedly. Across the river, a stork sat on its nest atop an old church tower. Its devoted mate stood next to it, not moving, though a breeze raised the feathers on its head.

"I found a book in your husband's library—"

I turned to her. "You mean the Dowager's library. Philippe does not read."

Her frown deepened, as if that might be significant. "Yes. That's true. He doesn't, does he?" She blinked in thought. "Well, as I was saying, I found this book—by Pliny the Elder, it turns out. It stuck out a little from its neighbors and so attracted my attention."

The spaniel stopped and, panting, turned to wait for the children. Leonor came upon her first and scooped her up in a chokehold, to which the dog, rear legs hanging down and belly exposed, responded by grinning like a fool.

"Pliny—one of your Romans," I said. "You must have liked that. Was it in Latin?"

"No. French. It was a miserable translation."

I raised my voice. "Leonor! Charles may pet her, too."

"Your Highness, Pliny was discussing some of the dangers to one's health from the metal lead. He felt it was particularly dangerous in the form of the white lead paint ceruse. The workers who used it to paint ships often succumbed to a sudden death."

"Charles, why would you hit your sister?" I ran over to Leonor, who sat in the grass crying, as Charles cuddled the dog.

"It'ff mine," he said, holding the spaniel away from me. "Everyffing iff mine. I'm to be King ffomeday."

"Kings must share," I said. "At least good kings do."

"Papa ffaid I get everyffing. Me and him."

I kissed him on his brow, wide and high, and with its silky blond widow's peak, so very beautiful. "Good kings like to see everyone happy. It makes them happier. Do you see how that works?"

He shook his head.

"You might try it. Be nice to someone, and see how it makes you feel. Here, give Leonor the dog."

Begrudgingly, he handed her the dog. She smiled, then buried her nose in its fur.

"See?" I said. "Just by something you did, you made Leonor happy. You had the power to do so. Doesn't that make you feel good and strong?"

"No."

"Think about it. You'll see." I gathered him in for a kiss, and then released him.

"Now what were you saying?" I asked Beatriz.

"There was a note in the book on Pliny. It quoted Vitruvius, mentioning that when lead in vessels comes into contact with a liquid, it leaches into the liquid. And lead, once ingested, is harmful to one's health."

I watched the children. "Why do you tell me this?"

"The symptoms of lead ingestion are weakness and lethargy. Not usually enough to kill, but to render a person helpless. Though in the case of white lead paint, the outcome might be even more dire."

"I still don't know why you speak of this. Do you think such vessels are used in our kitchens?" I had a sudden thought. "Is the health of my children endangered?"

"Your Highness, the goblet from which you took the Prince's potion was painted white."

Weakness, she had said the symptoms were, and lethargy. The bleak months of my wasting illness; my daily exhaustion; how hard it had been sometimes to walk and talk, even to breathe—all this played across my mind. "Do you think there was lead in the paint?"

Beatriz drew in a shuddering breath. "I wonder, Your

Highness, if the question is: Did someone wish for it to contain the poisonous metal?"

Hooves pounded. I started. Grasping my throat, I turned to see four German guards riding toward us with a riderless horse.

They reined their animals sharply. The commotion caused Isabel to latch on to my legs.

I looked up, shading my eyes. "Gentlemen?" I demanded, angry that they had frightened my child.

"Your Highness." The leader's pink skin and bristly yellow mustache were visible through his open visor. He dismounted and bowed. "His Highness asks that you return to the palace at once."

I picked up Isabel. She pushed away, making clear that she was still uncomfortable with me. "I am with my children now."

He frowned at Charles and Leonor, chasing the spaniel with sticks, their curiosity about the guards abated. "Your Highness, you are to come with us."

I looked at the riderless horse. It was saddled with a pillion.

Beatriz stepped next to me. "What is it that is so pressing?"

The men glanced at one another.

"I won't go," I said, "unless I am told why I must leave my children."

"We are under orders from the Prince."

"Tell the Prince that the Princess shall be there shortly." I turned toward Leonor and Charles, still running on the bank.

The guard laid his hand on my arm.

I stared at his gauntlet in shock even as I shifted Isabel away from him. "Do you know what you do?" I was incredulous.

He did not let go. "We are under orders from the Prince," he repeated.

Isabel started to cry. I handed her to Beatriz.

"Must you do this in front of the children?" I demanded.

He grabbed my other arm. Charles and Leonor stopped playing to watch.

"Beatriz, stay with the children. It's all right, Leonor. Charles, come and make Isabel smile. You have the power, remember?"

I let the guard seat me on the pillion before the children could become more frightened. The other men closed ranks around me. I was given the reins. The guard slapped my horse's flank; we were off as a group. I rode for the palace escorted as closely as if I were the most dangerous enemy of the state.

37.

19 May anno Domini 1504

The nightingale sang outside my window. Up and down the scale she warbled, calling for her mate, as she had been doing since I was escorted to my bedchamber and unceremoniously locked within it.

She had sung for her mate in the morning, while I pounded on the door, furious, outraged. How could Philippe treat me like this? I was heir to the Spanish crowns. I was the daughter of the Catholic Kings. My God, I was his wife.

She had sung for her mate in the afternoon, as I sank cradling my aching fists. Was no one to come free me? Where was Beatriz, or even Katrien?

The nightingale sang in the early evening, when I sat hugging my knees in terror. I was friendless. Powerless. My husband had made it abundantly clear that he could do whatever he wanted with me.

A key scraped in the keyhole. I rose, my heart thumping.

Philippe entered, a guilty smile on his face. "Knock, knock."

Even as he crossed the chamber, my relief that he had come hardened into fury. He kissed my hand, its flesh made tender from beating the door. I pulled it away.

The pouches by his mouth were set with a mixture of apology and stubbornness. "Don't be angry with me."

"I was walking with the children when your men came, Philippe. They frightened them. Leonor was crying. Did you not think of that when you ordered the men to seize me then?"

"You must understand my position. I could not have you leave a reception without my dismissing you. It made me look weak."

"And so you had me locked into my room like a dog?"

His contriteness dissolved. "You make it sound worse than it is. I will not be made to look like less of a man by my wife, as your father lets your mother do. I saw enough of that while in the Spains."

"I left last night because I wished to leave. It was not a show of power."

"That's not how it was construed." He went over to my table and picked up my pen. "Write me an apology. As soon as you show me deference, I will let you go."

"I will tell you now, then: I am sorry to have made you feel bad. It was not my intention."

"Not good enough." He held out my pen. "Write."

"I will not write. I am telling you: I am sorry." I turned to leave.

He dropped the pen and grabbed my arm.

"You're hurting me!"

His fingers dug into my flesh. "I said to write me a proper apology. You know how, with your fancy Latin training. The nun taught you how to turn a pretty phrase— do it."

"Let me go!"

"Not until you show me some respect."

I laughed. "Dear Philippe, don't you know that you can't force someone to respect you? You have to earn it."

He raised his hand. I flinched.

He patted my head. "There, there. I am surprised at you." He let go of me and then rubbed my arm. "You know I would never hurt you. Gyrfalcons are not trained by abusing them. They are given choice bits of meat and coddled until they realize that their masters will take care of them when they behave."

"Yes, and they come to that conclusion more quickly when their eyes are sewn shut."

He stared at me and, deciding I must be jesting, chuckled. "I should sew yours shut."

"Oh, mine were, for quite some time, by my lust."

He drew me to him. "Lust. Puss. Why can't you call it love? What's so wrong with desiring your husband?"

I kept my face turned away. "Nothing, when he treats you with care."

"I take care of you as much as any man takes care of his woman."

I broke from him and laughed. "I hope that is not true."

He caught my wrist. "You developed a smart mouth, being around your mother."

"Alas, if only I had a brain to match hers."

"She's not invincible, Juana. She can be defeated."

"Oh, she can be."

"I'm glad you are aware of that." He let go of me and reached inside his doublet. He took my hand and put a lump upon it. From my open palm, Diego's pearl glowed with a milky light.

"Just to show you that I am a reasonable man, I am giving it back to you."

But how will you remember your father without it? I had asked Diego when he had given me the pearl.

I saw his tender expression. *I am not likely to forget,* he had said.

I laid the pearl on a table. "I don't need it." Outside, the nightingale sang loudly. How long would she go on calling before she realized that her mate was not to come?

"I came here to free you. Damn it, Puss, I love you. Why do you want it to look otherwise?" He scowled at the window. "Damn bird. It's driving me mad."

I gazed into his beautiful face, now contorted with frustration. Yes, I believed that he did love me, in his unholy fashion, as Papa loved Mother in his own. Yet Papa had betrayed her, as Philippe betrayed me and would continue to betray me, the moment he stepped from this room. How many generations would this go on, as it had played out in my mother's life and mine? Would strong women forever find themselves undermined by their lovers should they appear too strong, cut down at their vulnerable roots—their need for trust?

I crossed over to my desk.

"You're writing the apology?" He sounded pleasantly surprised. "Good. Very good. Your attendants wait in the antechamber. I shall tell them to spread the word of my pardon and our reconciliation."

I sat down.

"I truly do love you, Puss. Next time, just think before you act, that's all."

I unscrewed the golden cap from a horn of ink, then paused. "Philippe, can you promise you will be true to me?"

"I can promise that I will love you."

"That's not the same. People can do horrible things to the people they love. Philippe, I am asking, will you be true?"

"Puss, I am weak. It does not mean that I don't love you."

"Weakness is a choice, Philippe."

He shook his head. "I don't know where you get these ideas."

I took up my pen. Swallowing back remorse so deep that I could scarcely breathe, I formed the first words.

My dear Mother. Can you forgive me? I am just now beginning to understand.

38.

13 November anno Domini 1504

It was butchering season, and the air seeping into my chambers in the Dowager's palace smelled of smoky fires, singed animal hair, and the cold. Charles sat on my lap in his little fur-trimmed gown and coif while Leonor stood next to him, as I showed them an illuminated book of letters.

"C is for—"

"*'Chat,'*" Charles said.

"That's right," I said, smiling.

"It is also for *'canard'* and *'chambre,'*" Leonor said smugly. "And *'chemise'* and *'cheval'* and *'cigogne.'* And you, too, Charles. 'Charles' starts with C."

I nodded. "Impressive, Leonor. *Cigognes*, even. I just so happen to like storks very much."

"I like storks," she said. "But they are very ugly."

I nodded. "Their faces might seem that way. But sometimes the ugliest things are beautiful inside. And the prettiest things, well, sometimes inside they are the ugliest."

Her fine wheaten hair tumbled over her shoulder as she cocked her head to consider this.

Charles blurted, "*'Cachot'* fftartff with ffee."

I looked at him in surprise. "*Cachot*. What do you know about dungeons?"

Nearby, Beatriz glanced up from her translation work spread on my desk. At her embroidery frame by the door, as far away from me as possible while in the same room, the Viscountess gazed my way, too. She was now my chief lady-in-waiting, to neither of our delights. After I had refused to write the apology, my husband had responded by sending my few Spanish ladies home and giving the Viscountess this highest honor. He had allowed Beatriz to remain in my attendance only after I had refused to eat for a week. Not that he cared about my hunger.

"I suppose your mother will take away my title if I let you starve," he had said on the seventh day. "And I do dislike bony women." He had scowled at the tray of uneaten fruit, then at me. "You can have your blessed nun—just eat."

Charles pointed to the Viscountess. "Ffhe told uff about them. There iff a dungeon in thiff palaffe. There iff a dungeon in every palaffe. Ffhe ffaid if we were bad, ffhe would have uff ffrown into it."

I turned around to glare at her. "How dare you frighten them!"

The Viscountess shrugged, and drove her needle into her embroidery. "I was only teasing. Children love tales of dungeons and giants and witches."

"Well, I don't appreciate it. You will frighten them."

"I'm not ffcared." Charles pointed up at me. "I'll ffrow you in the dungeon."

I kissed his dimpled finger. "That's not nice. Don't you want to be a good king and make people happy?"

"Papa ffayff I don't have to."

"Make people happy? Why wouldn't you want to? It feels so very nice."

The Viscountess smiled flatly as she tugged at her thread. On this day she wore a plain gown of gray. I had not known that she owned such a simple garment. She had not dressed to her usual standard in the past few weeks, the same period, coincidentally, that Philippe had been gone. He had traveled with his men and a few choice others to his pleasure palace in Hesdin, to see how the improvements he had ordered for its famous reception rooms fared. He was eager to see if the additional trick fountains had been installed, particularly those that sprayed the ladies from underneath. Such fun they were, he thought, since under our skirts we wore nothing. How he loved to sniff the air and smack his puffed lips as we dripped, and then cry, "Who smells fish?" I was glad to have not been asked to join him, though perhaps the Viscountess, now dressed like a sparrow and with her brow in a pucker, had not shared in my relief.

Leonor turned the page. "D is for—"

"'Dragonff'!" Charles broke in with a triumphant shout. "Big, mean, wicked oneff."

At that moment Katrien came in with a pile of pressed linens.

I could sense Beatriz stiffening at her desk. She had been wary of Katrien since reading of the dangers of white lead paint. She was convinced that it was lead in my cup that had made me ill, and that Katrien knew about and desired this effect. Her conviction was made stronger by Katrien's evasiveness when she tried to question her. There was also the fact that after abandoning the potion, I had gotten well. But it was not Katrien who frightened me. If someone meant me ill, it was one who had knowledge of insidious poisons, lead or otherwise, not an ignorant peasant girl—although, Beatriz argued, this did not mean that an ignorant peasant girl would not agree to deliver it. Perhaps Beatriz's suspicions would have been quelled if she had been able to examine the white cup. Katrien claimed that she didn't know what had happened to it, that she had not seen it since we had been in Segovia.

Now Katrien curtseyed to me, then, with a clack of her *klompen*, proceeded to pull back the cut-velvet counterpane and strip the sheets from my bed. I returned to the book and my children. We had reached the letter T when Katrien was gathering the sheets, readying to leave.

The Viscountess pulled at a stitch. "Girl, a little moment, please."

Katrien halted. She regarded the other woman, her expression as impassive as ever, except for her eyes, which tightened with sheer hatred.

The Viscountess did not see her disdain, or did not care. "I am thirsty. Get me a cup of water."

"Yes, Katrien," said Beatriz, "see if you can't find her a nice white cup."

I kissed the top of Charles's head, tired of the current of ill feelings swirling around me.

Philippe strode into the room. He bowled into Katrien, knocking her off her shoes and sending the wadded linens from her arms. He did not glance at her as she scrambled to gather them.

"Do you know what your mother has done?" he demanded of me.

"Children, say hello to your father." I gently pushed them toward him, though they were understandably reluctant. Their usually fastidious father's riding clothes were muddy, and his hair hung in dark, greasy strings. He slashed the air with his riding crop brought straight from the road, lowering it just long enough to receive their kisses.

Leonor had scarcely been able to peck his cheek when he bellowed, "You must set her straight this minute!"

My brave little girl pulled back, blinking to compose herself.

I kept my voice calm for the sake of the children. "I don't know what I am to set her straight about."

"That you, and only you, are to be her direct heir."

"Please, Philippe, can you stop waving that thing? It's terrifying the children."

He glared at them. Charles clung to my skirts as Beatriz rose from the desk.

"Sit down, nun, this has nothing to do with you."

"How do you know this?" I asked, rubbing Charles's back. "Did you receive a letter from Mother? She has not replied to me."

He glanced away with pursed lips. "Her ambassador gave me the news," he said after a pause. "Damn it, this word is not the greeting I expected when I returned from my journey."

"I'm sorry, Philippe, but it wasn't my doing."

"What really infuriates me is how she distrusts me. She wrote a codicil to her will that both you and I must be there to claim the crowns, or your father gets them."

"She writes this in her will? Why does she feel the need to write one now?"

He looked at me. "The old dame's not well."

"Not well?" I stopped comforting Charles. "What do you mean?"

"There's a growth in her stomach. They say she's not long

for this world. I doubt it—the old she-tiger won't be put down so easily."

"Why did no one tell me this?" But who would tell me? All those who were sympathetic to me had been dismissed for months.

He whipped the air again. "Why'd she have to make it difficult for us? You don't want to go—you want to stay with your children. Why drag you to the miserable Spains?"

I took my hand from Charles's back to cover my mouth. "My mother is dying," I said wonderingly, as if saying the words would give me more understanding.

Beatriz came over to me. "Señora."

"Write to her quickly," said Philippe, "before she goes. Convince her that you want me to take the crowns in your name. You want to stay with the children, yes? Tell her that. Tell her you won't go there—but you must be fast. Nun!" he barked.

Beatriz flinched.

"You're handy with the pen. Make yourself useful and dash off a letter now. Raymond!"

A page appeared at the door.

"Get a courier ready. I'll have a letter to send."

"Yes, Your Highness."

"Nun!" He poked her with his crop. "You're not writing!"

She would not leave my side.

"Why is everyone just standing there? You're as dumb as cows."

"Oh, Papa," Leonor cried, her voice breaking.

Philippe gazed down at her, then up at me. "You make me look bad in front of my children. That's just what you wanted, isn't it?"

"Where are her letters, Philippe?" I asked. "I never get them."

He pressed together his lips. "What does it matter? Her letters upset you."

"Have there been letters?"

He narrowed his eyes as though suspecting he had been tricked. "Damn it, why am I pretending? I've been doing you a favor. You were always unhappy after receiving them. When Grand-mère suggested that I keep them, I jumped at the idea. I was only trying to help you."

"So you have been keeping them," I said in disbelief.

"Yours to her, too." He shrugged. "Cat's out of the bag, so what? I acted in your best interest."

All those years before I returned to the Spains, and even now, I thought that she spurned me. And she had thought likewise of me.

"Nun!" Philippe cried. "Why aren't you writing?"

I sank back. Mother wrote to me. She wished to have me know her. She had tried to talk to me in the Spains, but I had been too afraid to encourage her. I had been too afraid to let her be a human, with all a human's frailties, because I needed her to be perfect. And now all my chances to make amends, all our chances to come to know each other, were dwindling like sand through an hourglass. "You had no right," I whispered.

Philippe snorted. "I have every right to do whatever I want. And you have none—not here, at least. You would think that would scare you into behaving better, but you don't seem to get it in your head."

I could write to her quickly, let her know that I didn't care whether she was perfect or not. That I admired and esteemed her no matter what, that I always had and always would. "I demand her letters."

He laughed. "You demand? *You* demand? Have you not been listening? My God, you are her daughter."

I swallowed against the lump searing my throat, then held up my chin. "You compliment me, Monseigneur."

"Always undermining me, aren't you, Puss?"

He threw his crop. The children cried out when it struck my shoulder.

The Viscountess flew over to entreat him as he marched for the door. He flung her away, even as Katrien covered her face.

39.

6 January anno Domini 1505

Charles reached into his shoes, so carefully filled with barley and hay and put by his bed the night before. He pulled out a little silver donkey the size of a mouse, and a little silver cart with leather leads. Instantly he jumped up and brought it to me. "Put it together!"

The sleeves of my night robe dragging, I reached over Isabel, sucking her thumb in my lap, to take it. "Look, Charles, the Three Kings took all of your hay for their camels. You must have been a good boy for them to bring you such a nice present." I worked the leads over the donkey's neck. "Leonor, are you not going to look in your shoes?"

She sat back on her heels, poised even with her hair crumpled from sleep and a stripe imprinted on her cheek from her bedclothes. How Mother would enjoy her, such a dignified little soul. How odd to think that they had not met. I hoped there would be time. "We did not have Three Kings' Day last year," she said.

"Ah, well, maybe we can make up for it this year."

"When I was a child," said Beatriz, "Día de los Reyes was my favorite day. I waited all year for the sixth of January. Once I got a book on the saints. I felt very rich and very good—no one got books. Too expensive."

"Those Kings knew you well," I said. "You would treasure a book. Go on, Leonor, look and see if the Kings brought you anything." Had Philippe and the Viscountess been so very busy with their lives that they could not remember this tradition, so important to the children?

Pursing her lips, Leonor reached into her shoe, then brought out a gold necklace with a pearl the size of an orange seed suspended from it.

"Pearls are special stones," I said. "They help you to remember someone."

"Who?"

"That is up to you."

"Grand-mère Margaret," she said with characteristic finality.

I drew in a breath. Of course she missed her great-grandmother. The Dowager had raised her during the time I was in Spain. "I'm certain she would like that."

I slid Isabel off my lap and led her to her shoes to see what was within. She was examining the miniature gilt dog she'd found, when I saw movement behind the lumpy glass of the window. I heard a nightingale sing. I frowned. There were no nightingales in winter.

Just then the Viscountess entered with a troop of Burgundian ladies. "There you are. We had gone to your chambers but could not find you."

"It's Three Kings' Day."

She looked blankly at the children. Outside, the nightingale burst into song. "What is that?" She crossed to the window and opened it. Cold air rushed in and the bird flew away.

Now Philippe entered, with Delilah on his wrist. He was in his night robe and his hair hung straight, as yet uncurled. "By Saint John, it's cold. Why did you open that window?"

"There was an irksome bird," said the Viscountess.

"Then by God, let me send Delilah after it."

"No!" I cried.

Philippe gazed at me, then made a little shooing motion at the Viscountess.

"But we've come to dress Madame."

"Go. Get. All of you." When she and the ladies had gone, he said, "You, too, nun."

She looked at me.

"What is this, Philippe?"

I nodded for Beatriz to leave. The bird returned. I saw its rippled image through the glass, hopping on the windowsill. I glanced away, hoping Philippe wouldn't see it, but he was sprawled on the floor with the children, admiring the gifts he had nothing to do with.

He encouraged Charles to pet Delilah, then looked up. "I thought I should be the one to tell you."

My stomach filled with dread. I did not want to hear.

"Your mother is dead."

On the other side of the wavy glass, the bird pecked at the sill. We would never get to talk. She would never truly know me, nor I truly know her.

It was too late.

"Happy Three Kings' Day." Philippe reached into his robe and drew out a packet of letters. He held them out to me.

"Mama, what are those?" asked Leonor.

I shook my head, unable to speak for the swelling in my throat.

"Mama has to get dressed," said Philippe.

"I'll be back," I whispered to the children.

Alone in my chamber, I stood by the light of the window, staring at my name written in my mother's hand.

"Knock, knock." Philippe entered. He came as far as my desk, stopping to toy with the writing things upon it. "Look, Puss, I know this is bad for you. Is there anything I can do?"

I shook my head.

He came over and put his arms around me.

Whether weakened by his act of kindness, or by the yawning chasm that had opened in my heart, I leaned against him.

He pressed his forehead against mine. "Is it too late to say I'm sorry?"

I kept my forehead to his. Gently, he began to sway with me.

It was all he knew to offer.

England

Possibly Catalina of Aragón

40.

12 February anno Domini 1506

*M*y fur sleeves brushed against my gown as I held out my arms. "Sweetest Catalina!"

My sister hesitated for an almost imperceptible moment, then launched herself across the frigid stone chamber within the forbidding English castle at Windsor. "Juana!"

We rocked each other in an embrace, then held each other out. How lovely my youngest sister had become. At twenty, there were no more gummy smiles, no trace of her girlish awkwardness. She had my mother's thick red-gold hair and Papa's well-shaped lips and a sparkle to her blue eyes that was all her own. It was hard to imagine that this vibrant young woman was a widow—she had lost her husband, the King's son Arthur, when she was sixteen. It was even more difficult to believe that another prince had not claimed her as his bride.

"You are well," she said wonderingly.

"Yes."

"I am so glad!" She hugged me to herself again. I drank in her oily-sweet smell, familiar to me since childhood. She let me go and beamed at me. "Thank God you are well."

"You act surprised."

"Your husband said—" She stopped, blinking blond lashes.

"Said what?"

She shook her head. "When you did not come to meet the King upon first reaching our shores—"

"I wanted to come. I wanted to see you! Philippe—" I took a breath, remembering how, the day after we had arrived, I had found the door to my chamber locked from outside when I had dressed, only to learn that Philippe had galloped off without me. "Philippe detained me."

She smiled apologetically. "He said you might say that."

"What else did he say?"

"Nothing, really. That you'd had a small incident that prevented you from accompanying him just then, that was all, but that sometimes, unfortunately, you were—"

"What?"

"I'm sorry—given to flights of fancy. But who isn't?" she added hastily. "After Mother died, I kept thinking I saw her at the window, but when I opened the casement, it was just a bird. Indeed, I went quite mad from my grief. I cried for days on end. None of us were there when she passed from this world, Juana. Not even Papa. It makes me feel so terrible. She did not deserve that."

Tears flooded my eyes. I had not known that Mother had died alone. No one had told me. To think what must have gone through her mind, abandoned, in her final hours.

She wiped at her eyes. "Only Fray Hernando was there."

I looked up. "Fray Hernando?"

"He had come from Granada for the last few months of her life. I suppose that was a comfort to her."

I thought of Mother's reply that day of her first illness, when I had remarked that Fray Hernando, as the holiest of men, cared not for earthly power. *No,* Mother had said. *He doesn't. He cares for me.*

"Yes," I murmured, "I suppose it was."

"Well, I don't know what is wrong with Papa. I shall not forgive him for marrying that girl. Mother was hardly cold in her grave! Have you met her?"

"Germaine of Foix? Yes, at the French court."

"What was she like?"

I winced, remembering that awful visit, where I had been abandoned by Philippe and left to fend for myself with the Queen's hostile court. "Of all of them, she wasn't so bad."

"I cannot believe you stick up for her."

"She wasn't cruel. At that court, that was quite re-markable."

"She's seventeen. Disgusting! How could he marry her? He and Mother were such lovebirds. Never has there been a couple as devoted as they. If I had a husband like that—"

"You sound like María—the starry-eyed romantic."

"Like how María *was*. I hear she does not find marriage as magical as she had dreamed. Her husband will have nothing to do with her beyond filling a cradle."

I thought of my newest infant at home, named for her once starry-eyed aunt. I, too, was but a filler of cradles. "No. Poor María."

Catalina's expression grew troubled. "How goes it with your husband?" she asked, watching my face.

"Surely you've heard."

"His ambassador tells us he's a benign ruler, gentle, kind. A friend to England."

I laughed in spite of myself. How Philippe's *grand-mère* had despised the Tudor King. She would have person-ally held his head in a butt of malmsey if she could have. She had brought up her grandson to hate him equally, though now Philippe, as a prince, was coming to admire the shrewd older man's political maneuvering. As for Philippe's being gentle and kind, I had bruises on my forearms where he had grasped me the night before. He had been so excited by his talks with the English King that he expelled his energy by bedding me roughly, against my wishes. But to admit to my miserable marriage was to confess my inability to earn a husband's love.

"The ambassador is well trained," I said in answer to her questioning gaze. "Tell me—what is the English King really like?"

"Old Henry? As sharp and cold as a dagger pulled from a snowbank. He won't let me go home and he won't let me marry his son Henry."

"Until he comes of age."

"No. It's a matter of the King's having lost interest in the Spanish alliance, but he suspects I might be too valuable to be let go of just yet. I did not mind being betrothed to young Henry." She sighed. "But now there's not even that."

I smiled. "María did have her influence on you."

"You would understand if you met him. He's tall, and handsome, with hair the color of a fox. He is very intelligent—he composes music—and he is exceedingly wise for his age—"

"Which is?"

"Almost fifteen."

I laughed. "A wise almost fifteen-year-old boy. I remember Juan at that age. 'Wise' was hardly a word to describe him. Loud, maybe, impertinent, cocky, vain . . ."

A merry voice came from the doorway. "Who is cocky and vain?"

Philippe entered with a slight man whose gray skin and hair belied the youthful sharpness of his eyes.

"Henry, please excuse the informal meeting. May I introduce you to my dear wife, Juana of Castile?"

The English King cautiously kissed my hand, then seemed surprised when I did not open my mouth and quack. What tales had Philippe told him about me? His campaign to slander and belittle me was astonishing. Yet he achieved his purpose. Because of my alleged incompetence, he had declared himself Mother's rightful heir before his court at Brussels, and no one had protested on my behalf. There was no one Spanish left to protest. My only hope was that once we arrived in the Spains, the Cortes would see through his lies. He would be my consort and nothing more, no matter what untruths he told.

He kissed my hand. "Are you feeling better, sweet?"

"I was never ill."

Philippe gave the English King a meaningful look. "You are so brave, darling," he said to me.

"You must have been, to survive a shipwreck," said the King. His smile was surprisingly courtly for such a plain little man. "Did you have a moment when you feared you would not make it?"

In my mind's eye I saw Philippe, drenched and sobbing, on the deck of the ship that was to carry us back to the Spains. A violent storm had struck when we were within eyesight of England's white cliffs. We watched in horror as the vessel next to us tipped, then was swallowed, sails and all. *Bring my jewels!* I had shouted. I waited for Beatriz to put them on me so that my corpse would be known, and had the captain lash me to the mast to keep me from being swept overboard. Meanwhile Philippe had bawled in terror, flailing his arms so that his men could hardly tie on the buoyant wings they had made for him of ladies' inflated skirts. Our ship broke up just offshore. We were plunged into the icy water. *Let me live for the children,* I prayed as Philippe thrashed next to me, his wings ballooning. Waves had crashed over our heads. *Let me live for them.*

"I think," I said, "that drowning was a reasonable fear for us all."

"She still has not recovered," Philippe said quickly. "She is weary, and needs to return to rest now. She will protest—brave girl that she is, she wants no one to know of her troubles."

"I'm not weary," I said.

"See?" Philippe laughed. "Just as I say. Sometimes you are not a good judge of your own fitness, sweet."

"His care for you is admirable," said the English King.

"Yes," I said. "He is Philippe the Good."

My husband flashed me a look of warning and then turned to the King. "Will you please excuse us?"

The King narrowed his miser's bright eyes. "I hardly got to speak with her. She doesn't seem that unwell. But if you insist." He kissed my hand, then that of my husband.

"Will I see you again?" cried Catalina.

"Of course," I said. Philippe let me kiss her before he led me away.

We walked down a chill hall, the silence broken only by our footsteps on the stone floor and the rustle of our clothing. Near the entranceway, a youth passed us, surrounded by armored attendants over whom he towered. He looked over his shoulder at me, his fox-red hair falling over his eyes.

Philippe took my arm to hurry me along.

Outside, he pulled me aside as we waited for our horses. "Did you think"—his breath came in furious clouds—"to make friends with the English King?"

"I should think you would want me to. We are in an alliance with the English."

"We? Who is 'we'?"

"The Spains."

"Oh? You are the Spains now?"

I held my tongue. It was best not to provoke him.

"Do you wish to enter in a secret alliance with him, to limit my power?"

"That is silly. Henry Tudor has no influence in the Spains."

"And neither will I, if you have your way."

"You will have power, as my husband."

"No. I shall have more. Your insufferably proud Cortes will beg me to take control when they see how incapable you are. People are already talking. They whisper about the fit you had on the ramparts of La Mota."

"Fit?"

"How you raged along the ramparts, unwilling to listen to reason and come inside, though it was a frigid night."

"Do you mean the night I went outside to catch my breath? I had no fit. My mother joined me. We talked."

"That's not what they say. They say she begged you to come inside."

"Who is 'they'?"

"They say after you gave birth to Fernando, you were weak and given to moods. They fear you have your grandmother's blood, that insanity runs through generations."

Realization swept through me in an icy wave. The flesh

of my arms and scalp tingled in painful alarm. "It's you. You started these rumors."

"Rumors? Even your mother was heard to say that you were lost in love without me."

I should not have let that lie stand when she said it. But I thought it was only words, and words can never hurt you.

"Oh, yes," he said, "they are saying all kinds of things. That I had to lock you up because you chased after the Viscountess and cut her long hair. That you threw a brick at me. That you set fire to your clothes."

"I did none of that."

"Jealous women are capable of anything."

"You are mad," I whispered.

"I can say that you must be locked up for your safety as well as that of others, and nobody will come rescue you."

"Why do you do this?"

"You know why."

A boy brought up our horses.

"Thank you, lad," said Philippe. "Take care of the lady. She's very fragile at present, and I wouldn't want anything to happen to her."

The Spains

Philippe I of Castile

41.

10 July anno Domini 1506

My view was of Papa and Philippe, swaying on their richly housed horses, their silk robes draped majestically over the haunches of their steeds. A hot wind sweeping off the Meseta and through the dusty streets of Valladolid stirred the scarlet brocade hangings of the Canopy of State held over their heads. A page walked before them, holding aloft the Sword of State, and before him clopped Philippe's German guards, whose apparent readiness to trample any stragglers cleared the road for our procession as efficiently as Moses at the Red Sea. I had witnessed such a scene before, riding into Toledo to greet Mother upon my first return to the Spains. I had thought it an innocent and touching expression of camaraderie then, a young husband riding with his wife's proud papa. I had been pleased to take a secondary position. Now, months after Philippe had started his campaign of lies questioning my fitness to rule, I knew better. Mother had warned me. How many more of her observations would come to haunt me, the damage already done?

Philippe looked this way and that, his perfectly curled hair swishing against the high collar of his satin robe. He was barely able to conceal his grin as men and women alike lowered to their knees as he passed. He clearly relished his role as King, even if it was of the Spaniards, whose restrained ways so perturbed him. He would happily be King of any peoples, be they Indios, Turks, or Cipangese, should they pay him enough deference. I saw now that he craved the enforced deference due him as King as a toddling child craves sweetmeats. He would crush anyone who was a threat to his supply, including his wife. Especially his wife.

How easy it was done. Just call me deranged, provide stories as proof, look solicitous, and then generously offer to take care of the kingdom as full King, not just King Consort, until my mind unclouded. Papa argued that, as my father, he should take care of Castile if I was truly unwell and thus preserve my rights until I healed. But Papa's appeal fell upon deaf ears. The nobles of the Cortes did not trust him. They feared that if he came into power, he would punish those who denied him a share in Mother's crowns. Would he? He was just trying to help me. He had his Aragón. Wasn't that enough?

Philippe snapped his fingers, breaking my reverie. Helmeted heads turned. He pointed to the side of the road, where a solitary man stood among those on their hands and knees.

"Why is he not bowing?" he asked, as querulous as a child being told that he must nap.

I looked closer at the man. His face was obscured by a broad-brimmed hat, though there was something familiar about the way he carried himself, so upright and proud. Papa leaned from his horse to whisper to my husband.

"Make him show respect," Philippe ordered the German guards who rode next to him. "Or seize him, I don't care."

The guards wheeled their horses around to confront the man. They barked at him to kneel, and when he did not, they pushed on his shoulders. He resisted, causing them to redouble their efforts. They knocked off his hat, revealing sleek dark hair drawn into a short queue. His face remained impassive as they tried—and failed—to shove him off his feet.

Philippe gaped at the scuffle as he passed. "The fool is mad. Seize him, if that's what he wants."

But when my horse neared, the man lowered himself to his knees. He bowed his head, but not before meeting my eyes with his searching gaze of grayest green.

My heart leaped.

Philippe turned around on his horse. I straightened my face and, with the slightest nod, acknowledged my subject before staring ahead. Philippe narrowed his eyes, then turned again.

My whole inner being sang with joy. If I had only one friend in Valladolid, let it be Diego Colón.

Later that afternoon, in the Palace of Pimentel, where we were to stay while the Cortes were in session to determine if Philippe was legally King, I could not get Diego out of my mind. I was alone, or nearly so. I had not had Beatriz's company in nearly three months. As soon as we landed in the Spains, she had continued ahead to Salamanca, where she was to present the translation of Aristotle over which she'd labored so hard. As for other ladies, I would not allow the Viscountess of Furnes within my sight, even though Philippe insisted that she remain my first lady-in-waiting in title. Nor could I stomach the other Burgundian ladies he had forced upon me. Which suited them—they were glad enough to be free to flirt with Philippe's men. Katrien was my only companion, and Philippe made much of this. *You see the extent of my poor wife's derangement? She fancies that a laundress is her boon companion.*

Though Katrien was hardly my boon companion, I was grateful for her presence. We had never recovered our former comfort together—I could not shake the feeling that she was withholding something from me—but at least she was not always scrutinizing the state of my mind. As she mended, scrubbed, or swept, I could think or feel whatever I wanted. And she doted on little Fernando, restored to me upon our return to the Spains, as patiently and tenderly as if he were her own.

And so, that afternoon, as I stood before an arched window opening onto the Plaza de San Pedro while she unpacked my traveling chest, I was left to dream of Diego. Swifts darted in the air, catching insects for the cheeping young that waited in their nests, built in the eaves of the church across the way. Had he thought of me during these past three years? Why should he? A man like him had surely married, had children, and become the affectionate father I knew he would be.

I heard footsteps approaching. I turned, holding my breath.

Papa entered and kissed my hand. "How are you feeling, Juana?"

I exhaled with a sigh. "I am fine, Papa. I have never felt unwell." I did not muddy the waters by mentioning that I was with child. I was well enough, though I was in the early months of my term, and I wished to keep my pregnancy a secret as long as I could. Katrien knew—a laundress knows everything about her mistress's person—but no one else. I did not wish to see Philippe preen at the thought of his having impregnated me once more. He would gloat about his potency for getting me with child the night he had forced himself upon me on shipboard, while sailing from England. Forestalling this pleasure was one of the few meager powers I had left over him.

"After little Fernando was born, did you not have spells of—"

"Papa, that was three years ago. Don't tell me you believe Philippe's lies. Can you not see for yourself that I am fine?"

He swept his gaze over me with a frown. "Your mother said that about herself, too, until the final weeks of her illness." He glanced pointedly at Katrien. She laid my hairbrushes on my table, as blank-faced as if she were deaf. "She sent me out to hunt the day of her death. She said that she would be there when I returned. God, I wish I had not gone."

"You were not there when she died?" I asked gently, knowing that he wasn't.

"No. Fray Hernando was. Of course."

I swallowed.

He looked up, wincing. "He always understood her. Her whole life, nearly. They were inseparable. He could make her laugh, or cry, more quickly than anyone. Sometimes I was painfully jealous of him."

I did not know if he was ready to examine the truth. "He was her priest, Papa."

"I know. I know." He tried to smile. "*Lo siento*. Look at me getting weepy here. Valladolid always makes me sentimental. We were married just down the street from here, in the palace of Juan de Vivero." He joined me at the window. "I came to her dressed as a muleteer," he said, shaking his head slowly. "She thought I was handsome. My God, I loved her."

The bells began to ring from the tower of San Pablo. We gazed across the plaza, the air between us thick with Papa's sorrow. I could smell his peppery scent, so dear to me in my youth. His black hair was mostly gray now; his gown hung from rounded, once broad shoulders. Time had reduced my dashing hero to a small, aging man.

He pulled away from the window. "You probably wonder how I could marry Germaine."

At my table, Katrien opened my Bible and spread my rosary upon it.

I said nothing.

"I'm lonely, Juana. I have been for a long time. I didn't think your mother loved me anymore."

"Of course she loved you, Papa."

"What a cruel jest it was—the symbol of our union plastered in churches and palaces all over the Spains. My arrows, her yoke. *Tanto monta, monta tanto.* Do you know what a fool it made me feel like to see them, knowing that she thought so little of me?"

"Papa—"

"Germaine, now, she thinks I am a god. Or at least a damn important king. She's young and easily impressed." He smiled to himself. "I feel like more of a man than I have for years."

"I've met her."

"Yes. She told me. She wished to come to see you, but I made her stay in Valencia. The Cortes are still not fond of the idea of our marriage—if I have a son, he is in line to be heir to the crown of Castile."

I had not thought of this. Surely any child of his would

be behind my Charles, and then my Fernando, for the throne. Even my daughters would have precedence. But who ever thought I, middling Juana, would be Mother's heir to the throne?

He chuckled. "Well, there can be no children without a father to make them. I must return to Germaine soon."

A footman entered and bowed. "A man is here to see you, Your Majesty."

I waited, thinking it was for Papa.

The footman rose. "Your Majesty," he said to me, "the visitor is for you. Don Diego Colón asks for an audience."

Heat surged into my face. "Colón?"

Papa crossed his arms. "I don't wish to see the man. He reminds me too much of Isabel. She did dote upon his father. She refused to be disappointed by him, even the time the charlatan was brought back in chains."

"I will send him away."

"No need. I am ready for a siesta. The heat is too much for me."

He left as Diego entered.

I was conscious of my thickening waist, of the imprint of another man upon me. Madness. I was married. It was my duty to carry my husband's child. Perhaps Diego was now wed, too. I looked for a ring as he kissed my hand. There was none.

"I have heard you are unwell," he said.

"It is just rumors."

He searched my eyes as he held on to my hand.

I glanced at Katrien. She closed the traveling chest and left.

"In truth," I told Diego after she'd gone, "my husband wishes me to look weak so that he can rule."

He said nothing.

I could not bear his troubled eyes. "How is your father?" I asked.

"I regret to tell you that he died. Just two months ago. That is why I am in this city, to settle his affairs."

"I did not know. I am so sorry."

"When he returned from the Indies the fourth time, he made his way posthaste to your mother, but she died before he got there." He lowered his voice, thick with emotion. "It crushed him. He had no other friend in the Spains. I think he gave up hope." He paused. "There were no mourners at his funeral."

"I'm sorry. I would have come if I had been in the Spains."

He squeezed my hand. "I know.

"Now it is my business to take up his claims," he said, releasing me. "From my years at your mother's court, I have supporters in the Cortes. They are sympathetic to my cause."

I stroked my hand, still radiating from his touch. "Did you tell them about your sugarcane?"

His eyes warmed. "You remembered."

"Of course. It is an elegant plan."

"You are too kind."

"You deserve to be Governor of the Indies. Indeed, as Queen I will make you that." I grew enthused. "Now I have a reason for being glad of the crowns. I can make you governor. Viceroy. You shall answer to no one—"

"But you." His face was full of tender regret. "Dear lady, you are most kind, but I cannot accept your offer. I wish to prove myself. If I am granted any title, it will be because I have earned it."

He opened his mouth as if to say something else, then

seemed to think better of it. He smiled. "Here I am, proud that I might earn the right to be Governor of the Indies. I realize now that it's nothing compared with being Queen of all the Spains. How foolish you must think me."

"No," I said quickly. "I don't think that. I'm—I'm not even Queen until the Cortes proclaim it. And even then, my husband is anxious to take precedence over me. Your role is the more exciting one. How wonderful to govern distant new lands! What marvelous things grow upon them—brilliantly colored birds, wondrous animals, strange fruits. Whenever I hear of your lands, I think of a painting I once saw at the palace of my friend Hendrik. It was filled with fantastical animals, and fruits as large as men. And the most beautiful birds."

He laughed with affection. "You do like your birds."

"I do!" Thank God to discontinue this comparison of our powers. "Have you seen your storks of late?"

"Oh, yes. I look for them every day." He drew closer, then gazed down upon me. "They remind me of you. They make me remember why I work so hard—to be worthy of you."

I gathered my pearl, hanging from the ribbon necklace Katrien had made me years before. "I have this to remember you, but I do not need it." I touched his hand. "I cannot forget you."

He took my hand and kissed it gently.

Shouts in French came from outside.

I sighed. "Philippe."

He let go of my hand. I curled it against my breast.

"You must tell me, Señora," he said quietly, "is he bad to you?"

I looked away.

He gently brought my face forward. "I can see the answer in your eyes. I never thought I could kill a man. I know now that I could."

"Do not say that."

"How could he dream of harming such a magnificent woman? He is mad not to cherish you." Gently, he tucked a stray lock behind my ear. "I do."

He brought his mouth to mine. Warmth filled me with such force that I moaned aloud.

I pulled away with difficulty. "Please, you must go, quickly. My husband has no qualms about harming anyone. If he saw me with you—"

"I don't fear him, but for your safety . . ." He grasped both my hands, then kissed them twice. "My love, until I can come for you." He released my hands by degrees, then, with a kiss to my fingertips, turned and left.

My heart was still aglow when, in half the turning of a quarter-hour glass, Philippe swaggered into the room.

"Looks like the Cortes are ready to make a good ruling," he said in a buoyant voice. "Tomorrow I shall be King with full powers, not some damn consort. God, I wish Grandmère could see me."

"Yes."

He peered at me. "What's wrong with you?"

"Nothing."

"No. Something is wrong. You look like you saw a spirit." His handsome face became pinched with fear. He glanced over his shoulder, then laughed. "As if old Isabel could rise from her grave. Not even that old battle-ax could manage that."

42.

11 July anno Domini 1506

Longing, I supposed, for the embraces of his teen-aged bride, Papa left the next day at dawn. And so as bells rang overhead, it was I who joined Philippe under the Canopy of State at the church steps that morning. With our fine robes trailing behind us, we processed from Mass to the palace, I searching the prostrate crowd for Diego, both hoping and fearing that he would be there, and Philippe looking down on his subjects with a satisfied smile curving his puffed lips. He insisted on parading across the plaza as if we were already King and Queen, though the Cortes had yet to rule. A decision was expected that day. For Philippe, final approval could not come quickly enough. I myself dreaded it. With full powers, what kind of monster would he become? The sweet Philippe, the youth who loved saying yes, had all but been subsumed within the imperious glutton to whom no one dared say no. Heaven help the Spanish people who would have him as their King.

Once inside the stone walls of the palace, we proceeded to the staircase that led to my quarters. There the canopy was lowered and pretense of our happy union was abandoned. Philippe turned his back to me as one of his men removed his robe. I made to go upstairs.

Philippe caught my wrist.

I turned around.

He smiled, almost nervously. "I wonder if you would like to go hunting. I'm training a new falcon."

"What happened to Delilah?"

"I like new things. So are you coming?"

I looked down at my captured wrist, then into his eyes. "No. Thank you."

His smile disappeared. "Yes. Stupid of me to ask. You hate birds."

I wished to laugh.

He let me go. "It won't do for my Queen to hate me, you know," he said coldly.

I was mindful of the gazes of his guards. "I don't hate you, Philippe."

He shrugged with a nonchalance that did not quite reach his eyes. "It won't do for my Queen to despise me, then."

"I don't."

"I'm not a fool, Juana."

"It's not that I don't wish for"—I sought words—"another way of being."

"I wish for that, too!"

I gazed at his lovely golden face, so cruel in its innocence. He seemed to have no recollection of the hurt and shame he had inflicted on me over the years. He was genuinely puzzled why I should be reluctant to be near him.

"I want to be closer to you, Philippe. I want us to be happy together. But I'm not sure that it is possible."

"Of course it is." He put his hands on my breasts, then nuzzled my neck.

I shied as does a horse newly broken. Knowing that the

guards were watching only heightened my discomfort. "Can we not ever simply talk?"

"Talk?" he said, his breath hot against my skin. "What is the fun in that?"

"You would be surprised."

"Plenty of women want to do more than just chat with me. But it's you whom I want to be with." He ran his hands down my body, then stopped.

"What is this?" He pulled back and placed his palms about my belly as if gauging its girth. "You are thick. I have felt this upon you before. Are you with child?"

The guards leaned on their halberds, watching with interest. I held my breath, enduring his examination like a mare in a marketplace.

"Why did you not tell me?" He stopped his groping. His surprise sharpened into angry suspicion. "Is it another man's? By God, I'll kill you both."

"There is no other. Remember," I said under my breath, "you took me by force on the ship."

The pouches by his mouth drew into tight lines. "It is hardly by force if it's one's wife." He glanced at his men. One side of his mouth curled in a smile. "Don't tell me you didn't like it."

I turned away my head. He pushed it forward.

"Be glad for this child. It makes me look good to have my wife fat with my seed. I will show you much honor."

He was taking the throne that was rightfully mine, the throne that my mother wished me to have, and I was to be glad to play the role of his broodmare? "How nice."

He waved at his guards. "Get out of here! All of you. Now." He turned to me as they clanked back in the direction from which we had come. "Damn it, woman, why can't you ever be proud of me? Would it kill you to acknowledge, just once, all that I have achieved?"

"I want to be proud."

"You 'want' to be?" His voice was sour now. "Isn't that kind? So damned high and mighty."

At that moment Katrien, head down and arms hugging her apron top, descended the stairs with Beatriz. Both drew up short at the sight of Philippe and me.

I pulled away from him. "Beatriz? You have come back!"

She did not smile. Not taking her gaze from Philippe, she told Katrien, "Stay where you are."

Katrien glanced about as if weighing her escape.

The strangeness of this scene was lost on me in my joy of seeing Beatriz. I held out my arms to her. "What is the matter with you? Come here! Oh, it's been too long."

Eyeing Philippe, she came down the steps, her nun's habit rustling. She dropped to her knees to kiss my hand.

"What are you doing?" I scolded affectionately. I lifted her and clasped her in an embrace. The coarse material of her veil was rough against my cheek as I pressed her to me. "I've missed you so much."

Philippe hung his hand before her. "Nun, do you forget to pay homage to your King?"

She looked at him from my arms. "I see no King."

I winced. Why did she risk giving Philippe offense?

I shifted her out of his reach. "Look at you! You are beside yourself with excitement. What is it? Did the scholars accept your translation?"

"I did not go to Salamanca."

"I don't understand," I said.

"I went to Segovia."

Katrien glanced up.

"Were the scholars in Segovia?" I asked.

"I did not go to see scholars, Your Majesty. I went to speak to the steward of the palace."

Philippe lowered his lids halfway over his eyes in a suave smile. "Nun, you appear to be overheated. Girl," he told Katrien, "bring this holy lady a dipper."

"I would take no drink from either of your hands," Beatriz said.

Philippe's smile faded. "I am a reasonable man. But you push me."

Beatriz removed herself from my protection to face him. "I found the cup from which you had My Lady served the 'healing' potion. The steward let me keep it, which was quite useful when I took it to an alchemist to test it for its properties. It seems the paint upon it was composed largely of lead."

"Interesting," Philippe said. He rolled his eyes. "Not really."

"Are you aware, Señor, of the properties of lead?"

Philippe turned to me. "I tire of her strange talk. My hunt awaits me." He patted my cheek. "Take care of my child."

"You are aware of these properties," Beatriz said, more shrilly now. "You have a book in your library in Malines that explains them. There was a note as well."

He laughed. "I don't care to read."

"I know. But others do. You knowingly gave My Lady a potion expecting that it would weaken her."

"Why would I weaken my own wife?" He put his hand on the small of my back, sending a chill up my spine. "Especially one who so readily grows my seed."

Beatriz's dark eyes flashed with ire. "Do not insult me."

"Why in the world would I care about insulting you? Indeed, I'm about to have you dragged away by my guards. But news of my wife's condition has put me in a good mood. So to answer your mad accusation, I wasn't even in the Spains."

"Yes. That was very convenient, wasn't it? But Katrien was."

"I didn't know," Katrien whispered.

Philippe looked up at her and snorted. "Don't worry, Round Eyes, there is nothing to know."

"I am going to the Cortes," Beatriz announced. "I have the cup."

Philippe's pretty lips deflated into a flat angry line. "Show me."

"It is not with me. I would not be so stupid. It's in a safe place. I'm not the only one who knows. Someone else knows, too."

"Oh?" said Philippe. "Too bad. This someone will come to regret that."

"I shall tell everyone."

He laughed. "Who are they going to believe? A false nun who is mad enough to think that she is smarter than a man? Or their King, who gives them gifts and feasts and his greatest love?" He raised his golden brows at me. "Who would you believe?"

My blood pounded in my head. To accuse him directly could only come to grief. I had to remove Beatriz from harm's way before he struck.

"I wish to rest now." I put my hand to my belly. "The baby."

A mongrel dog trotted into the passageway, its nails clicking on the tiles. It sniffed the floor, oblivious of the tense scene before it.

Philippe gazed at me, his eyes half closed. "Yes," he said. "Go rest."

I took Beatriz's arm. I could smell the fear radiating from the folds of her habit as I edged us toward the stairs.

I placed my foot upon the tread. I took one step, then another.

I felt a tug. Beatriz had stopped.

Philippe gripped the hem of her robe. "Just a minute."

"Philippe—"

"Go on, Juana. I need to have a word with your lady."

"No, Philippe!"

The mongrel looked up from its sniffing.

"Nun, why is it that you've never taken a husband? With that fire in your eyes, you are quite comely."

"Guards!" I screamed. "Help us!"

He grabbed Beatriz's ankle. "Damn it, Juana. You made me do this." He pulled Beatriz toward him as she tried to scramble up the steps.

Guards swarmed down the corridor, their armor clashing. The dog skittered off, tail between its legs. Katrien bounded up the stairs and was seized by a guard.

The men closed ranks around us. Panting, I looked from face to face—German, all of them. Was there not a single Spanish guard in all of Valladolid?

Philippe shook his head regretfully. "I'm sorry, gentlemen. The Queen is suffering from one of her"—he sighed—"jealous fits. Could you please escort her and her wench to her chamber? Be gentle, if you might."

A man with a thick ginger mustache wrapped his gauntleted hand around my arm. He smelled of steel and horse manure.

"Beatriz, you are coming, too!" I tried to calm my breathing. In my chambers, we could wait out Philippe's wrath. I would beg Beatriz to abandon her claim. No good could come from it. His revenge would be worse than any gratification gained from exposing him. She could recant, then we would be quiet. Soon he would be distracted by the Cortes' announcement of his kingship, and all might be forgotten.

"Not her." Philippe looked upon Beatriz, pinned before him by two guards.

He gestured distractedly at the men. "Leave us for a moment."

"Philippe," I said between gritted teeth, "no!"

Beatriz raised her chin in defiance. A solitary tear rolled down her face and soaked into the cloth of her wimple.

"Truly it is a pity," Philippe said to his men. "Why do so many of the women who have fallen across my bed go mad with possessiveness? No one can ever believe a word that they say."

He frowned up the stairs at the guards holding Katrien and me. "What are you waiting for? Help the Queen to her room."

I was led off, struggling.

He smiled at Beatriz. "So. Nun."

43.

25 September anno Domini 1506

Fall in Burgos is a melancholy season. Along the river, the leaves of the poplar trees curl, showing their silver undersides, as if surrendering to their imminent fate. In the woods, the wild roses are poor things, headless, brown, and dry, their former glory unimaginable. Storks pass overhead in the evening in groups of three or four, their departure made all the more wrenching by the beauty of the rising moon bathing their white bellies in a mellow amber light. A change is coming, and all of nature knows it. Even locked within my chambers, I could feel it, too.

Yet for a little moment that morning, the sorrow of impending change abated. Sunshine beamed through the arched windows of the Casa del Cordón, carrying with it a kind of forgetfulness of all things bad. Who could believe the long days of summer were shortening into winter when such soothing rays warmed one's face? The sunlight left me in its caress to spill in broad swaths across the tiled floor, across a sleeping dog, across Katrien's knees as she sat mending, across the back of my son Fernando, pulling a pair of bronze horses on wheels during the one daily visit that Philippe would allow him.

I heard the latch being undone at my door. Not turning from the window, I opened my eyes and gazed before me.

Down on the court beyond the garden, Philippe and don Juan Manuel, his new favorite, were engaged in a brisk game of tennis. Even from this distance, I could see the lean lines of Philippe's body, hardened by days devoted to riding and sport. At twenty-eight, he was in the prime of his life, as handsome, with his golden skin and laughing blue eyes, as any man in the kingdoms. He had got five children upon me; the sixth tapped from within my belly like a restless prisoner. I would have desired the man—so many did— had he possessed a beating heart.

The door opened. I saw the glint of the German guard's helmet behind Beatriz as she walked into the room.

"Beatriz, where have you been?" Unlike me, allowed to attend only Mass and other public functions, and only then to give the impression that I was free to come and go, Beatriz was truly at her liberty, and had been all summer.

Now she passed through a band of sunlight as she came to kiss my hand. We embraced. She smiled upon Fernando, pulling his horses and neighing to himself, before she spoke.

"I am sorry to have been away so long, Your Majesty. I don't like to leave you alone."

"I'm not alone," I said with cheerfulness I did not feel. We both glanced at Katrien, who looked up from her mending. Beatriz frowned. She never quite believed Katrien's insistence that she had no knowledge of the toxic properties of the white-painted cup, nor her claims that she was only acting on orders from her master to provide the healing tonic.

Fernando whinnied to himself, then crashed together his horses. A howl went up. I crossed over and knelt beside him. He showed me his hurt finger.

"Did you pinch it between your horses?" Kissing his sweat-dampened brow, I picked him up and took him to the window.

He pointed beyond the gardens. "Papa," he announced. He looked up at me with a watery smile.

"Yes." There was his papa, King of the Spains, Archduke of Burgundy, ruler of the most powerful dominions in the world. He was a man who had nothing to fear from anyone, certainly not one Beatriz Galindo, would-be Latinist, with her seemingly deranged accusation that he intended to sicken his own wife with a leaden cup. In fact, he allowed the poor mad woman to spout her theory to anyone and everyone, after which he would shake his head with a condescending smile. *This is what comes of a woman's seeking to untangle Latin like a man—her brain is quite undone. She has become fixed upon me in her madness.* He would wink before continuing. *I never should have given in to her,* n'est-ce pas?

Beatriz patted Fernando's plump arm. "Your Majesty?" she said to me.

"I want down," said Fernando.

One kiss more, and I returned him to his toy horses.

"Yes?"

"I have come to ask your permission."

"Yes, Beatriz, for what?"

"To marry Francisco Ramírez."

My mouth opened in delighted surprise. It was quickly tempered by the realization that I should lose her company. I pushed that thought from my mind. Better that one of us was happy.

"Of course, whatever you wish. It has certainly taken Francisco long enough to break you down. The man has been nothing if not persistent."

She smiled stiffly.

Seeing her discomfort, I asked uneasily, "What about your translation? Are you not going to present it at Salamanca? Have you lost your desire to teach?"

She lowered her eyes. "I have not bled for two months."

"You and Francisco . . . ?"

She shook her head. When she looked up again, her eyes were brimming with tears.

"Philippe," I whispered.

I rushed to her and cradled her in my arms. "Oh, my poor Beatriz."

We held each other, she shaking in silent sobs, I staring, sickened. How much damage could one unloved boy wreak?

I saw Katrien look up, all color drained from her round face. She put down her sewing, then went to the door and knocked resolutely. Her breast heaved silently as she waited.

The bolt scraped in the lock.

Her apron brushed against the guards' armor as she pushed past them, uncaring of their curious frowns.

I was still rocking Beatriz as the door closed with a resounding thud.

Later that day, in the heat of the afternoon, Beatriz lay upon my bed, sleeping. She had vomited earlier and, at my insistence, had taken to my bed to nap. I did not need it. I was too furious at Philippe, and at my own helplessness against him, to rest.

Against my better judgment, I went to the window, knowing it would only enrage me. Philippe had returned to the tennis court and again was pounding the ball as if it were truly important. Along the sidelines, the Viscountess of Furnes and my other ladies preened before him in their fetching best. Let them have him. Just keep him from me. And keep him from Beatriz.

A man dressed in simple black strode up to the court with a tray bearing a pitcher and a goblet. He made the astonishing, inexcusable error of interrupting the royal game. From this distance, I could see Philippe's pique in the way he mopped his brow when he grabbed his drink. The man turned and looked up in my direction as Philippe tipped his glass and guzzled.

I gripped the stone of the windowsill. No.

Diego. What do you do?

I watched in breathless disbelief as Philippe finished his drink and addressed Diego. Beatriz had told me that Philippe had turned down his claim for the governorship of the Indies, and refused to grant him an audience to discuss it. With no other access to the King, had Diego come to confront him on the tennis court? I feared for his safety—Philippe would be livid that he had been interrupted at his sport. He would make it unpleasant for both Diego and the servant who had allowed him to take his place at bringing refreshment.

I saw Diego point to the palace. Philippe turned and shaded his eyes. They peered in the direction of my window.

I shrank back. When I gathered my courage to look again, Diego was striding away, his tray in the hands of the shocked Viscountess of Furnes.

Philippe gestured to his guards. They rushed after Diego and seized him. To Philippe's apparent enjoyment, Diego fought back, five against one. When they had thrown Diego to the ground, Philippe waved them off with his cup. Laughing, he held out his goblet for the Viscountess to refill, then looked toward my window as she poured. Again shading his eyes, he tipped in a slight bow, then downed his drink as Diego stalked away.

I pulled away from the window.

Beatriz sat up. "What is it, Your Majesty?"

"I despise Philippe."

"Not a rare sentiment," she murmured.

I rubbed my temples. "Diego Colón was here. He just tried to claim an audience with the King at the tennis court."

She came to the window. "Dear Lord, is Diego Colón now dead? Does he not know that the fearful dog bites the quickest?"

Shouts went up within the palace. We looked at each other, listening. The noise grew closer. To our astonishment, Diego Colón pushed into the room, only to have guards try to shove him out.

"Unhand him!" I cried.

"Your Majesty, our orders are to—"

"My orders are for you to leave him be."

"But the King—"

"The King is not here. You obey me."

The guards backed out, scowling at Beatriz, who, arms crossed, enforced their reluctant retreat.

When they were gone, Diego kissed my hands. "Dear lady, I won't be long. I have come to bid you good-bye for a while."

I heard the door close behind Beatriz as she slipped out. "Good-bye?"

"I told the King something that he did not want to hear. I'm afraid he'll make it hot for me."

"What did you say?"

"That I could not stand by while he locks you away like a prisoner."

"You should not have risked it! There's nothing you can do to change Philippe's ways." I clasped his hands. "Take me with you."

"I would like nothing more. But I shall not steal you away like a lowly thief. I must make you mine by honor alone."

"Don't you know that I can never be yours, not as long as he lives?"

He squeezed my hands. "Have faith. Such evil cannot sustain itself. It will burn itself out soon. A man like that will bring his own early death."

"You do not know that."

"I know this." He gazed upon my lips, then bent down and sought them tenderly with his own. At last we each drew back. "I know," he said softly, "that I love you."

Cries went up outside. I looked toward the window.

"I must go. I will come for you when I am worthy. Soon, I pray."

"But—"

He put his finger to my lips, then replaced it with his mouth.

"Diego, take me with you."

"My love, be strong. Wait for me."

A scream sounded below. Trumpets blared in alarm.

He kissed me gently, then pressed my hands against his face. "Wait for me."

Beatriz pushed inside the chamber as he strode past. My mind in a blur, I followed her to the window.

Like ants in an anthill that had been kicked, guards

roiled upon the tennis lawn. Philippe was being carried between don Juan and another gentleman from the court, the
Viscountess weeping after them. His head lolled back as if
he was unconscious.

Shouts arose from inside the palace. Katrien burst into
the room like a bird blown before a storm, her clogs skimming the floor in her hurry. She slid down wordlessly against
a wall.

Before I could make sense of her, a page flew in. "Your
Majesty! You must come. The King has fallen ill."

With a glance at each other, Beatriz and I followed him
to Philippe's chambers. We arrived as the gentlemen shuffled in with their burden, then laid him upon the Bed of
State. Don Juan sank to the floor and crossed himself.

"What has happened?" I cried. I bent over Philippe. His
golden skin had turned the pale blue of skimmed milk.

"He asked for you, Your Majesty, when he fell."

"What do you mean? Did he stumble on the court?"

I took his hand. It was as cold as death.

"We had not yet resumed playing," said don Juan, "when
all of a sudden he clutched at his belly and dropped to his
knees."

"Where are his physicians?" I demanded.

I leaned down close. He smelled of metal, like blood,
though he had nary a scratch.

"Philippe!"

He opened his eyes, then, unseeing, closed them. They
seemed to sink back into his head.

"What brought him to this state?"

"We did nothing unusual!" don Juan cried. "I promise.
He drank water after our game—a pitcher of it, in fact, it
was so hot. He collapsed soon after."

The hair stood up on my neck. Diego had brought him the water.

"Philippe!" I said. "Look at me!"

He opened his eyes once more. He struggled to bring me into view.

"You are going to be well, Philippe. Don't give up!"

His eyes drifted closed, his lashes a pale gold fringe against the blueness of his skin.

I scanned the ashen faces of the men crowding the bed. How I wished for his old friend Hendrik— No. No! He might suspect Diego. I looked around wildly. The Viscountess was slumped near the door, sobbing into her sleeve. My ladies patted her back as if she were the grieving wife.

A physician whisked into the room, his long sleeves aflutter. I stepped back to allow him space, then crossed myself. Dear God, let Diego get far away. Let no one lay a hand on him. Spare him, God. Please. He did wrong, but he did it for me.

44.

18 August anno Domini 1507

*T*órtoles de Esgueva: a village named after the turtle doves that live in the cliffs above the River Esgueva. Such a soft name for such a harsh land. Here towering escarpments, beaten by the wind and the sun, crumble onto barren plains. Grasshoppers spring from dry stubble too sparse to sustain a herd of sheep. The acrid dust that clings to one's veil and teeth also fouls the river. Pure water is as precious as gold. Centuries ago, a band of Poor Clares seeking solitude built a monastery around a spring that bubbles up in this wasteland. Word of this miraculous place soon spread, for not only was the water from the spring without impurities, but it had special healing powers. Persons journeyed great distances for casks of this health-giving water. A village formed outside the walls of the monastery. Today the nuns support themselves by selling their blessed water, as they prepared to do that hot afternoon nearly a year after Philippe's death.

I sat with my baby, Catalina, watching two sisters draw a bucket from the well.

"Are you thirsty, Mevrouw?" asked Katrien. "May I get you some water?"

I looked up from Catalina, suckling at my breast. Beatriz

was not there to see the humor in Katrien's question. Beatriz had wed her longtime suitor, don Francisco, and the two had been blessed with a daughter who, some murmured, was oddly blue-eyed and fair, though both of her parents were dark. Of all my former attendants, only my humble laundress remained with me. It was as I wished. I had no need of ladies to accompany me on my journey to take Philippe's body to its final resting place.

"Thank you, Katrien—yes." Indeed, I found that as a nursing mother, I always had a great thirst. It was a small price to pay for the pleasure of watching my child tugging steadily at my breast. I had not experienced it with my first five children, as my body had always been made ready to receive my husband's seed as quickly as possible. So for this reason, and many others, I refused the offer of marriage from old King Henry of England. Although it might have been a good jest to wed the Dowager Duchess's great nemesis, I did not wish to be the King's broodmare to produce little English heirs.

And, too, I waited for someone else.

Katrien brought me a dipper. As I drank, she smiled wistfully upon the child at my breast. With Beatriz gone, Katrien had gradually become bolder, taking on new duties in assisting my person, edging closer to me, and to my little Catalina, each day. As with a wild animal, I did nothing to startle her, to discourage her advances. I needed her humble company, and appreciated her genuine interest in my baby. From the great care and love she showered on my child, I suspected that she yearned to be a mother herself.

I stroked Catalina's pale, wet wisps, stuck to her head with the sweat that came from the closeness of our bodies. "She woke several times last night."

"Yes, Mevrouw. I heard."

"Do you think it's her gums?"

She nodded, setting the wings of her headdress aquiver. "She cried out much when her front teeth came. Now there is another."

"I shall ask the sisters for oil of cloves," I said resolutely.

We heard a banging on the outer door.

The nun cranking down the bucket paused. The other, holding the cask, straightened. But neither grew as alarmed as Katrien, who glanced about, then slid her hands under her apron.

The pounding came again. "Open up, in the name of the King!"

The King? For a moment, I thought wildly of the coffin kept in the chapel. Philippe was just wicked enough to burst from his shroud to haunt me.

Her rosary thumping against her thigh, the abbess strode down the arcade. I could hear her undo the bolt, then throw open the door.

The sisters ran from the courtyard. I plucked my child, now sleeping after her efforts, from my breast. As I wiped the baby's milky mouth with my sleeve, Katrien quickly pulled at the laces of my bodice, throwing worried looks over her shoulder as she tied. I had risen from my bench, Katrien straightening my skirts, when my father strolled in.

"Papa?" I exclaimed. Katrien shrank against the arcade wall.

He opened his arms.

I went to him. He drew me up as I tried to kneel, then heartily kissed my cheeks. He tucked in his chin, grinning, to gaze at the child in my arms.

"So this is my new granddaughter."

"Yes, Papa. Catalina."

"She looks like . . ." He trailed off, frowning.

"Philippe." I was not afraid to say his name. Yes, I knew it was whispered that I had planted the pitcher of poisoned water on the tray. I knew it was said that I had been watching from the window and thus would have known when to send out the tainted drink. I knew it was murmured that I had every reason in the world to kill my cruel husband for taking my rights and imprisoning me. If I had killed him, who was there to punish me? Not even Papa ranked above me. I began to understand how the English King escaped punishment for drowning his brother in that butt of wine. And though I would never have killed a spider, let alone my husband, I did nothing to set the record straight. Let them blame me, as long as they did not think to blame Diego.

Papa gazed around. I could see him taking in the sight of the cask next to the well, the basket of uncarded wool, the infant shifts strung across the patio to dry. Katrien, I noticed, had vanished.

"You live like a peasant, Juana."

It was true. In my confinement at Philippe's hands, I had developed a taste for living simply. I wished to prove to myself—and to someone else—that though Queen, I had no more pretentions than any of my subjects.

"Why do you do this to yourself?"

"I am comfortable, Papa. I will settle down to a court when I am finished."

"Finished with what?" He grimaced as if he knew but did not want to hear my answer.

"When I have taken Philippe's body to be buried next to Mother, as is proper for the King."

"To Granada," he said quietly.

To Granada, where, against all expectation, Mother had insisted upon being laid to rest. She claimed that she wished to be buried in the city where she had had her greatest victory. What she did not mention was that it was in Granada that Fray Hernando lived and did his work with converts. That in Granada, there was a monastery where not only her yoke was carved upon the entrance arch, but Fray Hernando's family crest joined her symbol as well. In Granada, she could be near her heart's desire until the end of his days. In Granada, she could rest with him at last.

"You know that Fray Hernando was under interrogation by the Inquisition," said Papa. "He was brought to Valladolid for questioning."

I reddened. I do not know by what magic it is that thoughts can be heard, but it is potent just the same. "I was not aware of that."

"He always had too much sympathy for converts. Your mother used to protect him, but"—he spread his hands in regret—"that was no longer possible."

We stared at each other. It was then that I realized that he knew, oh he knew, exactly what Fray Hernando meant to Mother.

"Where is your wife?" I asked.

"In Barcelona. I have settled her there."

"I am surprised you were able to leave her."

"My daughter was in need."

"But I am not, Papa. I am fine."

He made a ring with his finger and thumb and held it out to me, smiling as if I were still a little girl.

My heart aching, I shifted my infant so that I could slip

my hand through. When it did not fit, he expanded the circle so that I could pretend it did.

"Still fits," he said. "Let me help you, Juana."

I swallowed back my sadness. Would that we could go back in time. "Thank you, Papa," I said gently, "but I truly am fine."

"Are you? Hiding in a remote nunnery. Keeping your husband's body nearby. People talk." He lowered his voice. "They say you open the coffin to look at him."

I laughed. "Papa. I hardly have a wish to see Philippe now. It was painful enough when he was alive."

He opened his arms, the concerned paterfamilias. "I only repeat what people say."

I smiled uneasily. "And what do you think would make them stop talking?"

"If I could take you home."

"Home?" It hit me hard—with Mother gone, there was no such place.

"Yes."

"Where would 'home' be?"

"I had thought perhaps Tordesillas. The palace has been recently refitted and has a beautiful view of the river. It is quite comfortable."

"Papa, Pedro the Cruel locked up his wife there."

He frowned, then cleared his face. "Very well," he said soothingly, as to an unreasonable child. "Where would you like to go?"

I rubbed my brow. Why did Diego not come to me? Had he regrets for what he'd done? Surely he had heard where I now stayed, remote as it was. Talk, I had learned, traveled fast. "I don't know."

"Obviously you are"—he smiled with concern—"not yourself. Please, Juana, I want to help."

"I don't need it."

"Surely you do." He gazed at baby Catalina in my arms, her mouth wetly ajar as she slept. "You have the infant. Fernando calls for his mother in Burgos. And you must be busy making arrangements for your other children to join you."

A black pall of sadness descended upon me. He had struck my Achilles' heel. I was miserable with guilt over leaving my children for so long. Why did Diego not hurry?

Papa saw his advantage. He drew himself up. "Until you have restored order in your life, I would like to offer my services. I can manage all your duties. You know that I know how. You wouldn't have to worry about anything." When he saw my frown, he added quickly, "It would be only temporary. Just until you are yourself again."

When I said nothing, he drew in a deep, regretful breath. "It would mean so much to Germaine. She can't get the French court out of her head. She complains that compared with it, Aragón is a pitiful backwater."

A chill raised the hairs on my head: Did he want my crowns?

"I know," he said, "I should not care what she says. But I'm an old man with a young wife—there is no more foolish creature in the world."

My heart beat faster as I pondered the possibilities. What if I did turn over my duties to Papa for a while, if I asked the Cortes to temporarily grant him my crowns? It would certainly make him happy. And it was true, he did have experience in ruling, albeit over little Aragón. Still, my people would do well by him. What harm was there in his managing the kingdom until I was ready to resume my reign?

Until Diego could become governor, and rule the Indies, and feel that I was not above him. Until I could be Diego's wife.

"It would be only for a little while," Papa said. "You could have your say in whatever you want. I would just—"

"Papa?" I touched my bodice, behind which the pearl hung from its ribbon. "When can we speak to the Cortes?"

45.

March 2 anno Domini 1509

Katrien came to the door with two-year-old Catalina on her hip. "You have visitors, Mevrouw."

I stopped playing the organ. It had not been a very satisfactory experience. The damp air rising from the Duero wreaked havoc on the instrument. It had lost its tune within days of arriving in Tordesillas, and the music master I had sent for from Toledo had yet to arrive. I was learning with even greater clarity since leaving Arcos, where I had cloistered myself for the past year and a half in hope that Diego would come, that my orders did not carry the same urgency they'd had before I asked the Cortes to let Papa rule as regent. I had thought I had been left alone by my courtiers out of respect for my wish to play the part of a mourning widow. But after finally giving in to Papa's demand that I move to a palace more suitable for a queen, I found that I had little staff to relay orders to, and the staff I did have looked at me with a blankness behind their eyes that made me uneasy. It was as if they took their orders from someone else, and had been told to act as though they were serving me, while they actually weren't. I would wait for Diego as long as he needed, but I feared that the longer I waited, the harder it would be to undo the constraints in which I was finding myself.

"Who is it?" I asked Katrien.

Her pursed lips indicated her disapproval of whoever it was. Nonetheless, I must greet them properly. I received so few visitors those days.

I had straightened my headdress and corset, and was pulling the painted cover over the keys of the organ, when my father and his young wife entered the room.

"Juana, dear!" Papa called.

My skirts swished as I rose to greet them.

"Papa."

We exchanged kisses. He had gained weight since I had seen him last, and had a glow that I chose to attribute to his marriage.

"Juana, I am pleased to present my wife. Germaine, may I present the Queen of the Spains? This is my dear daughter, the lovely Juana."

Germaine, heavily pregnant, came forward. She craned her neck over my shoulders, giving me a dose of her flowery perfume at each ear, but no contact with her lips.

I pulled back and smiled. "I am pleased to see you again."

She nodded regally. Although her girl's sweet features had changed little in the seven years since I had seen her, she held herself with the pompous authority of a child playing at Queen.

"Yes," she said. "It has been a long time."

"And do you like the Spains?" I asked.

"Well enough. Some of the churches are very nice."

Papa chuckled. "She wishes to claim the cathedral in Toledo as her palace."

She swatted at him. "I do not."

He dodged her like a youth, belying, for the moment, the man who'd gone white at the temples and sported wrinkles that fanned from his eyes. "You do!"

"I only asked how we might have a few of the carvings in the choir screen moved to my rooms at our palace. No one would miss them—there are so many. They reminded me of Notre Dame in Paris. I so love the carvings there. It is the most beautiful church in the world." She stuck out her lower lip. "But *he* doesn't care about what I think."

Papa took her hand, kissed and then rubbed it. "Yes, I do." Tucking it under his arm, he said to me, "How are you, Juana? How do you like Tordesillas?"

"I don't know where my regular staff has gone. I am left with servants who stare at me oddly, as if I might be speaking in a language they do not know."

He rubbed Germaine's arm. "I am sure that you imagine it. You are Queen. I suppose they are simply not used to serving such a lofty personage here."

"Perhaps. It's not as if I require much." I sighed. "I'll like it better when you return Fernando to me, as you promised, and when the other children have finally come."

"Well," he said cheerfully, "that shouldn't be long. I've arranged for an entourage to bring the children from Flanders, but you know how long outfitting such an expedition can take. They are not just any children, but future kings and queens. We must be careful."

"Oh, yes." Germaine rubbed her swollen belly. "They are very valuable."

"Like nuggets of gold," I murmured.

Papa gazed at me as though ascertaining whether there might be disrespect in my words.

Germaine extricated herself from Papa to stroll over to dab Catalina's nose; the child responded by clinging tighter to Katrien. "Aren't you a pretty girl? I do love children. I thought I'd have several by now, but Fernando . . ." She produced another excess of lower lip.

Papa's dark face went purplish-red. "Patience, woman. There's a tadpole in your belly now, isn't there?"

She flashed him the closed-eye smile of a contented kitten. "A prince."

She went over to the organ. "What a charming instrument! It must make the sweetest little music. In France, we play upon loud old beasts the size of a coach—oh, sorry—do you know what a coach is? A conveyance to ride in, pulled by horses?"

"She knows," said Papa.

"Well, it's not such a foolish question," Germaine said petulantly. "I have not seen a single coach since crossing into our lands. I don't know how you can live without them," she told me. "Fernando, you must order me one this moment."

"*This* moment we must talk to Juana," he said, rather more sternly. He smiled at me. "We have news."

"News?"

"The Cortes of Castile and León have made their ruling. I have been officially granted full powers to use in your stead. You need not worry about anything."

"Ever," Germaine chimed in.

Papa cleared his throat. "Well, at least however long you want."

"That is good, Papa." I smiled as if pleased to hear this news, although word of it had trickled into my cocoon many months before. I tried not to be hurt at how long it had taken Papa to come to discuss it. I supposed that the production of tadpoles did take time.

Germaine returned to him and clung to his side like a child at her nursemaid's skirts. He patted her as he spoke. "I have recently made a minor appointment when meeting with the Cortes. I tell you only because you seem to have taken interest in the family. Like your mother, you have always been partial to the Colóns."

My heart lurched. "Colón?"

"I granted the elder son, Diego, governorship of the Indies. I had promised Isabel I'd do so, and God knows that he'd been pushing for it."

For me. Diego had been pushing for it for me.

"Truly, I have never seen a man so hell-bent on proving his nobility. But that often seems to go hand in hand with those who feel inferior, doesn't it? He told the Cortes that he wanted to be worthy of a most noble wife. That raised a few chuckles, that."

I struggled to keep my voice level. "Those were his words?"

"As I thought—you do seem quite interested in that family. So I thought that just for you, since you have been so"—he glanced down at Germaine, picking at the buttons of his tunic—"supportive of me, I would do him a favor."

My pulse pounded in my ears.

"If the lad wanted a noble wife, I thought I would give him one. The Duke of Alba had a daughter he'd been needling me to settle upon someone. You know María de Toledo y Rojas—your second cousin. A pretty-enough girl. She'll be a marquise in her own right. I gave her to Colón."

I could not see, or hear, for the blue-black roaring in my head.

"No," I whispered. "He did not take her."

"Strangely enough, he did resist. Here I gave him what he wanted, and he rejected it. I had a notion to rescind my offer, but the girl was quite set on it and so Alba would not relent. You have never seen a groom with colder feet. Alba had to hold him at the church step at knifepoint. I would not have wanted to be in their marital chamber that night."

I felt my lips move. "They wed?"

"Oh, yes. I suppose they'll have plenty of time to sort it out on the ship. Both bride and unhappy groom leave for the Indies in a fortnight."

"The Indies."

"Where else is its governor to go?"

Germaine reached up to peck Papa's cheek. "My shining knight."

Papa grinned, then peered at me.

His smile faded to a frown. "Juana, are you unwell?"

2 May anno Domini 1543

*T*he woman looks up to see her grandson, twitching his jaw—
that jaw, and those terribly familiar puffed lips—with
concern.

"I'm sorry," she says. "I get caught up in my thoughts. It is a
hazard of spending so much time alone."

He frowns guiltily.

She truly must be more careful. She is frightening him.

"So you've come to get my approval for your marriage?" she says
as brightly as she can manage.

"Yes, Abuela."

She refuses to let her mouth turn down, though. Hostias, this
sham has gone on too long. Sometimes it is all she can do to bear it.
If she had not promised Diego that she would wait, she would have
gone mad. Her smile becomes more genuine as she savors the humor
of that thought.

She looks around her grandson, at his nobles. "Is there something
I'm supposed to sign? Quick, quick, get it out. I don't want to waste
the time I have with Felipe."

Her grandson's melon-haired fool scoots out of the way like a
kicked dog, as a noble steps forth with a parchment. She goes to her
desk and holds out her hand. He gives it to her, then backs away with

such a flowery show of deference that she nearly laughs. Hostias santas, *the man overacts. She is not the Great Khan, you know.*

She uncaps her inkhorn, dips her pen, then signs.

The youth glances from her to the parchment in astonishment. "Are you not going to look at it?"

"No." *She sits back.* "Does it matter?"

"Yes. I could have put anything in there."

The woman smiles affectionately. Dear boy, does he not know how many documents she has signed over the years that have been filled with lies and misrepresentation? What bothers her most about them is that the perpetrators always think that they are pulling the wool over her eyes. Do they never suspect that she sees through all of their duplicity, that she lets it go because her life is as she wills it?

"My father says that I should read every document carefully. That a king—or a prince—must not trust anyone. Not even his advisors—perhaps especially his advisors." *He glances at his men, who stare back in innocence.*

"That would be just like my Charles." *The woman does not add the rest of her thought: Those who mistrust most should be trusted least. Neither her son nor her father nor her husband could ever believe that what was hers was theirs, just for the asking. They thought they had to take it by force, then guard against her taking it back. It hurt her especially that her Charles would treat her thus. Perhaps it was his deformity that had turned him cold, though she would rage against anyone who dared to trouble him about it.*

She holds out the parchment. "I am done." *The noble comes forward once more, bowing and scraping, again drawing a smile from her lips. When she glances at her grandson, she sees that he is scowling at the falsely humble supplicant. A spark glimmers in her heart. Could the boy hate this cruel jest, too?*

After a moment, she says, "Felipe?"

"Yes, Abuela."

"Felipe, would you like my crowns?"

"Your crowns?"

"Of Castile, León, Aragón, Granada, Gibraltar, Sicily—all of that."

"No, Abuela," he says sheepishly, "but thank you."

She thinks of her mother, once brought upon a mountaintop and offered, as was Christ, a kingdom that was not rightly hers. She had taken it. How she came to regret it. So much heartache it brought her, and so little joy. What was the use of such power when it could not bring her what she truly wished, the man who held her heart? Was this why her mother sent her off to marry a mere duke? To spare her from the knives of power?

She turns her attention to the youth before her. "Felipe, if I made a big-enough stir, I could get the pack of crowns for you. I have much more power than you know."

The men behind him pale. Once rebels came to free her. The Comuneros shouted that she was the true king, and that they dedicated themselves to restoring her power. She thought about it. Escaping from her rooms did have its appeal. But when she heard that Diego Colón was not behind the rebellion, she let Charles's men seize her and toss away the key. She would wait. She had said she would.

"Please, Felipe. I want you to have them. It would be my one true act as Queen."

From a back door, two women enter, their arms full of canes of roses. The younger one, a woman of perhaps thirty, barely flinches, her face impassive within the white linen wings of her Flemish headdress. She is a cool blond beauty, apparently used to taking her mistress's catastrophes in stride. The slight pouches by her mouth remain slack with dispassion. But the older woman, a dame old enough to be the other's mother, gasps in surprise. The white wings of her headdress nearly quiver with her dismay.

"Don't stop," the woman tells them. "Come in. Please." She turns to her grandson as the two women take their armfuls to the window, where a pitcher awaits on the sill. The youth stares at them in astonishment.

"What is it?" asks his grandmother.

He lowers his voice. "The younger of your servants looks much like the portrait of my betrothed. They—they could be sisters."

"I see the resemblance. Yes, one might say they could be related."

The older woman casts a glance over her shoulder, her eyes round with alarm. The boy's grandmother sighs. Poor Katrien, she thinks, rubbing the crucifix on her rosary. Will she ever stop worrying about being found out? Even after I fetched her child from the nunnery in Segovia—the same one where Mother had so lovingly doted on Papa's bastards—and helped her raise the girl, she still disbelieves my goodwill. But how could I punish her for doing what so many people wished to do? Philippe's use of her, and then his abandonment, pushed her to madness. She did not wittingly poison me, but she knew, oh yes, she very much knew, what a deadly draft she had given him.

"Last chance, Felipe," the woman says. "I do wish you to have my crowns."

"No, Abuela. They are Papa's." He steps up to her desk and pats her hand. "But thank you for your trust in me."

"Then take this."

She lays back the humped lid of a coffer on the desk. Carefully, as if she were lifting a chick from a nest, she takes something from its velvet depths. It is a pearl the size of a pigeon's egg.

"Give this to your bride. Let it help you to remember."

"Remember what?"

"Whatever you need to."

"I can't," he says. "Obviously, it is special to you."

She beckons him near. "Hold out your hand."

Reluctantly, he holds it forth.

She closes her hand around the pearl, then puts her fist on his hand. "Listen to me, Felipe. If you love this bride, you must cherish her. Forget your hunts, your sports, your pursuit of lands—everything—and savor her. You will think you will have plenty of chances to do so, but you won't. I promise you, you won't. Life is odd that way." She opens her fingers and, turning her hand, lets the pearl fall to his palm. "Very well?"

Seeing he is beaten, he smiles. "Very well."

As he surveys it, a noble takes a brand from the banked coals in the brazier and lights a taper of wax. The woman watches as hot red drops pool on a ribbon affixed to the document she has signed. She presses her seal into the liquid center.

When the wax has cooled, she gives the document to her grandson. "Go, Felipe. Be a good husband and be a good king."

He kisses her hand and, with tears in his eyes, leaves, his gentlemen following after.

When they are gone, the woman slumps back into her seat. It is so hard to see the young ones come and go. Her son Charles was brought to her only when near Felipe's age, and her other children, later, or more heartbreakingly, never. Why she was denied even her children, she does not know. It was the cruelest trial of all.

She feels something on her arm. When she looks up, the older of the two women is patting her.

She smiles. "Thank you, Katrien."

The woman places the pitcher of roses on the desk. "No." The white wings of her headdress waver when she shakes her head. "I thank you, Mevrouw. You are too good to me. I do not deserve—"

"Shhh. Shhh. I have told you—people do mad things for love. Just as they say."

The woman's smile fades into a look of concentration as she pulls on the lining of the coffer, revealing a hidden compartment. From within a nest of red velvet, she carefully plucks a ruby the size of a hazelnut. She holds it to her throat. She remembers the feel of her papa's skin when she slipped her hand through his fingers. She remembers the smell of her mother's hair, her stern smile, her laughter. She remembers the feel of the cold air as she and Philippe flew their sheets from the balcony; the chuckling sound of Leonor's first laugh.

She remembers Diego, his face aglow with youthful certainty as he talked of his plans for their future.

She opens her eyes and leans forward, then smells deeply of the roses. Such a brief bloom, so unforgettably sweet. It is a comfort to her as she waits.

Author's Note

Reign of Madness is a work of fiction, based on history. The challenge in writing this story was to make sense of the lives of actual people who lived in the past, on the basis of the records we have of them. My primary goal was to understand how Juana "the Mad," Queen of Castile and León, heir to the most powerful and extensive kingdom in the Western world at the time, came to live under house arrest for more than fifty years, a confinement that began during her marriage to Philippe "the Handsome," Archduke of Austria. How did her husband, a noble of lower standing than she, manage to take over her lands? This pattern would be repeated by her father, Fernando of Aragón, ruler of a kingdom smaller than the one Juana inherited, and later by her older son, who became Charles V, Holy Roman Emperor. Not only did they usurp her power; they also allowed her to be grievously mistreated. In her final place of incarceration, the palace at Tordesillas, where she languished from 1509 to 1555, she was continuously lied to by her jailers about the whereabouts and status of her family, and about current events. They kept up the elaborate ruse that she was still Queen, having her sign documents, many of them false, even as they enforced her isolation. Her only

companions were her youngest daughter, until she was sixteen, and a lowly servant or two, one of whom was the laundress Catalina Redondo, on whom the character Katrien is
based. Juana was treated as dangerously insane, and had
to endure exorcisms and frequent solitary confinement. Yet
when a group of citizens loyal to Juana, the Comuneros,
stormed the palace in 1520 to free her, she would not take
the reins of power from her son. I had to wonder: Could it
be that Juana *chose* to remain imprisoned?

Then, into my research marched the older son of Cristóbal Colón (Christopher Columbus), Diego. It is known
that Diego spent many years as a page in the court of Isabel
of Castile and then served in her husband's court after she
died. Before that, he was a page to Juan of Castile, son of
Isabel and brother of Juana. Diego was about the same age
as Juana, and there were plenty of opportunities for their
paths to cross. Add the known fact that Diego spent his life
fighting to defend his father's honor and titles—even after
he himself became Governor of the Indies in 1509 and built
the palatial Alcázar de Colón in Santo Domingo (now the
oldest remaining viceregal residence in the Americas)—and
a possible explanation for why Juana allowed herself to be
imprisoned began to take shape. Besides wanting her son to
have her titles, could it be that she wished to lower her
standing, to be acceptable to someone of lesser rank?

The relationship between Isabel of Castile and Fernando
of Aragón, that famous pair who bankrolled Colón's voyages of discovery, was my inspiration for this theory. During their reign, much was made about the equality of their
power. Even today, a brief visit to Spain affords a view of
five-hundred-year-old propaganda touting their glorious

union. Isabel's *yugo* (yoke—Isabel was spelled with a Y then) and Fernando's *fechas* (arrows) are carved, painted, or plastered on buildings in many cities and towns. My favorite example is at the monastery of San Juan de los Reyes in Toledo, which is essentially a Gothic billboard advertising the fabulous marriage of Isabel and Fernando. Almost all the walls and ceilings there are emblazoned with their motto and symbols. I particularly like the chains draped over the façade of the church, supposedly the bonds worn by Spaniards incarcerated in Moorish prisons. The chains have been there since the late 1400s, hung as a potent reminder that Isabel and Fernando freed imprisoned Spanish men, women, and children when they conquered the Moors and united the Spains. Isabel and Fernando were *the* power couple of the world, and were even named the Catholic Kings by Pope Alexander VI.

I couldn't help wondering how a proud man like Fernando of Aragón would react to having his wife considered his equal or, worse, to the reality that she was the main decision-maker in the realm. Early on, the couple had marital troubles when Isabel allowed herself to be crowned Queen while Fernando was away. They did not speak to each other for weeks. Fernando strayed. Even after they patched things up, his eye continued to wander. While Isabel made a point of cloistering herself with her ladies in his absence, he was out producing bastards—six that he recognized. They were billed as the happiest power couple in the world, yet there is evidence that their inequality didn't sit well with either of them. Almost all of the incidents in the book alluding to their discord have been taken from contemporary accounts.

But history can be slippery. Much general historical

knowledge, even the history taught in schoolbooks, may be more legend than fact. For example, many people in the United States can tell you that Christopher Columbus discovered America on October 12, 1492. And that he was extraordinarily brave, daring to think the world was round at a time when everyone else thought it was flat. No wonder he was soon celebrated around the globe for his great discovery.

Truth: Colón hoped to find a passage to the Indies. He was even equipped with a letter of greeting from Isabel and Fernando addressed to the Great Khan, should Colón find him. When Colón sighted land (in fact, one of his sailors did; Colón took the credit and reaped the subsequent reward in gold coin from Isabel and Fernando), he felt sure it was one of the outer islands of the Indies—perhaps part of the famed Cipango (Japan)—hence his name "Indios" for the natives he encountered. He made a total of four voyages from Spain and back, but even after probing the coasts of what are now South and Central America on his third and fourth journeys, he never realized that he had struck upon new continents. To have admitted that he'd come across something other than the Indies would have been to admit failure. So he did not call the areas that he'd bumbled onto the "New World."

Truth: It was generally known by cartographers in Columbus's day that the world was not flat. What was not known was how far the "Ocean Sea" stretched from the edge of Europe. Sailors were afraid of sailing beyond the capacity of their food supplies, a reasonable fear, but not afraid of dropping off the edge of the world.

Truth: Colón's "discoveries" were not immediately heralded as great feats. He brought back relatively little gold

from his voyages. He found no spices or precious woods—
among the main trade items from the real Indies—and Spanish crops like wheat went to ruin in the semitropical climate.
After his second voyage, disappointed colonists returned to
Spain calling Colón the "Lord of the Mosquitoes." The joke
was made only richer by his visibly high self-esteem. When
he returned from his third voyage under arrest and in chains
for his harsh treatment of the colonists, he received little
sympathy in Spain, although Isabel ordered him released
upon hearing of his imprisonment. As the historical record
shows, and as I hope to convey in *Reign of Madness*, the
Queen saw something in Colón that most of his contempo-
raries did not.

Colón did find some pearls. I like to think that one of
them was the Great Pearl in the story, which came to be
known as La Peregrina (the Wanderer or Pilgrim). It was
brought from the Americas during Juana's lifetime, and
was part of the crown jewels of Spain for centuries. We
have a visual record of it in a 1554 portrait of Mary Tudor,
the second wife of Prince Felipe (Philip II), Juana's grandson. It was owned by Elizabeth Taylor, a gift from her husband, Richard Burton—a power couple from another time
and sphere.

Aside from some pearls and a bit of gold, Colón's voyages did not prove to be the moneymakers he had hoped. To
make up for the paucity of profits, he pushed to capitalize
on "human gold." It was Isabel who put her foot down about
trafficking in slaves. She thought of the indigenous people as her subjects, and repeatedly stated that she wished
for them to be treated humanely. Though her wish to convert them to Catholicism might seem bigoted today, she

acted with the best intentions. Her sincere religious faith gave her peace and strength, and she felt it was her duty, punishable with her own damnation if she failed, to bring all others to her beliefs.

It was this same well-meant but ultimately disastrous desire that would inflict so much pain on her Islamic and Jewish subjects. Under her rule, Jews who would not convert to Christianity were ordered to leave Spain in 1492. Some historians think Isabel felt that her threat to expel the Jews from Spain would be enough to make them convert to Catholicism; she never believed they would actually go. But leave Spain they did, by the hundreds of thousands. During this same period, she allowed the Spanish Inquisition to operate as a means to root out those converts who were not true to their new faith: These backsliders practicing Judaism or Islam would supposedly weaken the faith of the "good" converts. She never imagined how much the inquisitors would come to enjoy their power, jealously guarding it against those like Fray Hernando de Talavera, Archbishop of Granada, who opposed this new mandate from Rome. He argued that converts must be encouraged and nurtured in their new faith, not tortured if they had doubts. Nor did Isabel foresee how ordinary people would come to use the threat of the Inquisition to bring down their enemies. She could not fathom that something initiated with such pious intentions might spiral into the corruption and misery that would dim Spain in the eyes of the world for centuries. Even Fray Hernando would himself fall to the Inquisition, in 1505, the year after Isabel died. He and his extended family were hounded by people who did not agree with his "soft" attitude toward converts and who resented his opposition to the movement. He died after two years of harassment. Isabel was not there to protect him.

Whether Isabel and Hernando de Talavera enjoyed a deeper relationship than their official one of queen and confessor is a matter of my own conjecture. What is apparent to me is that the two were matched in intellectual power, in their beliefs and outlook on the world, and in charisma. How could she have not fallen in love with him? As a rule of thumb in this novel, the more unbelievable an episode seems, the more likely it was drawn straight from historical records. I constructed the story around actual events, taking most of my liberties when exploring relationships between characters.

Which brings us back to Juana. Just as children in the United States have been taught that the brave sailor Christopher Columbus discovered America, Spanish schoolchildren have heard that the mad queen Juana la Loca was locked in a tower in the little town of Tordesillas because she was too insane to rule. She loved her handsome husband, Philippe, so much that when he died, she went off the deep end. She traveled around Spain at night, opening his casket to gaze lovingly upon his remains until finally, for her own sake, her father locked her up and ruled Spain for her; when he died, her son Charles took over. Even worse, she had a tempestuous relationship with her saintly mother, shortening that good queen's life. But like the legends surrounding Columbus, most of the legend of Juana the Mad is false.

Truth: Juana may have loved Philippe, but if so, he certainly must have tried her patience with his callous treatment of her. It is true, as recounted here, that he didn't pay

Juana's ladies-in-waiting or her household expenses, as was agreed to in their marriage contract. He withheld gifts to her until she produced a son. He was generous again when they embarked on their trips to Spain, but only for the sake of appearances. He spent much time apart from her, pursuing his love of sport, feasting, and the company of other women. As soon as Juana became heir to the Spanish crowns, he started to make deals with her father to undercut her power. He claimed that she had gone mad from an excess of love and jealousy, and therefore was unable to rule.

Court visitors backed this up by writing about instances of her madness, but their reports would have been shaped by the tales Philippe fed them. It was his word against hers, and he, not the isolated Juana, had the ear of the courtiers. All Philippe had to do to take the power that was rightfully Juana's was to make the story of her madness stick, and it has, for half a millennium.

Yet records indicate that Juana was one of the most intelligent of Isabel and Fernando's five children. She studied under the famed Latinist Beatriz Galindo, whom I tried to portray much like the real-life scholar, although I altered the date of her marriage to fit the story. (You may be happy to know that Beatriz became a professor at the University of Salamanca, where she taught rhetoric, philosophy, and medicine. She founded the Hospital of the Holy Cross in Madrid, still there today, and had five children with Francisco Ramírez. She is commemorated by a district in the capital named after her, La Latina, as well as by statues in that city and Salamanca. And yes, it is said that she dressed in the habit of a nun.) Juana was a gifted musician, and so poised and well-spoken that Henry VII of England, who had met her when her ship sank off the coast of Portsmouth, sought her hand in marriage after Philippe died; "old Henry" judged her a sensible woman. Hostile sources claim that Juana was a poor mother who did not care to see her children after leaving the Low Countries, but I doubt this, not when she kept her youngest daughter, Catalina, with her until her son Charles had the girl forcibly taken away as a teenager. It was Philippe and then Juana's father who would not allow her children to be brought to her; court records are full of her pleas to see them. I wonder whether Juana allowed Charles to have her power because he was a sickly child, with a defect that threatened his health, and she was trying to protect him. Although he had the world's best portraitist, Titian, to tidy him up in one picture by reducing his misshapen jaw and placing him on a magnificent stallion, the fact remains that Charles suffered from a deformity that caused him difficulty in eating and speaking all his life. But who dared mock a man who, with his titles in Spain and Austria, would become Holy Roman Emperor? This, I believe, is one of the reasons Juana did not throw her weight behind the Comuneros who wished to free her and restore her to the throne in 1520. She did not want to undermine her son. Charles showed little mercy to the rebels. He hunted them down and had them hung. A statue of Juan Bravo, one of their leaders, still stands in Segovia and is decorated with wreaths every April. To this day, not everyone in Spain believes the history found in old schoolbooks.

In May 2008, I visited the town of Tordesillas, the scene of Juana's imprisonment of forty-six years. As I entered the Plaza Mayor, a quiet space surrounded by crooked plaster-and-timber buildings and given to flocks of bobbing pigeons, my husband pointed to the window of a narrow shopfront.

"Isn't that a picture of your Juana?" he asked.

I couldn't believe it. The windows of the store were crowded with what looked like posters of the Mad Queen of Spain, "my" Juana.

A Juana shop? It seemed as unlikely as it sounded.

I hurried across the bricks of the square, passed under the sagging timbers of the arcade, and pushed open the battered door. There, on the ocher walls of the shop, were scores of hand-tinted woodcuts of Juana, and views of Tordesillas as drawn in 1543 by Anton van den Wyngaerde, along with smaller prints of Philippe and Charles V. I was greeted by a handsome young man with long, curling dark hair—Carlos Adeva, the artist, I learned, who hand-reproduced the woodcuts, among other works of art displayed around the shop.

Señor Adeva was delighted by my interest in Juana, and soon launched into legends of her intelligence and bravery—my favorite being the one according to which Juana gave birth to Charles while dancing at a party. She had popped into a privy and came out smiling (although surely a bit careworn) with her newborn son. When I asked señor Adeva if he believed Juana was insane, he bristled at the suggestion. She was made to look that way, he told me, so that others could take her inheritance. Calling her Juana la Loca was offensive to him and many others in Spain, especially in this town.

"What should she be called?" I asked.

He pointed across the square, to the plaza entrance under which I'd just walked. A banner, wafting in the spring breeze, stretched across several storefronts. Its letters, each as tall as a child, spelled out the five-hundred-year-old signature:

JUANA LA REINA

Acknowledgments

So many people have helped me on my journey to bring Juana of Castile to life. At the start was my agent, Emma Sweeney, upon whose calm and sage advice I always depend. I am grateful to Peternelle van Arsdale for nurturing the story (and me) in the early drafts. I count myself as lucky indeed to have benefited from the sure editorial hand of Christine Pepe as the book took shape. Her confidence in me and in the story has meant the world to me. She promised that we would have fun working on this book, and she was right.

My deepest gratitude goes to Ivan Held for his unwavering support for the project at all stages. I must thank Marilyn Ducksworth, Catharine Lynch, Meredith Phebus, Kate Stark, Katie Grinch, Rich Hasselberger, Meaghan Wagner, and the design team of Claire Vaccaro and Chris Welch, all indispensable in their various capacities in bringing this book along. I owe a huge debt of thanks to Anna Jardine, upon whose expert copyediting skills and knowledge of everything under the sun I greatly depended. I would also like to thank Leslie Gelbman, Jackie Cantor, and Caitlin Mulrooney-Lyski at Berkley. To the energetic Penguin sales force, I owe my appreciation, as well as to the stalwart

Eva Talmadge and Suzanne Rindell at the Emma Sweeney Agency. And thank you, John Burgoyne, for creating the evocative endpaper maps.

One of the best parts of traveling the road to discover Juana is the fascinating and unforgettable people I have met on it. In Belgium, I had the good fortune of being taken under the wing of Rudi van Poele and Marie-Paule Rombauts, who welcomed me into their hearts and home while opening my eyes to the richness of their Flemish heritage. Thanks to Rudi, I met Paul Behets, Dieter Viaene, and Axel Vaeck at the city archives in Mechelen (Malines), who kindly showed me documents pertaining to Philippe the Handsome and Juana. What a thrill it was to hold in my hands a five-hundred-year-old paper, complete with its crumbling wax seal, that had been signed by the archduke himself—a loan agreement, unsurprisingly. (Philippe needed money to support his appetites.) Thanks to Rudi, I had the opportunity to bicycle through the Flemish countryside to Lier, where the church in which Juana and Philippe were married still stands, little changed. Rudi also arranged an instructive afternoon in Damme with Gustaaf Dierckx, to whom I am grateful for sharing his time and his knowledge of the Burgundian court, and a visit to the Cathedral of Our Lady in Mechelen for an impromptu concert by the brilliant organist Wannes Vanderhoeven on a centuries-old instrument. I am grateful for the friendship of Peter Meuris and Patricia Gobein, also from Mechelen. The many hours spent chatting with them at their lovely B&B, Luna Luna, were informative and entertaining. Both Peter and Rudi are official city guides in that fabled place—if you have the luck to go to there, ask for them!

In Spain, I was greatly helped by the talented artist Carlos Adeva. He, like his shop in Tordesillas, is a treasure trove of Juana lore. It was a joy to meet someone who loves her as much as I do. I would like to thank Laura Martín Velasco for sharing her knowledge of Segovia and the Monasterio de San Antonio el Real. I am grateful to José L. Ardura for hosting a magical evening at the Posada Monasterio Tórtoles de Esgueva, the very place where Fernando caught up with Juana after Philippe died. At dinner, Rosa Guillén generously shared her knowledge of Spanish history. Besides having the best meal of my life, I learned much that night.

I would like to thank my companions on my trips to Spain, Steve and Ruth Berberich, and my husband, Mike. Because of their unflagging energy, no road, village, church, or monastery was left unexplored as we traced Juana's steps. I am grateful to Steve for often rallying us with his cry "What would Juana do?"

Stateside, seeking Juana took me to Columbus, Ohio, where I was able to board a replica of Columbus's ship the *Santa María*, my trip made easier thanks to my sisters, Jeanne, Margaret, Carolyn, and Arlene. I am deeply grateful to my brother David, who was among the first to encourage me to tell Juana's story, and who continues to be one of my staunchest supporters. I am fortunate to have had constant encouragement from the members of my long-standing book club—thank you, ladies. I'd like to thank in particular Sue Edmonds, Jan Johnstone, and Karen Torghele for nourishing me in mind and spirit.

Although my quest to know Juana has taken me across the globe, it started at home, when I first read Bethany Aram's *Juana the Mad: Sovereignty and Dynasty in Renaissance Europe* (The Johns Hopkins University Press, 2005.) Informed by that definitive work, and by the biographies on Isabel of Castile by Peggy K. Liss and Nancy Rubin, my story took root and grew. But none of it would have been possible without the love and encouragement of my daughters, Lauren, Megan, and Ali, who not only inspired this story about mothers and daughters, but are the shining lights of my life.

List of Illustrations

REIGN OF MADNESS

Discussion Questions

1. From a young age Juana and Diego are drawn to one another. What similarities do they share that enable them to identify with each another? What could have inspired Diego's loyalty to stay so strong even during Juana's marriage and long absence?

2. *Tanta monta, monta tanto, Isabel como Fernando.* "Isabel and Fernando, they amount to the same thing." Both in historical and fictional representation a great deal of emphasis was placed on the equality of Isabel and Fernando. In what ways did this emphasis create inequality between them? Did it create an imbalance solely in their personal lives, or was a disparity evident politically as well?

3. Philippe's own grandmother characterizes him as "a man whose appetite grows larger from eating." Discuss what could cause a man who was happy with his status as an archduke to be unsatisfied with his role as a King-consort?

4. Throughout the story, how does Juana's perspective of marriage change, particularly her views of the role of a wife in relation to her husband? How does becoming a mother affect her marriage?

5. In what ways does Isabel admitting her shortcomings affect Juana's perspective of her parents? Of her own situation?

Is it possible for even grown children to fully understand and accept their parents' strengths and weaknesses?

6. Through the romantic relationships depicted, *Reign of Madness* takes a close look at the gray areas of love and fidelity. Isabel, Fernando, Philippe and Juana each have some form of extramarital affair or attachment. How do these affairs differ from one another? Due to the political contexts of arranged court marriages, would you consider love or happiness possible within one of these marriages?

7. Balancing power and love in a relationship is not a problem isolated to kings and queens. How does this struggle manifest itself in modern relationships?

8. In what ways are Juana's roles as wife and ruler at odds with one another? What kind of conflict does this create for her?

9. In the author's note, it is stated that Beatriz did, in fact, become a professor at University of Salamanca in addition to marrying Francisco Ramirez. In the novel, how does Beatriz's quest for academic achievement stand in contrast to the romantic relationships occurring around her and Juana?

10. One of the themes of *Reign of Madness* involves the power of perception over reality. The strength of the Spains, Isabel's claim to her crowns, and Juana's own stability are all subject to public perception. In Cullen's imagining, creating a perception of the young queen as unbalanced was frighteningly easy. How important is perception? Can it be more important than reality?

NOTES

NOTES